THE PRICE OF SILENCE

THE PRICE OF SILENCE

An Anthony Brooke Espionage Thriller

Dolores Gordon-Smith

This first world edition published 2017
in Great Britain and the USA by
SEVERN HOUSE PUBLISHERS LTD of
19 Cedar Road, Sutton, Surrey, England, SM2 5DA.
Trade paperback edition first published
in Great Britain and the USA 2017 by
SEVERN HOUSE PUBLISHERS LTD

British Library Cataloguing in Publication Data
A CIP catalogue record for this title is available from the British Library.

ISBN-13: 978-0-7278-8726-9 (cased)
ISBN-13: 978-1-84751-838-5 (trade paper)
ISBN-13: 978-1-78010-901-5 (e-book)

All Severn House titles are printed on acid-free paper.

Severn House Publishers support the Forest Stewardship Council™ [FSC™],
the leading international forest certification organisation.
All our titles that are printed on FSC certified paper carry the FSC logo.

Typeset by Palimpsest Book Production Ltd.,
Falkirk, Stirlingshire, Scotland.
Printed and bound in Great Britain by
TJ International, Padstow, Cornwall.

Dedicated to Dr John Curran, author of *Agatha Christie's Secret Notebooks* and a really 'mint' bloke!

ONE

Mrs Rachel Harrop stood at her sitting-room table, sorting out the bed linen that had arrived from the laundry that morning. Mrs Harrop, housekeeper to Mr and Mrs Jowett, of 4, Pettifer's Court, Northumberland Avenue, believed in a strict hierarchy in all things. There was, in her opinion, a place for everything and everything in its place.

That applied equally to God, social class, the household and the laundry. The lower servants' sheets and pillowcases of inexpensive American cotton went in the bottom of the basket, to be placed on the bottom shelves of the linen cupboard. Her own bedding and that of Mr Hawthorne, the butler, was made of hardwearing Irish linen and went in the middle, whereas Mr and Mrs Jowett's sheets and pillowcases, made of fine Egyptian cotton, destined for the upper shelves of the cupboard, went on the top.

Mrs Harrop had been housekeeper to the Jowetts for nearly ten years. She had come to work for them when Mr Jowett, a bachelor in his early forties, had married Mary Knowle, a pretty young widow with a thirteen-year-old son, Maurice.

She liked the Jowetts. Mrs Jowett and her husband, Mr Jowett, the chief cashier of the Capital and Counties bank, were a nice, respectable couple to look after.

Mrs Jowett, in particular, always appreciated any little extra effort. Mrs Harrop smoothed the sheet on top of the laundry basket absently, her hands slowing. At least, Mrs Jowett *had* appreciated any little extra effort, but for the last few weeks she'd seemed too worried and abstracted to notice.

Maybe, thought Mrs Harrop, she was anxious about Maurice, and no wonder, poor boy. When Mr Maurice had called that morning he seemed worried to death. Young Mr Maurice usually had a friendly word for her, enquiring about her knee (Mrs Harrop always appreciated an enquiry about her rheumaticky knee) and listening to her lamentations about how difficult it was to furnish the table with the sort of foodstuffs a gentleman's table should be furnished with in this dreadful war.

This morning, however, Captain Maurice had hardly seemed to notice her. He'd rushed past her into the house, scarcely said 'Hello' even, and greeted his mother with the words, '*It's true!*'.

Then Mr Maurice and his mother said something about chocolate. Mrs Harrop couldn't quite hear what it was about chocolate, but whatever it was, they were unhappy. Mrs Harrop shrugged. Whatever it was, it'd all come out in the wash.

The wash. Mrs Harrop's hands unconsciously twisted in the smooth sheets. Poor Mr Maurice. He had been so keen to be a soldier, too, just like his father.

Maurice Knowle's father, Mrs Jowett's first husband, had been Major-General Knowle of the Royal Artillery but poor Mr Maurice's army career had been cruelly short-lived. He survived the nightmare known as the retreat from Mons, and stuck out a horrible winter in the trenches. Trenches! thought Mrs Harrop with a sniff. A hole in the ground, that's all a trench was, and frozen solid, too. It seemed all wrong that gentlemen's sons should be called on to live in holes. Then, after all that, he had been in a battle for somewhere called Aubers Ridge and been invalided home with a shattered left arm and a permanent limp.

A place for everything and everything in its place. But poor Mr Maurice, an officer, was in the wrong place, here in London, while his young lady, Miss Edith Wilson (and she was a real lady too, related to Sir Horace Wilson) was out in Belgium, nursing wounded soldiers.

It was, thought Mrs Harrop, obscurely but definitely, all wrong.

With a sigh she picked up the linen basket, came out of her sitting room, and, panting slightly with the effort, went up the back stairs to the top floor.

She opened the linen cupboard door, then paused, her head on one side, listening. The linen cupboard stood beside the door that separated the servants' bedrooms from the main body of the house. From the other side of the door she could hear voices. With a jolt of indignation she recognized Eileen Chadderton, the parlourmaid, and the two housemaids, Winnie Bruce and Annie Colbeck. What on earth were they doing, upstairs at this time of day?

Frowning, she pushed open the door and gaped in amazement.

Outside Mr Jowett's study – Mr *Jowett's* study, mark you – the three women were unashamedly listening at the door. To Mrs Harrop's amazement, there was a fourth listener at the door, none other than Hawthorne, the butler.

'What's . . .' she began when Winnie Bruce turned, saw her, and put a finger to her lips.

It was only the astonishing presence of Hawthorne that kept Mrs Harrop quiet.

Mr Hawthorne, as he liked to remind the staff, had been with Mrs Jowett's family since he was a boy and was, as he put it himself, proud to be one of the old school.

Unwillingly accepting retirement two years ago, he had insisted on taking up his post on the outbreak of war. Mrs Jowett, driven to near distraction by the patriotic, if inconvenient, urge that had possessed her young and energetic butler to join up, mentally crossed her fingers at the thought of Hawthorne's dodgy heart and accepted his services gladly.

Arthritic, elderly and with an immense pride in the family, Hawthorne was the very last person who would stoop to listening outside doors.

Mrs Harrop might have believed in a place for everything and everything in its place, but she was only human. Impelled by curiosity, she joined the little knot of servants outside the study door.

The study door was solid, but she could distinguish Mr Jowett's voice, sharp with anger. Whatever was the master doing here? He was never at home this time of day. Then she caught the name 'Maurice' followed by a shrill yelp of protest. That was the mistress.

Another few words reached them. 'The police . . . law . . . disgrace.'

It was Mr Jowett speaking. Mrs Harrop drew in a horrified breath. What on earth did the police have to do with things?

Mr Hawthorne, alerted by Mrs Harrop's gasp, turned and caught her eye. He suddenly seemed to become aware that he was not the only listener at the door. 'We should all disperse,' he said. Behind the door, Mr Jowett's voice rose. Hawthorne drew himself up and, very much on his dignity, started to shoo the servants away like so many chickens.

'Bruce, Chadderton, Colbeck, I believe you should be attending to afternoon tea . . .'

There was a sharp crack from the room.

'That's a gun!' yelped Eileen Chadderton. 'He's shot her!'

Hawthorne turned slowly, gazing at the door in astonishment.

All four women screamed as another shot cracked out inside the study. Hawthorne groaned, blanched, clutched at his chest, and, falling against the door, slid to the floor.

For a moment Mrs Harrop thought that Hawthorne had been shot, but the door was undamaged. He *couldn't* have been shot . . .

Then the truth hit her. Hawthorne's heart, never strong, had given way under the strain. She quickly pushed past the girls. 'Mr Hawthorne!' she cried, putting an arm under the old man's shoulders. She looked wildly at the other servants. 'It's his heart!'

Eileen Chadderton, torn between Hawthorne's condition and what had happened in the study, banged on the door. 'Open this door!' she yelled. 'Open it!'

'Never mind that!' cried Winnie Bruce. 'What about Hawthorne?'

Eileen Chadderton ignored her, rattling the handle of the study door. The door was locked. Annie Colbeck did nothing, but, hanging back, repeated, 'He's shot her. He's shot her.'

'Open this door!' yelled Eileen, banging on the woodwork. 'Open this door, I say!'

'Leave the door!' said Mrs Harrop, her voice sharp with worry. 'Mr Hawthorne needs help. He needs a chair.'

'Eileen!' shouted Winnie Bruce. 'Help us!' Then, driven to distraction by Annie's constant wailing, yelled, 'Annie! Help Eileen and *shut up*!'

Annie subsided into a series of sobs. Eileen Chadderton took one look at Annie, gave her up as a bad job, and ran down the corridor to the nearest bedroom. Seizing hold of a chair, she dragged it to where Mr Hawthorne was slumped.

Together they got the old man into a chair. They *couldn't* have heard shots from Mr Jowett's study, thought Mrs Harrop in terrified bewilderment. It was utterly incredible and Mr Hawthorne – poor Mr Hawthorne with his weak heart – was suffering. His face was paper white and his lips had a bluish tinge. He reached up and grasped her hand convulsively, trying to speak, but, with Annie's wails rising to a new crescendo, Mrs Harrop couldn't make out the words.

'Quiet, girl!'

Annie gulped into stuttering sobs. In the brief moment of silence, Mrs Harrop made out what Hawthorne was saying.

'My drops,' he croaked. 'I need my drops.' He made a huge effort. 'Drops . . . In my bedroom.'

'I'll get them,' offered Annie, clearly anxious to get away.

'Off you go, girl!' snapped Mrs Harrop.

Annie, white-faced, nodded and, opening the door into the servants' quarters, went to search.

It seemed a long time before she returned, holding a small bottle and a glass of water. The study door remained firmly closed. Hawthorne sprawled in the chair, his breath coming in fluttering gasps.

'The bottle was in his dressing-table drawer,' Annie explained as she handed the glass and the bottle to the housekeeper. She seemed on the verge of tears. 'I couldn't find it at first, then I thought as how they probably needed water, so I read the label and they do, so I had to go down to the kitchen for the water because we can't use bathroom water, can we?'

Mrs Harrop took the bottle impatiently and, screwing up her eyes, read the label. 'For once, you're right.' Annie whimpered at the sharpness of her voice. '*Stop crying*!' commanded Mrs Harrop.

'What about the door?' asked Eileen Chadderton. She bent down and peered through the keyhole. 'The key's in the lock. We'll have to break the door down.'

Mrs Harrop shrieked in protest. Already the noise they had heard from the study – surely it couldn't really be shots? – had receded in her memory. There had to be some innocent explanation, of both that noise and the ominous silence from the study. To break down the door was utterly unthinkable. Normally she'd ask Mr Hawthorne what should be done, but poor Mr Hawthorne wasn't capable of any decision.

'He needs a doctor,' said Eileen.

Mrs Harrop nodded. There was no scandal in calling for the doctor. 'Go and do it, Eileen,' adding in a worried way, 'you'd better use the telephone in the hall.' The telephone was usually off limits to the housemaids, but the circumstances were anything but usual.

Eileen went downstairs, leaving the three women alone with Hawthorne.

It suddenly seemed very quiet. The only noise was that of Hawthorne's laboured breathing and Annie's sniffles.

From down below, they could faintly hear Eileen's voice, then there was silence. That seemed to last for a long time when suddenly, from downstairs, came the low rumble of a man's voice, followed by the heavy tread of feet on the stairs.

Eileen came up the stairs, followed by a burly policeman.

Mrs Harrop was shocked. 'Eileen! What is the meaning of this?'

The policeman cleared his throat. 'This young woman tells me you heard shots, missus.'

'Nonsense!' snapped Mrs Harrop. She glared at Eileen. 'You were sent to summon the doctor.'

'The doctor's on his way,' said Eileen. 'I telephoned him first but then I went outside and saw this policeman, so asked him to come in. What else could I do?'

'Consulted me,' said Mrs Harrop stiffly.

Ignoring her, the policeman eyed up the door, rapped smartly on the panel, rattled the handle, then looked through the keyhole. 'The key's in the lock,' he said stepping back.

'As I said,' murmured Eileen.

'We need this door open,' said the policeman ponderously. Annie's sniffles increased in volume. 'Now, my girl, be quiet! We'll have to break the door down.'

Hawthorne spoke for the first time. 'No!' he protested feebly. 'We can't damage the property.'

'Needs must, sir,' said the policeman. Retreating down the hall, he sized up the door and ran at it.

Mrs Harrop cried out and Hawthorne gave a convulsive shudder as the door shook.

The policeman retreated once more. 'This should do it,' he said and, lowering his shoulder, charged the door once more. The lock gave way with a splintering crash.

The policeman, carried forward by the momentum of his charge, burst into the study.

Everyone crowded into the doorway, then Annie let fly with an ear-piercing shriek. Mrs Harrop clapped her hand to her mouth, feeling sick.

Mrs Jowett, the mistress, lay on the carpet. Mr Jowett, gun held loosely in his hand, was sprawled by the hearth.

The policeman drew a deep breath. 'They're goners. He must've shot her, then shot himself.'

Hawthorne appeared in the doorway, clutching onto the frame for support. 'Oh, dear God,' he muttered. 'No!' Stumbling forward, he fell into the room.

Mrs Harrop went to his side. Lying on the floor, with Mrs Harrop kneeling beside him, he groped feebly for her hand. 'It's my fault,' he muttered. She could see the immense effort the words cost him. 'My fault . . . *Maurice.*'

Mrs Harrop felt his hand tighten, then relax. His eyes rolled up, then fluttered shut and he slumped back on the floor. He was dead. She tried to get him to wake up but she knew he was dead.

Mrs Harrop felt the policeman's hands on her shoulders as, with rough kindness, he helped her to stand. She saw Eileen Chadderton, Winnie Bruce and the policeman stooped over Hawthorne, heard Annie's wails of shock and grief as something very far away. Then there was a buzzing in her ears and everything went black.

TWO

S ir Douglas Lynton, Assistant Commissioner of Scotland Yard, pushed the cigarette box across the desk to Inspector Tanner. It was six days after the deaths in Pettifer's Court.

'Help yourself,' said Sir Douglas absently, as he read through the inspector's report.

He finished reading, sat back and lit a cigarette. 'So your conclusion is that Edward Jowett argued with his wife, shot her and then shot himself?'

The inspector nodded. 'Yes, sir. There's no other conclusion possible. The gun Jowett used was a Browning automatic. The housekeeper, Mrs Harrop, said he'd bought a gun at the start of the war.' He gave a superior smile. 'Apparently he wanted to be prepared, in case of an invasion.'

'As did many others,' agreed Sir Douglas, rubbing the side of his nose. 'There's no doubt, I suppose, that the gun was his?'

'It's as certain as it can be,' said the inspector with a shrug.

'Mrs Harrop and Eileen Chadderton, the parlourmaid, said they'd seen a gun in Mr Jowett's desk but couldn't swear to it being the Browning. Eileen Chadderton thought the gun she'd seen was different, but couldn't say how. Annie Colbeck, on the other hand, had also seen a gun in the study and was sure that it was the Browning, but you know what women are, sir.' He laughed tolerantly. 'A young lad, now, that would be different, but I wouldn't trust a woman to know anything about firearms.'

'It's an odd business though,' said Sir Douglas reflectively. He tapped the report. 'All Mr Jowett's friends and acquaintances have said he was the last sort of man to resort to such violence.'

He leaned back in his chair. 'I've read your official report, Tanner, but I'd like you to give me your own impressions. For instance, what were the relations between Jowett and his wife? And where does Maurice fit into the picture? Hawthorne, the butler, said his name before he died.'

'I know he did, sir, but what he meant by it is anyone's guess. Maurice is Captain Maurice Knowle, Mrs Jowett's son by her first marriage. His father was Major-General Knowle, who died in Honduras in 1898. The Jowetts married ten years ago and, as far as I can ascertain, the relations between all three of them were always very good. Having said that, the housekeeper thinks that her mistress had been worried recently and she thinks it was something to do with young Knowle.'

'Has she any idea what worried Mrs Jowett about Knowle?'

'Not really, sir,' said Tanner. 'The housekeeper says that Captain Knowle called to see his mother on the morning of the shootings, but he only stayed for half an hour or so. Apparently he seemed unusually anxious, as did his mother, but heaven knows what about.'

'Hasn't the housekeeper got any idea?'

Inspector Tanner grinned. 'She heard them saying something about chocolate, but that's all.'

'Chocolate?' repeated Sir Douglas, puzzled. 'What on earth has chocolate to do with it?'

'Search me, sir. I must say, I felt sorry for Captain Knowle. He seemed a very nervy type, but he's probably got good cause. He was commissioned into the Royal Artillery a couple of years before the war and received his captaincy in time to take part in the retreat from Mons.'

Sir Douglas Lynton winced. 'Poor devil.'

'Exactly. He saw out the winter in Ypres, then sustained a shrapnel wound at Aubers Ridge. His left arm was taken off at the elbow and he's got a damaged leg. He's still recovering but he hopes to take up a post at the War Office in a couple of months.'

'Is he hard up?'

Tanner shook his head. 'Not as far as I can tell. He has some money of his own. The late Major-General Knowle left both his wife and his son a tidy little sum.'

'Did he, by Jove? That probably accounts for where they live. I would've thought a house off Northumberland Avenue was a bit above a bank employee, but if Mrs Jowett had money, that explains it.'

'You're right, sir,' agreed Tanner. 'The house belonged to the Knowle family as did, in a manner of speaking, Hawthorne, the butler. He'd been with the Knowle family all his life.'

'Mr Jowett seems to have done very well from his marriage,' commented Sir Douglas. 'Did that lead to any strain between them?'

'Not that I've been able to find out,' said Tanner in a disgruntled way. 'They seem to have been a devoted couple. Edward Jowett, by all accounts, was a kindly man, popular and well-liked, as was Mrs Jowett. She's done a good deal of practical welfare work since the war started. She was particularly keen on Belgian relief work. Maurice Knowle is engaged to be married to a Miss Edith Wilson, who's nursing in Belgium.'

Sir Douglas grunted in dissatisfaction. 'And yet this exemplary couple clearly had a violent argument concerning Maurice which ended in murder and suicide.' He ground out his cigarette in the ashtray. 'I don't like it, Tanner. As the affair stands, it's inexplicable.'

Tanner put his hands wide. 'We don't know what goes on behind closed doors, sir, and that's a fact.'

'I wish we did have some facts,' said Sir Douglas grumpily. 'They seem to be like hen's teeth. We know what happened but we don't know why. What about Jowett's colleagues at the bank? What do they have to say?'

'They seem to be as shocked as the rest of the Jowetts' friends and acquaintances, sir. Having said that, I was a bit unhappy about the bank itself.'

Sir Douglas looked startled. 'The bank? The Capital and Counties, you mean? I know it was ailing a few years ago but it seems in perfectly good order now. Why are you unhappy?'

'Jowett was the chief cashier at their head office, in Throgmorton Street, in the City . . .' Inspector Tanner paused. 'It's not an English bank.'

'The Capital and Counties?' repeated Sir Douglas. 'Of course it's an English bank.'

'It was, sir. It was bought out five years ago by a Chicago concern, the Midwest Mutual and Savings.'

'Well? What of it? London's the greatest financial centre in the world, Tanner. Naturally the Americans want a hand in it.'

'Do you know the owner's name, sir?' Tanner paused significantly. 'It's Diefenbach. Rupert Arno Diefenbach. His son, Paul Diefenbach, is the chairman of the London bank. They're Krauts.'

Sir Douglas laughed. 'For heaven's sake, Tanner! They might have German names, but you said yourself, they're American.'

'They're German-Americans,' persisted Tanner stolidly, unmoved by his chief's derision. 'Rupert Arno Diefenbach made a fortune in the Chicago cattle markets and also has considerable interests in oil and railways. He's a millionaire a good few times over.'

'Lucky beggar,' commented Sir Douglas. He looked at Inspector Tanner and sighed in half-humorous exasperation. 'You're surely not suggesting that this American millionaire, Diefenbach, or whatever his name is, is responsible for the Jowetts' deaths?'

'Well, no, I wasn't suggesting that.'

'Was he even in this country when the Jowetts died?'

'No, he wasn't,' Tanner grudgingly admitted. 'I don't know if he's ever been to England. I bet he's been to Germany a few times though,' he rumbled defiantly.

'What about Paul Diefenbach?' asked Sir Douglas. 'The man who actually runs the bank?'

'I wondered about him, sir. Apparently he was very friendly with Mr Jowett. I thought that was odd, as there's such a difference in age.'

'Have you questioned him, Tanner?'

'I can't, sir. He sailed for America three weeks ago.'

'That rules him out, however German he is. Paul Diefenbach? The name's vaguely familiar for some reason.'

'He's a bit of a character, as far as I can make out. He goes in for motor-racing and mountain climbing and such-like.'

'That's right,' said Sir Douglas. A memory of a lean-faced, fair-haired man holding a flying helmet, grinning from the pages of an old newspaper, rose to mind. 'I've placed him now. He attempted to fly across the North Sea before the war.'

'Some people have got more money than sense,' grunted Tanner. 'It seems an expensive way of trying to break your neck. Apparently that's why he's gone to America, to go off on an expedition up the Amazon, to the Matey Grocer or some such place.'

'The Matey Grocer?' Sir Douglas smiled. 'I think you mean the Mato Grosso, Tanner.'

'I daresay I do,' said Tanner, unmoved. 'It's somewhere foreign, that I do know.'

Sir Douglas laughed. 'The spirit of adventure evidently doesn't appeal to you. Like you, I'm surprised he was friendly with Mr Jowett, though.'

It was an odd friendship, he thought. From the description he'd read, Edward Jowett was a precise, portly and utterly conventional, if kindly, man. 'He sounds to have been a staid sort of chap for an American daredevil to take up with.'

'Nevertheless, sir, that's what I was told. They'd often have dinner together. I tell you sir, it's odd. And I don't like the bank. It strikes me as all wrong they should masquerade as British when there's German money behind it.'

'American money,' corrected Sir Douglas. 'Look, Tanner, forget about international finance. When I asked you about the bank, what I actually wanted to know was if any of Mr Jowett's colleagues had noticed any change of mood recently. Was he worried or concerned about anything?'

'He certainly had something on his mind, sir. On the day of the incident, he was noticeably distracted and very much below par. He told his colleagues he felt very seedy, so he went home early. He doesn't seem to have been himself for about a week or so before he died.'

'Was he sickening for something?'

'If he was, he hadn't consulted his doctor about it.'

'Then was it something wrong at the bank? Any suggestion of fraud or theft, perhaps?'

'Nothing's come to light,' said Tanner.

'So we're back to something wrong at home. Which, I must say, is where I thought the problem was in the first place. Both Mr and Mrs Jowett were worried in the week or weeks leading up to their deaths. It could be that Mr Jowett had some sort of illness – although, as you say, he hadn't consulted his doctor – but we're guessing it had something to do with Maurice Knowle.'

'The servants heard him shout "Maurice", before the shooting,' agreed Inspector Tanner.

'Indeed they did.' Sir Douglas tutted impatiently. 'And, of course, the butler said "Maurice" before he died.' He flicked open the report and thumbed through it. 'Maurice Knowle benefits from his mother and stepfather's death to the tune of fourteen thousand pounds. It's a tidy sum.' He leaned back and steepled his fingers. 'You're sure we're not being led up the garden path?' he asked abruptly.

Inspector Tanner was startled. 'How d'you mean, sir?'

'Are you certain that Mr Jowett shot his wife and then shot himself? You see, Tanner, for one thing, the butler, Samuel Hawthorne, said, literally with his dying breath, that it was his fault. What did he mean?'

Tanner shrugged. 'I couldn't make sense of that, sir. It can't possibly have been the butler's fault. Hawthorne was with the other servants outside the study door. The housekeeper, Mrs Harrop, stated that, not only was he in service with the family since he was a boy, he was devoted to Mr Jowett and to Mrs Jowett in particular. I may say that the Jowetts were highly regarded by both Mrs Harrop and Hawthorne. Mrs Harrop has been with the Jowetts for nearly ten years and was very happy with them.'

'The cause of Hawthorne's death was heart failure, I believe.'

'Yes, sir. It was a long-standing condition.'

'What about the other servants? Have they been with the Jowetts long?'

'No, sir. All the rest of the staff have only been in their places a few months, but according to the housekeeper, the Jowetts counted themselves lucky to get anyone, what with the wages these women can earn nowadays in the factories.' The inspector grinned. 'Mrs Harrop doesn't approve of factory work. She's very old fashioned and hates the idea that Jack – and Jill – are as good as their masters.'

'She's out of tune with modern thought,' grunted Sir Douglas. He sighed impatiently. 'It doesn't make sense. Edward Jowett seems a kindly, well-disposed man who cared for his wife and stepson. He was a moderate drinker and there's no history of domestic disputes. And yet this kindly, well-regarded man apparently murdered his wife.'

'We know they quarrelled, sir. The servants heard them.'

'Even so . . .' Sir Douglas broke off impatiently. 'Look, Tanner, not to beat about the bush, was there a third party in the room? A third party who murdered the Jowetts? Furthermore, in light of what the butler said, was that third party Maurice Knowle?'

'It's not possible, sir.' There was no doubt in Tanner's voice. 'As I've stated in my report, the servants heard the argument, heard the shots, and stayed outside the door until it was broken open.'

'Could a murderer have killed the Jowetts, then escaped out of the window before the door was forced?'

Inspector Tanner shook his head. 'No, sir. The study is on the third floor, overlooking the front of the house and it's a sheer drop to the ground. Besides that, there were no marks on the windowsill. Granted his injuries, it would be a complete impossibility for Maurice Knowle, no matter what the butler said.'

Sir Douglas nodded in agreement. 'I have to agree with you on that score. You seem to have gone into the thing pretty thoroughly.'

Tanner looked understandably pleased. 'I did, sir. In view of the importance of the case, I didn't want there to be any doubt. PC Coltrane, the officer who broke the door down, left the servants in the room and telephoned the station for instructions. Acting on advice from the inspector of the division, Inspector Carhew, Constable Coltrane remained on duty inside the room until Inspector Carhew arrived with his men. The local doctor, Dr Simmons, arrived before Inspector Carhew. He saw to Mrs Harrop and pronounced Hawthorne and both the Jowetts dead. Although Inspector Carhew was satisfied in his own mind that no third party was involved, in view of the gravity of the case, he called in the

Yard. He didn't want there to be any question that the police had failed in their duties.'

'Quite right too,' murmured Sir Douglas.

'When I arrived, Inspector Carhew was still there. We naturally discussed the possibility of an intruder but we were able to dismiss the idea.'

'You're completely certain?'

'Completely, sir. In view of the evidence from the servants, I can't say I had any real doubts as to the truth of the matter, but, to be on the safe side, I conducted a thorough search.'

'There wasn't anywhere an intruder could've been hiding?'

'Not that I could see, sir. It's not a big room and there aren't any cupboards or anything of that nature.'

'I see there were papers on the table. Where were the papers kept?'

'On the bookcase, I presume, sir. There was a box file, the sort of file that's kept on a shelf. There are bookcases, but they're solid oak, flat against the wall, and can't be moved. No one could hide behind them.'

Sir Douglas drummed his fingers on the table. 'I wish I knew why the butler said "Maurice" before he died.' He tapped the report once more. 'I see that, despite him being a cripple, you did check up on Maurice Knowle.'

'Of course, sir. In view of what Hawthorne said before he died, I felt it my duty to do so. I didn't know the extent of his injuries, otherwise I'd have probably dismissed him out of hand. He seemed genuinely shaken.'

Sir Douglas smoothed his moustache thoughtfully. 'He could have been putting that on, I suppose, but in light of what you say, I don't see how it's possible for him to be involved.' He lit a cigarette and heaved a deep sigh. 'Is there anything else? Anything, that is, that we haven't spoken about?'

'Nothing, sir . . .' began Tanner, then stopped. 'There's just one thing, sir. The housekeeper mentioned it. About a fortnight before the shooting, Mr Jowett complained that someone had been in his study. He was far more upset than the occasion seemed to warrant. It blew over, but it was about that time that Mrs Jowett seemed to become worried, as if she had something on her mind.'

'Was anything taken?'

'No, sir, but I did wonder if someone in the house – perhaps even Captain Knowle – had tried to get hold of confidential bank documents.'

'It's a thought. Are we certain Jowett wasn't involved in a fraud?'

Tanner shrugged. 'As certain as I can be, yes. Everyone who worked with him has said he was an honest and dedicated man. There's the other point, too, that no irregularities at the bank have come to light. Mr Jowett's been dead for the best part of a week. If anything was wrong, it'd have been discovered by now.'

Sir Douglas nodded. 'I agree.' He blew out a cloud of smoke, closed the file and drummed his fingers on the manila folder. 'So there we have it, Tanner. You seem to have acted very efficiently.' He paused unhappily. 'We're missing something though. Something happened to cause Edward Jowett to lose his temper so completely that he murdered his wife. I wish we knew what.'

THREE

I t was a week after the three deaths that had ripped the Jowett household apart. With the press dominated by news of the war, the case, which would have merited columns of newsprint before the war, was relegated to a brief recital of facts under the headline of 'Tragic [or Mysterious or Sudden or Violent] Death of Banker and Wife'.

Father Emil Quinet read of the deaths as he diligently scoured the papers for news of his beloved Belgium, which was so scarred by war. Then, as habit and training lead him to do, he said a prayer for the souls of the departed, and forgot all about it.

Behind the screen of the confessional, he yawned and rubbed his face with his hands. He was old, he had slept fitfully, and the church was very quiet, this Saturday lunchtime. From outside, filtered by the thick walls, came the restful, muted, sound of London traffic.

From outside the confessional came the creak of a pew. He sat up, unconsciously readying himself into a listening pose. Someone was sitting or kneeling down, gathering their thoughts or saying a prayer before entering the small, dark space on the other side of the screen.

Bless me Father, for I have sinned . . .

He had heard those words thousands of times. Would they be spoken in French or English? His English was good but slow and he understood far more than he could speak. At home, in Liege, they had been spoken in French. Here, in London, it was still said, as often as not, in French, as his fellow refugees came to the Belgian priest to whisper their faults and be granted absolution. For the most part the faults were very minor and if Father Quinet's speech was gentler and his manner more gracious with his unseen Belgian penitents than with the Irish, Italians and English, it was only to be expected that he should favour his fellow Belgians who had suffered so much in this terrible war.

He waited a few minutes for the creak of the door, but no creak came. Should he, perhaps, go into the church? There was no door into the priest's side of the confessional from the church, only a blank wall. The priest entered the confessional from the sacristy and newcomers sometimes didn't realize the priest was there, waiting to hear their confession. Then he heard footsteps and relaxed. They would come in soon.

They didn't.

Instead he heard a voice. It was a man's voice, quiet but sharp with anger. 'You're late.'

Father Quinet blinked in surprise. Anger was an unusual state of mind in which to approach confession. It was a fault he would have to bring to the unseen's attention.

A woman answered. Her voice was also quiet but indignant, made sharper by her shrill London accent. 'Don't you take that tone with me. I didn't know where this place was. It took me ages to find it.'

Father Quinet found himself nodding in unconscious agreement. St Mark the Evangelist, like all Catholic churches in this foreign land, hid itself away down a side street, away from its Anglican neighbours.

'Don't be late again.' The man's voice was curt and he had an accent Father Quinet found hard to place. Was he an American? Perhaps. 'There's a lot at stake. He's worried by recent events.'

'It wasn't my fault the Jowett business went wrong.'

Father Quinet frowned. Jowett? The name rang a very faint bell.

The man sighed impatiently. 'That's all over and done with. I've managed to convince him it was just bad luck.'

'Bad luck? It's thanks to me that it wasn't more than bad luck. Without me, we'd have been up the creek and no mistake.'

'All right,' said the man grumpily. 'You've had a reward. What more d'you want?'

'A few manners would be nice,' said the woman with a sniff.

'Can it, will you? I don't mind telling you I'm worried. We've never handled anything as big as this before. We have to show him we mean business.'

If Father Quinet had been a younger man, he would have risen indignantly and shooed away this couple who seemed to think the church was nothing more than a handy free space to hold a business meeting. Visions of Christ driving the money changers from the temple rose in his mind. He tried to stand, but his arthritic knee jabbed an agonizing protest and he sank back in his chair, gathering his strength.

'I don't know why we've come here,' said the woman petulantly. 'I've never had nothing to do with churches.'

'I've used this place before. It's quiet and he wants to be private. Jowett worried him. That's why he wants to meet you. He wants this kept completely private, you understand? This is between you, me and him. If one word leaks out—'

'I know how to hold my tongue. Where is he, anyway?' she added aggressively. 'If anyone's late, he is.'

'He's the client. He's allowed to be late.'

Father Quinet's eyebrows rose in disbelief. Was it possible that the church – *his* church – was being used not merely for business but for a sordid assignation? He gathered his cassock around him and, gripping the arm of the chair, made another move to stand up, when more steps sounded outside.

He paused, listening keenly, wanting to hear details of the transaction, wanting to assure himself that he was right, that his grasp of English had not misled him.

There was a creak as the newcomer sat down.

'*Bonjour, Monsieur.*' It was the woman. Father Quinet blinked.

The woman still spoke in unmistakable cockney, but the language was French.

There was a satisfied laugh. '*Tres bien.*'

Why on earth were they speaking French? No matter what language they spoke, this had to be stopped. It was a man's voice but, Father Quinet was sure, not the first man. This must, he thought with a shudder of fastidious disgust, be the client. Once again he was about to stand up, when the client spoke once more, again in French.

'So you speak the language?'

'We both do,' said the first man. Astonishingly, he also spoke in French. 'We lived in Paris for five years. The language isn't a problem.'

'Do you speak it well enough to look after the child?'

The child? What child? Curiosity kept Father Quinet in his seat.

'And the journey?' continued the client. 'That will not bother you?'

'Not if you arrange things. As he told you, we lived in Paris.'

'Good.' The client was evidently satisfied. 'You are competent to deal with children?'

Again, the woman spoke in French. 'How difficult can it be?'

The first man intervened. 'She's a quick learner.'

Father Quinet could hear the doubt in the client's voice. 'If we're recommending her, she must be good.'

'I'll be fine,' said the woman. 'I want to be paid in English money, mind. None of your foreign stuff.'

'You will be well rewarded!' The client's voice was thin with impatience.

'That's what you say, but you can't tell me there isn't anything dodgy going on. I want to know what I'm letting myself in for *and* how much I'm getting.'

'You will both receive two hundred when you start and another eight hundred when the job is completed.'

There were a few moments of dead silence.

The man whistled appreciatively, but it was the woman who spoke. 'A thousand quid?' she said in an awed voice. 'All for me, you mean? That's a lot of money.'

The client gave a short laugh. 'Enough to ensure you keep quiet and obey orders, yes?'

'Well . . .' The woman hesitated. 'What's going to happen to the kid? I don't want it killed.'

Father Quinet's eyes widened in horror. This wasn't business or even a sordid assignation. This was downright wickedness.

'You would care about the child?' asked the client quickly.

'If I'm involved, yes. It's too risky, even if the money's good. People get funny about kids.'

There was a long pause, then the client said, 'You will take her to Jane Fleet.'

'Jane Fleet?' repeated the woman. 'Who's she?'

The first man laughed. 'Never you mind. I know all about Jane Fleet.'

Jane Fleet, Father Quinet repeated to himself. That was a name to remember.

The client spoke again. 'The child will not be harmed.'

With a shrinking of his flesh, Father Quinet knew the man was lying.

'However,' continued the client, 'although the reward is great, there is only one penalty for failure.'

There was dead silence.

'Are you threatening us?' said the man.

The client's voice was icy. 'I am pointing out the obvious. We cannot tolerate another failure such as Jowett.'

Jowett? thought Father Quinet. He knew that name but from where? He dismissed the elusive memory and concentrated, listening hard.

'The Jowett affair was bad luck,' said the first man. 'I did what I could.'

'A very valuable resource was lost. This must not happen again.'

'All *right*,' said the first man. He sounded harried.

'If the police had not been stupid, our entire operation would have been compromised. Jowett—'

'Thanks to me, we got away with Jowett,' interrupted the first man.

'Thank to me, actually,' put in the woman icily. 'The police get a bit too nosy for my liking when there's a sudden death. I don't like deaths.'

Death! With a sudden rush of memory, Father Quinet remembered pausing as he read the newspaper. He had joined his hands in prayer. *Requiem aeternam dona eis, Domine, et lux perpetua luceat eis . . . Eternal rest give unto them, O Lord, and let perpetual light shine upon them.* They were the first lines of the mass for the dead. The Jowetts were dead.

There was an exasperated sigh from the church. 'Look, it's better if we put our cards on the table.' It was the first man. 'There'll be at least one death. It's better to have this out in the open now. I don't want you to have anything to complain about.'

'Murder?' asked the woman.

Father Quinet could hardly restrain his gasp of horror. There was silence from the church.

'You could call it murder, I suppose,' said the first man eventually.

The woman was silent for a while. 'Any chance I'll be nabbed for it?'

'None whatsoever.'

Again, she was silent for a while. 'All right,' she said grudgingly. 'You've always played square with me before. Mind you, I could mention a few things if I was nabbed.'

'It would be much, much better for you if you didn't.' It was the client and his voice was silky with menace.

'Don't you threaten me,' said the woman petulantly. 'All right, I'm in. I'll have to learn the ropes, though.'

The client sighed impatiently. 'It would be better to find a woman who is already trained.'

'Where from?' demanded the woman. 'If you can find someone else who speaks the lingo, can look after kids, and who isn't squeamish about murder, you're welcome to them.'

'She's right,' said the first man.

'How long will it take?' demanded the client. 'Time is short.'

'I'd like a month.'

'A month! This needs to happen within days. I can let you have a fortnight, and even that might be too long.'

'What about the kid?' asked the woman. 'What if she talks?'

She, Father Quinet noted. It was a little girl who was in danger.

The client made a dismissive noise. 'It's up to you to keep her quiet. How you do it is your affair.'

'And the orphanage won't kick up? They're nuns, aren't they? I don't know nothing about nuns.'

'These nuns will not complain,' said the client and something in his voice made Father Quinet shudder.

'You're sure?' asked the first man. 'I don't want it to go wrong because of some snivelling nun.'

'It will not go wrong. We have used this particular child before, you understand? Sister Marie-Eugénie has enjoyed certain privileges because of her co-operation.'

Marie-Eugénie. Father Quinet hung hungrily onto the name. That was a real fact. Sister Marie-Eugénie and Jane Fleet. He must remember those names.

'Such as what?' asked the woman suspiciously.

'You ask too many questions,' said the client curtly. 'The orphanage has been allowed to continue and Marie-Eugénie has been left unmolested. That is enough.'

There was a creak from the pew and a shuffle of feet. He'd evidently stood up. 'We are agreed then?'

'We're agreed,' said the first man. 'I'll let you know in the usual way when we are ready.'

'Time is short,' said the client. 'Remember that.'

Father Quinet heard the sound of feet on the stone flags as the client left. As quietly as he could, he levered himself to his feet. He needed to be quick. The client had gone but he wanted to see this terrible man and woman who had so calmly plotted murder. Yes, he needed to be quick, but age and stiffness took its toll. By the time he got out of the sacristy and into the church, the church was empty and the street outside, once he had hobbled to the door, was deserted.

FOUR

Father Quinet had never felt so handicapped by his position and his nationality. If this was Belgium, he would have consulted his bishop. As it was, he had to consult the parish priest, his superior, Father Croft.

Father Croft was sceptical. He suggested that the old man had fallen asleep and dreamt it all. That, in Father Croft's view, would be the most convenient explanation.

Father Croft liked convenience. He was a brisk, no-nonsense man with a large, poverty-stricken parish that had quite enough problems of its own before it had swelled alarmingly with the flood of Belgian refugees.

Father Croft, who marshalled his curates like a general deploying his troops, found Father Quinet an inconvenient anomaly. After all, Father Quinet had had his own parish for many years, even if it was in Belgium. He was far too old to be treated as a curate but not old enough to be safely retired. Father Croft assigned him the care of the Belgian refugees and – this *was* convenient – let him run their affairs as a parish within a parish. Father Croft was dismissive of the idea of going to the police and was annoyed when Father Quinet, with the help of a Belgian parishioner, who had been a lawyer before the war, insisted on going to Scotland Yard.

Father Quinet's statement gave the Deputy Commissioner, Douglas Lynton, a problem.

If it hadn't been for the mention of the Jowett case, he would have probably filed the statement away and waited on events. The trouble was, although there was certainly something criminal afoot, exactly how it could be prevented was anyone's guess.

But then there was this odd connection with the Jowett case.

The police had apparently been stupid over the Jowett case, but for the life of him, he couldn't see how. The Jowett case troubled him. Even though he couldn't fault the way Inspector Tanner had handled the case, he had been uneasy with the obvious conclusion. Now, in light of what Father Quinet had stated, it seemed as if he'd been right to doubt the obvious.

Not only that, but it sounded as if some further devilry was being planned. Whatever it was, it sounded as if it was going to happen in France or, possibly, Belgium. The reference to a journey, the fact that part of the conversation had been in French and the insistence that the woman spoke the language certainly suggested as much. Should he report it to the War Office? The lack of details made him pause and then he suddenly thought of Sir Charles Talbot.

Talbot had been a policeman, a colleague, a big, affable, Irishman and one of the shrewdest men Sir Douglas had ever met. He had been knighted upon his retirement from the force and was now supposedly in a sinecure of a post that was vaguely described as something to do with police pensions.

The truth was, as Sir Douglas and a very few others knew, that Charles Talbot had been picked to set up an intelligence service. Its aim was to counter threats from Fenians, anarchists and revolutionaries who promoted their cause with gunfights and bombs in the London streets. As his own name was far too familiar to the various Fenians, anarchists and revolutionaries, Charles Talbot worked from a small office in Angel Alley off Cockspur Street under the name and description of Mr W. Gabriel Monks, General Agent.

When war was declared, the tiny service had taken on a new role, gathering information about the enemy.

Charles Talbot, thought Sir Douglas, wouldn't take too much notice of that crack about police stupidity. Inspector Tanner was nobody's fool and, in light of the evidence, there was no other conclusion possible about the Jowett case. Talbot would understand that.

Talbot did. It was interesting. Very interesting. And what, perhaps, was the most interesting of all was the mention of Sister Marie-Eugénie. Because, he thought, as he walked from Whitehall to the War Office, the mention of Sister Marie-Eugénie could only mean that this was a case for Dr Anthony Brooke.

Tara Brooke was trying hard to keep her spirits up. After a three-day leave, Anthony was going back to France. They'd been married for seven weeks and he was going back to France.

If the wind was in the right direction, the sound of the guns could be heard in London.

Anthony had to go back to the guns. Anthony, who could make her heart turn over, Anthony with his kindly grey eyes and wonderful smile, was going back. Back to a Casualty Clearing Station, back to the bombed-out cellars just behind the front line.

The lunch – a special lunch, with as many of Anthony's favourite things as she could manage – tasted like dust. Tears were very near but she *wasn't* going to send him off in tears. She was fiercely proud of who he was and what he did and her own small sacrifice to the war was to be as brave in remaining as he was in leaving. Tears were for later.

If only this was a normal day! She knew that later she'd think of so much she should've said, but anything 'normal' sounded trite and all the things she really wanted to say were awkward, weighty and embarrassing. To say the conversation was stilted was an understatement.

The doorbell rang. Tara clutched the tablecloth convulsively as Anthony looked up, puzzled.

'We weren't expecting anyone, were we?'

'Certainly not,' she said, and was relieved to hear her voice sounded steady. She could hear Ellen, the maid, open the door. 'No one would interrupt us on your last day.'

Ellen had been given instructions that they were not at home. It was unendurable that Anthony's last few hours should be shared with anyone else but her. Unendurable, yes, but – she twisted with guilt – she couldn't help feeling slightly relieved.

There were voices in the hall. Was that Charles Talbot? What on earth did he want?

Tara liked Sir Charles very much but they had seen him yesterday. Resentment flared. After all, he knew this was Anthony's last day. She expected Ellen to show Sir Charles into the sitting room, to wait until they finished lunch at least, but to her absolute astonishment, the door opened and Sir Charles walked in.

'I'm sorry to interrupt,' he said, as Anthony stood up. 'Mrs Brooke,' he added with a smile, 'I'm not surprised you're looking daggers at me, but I really needed to catch Brooke before he left. Please, go on with your meal.'

'Take a seat, Talbot,' said Anthony. He gave Tara a what-can-I-say look as he sat down. 'What can I do for you, old man?'

Sir Charles lent forward. 'Before I say anything else, let me tell you that I've spoken to the War Office, and they've agreed to let me borrow you, so to speak, for an indefinite period.'

'Borrow me?' asked Anthony with a frown.

'And an uphill job it was too, my dear fellow, to get them to agree.' He smiled at Tara. 'You'll perhaps look at me a little kinder, Mrs Brooke, when I tell you that your husband is not going back to France. He's very much needed here.'

'Not going back?' Tara repeated blankly. '*Not* going?' There was a buzzing in her ears and her eyes seemed misty as she looked at Sir Charles. He nodded agreement and suddenly, through the mist, Charles Talbot looked like the most wonderful man in the world.

'But why?' demanded Anthony.

'I've got a job for you. I can't command, of course, only ask. It's fortunate that you're in London, but if you weren't, I'd request your return.'

'What on earth's happened?' asked Anthony in bewilderment.

'I'm sure Mrs Brooke has heard of the Jowett family,' said Sir Charles, turning to her. 'Their deaths were reported in the papers, but you, Brooke, were in France when the tragedy occurred.' He hitched closer to the table. 'Let me tell you about the Jowetts and a certain Father Quinet.'

Sir Charles couldn't complain about any lack of attention from his audience.

'I don't understand,' said Tara slowly, when he'd finished. 'Is this priest, this Father Quinet, *certain* he heard these people mention Sister Marie-Eugénie?'

Sir Charles nodded.

Tara stared at Anthony. 'Anthony, this is incredible. The child they spoke about, the little girl who's in danger – if she's looked after in an orphanage by a Sister Marie-Eugénie – they just have to be talking about Milly.'

Anthony felt stunned. 'I can hardly believe it, but you have to be right. The enemy must be planning to use Milly. They've used her before, as we know.'

Earlier in the year, in May, Anthony had brought the affair that in his own mind he labelled as Frankie's Letter to a conclusion. Although the danger posed by Frankie had been averted, there were – there always were – unfinished elements and messy threads.

Perhaps the most unfinished and messiest element left unresolved was the little girl called Milly. Milly was about five years old, an orphan, who had been used by the enemy as a tool for blackmail. Anthony had never met her; he had only seen a photograph, but the picture of the child with her dark, solemn eyes had captured his imagination. He knew very little of her but what he did know was that she was behind German lines in the occupied territory and in an orphanage in the care of a nun, a Sister Marie-Eugénie. The trouble was, that was all he did know.

'And so you see, Brooke,' said Sir Charles, 'once I'd heard what Douglas Lynton had to say, I knew you had to be involved.'

'You're absolutely right.' Anthony still felt stunned. 'Well, I suppose the first thing to do is to see Father Quinet. Which church is it again?'

'St Mark the Evangelist, Hob Lane, Soho,' said Sir Charles quickly. 'But you must finish your lunch before we go.' He grinned. 'Otherwise I really will be in the doghouse with Mrs Brooke.'

Father Quinet didn't know what to make of his visitors. He'd expected an official in uniform, but neither of his guests wore uniform. Mr Monks was an Irishman and had, apparently, been a policeman, for all that he looked like a well-to-do farmer with comfortable proportions, an infectious smile and a healthy out-of-doors complexion. Dr Anthony Brooke was taller and leaner, a thoughtful looking man in his early thirties, with fair hair and grey eyes.

Father Quinet started, at his guests' request, by showing them the confessional in the church. Mr Monks immediately endeared himself to the old priest by genuflecting in front of the tabernacle. 'I'm a Catholic, Father,' Mr Monks explained. 'If not, I'm afraid, a very good one.'

'That can be said of most of us,' said Father Quinet, feeling immeasurably reassured.

Anthony and Sir Charles examined the confessional from the sacristy.

This was where the priest sat. It was a small space containing a chair, a wooden prie-dieu or prayer desk with a sloping shelf, pinned to which were the words of absolution and holding various prayer cards and a set of rosary beads. The prie-dieu stood against the stone wall separating them from the other half of the confessional. The wall was pierced by a small unglazed window, masked by a black linen curtain.

Sir Charles went to sit in a pew in the church, beside the open door of the confessional.

The entrance to the confessional was the only door in the solid stone wall. A glance inside the confessional showed it was empty. From this side, the confessional was a small stone room with a place to kneel in front of a black linen curtain. To anyone unacquainted with Catholic practice or architecture it would seem impossible that there was anyone there to overhear what was said in the church.

Anthony, behind the curtain in the sacristy, drew the curtain aside and put his head through. 'Can you say something, Mr Monks?' he called to Sir Charles in the pew. 'A poem or a nursery rhyme, perhaps? I want to see how the sound carries to someone behind the curtain.'

'I can think of something more suitable than a nursery rhyme,' said Sir Charles. '"Hail Mary, full of grace . . ."'

He completed the prayer, speaking clearly but quietly.

Anthony came out of the sacristy and into the church. 'I could hear every word,' he said. 'It's an odd effect. I think the sound is amplified by the stone.'

'You can hear nothing when the door is shut,' said Father Quinet rather defensively. 'The secrecy of the confessional is absolute, you understand?'

'You don't feel bound by secrecy in this case, Father?' asked Sir Charles.

The old priest shook his head gravely. 'No, indeed. They were not seeking absolution. Nor were they – how shall I say it? – seeking *aggrandizement,* to impress each other.' He shuddered. 'It was a cold-blooded plan to murder a man and to harm a child. I am certain they mean to harm a child, a little girl, you understand?'

'Harm a little girl,' Anthony repeated. 'That must not be allowed to happen.' He spoke quietly but there was a steely glint in his grey eyes. Father Quinet glanced at him sharply. This English doctor was angry but Father Quinet felt warmed by the emotion. Father Quinet was used to discerning emotions and this was a righteous anger.

'You said part of the conversation was in French,' asked Sir Charles. 'They weren't French, were they?'

Father Quinet shook his head vigorously. 'The man, I think, was American. I have heard Americans speak before. The woman was English. She spoke as people from London speak, you understand? The second man, the client, as they called him, I do not think was French, but not English either.' He shrugged helplessly. 'I wanted to see them!' he added desperately. 'I would have stopped them, challenged them, confronted them with their crime.'

It was just as well, thought Anthony, that the fearless old man had been unable to do any such thing, otherwise they would have his actual murder rather than a hypothetical crime on their hands.

'I searched the church,' Father Quinet went on. 'I thought perhaps they might have left a glove or a notebook or something to say who they were, but there was nothing. I wrote everything they said down as soon as I could, so I would not forget.'

'That was very far-sighted of you,' said Sir Charles. 'Now, Father, you have a study, yes? Perhaps we could sit down in there and you can tell us everything you can remember. Then Dr Brooke and myself are going to do our level best to see that these people are stopped.'

FIVE

I t was probably extreme circumspection on Anthony's part, but he didn't want to discuss Father Quinet's story until he and Sir Charles were safely behind closed doors in Sir Charles' office in Angel Alley.

'Are you happy to talk about the matter now?' asked Sir Charles with an ironic twist to his voice.

Anthony laughed. 'I'm not going to apologize for being cautious, Talbot,' he said, picking up his cup of tea from the tray that Sir Charles had sent for.

Sir Charles winced. 'Monks, m'lad, if you please, although we're safe enough in here.' Sir Charles had made sure the door to his private office was firmly shut. 'Remember I'm known in the office as Mr Monks.'

'That's exactly what I mean,' said Anthony. 'The wrong word out of place can be dangerous. We don't know much about the scheme Father Quinet overheard, but one thing we do know is that our precious trio must've had some reason for picking St Mark's. The most obvious reason is that it's near at hand for either one, both, or all of them. There was a dickens of a crowd on Charing Cross Road. We could've been easily overheard and we'd never know.'

'That's true,' agreed Sir Charles, stretching back in his chair. 'On the face of it, the fact that at least one of them has to be near St Mark's seems like a clue, but Soho is one of the most densely populated areas of the globe. Still,' he added with a shrug, 'it might lead us somewhere eventually. What d'you make of the whole thing? Is the child they're after really Milly?'

'I think so,' agreed Anthony. 'It just has to be Milly. "We have used this particular child before",' he quoted thoughtfully.

'There are thousands of children in occupied France and Belgium, poor little devils,' said Sir Charles.

'Yes, but not looked after by a nun called Marie-Eugénie. But why on earth should Milly be worth a couple of thousand quid to anyone?'

Sir Charles shook his head. 'On the face of it, there isn't any reason. What I am going to assume, though, is that this isn't an ordinary criminal enterprise. Like you, I'm going to take an educated guess that the child involved is Milly. It's a fair presumption that Milly can't speak English, which explains why it's important the woman speaks French.'

Anthony nodded. 'That would account for it, yes.' He gave a quick, frustrated sigh. 'Dammit, Talbot, I wish we had more facts! I don't suppose the name of this other woman, Jane Fleet, means anything to you, does it?'

'No, it doesn't. More to the point, it didn't mean anything to Douglas Lynton either. There's no mention of her in the records department at the Yard.'

Anthony clicked his tongue. 'If we knew where Milly was, the simplest thing to do would be to go and get her. That'd spike their guns sure enough, but I can hardly wander round behind enemy lines looking for a Sister Marie-Eugénie.'

'No, you can't,' said Sir Charles firmly. 'However, we've got to do something and, what's more, do it quickly. It's two days since Father Quinet overheard our precious trio. The woman was told she had a fortnight, which doesn't give us long. In the time we've got, I think it's hopeless to imagine we'll find out where Milly is. On the other hand, we do know about the Jowetts.'

'Judging from what Father Quinet overheard, it's obvious there's more to that business than meets the eye.'

'Indeed it does. I may say that Douglas Lynton, who's a very sound man, is perfectly happy to believe that the police were forced to accept the wrong conclusion about the Jowett case.'

Anthony nodded. 'The wrong conclusion being that Edward Jowett shot his wife then shot himself. In fact, we're saying the Jowetts were murdered.'

Sir Charles lit a cigarette. 'That's the size of it, yes.'

Again, Anthony nodded. 'OK . . . So why kill the Jowetts? All I've gleaned from the police report is that they were a devoted couple who lived quiet lives. There doesn't seem any reason to kill them.'

'That's just it,' said Sir Charles in frustration. 'Nevertheless, there must be a reason and a pretty urgent one at that.' He shook his head impatiently. 'I wish I knew why the butler said "Maurice" before he died.'

Anthony drummed his fingers on the table. 'It's unfortunate that the butler died.'

Sir Charles raised his eyebrows. 'I'll say this for you, Brooke, you don't go in for hyperbole. You wouldn't like to use a stronger word than unfortunate, perhaps?'

'All right, it's very unfortunate,' said Anthony with a quick smile. 'And tragic for the butler, poor beggar. He obviously felt guilty about something. I think I need to talk to the servants.'

'Very well.' Sir Charles picked up the Scotland Yard report. 'Here we are. There's a list of the servants' names. The housekeeper is a Mrs Harrop. She's the woman who collapsed at the scene.'

'Right-oh. Do I use my own name?'

'No,' said Sir Charles after a couple of moment's hesitation. 'We don't know who she might talk to.' He smiled. 'I think this is a job for Colonel Ralde.'

Anthony grinned. There was no such person as Colonel Ralde, but, all the same, the colonel was known to the War Office.

Talbot had dreamed up the name. His office was in Angel Alley. Sir Charles liked an angelic touch to his choice of pseudonyms, so Colonel H.E. Ralde was born. He was, as Sir Charles explained, with a laugh, a 'Heralde' angel. Puns aside, if anyone left a message for, or wanted to get in touch with, Colonel Ralde, the War Office knew to refer them to Talbot. It was a device that had been very useful in the past.

'Colonel Ralde it is,' said Anthony, pushing back his chair. 'I've got his visiting cards.'

Number 4, Pettifer's Court, was a typical London town house, tall and thin and guarded by iron railings. A short flight of steps over the basement below led up to a blue-painted front door. The lion's head brass door knocker had a length of black ribbon wrapped around it, bearing mute witness to the recent tragedy.

The door was opened by a plump, middle-aged woman with a worried, kindly face. She eyed Anthony's uniform with respect and a certain amount of caution.

Anthony had very mixed feelings about his uniform. He wasn't a soldier; he was a doctor. He had his doctor's uniform, of course, but Talbot had arranged a commission for him, complete with a uniform with a colonel's insignia from the Intelligence Corps, to go with it. It gave him, said Talbot, a right to ask questions.

'Can I help you, sir?' asked the woman.

'I hope so,' said Anthony, raising his cap. 'I was hoping to speak to Mrs Harrop.'

The woman looked surprised. 'Why, that's me, sir. Did you want to ask about the poor master and the mistress? I seem to have answered no end of questions about it, but I thought all that had stopped now.'

'I can only apologize,' said Anthony. 'I realize you must be very busy, but I really would appreciate a few minutes of your time.'

The housekeeper eyed his uniform once more and nodded. Talbot had been right about the uniform. 'I suppose you'd better come in, sir,' she said reluctantly. She stood aside for him to enter the hall, a cheerless passage with the furniture swathed in brown holland covers.

'You'll excuse the state of the house, I'm sure, but with the master and mistress gone, Captain Knowle – he owns the house now, of course – asked me to stay on, until we can find a nice tenant, and, of course, the covers help to keep the dust off.'

'It must be very difficult for you,' murmured Anthony.

She warmed to his sympathy. 'Indeed it is, sir. The thing is, I'm not sure where to ask you to sit down. The master and mistress always entertained their visitors in the drawing room but everything's

boxed up and packed away.' She looked at him, perplexed, then said
dubiously, 'I usually have visitors in my own sitting room, but that
doesn't seem quite right, somehow, for a gentleman like you. I
wouldn't suggest it, but I don't see where else we can sit, and that's
a fact.'

'I'm sure that'll be fine,' said Anthony easily. 'I'm very much
obliged to you for sparing the time.'

Inwardly he was very pleased with the suggestion. In her own
room, Mrs Harrop would probably feel a lot more forthcoming
than in the cold formality of the drawing room surrounded by
shrouded furniture.

Mrs Harrop was unconvinced but willing to be persuaded. 'Well,
if you're sure.' She led the way down the hall, through the green
baize door and into a pleasant, bright room with a fire in the grate,
a brass kettle on the hob, oilcloth-covered table and chairs, and a
well-worn but comfortable looking sofa.

'Please sit down,' she said, shooing the cat off the sofa and
moving the kettle onto the hob, where it started to whistle almost
immediately. 'The kettle was just on the boil when you rang the
bell. You'll have a cup of tea, won't you? I always have one about
this time in the afternoon.'

Anthony, mindful of cat hairs on his uniform, chose one of the
kitchen chairs in preference to the sofa. 'The day of the tragedy
must have been very sad for all of you,' he said, as she poured
the boiling water into a stout brown teapot. 'I understand that as
well as poor Mr and Mrs Jowett, you lost the butler as well.'

She turned to him, blinking back tears. 'That was shocking,'
she said, taking two cups from the dresser. 'Poor Mr Hawthorne.
He was that pleased to be back in service – not that he could do
as much as he liked because he really was very frail – but he
insisted on coming back.' She sighed and dabbed the corner of
her eye. 'I remember the mistress saying to me, as how she hoped
as how it wouldn't be the death of him.' She gulped. 'I suppose
you could say it was, not that she had any idea of what was going
to happen.'

'You heard the shots, I understand.'

She nodded vigorously. 'We all heard them, sir, not that we
knew what they were. I mean, you don't expect shooting, do you?
Not in a respectable house.'

'Certainly not,' agreed Anthony. 'It must've been a terrible shock.'

'It was! You mustn't think that we usually listened at doors,' she added defensively. 'I wouldn't dream of it, and Mr Hawthorne, he'd never tolerate such a thing, but we could hear an argument, and I couldn't believe my ears. I must say, I was surprised to hear the master. He was never at home at that time of day but we heard afterwards that he'd felt seedy, so he'd come home early. I suppose that was what made him tetchy-like, because in all the time I've been here, I've never heard the master raise his voice, nor the mistress either, but they were going at it hammer and tongs.'

'You couldn't hear what was said, could you?'

Mrs Harrop shook her head. 'Only bits and pieces and odd words here and there, as you might say, sir.' Thanks to Sir Douglas Lynton's report, Anthony knew what those odd words were: 'the police . . . law . . . disgrace'. They were, thought Anthony, suggestive.

She looked at him hesitantly. 'The thing is . . .' She broke off. 'I don't know what you've heard, sir.'

'I understand Captain Knowle's name was mentioned. As a matter of fact, Mrs Harrop, that's what brings me here today.'

She looked at him warily. 'Mr Maurice knows nothing about it. He called to see his mother that morning, but he only stopped about half an hour or so.'

'How did he seem? As usual?'

Mrs Harrop frowned. 'I wouldn't say he was as usual, exactly. He was worried about something, that I do know.'

'Have you any idea what he was worried about?'

'Chocolate.'

Anthony blinked. 'I beg your pardon?'

'Chocolate,' repeated Mrs Harrop. 'Don't ask me what about chocolate, because I can't tell you, but that's one of the first things he said to the mistress. "It's true," he said and then something about chocolate. After that they went into the mistress's sitting room. But you can take it from me, that Mr Maurice is as innocent as the babe unborn, especially with him being crippled and all.'

'Of course he is,' Anthony reassured her. 'But you know how gossip gets about. It's become known what poor Hawthorne said before he died and, as you can imagine, there are those who've put the worst possible construction on his words.'

Mrs Harrop bristled. 'It's just shocking what some people say.'

'I couldn't agree more. Captain Knowle is a very gallant officer and the regiment feels it's their duty to do all they can to prove his complete innocence.'

'I'll do anything to help Master Maurice. I've known him from a boy and a nicer lad you'd never meet.' She sighed heavily. 'I know he was an officer, but he was so young to have gone through so much. You know he lost his arm? You'd think folk would be shamed to think ill of him.'

'If more people thought like you, Mrs Harrop, there'd be a lot less ill-natured gossip in the world.' She was clearly pleased. 'Why don't you,' said Anthony in what he thought of as his 'I'm a doctor, you can trust me voice', 'tell me all about it?'

The voice worked. Clearly reassured, Mrs Harrop told him the story, starting from her initial surprise at seeing Hawthorne – Hawthorne, of all people! – outside the study, listening to the quarrel.

'Can you think of any reason why Mr and Mrs Jowett should have quarrelled?' asked Anthony.

Mrs Harrop looked distressed. 'I can't, sir, as true as I'm sat here. I've gone over it time and again, but it defeats me.'

There must have been something though, thought Anthony. His impression of Edward Jowett was of an even-tempered, thoughtful man. Inspector Tanner had established that Mr Jowett had been feeling under the weather when he'd left work, but not angry or distressed. Therefore it must have been something at home that had made him angry. That was a fair deduction but what was it, for heaven's sake?

'How was Mrs Jowett that morning?' Maybe she had learned something, some bad or worrying news. Some news that could, perhaps, make her husband lose his temper.

'Much the same as usual, sir. I spoke to her that morning about meals for the week, and she said there was nothing for it, but that if we couldn't get hold of chops, we'd have to make do with heart and liver and make the best of it. Wrong, I call it,' said Mrs Harrop with a sniff. 'Having to eat the inside of animals. It's not right.'

If Mrs Jowett was concerned about offal, it didn't sound as if she had any bad news to impart.

'Mind you,' continued Mrs Harrop, 'I wouldn't say she was exactly at ease. I told the policeman about this. About a month before . . .' she hesitated. 'About a month before it happened, Mr Jowett was upset and said that someone had been rooting around in his study. Nothing was taken, but my word, he was upset! He took to locking the door of the study afterwards. Mrs Jowett was ill at ease after that.' She sighed. 'It's just as well we don't know what's in store for us, isn't it?'

'Those are very wise words, Mrs Harrop,' said Anthony with shameless flattery. He was still trying to work out what had caused Mr Jowett's anger. 'Had any letters arrived for Mr Jowett by the midday post? I wondered if he'd been upset by a letter he'd received.'

'There were two letters,' said Mrs Harrop with a sniff. 'A bill from the electric and a bill from the telephone.'

Electricity and telephone bills were more likely to cause complaint than violent anger. So letters were out then. 'Had there been any visitors to the house that day?'

She shook her head. 'Not as far as I know, sir, except Mr Maurice that morning.' She hesitated. 'I don't know what Mr Maurice said to the mistress, but she wasn't herself afterwards. She seemed mithered, as if she had something on her mind.'

Something on her mind. That had to be it, surely. Maurice Knowle had brought some news, something that had worried his mother. Was it enough though? After all, what had apparently only worried Mrs Jowett had driven Mr Jowett to fury.

'Would you say Mr Jowett was a quick-tempered man?' asked Anthony.

Mrs Harrop looked shocked. 'Oh no, sir. They were such a quiet couple. They used to have the occasional bridge party and guests to dinner occasionally, but not so much recently. It's difficult, as you know, with any sort of food that's fit to put before guests being so short and hard to get hold of. The last dinner party wasn't really a dinner party at all, more a supper, with just one guest, a gentleman who Mr Jowett knew. That was about three weeks before . . .' She caught her breath. 'Before it happened. That was Mr Diefenbach from the bank.'

Diefenbach? Anthony remembered the name from Inspector Tanner's report. 'Mr Paul Diefenbach, you mean? He runs the bank, doesn't he?'

'Yes, sir, for all that he's only a young man. I should say he's not out of his thirties yet. He and the master always got on. The master was the uncle of one of Mr Diefenbach's friends. You know he used to get up to all sorts of harum-scarum tricks, flying and such like?'

Anthony suddenly realized why the name Diefenbach was vaguely familiar. Of course, Diefenbach was a real adventurer. It wasn't just flight – although hadn't he attempted to cross the North Sea? – but surely he'd been on an expedition to the Pole and he was pretty sure he'd explored Yucatan as well. Quite a bloke. 'Yes, I think I've placed him,' he said.

'Well, as I say, Mr Jowett, he was uncle to Richard Cooper, who went off with Mr Diefenbach on one of his trips, and poor Mr Richard, he was killed. A few years ago now, it was, but Mr Diefenbach, he came to see Mr Jowett to tell him all about it, and how sorry he was. It was about that time there was a bit of uncertainty at the bank, and Mr Diefenbach, he told his father, and his father ended up buying the bank. So you could say it all worked out for the best, but it's tragic that the poor master and mistress should end like this.'

She sighed deeply. 'I've wondered a few times if I should try and get in touch with him, to tell him what happened, but apparently he's gone off exploring somewhere, so I don't suppose he was able to send his condolences. He'll be upset, that I do know. He and Mr Jowett were very close. I think he saw Mr Jowett as an uncle, I do indeed. You know he was separated from his wife?'

As Anthony had only really just become aware of Paul Diefenbach's existence, he could hardly be expected to know that he was married, however unsatisfactorily. He shook his head.

'I think he appreciated Mr Jowett's advice,' continued Mrs Harrop with a sigh. 'The master, he was all for peace in the home and thought Mr Diefenbach should make an attempt to make up, but there! You can't live other people's lives for them, and that's a fact. I think this was his little bit of home, if you see my meaning, with him not having a proper home himself, just a couple of rooms in a club. He often dined here. I've heard him say that he felt that

Mr Jowett was the only one he could rely on. He said that as he
left,' she said with a reminiscent sniff. 'Poor Mr Hawthorne,
he should have stayed up to see Mr Diefenbach out, but he was
that weary, I told him to get to bed and I'd step in for him, as the
master wouldn't mind, with it being just the one guest and him
an old friend. Yes, Mr Diefenbach shook the master by the hand
as he left and said he could rely on him.'

'Rely on him? Rely on him for what?'

'I don't know, but there was something going on. It perhaps
had to do with this trip of his, running off to the ends of the earth,
and he wanted Mr Jowett to support him.'

'Perhaps,' said Anthony, making a mental note to find out more
about Paul Diefenbach. However, a supper party three weeks before
the shootings wasn't the event he was looking for. 'I don't want
to distress you, but I'd be grateful if you could tell me what
happened on the day itself.'

Mrs Harrop, dabbing her eyes occasionally, plunged into her
story.

First of all the shots and then Hawthorne's collapse, with that
wretched girl, Annie, who was as much use as a wet washday,
sobbing and crying and carrying on, and how, despite everything
she, Mrs Harrop, had said, that officious young madam, Eileen
Chadderton, had insisted on bringing a policeman into the house
and how he had shouldered down the door.

Anthony had the distinct impression that in her heart of hearts,
Mrs Harrop believed that if PC Coltrane hadn't broken down the
door, everything would somehow and mysteriously have been all
right.

'After all,' said Mrs Harrop, with an air of finality, 'Mr
Hawthorne didn't want the door broken down. That's what upset
him so.'

There was a bit more to Hawthorne's collapse than his distress
at the destruction of Mr and Mrs Jowett's property, thought
Anthony, finishing his tea. So far he'd heard nothing new, but Mrs
Harrop's story breathed life into what had been a bald recounting
of the facts in the police reports. He felt sincerely sorry for the
housekeeper. 'Poor Mr Hawthorne,' he said sympathetically.

Mrs Harrop wiped her eyes. 'I know he was old, and if he was
going to be taken, he'd have wanted to have been taken in service,

but when I think of how it happened, and how he blamed himself
– well, it breaks my heart.'

'Blamed himself?' Anthony repeated innocently, as if it was
the first time he had heard it. 'How could he possibly be to
blame?'

'I don't know, sir,' said Mrs Harrop, her plump face crinkling
in distress. 'I've teased myself with that. It's come between me
and my sleep many a time since. All I can think of is that poor
Mr Hawthorne felt guilty about listening at the door.'

As a reason for Hawthorne's undoubted distress, that seemed
weak, to put it mildly, but those last words of the butler's had to
be explained somehow. 'It really was so unusual for Mr Hawthorne
to listen at a door?' questioned Anthony.

Mrs Harrop's eyes widened. 'Unusual! You could have knocked
me down with a feather and no mistake, when I opened the door
onto the landing and saw Mr Hawthorne and that gaggle of girls,
all outside the study door. I can tell you this much though. Samuel
Hawthorne never did anything wrong. He was one of the old
school, as they say, devoted to the master and mistress and punctilious to a fault. That's what the master, God rest him, used to
say. Punctilious to a fault. It used to tickle the master, how correct
poor Mr Hawthorne was. He had better manners than a duke, the
master would say.'

Considering that Mr Jowett had, in the eyes of the world at
least, murdered his wife and then shot himself, it didn't seem to
have dented Mrs Harrop's affection for her late employer.

'So you were fond of Mr Jowett?' he hazarded.

Mrs Harrop nodded vigorously. 'I was, sir, despite what
happened. *If* it happened as they say,' she added portentously. 'Not
that I believe it. The police don't know everything and don't tell
me they do. You mark my words, Mr Jowett might have been
upset, but he'd no sooner raise a hand to the mistress than he
would have flown to the moon. That's God's own truth.'

'I agree,' said Anthony, to her obvious satisfaction. 'Like you,
I can't believe in the story the police told.'

'You've never said a truer word, sir,' she said earnestly. 'We've
been asked to believe wicked lies, but I knew the truth would out.'

'The trouble is, Mrs Harrop, the truth isn't out yet.' Anthony
smiled encouragingly as she gave him a puzzled look. 'We'll have

to give it a helping hand. What I mean is, that somehow we're going to have to prove the truth as both you and I know it.'

'Anyone who can believe wrong of the master isn't worth bothering about,' she said stiffly.

'I'd still like to convince them,' said Anthony gently. 'Tell me, where are the other servants who were here that day?'

'Them!' said Mrs Harrop with a snort. 'Gone to work in factories, if you please. Flighty, I calls it. It's sinful what these girls can earn nowadays. I did hear as they can earn five pounds a week.' She bridled in indignation. 'Five pounds! *And* all spent on rubbish, I'll be bound. It's no wonder that girls are getting ideas above their station. Service isn't good enough, oh no, not any more. Obviously we don't need a full staff, but I'm here by myself and I don't like it. One of those young women should've stopped on but we can't get anyone, not with these factories paying the wages that they do. It wouldn't have happened before the war.'

Anthony had a great deal of sympathy for the absent girls' point of view, but he thought it politic not to express it. 'It's a great pity the other servants have left. I'd like to speak to them.'

'Why?' demanded Mrs Harrop belligerently. 'I'm the house-keeper. I can tell you anything you care to ask.'

The last thing Anthony wanted to do was put Mrs Harrop's back up by seeming to undermine her authority. 'That's not quite so, though, is it?' he said with a disarming smile. 'After all, Mrs Harrop, when the door was broken down and Mr Hawthorne collapsed, you fainted, didn't you? I'm sure it does credit to your feelings, but it does mean you can't tell me what happened after you were taken ill.'

'Mortal bad, I was,' she said earnestly. 'I'd tell you if I could, sir, but I was taken mortal bad.'

'And did someone look after you? You weren't just left on the floor of the study?' His voice betrayed nothing but concern.

'Well, no, I was helped up to my bed,' she admitted. 'It wouldn't have been seemly otherwise.' She shuddered. 'I can't think of that room without going cold all over and that's a fact.' She lowered her voice. 'I haven't been able to bring myself to go in there ever since it happened and never mind the dusting.' She moved uneasily in her seat, obviously wanting to say more.

'Go on,' prompted Anthony gently.

'The room's *haunted*!' She glared at him defensively. 'It's true. I'd swear it on my mother's grave. I know there's many who'd laugh, but that study's haunted.'

Anthony didn't believe in ghosts but couldn't doubt her sincerity. 'Have you seen anything?'

She shuddered. 'No. I won't go near that room again and that's a fact. I've heard groaning and, what's more, heard gunshots, too. I can hear it at night and sometimes in the day too. I tell you, there's something in that room that's not natural.' She poured herself another cup of tea with trembling hands. 'I don't care what anyone says, I knows what I've heard.'

What on earth had she heard? A room that had been witness to sudden death virtually demanded to be haunted but . . . 'That's very interesting,' said Anthony slowly. 'Can I have a look at the study?'

She shuddered once more. 'If you must. There's something in that room that shouldn't be there.' She drank her tea broodingly. 'Do you want to know anything more, sir?'

'Yes, if you don't mind. Mrs Harrop, who helped you to your bed after you fainted? Can you remember?'

She looked puzzled. 'I think – mind I say I *think* – it was Eileen Chadderton and Winnie Bruce. Yes, it was,' she added, sounding much more like her old self. She made a sound between a sniff and a snort. 'No one would've asked Annie Colbeck to help, if I know anything about it. When we were stood outside the door and poor Mr Hawthorne was took so bad, all she did was sob and wail. She couldn't even go and get his drops and a glass of water without taking till doomsday to come back.'

'So Annie Colbeck was left in the room while Eileen Chadderton and Winnie Bruce saw to you?'

'Someone had to stay,' said Mrs Harrop, shocked. 'It wouldn't have been right to leave them alone.'

'No. No, of course not. Will you show me the study?' he added, after what he thought was a suitable pause.

Mrs Harrop shuddered. 'If you insist, sir,' she said reluctantly.

SIX

Mrs Harrop wouldn't come into the study; in fact she wouldn't venture along the corridor but pointed out the door from the stairs before she departed back to her sitting room.

Once in the study, Anthony was able to see for himself the truth of Inspector Tanner's assessment of how difficult it would be to escape from the room. The sash window opened onto Pettifer's Court with a sheer drop to the basement area three stories below. Not only was it overlooked by the neighbouring houses, but Pettifer's Court was well populated. If anyone had dropped a rope ladder, say, out of the window, they would certainly have been spotted. There was, as Inspector Tanner had stated, no fire escape or balcony and, noted Anthony, no drainpipe either. No; there was no exit that way.

A pair of fine Turkish rugs – they must be worth a good deal, thought Anthony – hung on wooden rails in the alcoves, one either side of the fireplace. The two other walls were lined with deep bookcases that nearly reached the ceiling.

The bookcases, sturdy constructions of oak, had evidently been built to fit the room. The upright junctions between the sets of shelves were masked by slim carved panels which slid upwards, leaving a gap of eight inches at the most. No one could have hidden between the shelves or, for that matter, behind or on top of them.

The study itself was a pleasant enough room, panelled to shoulder height in oak. There was a substantial oak table, with a brass ashtray, a bunch of keys, a desk-lamp, pens, blotter and a quire of writing paper. A box file, with papers beside it, covered with dust, lay on the table. The carpet, which covered most of the floor, was a rich Indian design, evidently old but of good quality.

Against the fireplace was a comfortable chintz armchair, flanked by a standard lamp and a small table, on which was a litter of pipes, a tobacco jar and an upturned book, a nurse's account of life in Belgium. Anthony remembered from Sir Douglas's report that Maurice Knowle's fiancée, Miss Edith Wilson, was nursing in Belgium.

Anthony settled himself in the armchair, coughing as a cloud of dust puffed up from the cushions. Mrs Harrop wasn't joking when she said she hadn't dusted. A fine layer of dust covered the entire room.

Despite Mrs Harrop's forebodings, there didn't seem to be any ghostly chill in the atmosphere, but a murder – two murders and a sudden death – had certainly occurred. It was clear, from the conversation that Father Quinet had overheard, that someone had been in that room and that someone had murdered both Edward Jowett and his wife. It wasn't, thought Anthony, a planned murder. The servants had clearly heard Mr Jowett's furious voice and a snatch of what he'd said: 'The police . . . law . . . disgrace . . .'

Then, when the argument had reached a point where there was nothing else for it, the killer had struck. The kerfuffle outside the door had given the killer time, but he simply couldn't have escaped. Therefore he had hidden himself in the room. So far, so good, but *where*? Where had he managed to hide so successfully that he escaped Inspector Tanner's thorough search?

From the moment the door was broken down until the police had departed, some hours later, there had been at least one person in the room, either the doctor, a member of the household or the police.

After he'd broken the door down, Constable Coltrane had left the servants in the room and telephoned the station for instructions. Inspector Tanner had established that the only telephone in the house was downstairs in the hall. However, once Constable Coltrane was in the hall, the servants didn't stay in the room. Two of them had helped the fainting Mrs Harrop to her bed, leaving Annie Colbeck alone.

Annie Colbeck; the inefficient Annie Colbeck, as much use, Mrs Harrop had said, as a wet washday. Annie who had cried and sobbed outside the door and took as much time as she possibly could to fetch Hawthorne's drops. Was she trying to give the killer time? Was she the woman in the church, the woman who Father Quinet had overheard?

What had Father Quinet actually heard? The woman had lived

in France for five years and spoke good French. She was asked to look after a little girl who more or less had to be Milly. The woman had never looked after children before but she had promised to be competent within a fortnight.

So who looked after children? In Milly's case, it was the nuns who ran the orphanage, but there were also teachers, nurses, governesses and nursemaids. Nursemaids. Servants. Annie Colbeck was a servant, a housemaid. Was she a housemaid who could switch roles to that of nursemaid within a fortnight? Anthony rather thought she was. After all, he added to himself, his stomach tightening, it wasn't, by the sound of it, a role she'd have to keep up for very long.

All that, however, was in the future. Granted that Annie Colbeck had managed to usher the killer out of the room in the time she was alone in here, he'd still managed to escape detection when the door had been broken down.

How? There was no sofa to hide behind and the table, sitting squarely a few feet from the wall in the middle of the room, had no cloth to conceal anyone underneath.

For an ordinary room, the place was as devoid of hiding places as a billiard table. Where the devil had he been?

He got up and strolled round the room. Something about the room seemed wrong, but he couldn't put his finger on what it was.

Idly he glanced at the papers beside the open box file on the table. The papers were contained in manila cardboard sleeves. Anthony read the names on the sleeves. Douglas, Denshaw, Drake and Sons, Dauntless Insurance, Dobson, Dreadnaught Iron Ltd., Dysart . . .

They seemed to be banking records, confidential documents relating to loans and businesses, copies, Anthony thought, of records that were probably in the bank. These were the papers that Mr Jowett had needed at home, papers he wanted to study . . . That was it!

That was the thing that seemed wrong. For a room that was called 'the study' there seemed to be an absolute lack of things to actually study. There should have been a filing cabinet or a shelf at least, devoted to working papers.

Anthony flicked back the lid of the box file and wasn't, granted the names on the manila folders, surprised to see the initial D.

So if this was the box file containing the papers for clients whose name began with D, where were the others? A, B, C and through to Z, if there were any clients whose name began with Z. There weren't any box files on the bookcase.

Anthony looked round the room. There weren't any box files anywhere. Edward Jowett could, he supposed, have brought this one file home, but surely the bank would have missed it and would have asked for its return?

Then he froze. A low groan sounded behind him, then another groan. What the devil? He jumped as the groan was followed by a sharp *crack!*

The hair on the back of his neck stood up. Could Mrs Harrop possibly be right? Was the room haunted?

The room seemed exactly as before. It was quiet, almost mockingly quiet. Anthony took a firm grip on his nerves. Something had groaned and something had cracked. What?

The sun streamed through the window, glinting diamond sparks off the dust on what had once been the highly polished table. The light brought out the deep reds of the Indian carpet, the rich golden browns of the oak panels, touching the oak floorboards, not quite catching the fringe of the Turkish carpet on the wall. Everything, absolutely everything, was filmed with dust, except the oak floorboards in front of the hanging carpet on the far side of the fireplace. Here the dust was shaped into little tracks and tiny mounds.

As Anthony watched, the fringe of the carpet lifted slightly, then flattened. The dust on the floorboards in front of the carpet swirled, lifted, then settled.

He walked to the hanging carpet and drew it back. It swung outwards on its rail, revealing the oak panels underneath.

Anthony stepped back, then, taking a box of matches from his pocket, lit a cigarette. The smoke from the cigarette curled upwards. Holding the cigarette between his thumb and forefinger, he reached out to the panelling, watching the smoke as it drifted up beside the panels. Nothing. He started on the adjacent panel.

The smoke blew out into the room.

That was it! Despite looking exactly like its neighbour, that panel had to open. He ran his fingers round the edge. There had to be a catch or a lock somewhere. Nothing opened to his touch but surely, outlined in the dust, was the faint impression of a hand.

He pressed down against the outline and with a click, the panel swung back.

Sunlight streamed into the room from the open panel. Behind the door, for that was what it was, was a low space about six-foot-long and four across, illuminated by a skylight. It looked like the end of the eaves of the attic, partitioned off to make a separate room.

This was where Mr Jowett kept his files. There were shelves with initialled box files on them (Z was part of V to Z) and other documents, all neatly arranged. There wasn't, Anthony thought, anything necessarily mysterious about the room. At a guess, the cupboard was as old as the house and used by Mr Jowett to keep confidential files neatly out of sight and away from prying eyes. There was something else in there, too. A stumpy Webley Bulldog revolver together with a box of ammunition that presumably was Edward Jowett's own. So there had been two guns. Anthony didn't need any more proof that the Jowetts had been murdered, but here it was, all the same.

The skylight wasn't properly shut. Anthony could see the outline of a chimney stack outside of the skylight. The wind gullied round the stack and, as Anthony watched, the skylight lifted in its frame and slammed down with a bang. The long arm of the metal latch was hanging loose, preventing it closing properly.

Anthony grinned and, lifting the latch, fastened the skylight firmly in position. He had exorcized Mrs Harrop's ghost for her. It seemed the least he could do.

SEVEN

'**A**nd there it was, Talbot,' said Anthony pouring out a glass of whisky. He added a splash of soda and handed it to Sir Charles. They were in Anthony's sitting room in the flat in Grosvenor Road.

Tara, after listening enthralled to his story of ghost-hunting had, with some reluctance, gone out to a meeting of the Belgian Relief Aid.

'A secret cupboard?' said Talbot.

'As a matter of fact, it wasn't so secret. Mrs Harrop knew all about it. However, Inspector Tanner didn't ask her if she knew of such a thing and it never occurred to her to mention it.'

'Wonderful,' commented Sir Charles ironically. 'I thought Tanner was meant to be one of the best.'

'To be fair to him, I didn't ask Mrs Harrop how an intruder could conceal himself in that room and I don't suppose he did, either. It's a lesson to us all, I suppose, to ask the obvious question.'

Sir Charles grinned. 'To take you at your word, I'll ask it. What do you think happened that day?'

Anthony took a thoughtful sip of whisky. 'I don't think it was a premeditated murder. No one in their right mind would plan a murder that had so many opportunities to go wrong. I think we have to go back to a few weeks before when Mr Jowett complained that someone had searched his study. He kept the door to the study locked after that. He was unhappy and Mrs Jowett was unsettled and worried.'

'Who searched the study? Do you know?'

'I'm fairly sure it was Annie Colbeck, the maid. However, on that occasion she was unsuccessful. I don't think she found the cupboard. Mrs Harrop, when I questioned her afterwards, told me she'd never mentioned it to anyone and she certainly didn't chat about it to Annie Colbeck. The cupboard wasn't of any importance to her, you see, and it's very well concealed. A searcher would have to be very lucky indeed to stumble across it. If the skylight hadn't been left open, I doubt I would have found it.'

'I think you're underestimating your abilities, but go on.'

'Thanks,' said Anthony with a grin. 'In a way,' he said, picking up his pipe and stuffing tobacco into it, 'it's a great pity that Annie Colbeck didn't find what she was looking for. If she had, I'm sure that both the Jowetts and that poor beggar, Hawthorne, would be alive today.'

'That poor beggar, Hawthorne,' repeated Sir Charles thoughtfully. 'He said, "It's my fault, Maurice." Have you any idea what those last words meant?'

Anthony nodded. 'I think so. Tell, me, Talbot, what does a butler do? What's his job?'

'He does various things,' said Sir Charles with a shrug. 'His main role is looking after the wine, fining it, bottling it and corking it and so on. It's quite a responsibility. My uncle served as a butler in Ireland and it's no sinecure, believe you me. What else? You could say he's in charge of the house. He pays the bills, takes charge of the valuable plate, he waits at the table and carves the joint, gets up first thing and sees that everything is safe and sound at night. It's early mornings and late nights, but if the butler's doing his job, there shouldn't be a problem with burglars.'

'A butler also answers the door to visitors, doesn't he?'

'Yes, of course. He takes the visiting cards into the master or mistress, helps the guests with their coats and shows them in.'

'Exactly. He opens the door to visitors. A lot of Hawthorne's duties were taken over by Mrs Harrop, as his health was so poor, but what I think happened is this. A visitor came to the door – and if that visitor wasn't Father Quinet's first man in the church, I'm a Dutchman. The man wanted to see Mrs Jowett.'

'*Mrs* Jowett?' questioned Sir Charles.

'That's my guess. I haven't got any direct proof but I think the man handed Hawthorne his visiting card and, in order to ensure Mrs Jowett did receive him, I think he'd scribbled a note on the card saying words to the tune of "Concerning Maurice Knowle", or something similar.'

'Where's the card?' began Sir Charles, then stopped. 'He'd have taken it with him, of course. Go on, Brooke.'

'I think Hawthorne was uneasy about the visitor. Hawthorne had served Mrs Jowett's family all his life and, according to Mrs Harrop, felt very protective towards her. I think he would have kept as close a watch on things as he could, in order to step in if necessary. I know and you know that he was a frail old soul, but he didn't see himself like that. He was the Jowetts' butler and it was his duty to protect the house. He would have certainly known that Mrs Jowett had gone with the man from the drawing room, where she usually received visitors, into Mr Jowett's private study. I know it was kept locked but if anyone could get hold of the key, she could. Hawthorne wouldn't like it.'

'He wouldn't like it at all,' agreed Talbot. 'What were they doing in the study? Was it something to do with that box file on the table?'

'I believe it was. All the folders in that file related to businesses and people with the initial D. Who do we know who's got the initial D?'

'Diefenbach!' exclaimed Sir Charles. 'Paul Diefenbach!'

'Exactly. Paul Diefenbach, the head of the Capital and Counties bank, who trusted and relied on Mr Jowett.' Anthony briefly recounted the facts he had gained from Mrs Harrop. 'So you see, Talbot, granted that Edward Jowett was a trusted colleague, as well as a friend, it's possible that Diefenbach kept any confidential papers and so on lodged with Jowett for safekeeping.'

'That's perfectly possible,' agreed Sir Charles. 'You say Diefenbach's married?'

'Yes, but separated, according to Mrs Harrop. Apparently he lives in his club. Which one, I don't know.'

'Leave it with me, Brooke. I'll make a few enquiries. I'd like to talk to the man himself but, as Inspector Tanner found out, he's *en route* for God knows where.'

'I suppose he really is abroad?' asked Anthony, suddenly uneasy. 'There seem to be some very sinister types who are determined to get hold of him. I'd like to know why.'

'Yes.' Sir Charles took a cigarette from the box on the table and lit it thoughtfully. 'Usually when someone in his position disappears, the first thing that springs to mind is that he's absconded with the cash, but there's nothing untoward been reported at the bank.'

He shook himself. 'To stick to what we do know, let me sum up what you've worked out so far. Annie Colbeck searched Jowett's study a month before he died. We're assuming that she was looking for information about Paul Diefenbach.' He gave Anthony a quizzical look. 'Why did our man wait a month before he called?'

'Again, this is guesswork, but it fits. I think it took that long to find out something about Maurice Knowle, something that could be used to put pressure on Mrs Jowett to let our man see Edward Jowett's confidential papers about Paul Diefenbach.'

'Blackmail?' asked Sir Charles sharply.

'That's about the size of it,' said Anthony, picking up his whisky and swirling it round in his glass.

'But Maurice Knowle sounds like a first rate sort of man,'

objected Sir Charles. 'Apart from anything else, he's crippled. What could he have done to be blackmailed?'

'I don't know, but I intend to find out,' said Anthony, pulling on his pipe. 'Maurice Knowle called on his mother that morning. Mrs Harrop said that he was distracted and worried, quite different from his usual self. All she actually heard him say was something about chocolate, which doesn't seem to make any sense, but the effect of the visit was that Mrs Jowett was on edge afterwards. I think Maurice Knowle had warned his mother to expect the man to call.'

'He was warning her to expect a blackmailer?'

Anthony nodded. 'What's more, it worked. The fact that Mrs Jowett took the man into the study and got the box file out of the concealed cupboard proves that. Then, of course, it all went wrong. Edward Jowett returned from the bank early. Presumably Hawthorne met him in the hall. Jowett enquired if his wife was at home – he would, you know – and Hawthorne, who was probably very relieved to see his master, told him that Mrs Jowett was indeed at home and, what's more, in the study with a dubious visitor.'

'So Jowett goes into the study to see for himself what's afoot,' completed Sir Charles.

'And Hawthorne, worried about what will happen, breaks the habit of a lifetime and listens apprehensively at the door.' Anthony got up and stretched his shoulders. 'You see why Hawthorne would feel guilty? One of his main duties, as a butler, is to guard the house. Against his better judgement, he's admitted this man instead of sending him packing. The fact he listened at the door shows how unhappy he was. He didn't intervene, as perhaps he felt he should, but let the situation continue until, as we know, it got out of control. After the shots rang out, poor Hawthorne must've been in despair.'

'That adds up,' said Sir Charles.

'Now, once Edward Jowett went into the study, he was horrified. I don't know if Mr Jowett knew who the man was, but it's clear that his wife has shown him confidential papers. As we know, Jowett lost his temper. The servants heard Mrs Jowett say "Maurice" – I imagine she was protesting that she'd acted for Maurice's sake – and Mr Jowett responded with the words the servants overheard. "The police . . . law . . . and disgrace" .'

'I think I can fill in the gaps,' said Sir Charles. 'Jowett must've said something along the lines of, "I'm going to call the police. I'll have the law on you." And then he would've added to his wife something about how she's brought disgrace on them all, by showing this crook Diefenbach's confidential papers.'

'That's it, I think,' agreed Anthony. 'Which means, of course, our pal's in an awkward situation. If the police are called, not only will he be arrested for blackmail, but whatever plan it is he's concocting will be down the Swanee. So, not to beat about the bush, he pulls a gun, the Browning that was found at the scene, and shoots both Mr and Mrs Jowett.'

Sir Charles drank his whisky grimly. 'It must be big for him to resort to murder. So what then? Presumably he takes the Diefenbach file and hides in the cupboard. What makes you pick out Annie Colbeck as his accomplice, by the way?'

'Of the three women there, Annie Colbeck positively identified the Browning as Mr Jowett's gun, which we know is false. She was the one who was the least effective in trying to get the door open. After it was broken down, she was left alone in the room. She might not have known about the cupboard, but she knows or guesses her accomplice must be hidden somewhere. As soon as she's alone, she would have called out, told him it was safe, and hurried him out of the room. The door to the servants' quarters is next to the study. It would only take minutes to get the murderer through the door and away to safety.'

'I can see a flaw,' said Sir Charles after some thought. 'The sequence of events you've described works because Hawthorne died and couldn't tell us Mrs Jowett and the man were in the study. I grant you Hawthorne was old and frail, but Annie Colbeck and her partner couldn't know he was going to die.'

'Couldn't they?' said Anthony grimly. 'I told you it was unfortunate that the butler died.'

Sir Charles stared at him. 'Hawthorne was murdered, you mean? But how?'

'I think it was very simple,' said Anthony. 'I checked the medical evidence. Hawthorne was suffering from mitral disease, a condition which affects the valves of the heart. The thing about mitral disease is that a sufferer can live with it for years until, that is, they become elderly. It's often only then the condition is diagnosed.

There's various stimulants and tonics, all of which contain either digitalis, strophanthus or strychnine. All these medicines, I need hardly tell you, have to be treated with caution. Hawthorne had been prescribed strophanthus, the medicinal dose of which is two to five minims, or drops. Annie Colbeck went to get Hawthorne's drops and came back with both the bottle and a glass of water.'

'I see,' breathed Sir Charles.

Anthony nodded. 'It's simple, isn't it? Annie Colbeck probably didn't know what the proper dose was, but she'd know that an overdose was dangerous. All she'd have to do, in the privacy of Hawthorne's bedroom, was to shake a generous amount of the strophanthus into the water. She then gave it to Mrs Harrop, who'd shake even more strophanthus into the glass, before she helped Hawthorne drink it. The result?' Anthony drew his forefinger across his throat.

'Three murders,' said Sir Charles quietly. 'And one of them completely unsuspected.'

'Untraceable, too, I imagine. There was no post-mortem carried out on Hawthorne, as it seemed obvious that he'd died of natural causes, but, even if it had been, the presence of strophanthus wouldn't ring any alarm bells.'

Sir Charles picked up his whisky and drank it sombrely. 'So how do we get hold of this appalling woman? Did Mrs Harrop know where she's got to?'

'To the best of her knowledge, Mrs Harrop says that Annie Colbeck, along with the other two girls, have given up domestic service and gone into factories. It might be true of the other two girls but I doubt very much if it'll be any help in tracing Annie Colbeck.'

'So do I. Where did this Annie Colbeck come from? How did she get the post? Was it a personal recommendation or an agency or what?'

'She came from a domestic service agency, but Mrs Harrop couldn't recall which one. What's more, her book of household notes, in which she kept a record of the domestic staff, was mysteriously missing.'

Sir Charles breathed dangerously. 'Damnit, there has to be some way of finding out about this woman! She's colluded in two murders, committed another and, in some way we don't understand, is a threat to Paul Diefenbach.'

'And Milly,' Anthony reminded him.

'And Milly,' repeated Sir Charles quietly. 'I feel for that child, Brooke.'

There was no doubting his sincerity. After all, Anthony reminded himself, Talbot had four grown-up daughters of his own and was a generous subscriber to at least one children's charity.

Sir Charles sat broodingly for a moment. 'I could enquire about the other two servants,' he said. 'Winnie Bruce and Eileen Chadderton. They might know something useful. I'll put an advert in the papers for them, asking them to contact Mayer and Galbraith, the solicitors. Stephen Mayer's done the occasional job for me before. Servants are often left small legacies. If I say they'll hear something to their advantage, that shouldn't arouse anyone's suspicions.'

'That'd probably work,' agreed Anthony.

'Right,' said Sir Charles, standing up. He glanced at his watch. 'It's half past six. I can probably catch Mayer at his club. I'll have a word with him, then put the advert in the papers. In the meantime, Brooke, make it your business to meet Maurice Knowle. If you're right, his mother was prepared to submit to blackmail on his behalf. I want to know who the blackmailer is and what he was threatening. If we can crack the Jowett murderers, we have a chance of getting to grips with what the conspirators in the church were planning. And remember – we haven't got much time.'

EIGHT

A t half seven that evening Anthony rang the bell of Maurice Knowle's flat. Sixteen, Torpoint Mansions was a purpose-built, three-storey, smoke-blackened building on the corner of Gower Street and Pipewell Lane. He was wearing his colonel's uniform. It gave him the authority to ask questions. Maybe Maurice Knowle would provide some answers.

A square-faced manservant answered the door.

'Good evening,' said Anthony, reaching in his coat pocket for his card case. 'Is Captain Knowle at home? My name's Ralde, Colonel Ralde. I'd appreciate a word with him.'

The valet eyed Anthony warily, then took the visiting card Anthony held out to him. 'I'll enquire if he is at home, sir.'

His words were unremarkable and the valet was dressed conventionally enough, in pinstriped trousers and a black jacket, but his shoulders were broad and Anthony could see the bulge of muscles under his coat. His nose was out of true and his ears were oddly lumpy and flattened.

One glance at the man's ears told Anthony he had been affected by hematomas. The walls of the blood vessels had been damaged and blood had leaked into the tissues, resulting in the tissue becoming misshapen.

The common name for the condition was cauliflower ear. Any footballer or rugby player was at risk from such an injury, but, in Anthony's experience, the men most likely to carry such scars were boxers. The manservant may be a valet now, but sometime in the not too distant past, Anthony was prepared to bet he'd been a prizefighter.

Leaving Anthony by the door, the man went into the room at the end of the hall. Anthony heard a brief buzz of conversation, then the man returned. 'Captain Knowle is going out for the evening, but he can spare you a few minutes. Can I take your coat, sir?'

It happened so quickly that Anthony nearly missed it, but as the valet took his coat, the hall light caught the green tabs of the Intelligence Corps on the shoulders of his uniform. For a fraction of a second, the man stiffened and his eyes narrowed as he opened the hall cupboard and hung up Anthony's coat. 'If you would follow me, sir, Mr Knowle will be with you in a few moments.'

Anthony followed him into the sitting room. The first thing that struck him was how oddly untidy everything was. The cushions were rumpled, there was a mess of pipes and glasses on the sideboard, the ashtrays were full and newspapers were scattered on the floor.

As an employer, Maurice Knowle must be tolerant to a fault. The manservant was clearly not doing his job.

He shot a glance at the valet, standing with arms crossed by the fireplace. Servant? Not ruddy likely, thought Anthony. The man was a professional thug.

The door opened and Maurice Knowle came into the room, walking with the aid of a stick.

He was a tall, fair-haired man in his early twenties. He was wearing evening dress, with the fresh appearance of someone who had just washed, but his face was lined and anxious, making him seem older than his twenty-three years. That could, thought Anthony, be a result of his injuries – he could see the empty left sleeve of his coat pinned close beneath the elbow – but Anthony was immediately struck by how tense he seemed. He held Anthony's card in his hand. His hand trembled and he swallowed convulsively before speaking.

'Colonel Ralde? It's good of you to call.' He gave a quick, nervous glance at his valet and said, with a little laugh, 'I suppose this is to do with my application for a post at the War Office.'

Anthony's denial stuck in his throat. He'd been about to explain that he'd called on quite another matter, a private matter, when he suddenly caught the expression in Knowle's eyes.

The pitch of Knowle's voice rose slightly. 'My post.' Anthony could almost feel the man's anxiety. Knowle swallowed once more, and gave an almost imperceptible nod, willing him to agree.

Anthony decided to back him up. He wanted to see how this would work out. 'Yes, that's right.'

He could see the tension ebb out of the man. 'If I could just have a few minutes with you alone . . .?'

The manservant didn't move.

Knowle turned to him. 'Thank you, Blatchford, that will be all.'

Anthony could see the man was reluctant to go, but he really didn't have any choice. 'Very good, sir.' He cleared his throat. 'I'll be close at hand if you need me.'

It sounded like a threat.

Blatchford walked to the door but before he left he turned. 'Don't forget the chocolate, sir.'

Knowle flinched as if he'd been struck.

Apparently satisfied, Blatchford left the room.

Anthony stared at Knowle. 'Chocolate?' he mouthed.

Knowle raised his hand instinctively, fending off the question, then shook his head vigorously. When he spoke, his voice was so quiet, Anthony could scarcely hear him. 'I can't tell you.'

It was obviously useless to press for more information. 'Do you mind if I smoke?' asked Anthony, in an ordinary voice.

Grasping at the mantelpiece, Knowle took a deep breath. 'Yes, please do.' He shook himself then looked up. 'Play along,' he mouthed, adding out loud, 'help yourself to a cigarette, Colonel. The box is on the table.'

'Thank you,' said Anthony, walking over to the table. 'There's just a few points we need to clear up before we proceed any further with your application.'

'Nothing too tedious, I hope,' Knowle replied in a strained voice. He had taken a pencil from the sideboard and scribbled on the back of Anthony's card. He put the card back on the sideboard and indicated Anthony should pick it up.

'Nothing to bother about particularly,' said Anthony, taking a cigarette from the box. 'Are the matches on the sideboard?' He strolled across the room and, picking up the matchbox, lit his cigarette.

His card was face down on the wooden surface. The note consisted of three words.

Help. He's listening.

Anthony looked quickly at Knowle. The man was quaking with nerves. Anthony nodded, mouthed the word 'OK' and gave him a silent thumbs-up sign. 'Would it be possible for you to pop along with me to the War Office now? I realize it's a beastly nuisance, but the quicker we get these details sorted out, the quicker we'll be able to get you back into harness.'

Maurice Knowle looked horrified. He shook his head, mouthed the word 'No' and jerked his head in the direction of the door. The implication was obvious. The valet wouldn't let him go. 'I'm sorry, Colonel, but I've got an appointment for this evening.'

Anthony bit his lip. The easiest solution would be to simply walk out of the flat with Knowle in tow. He weighed up the odds.

Knowle, poor devil, wouldn't be much use in a fight against a professional bruiser like the valet, but Anthony reckoned he could take him on if necessary. However, judging by the state of Maurice Knowle's nerves, his own fear was a more effective imprisonment than anything Blatchford could devise.

'Perhaps tomorrow?' suggested Knowle. 'I could call at the War Office tomorrow.'

So he was allowed out of the flat then. Presumably after the valet had given him his instructions as to what he could and couldn't say.

Picking up a newspaper from the floor, he took a pencil from his pocket and wrote in the margin, *Why are you afraid?*

Knowle took the pencil. With trembling fingers he wrote *Edith*, then, his eyes wide, ran his finger across his throat.

Anthony understood. Edith Wilson, Maurice Knowle's fiancée, had been threatened.

Knowle added another note. *Protect her.*

Anthony nodded and then, for the benefit of the listening Blatchford, said, 'Can I trouble you for a drink, Knowle?'

'Of course,' said Knowle. 'Help yourself, Colonel. All the fixings are on the sideboard.'

'Thanks.' Anthony stood up. 'Shall I pour one for you?' He scribbled another note on the margin of the newspaper. *She's safe in Belgium.*

'Please do,' said Knowle, with an attempted laugh. 'I find the soda siphon a bit tricky. I always manage to splash it.' He read the note and shook his head vigorously. Seizing the pencil, he wrote *No!*

Anthony took the pencil back. *They killed your mother?*

Knowle read the note and gazed at Anthony. He swallowed hard then, seeming to come to a decision, mouthed the word, 'Yes' .

There was a creak outside the door. Anthony picked up the newspaper. 'Do you mind if I keep this newspaper, Captain? There's an article in it I wanted to read.'

'Please do,' said Knowle, as the door opened and Blatchford came back into the room.

The manservant looked at him suspiciously, then turned his attention to Maurice Knowle. 'It's about time you were leaving, sir.'

'I'd better be off,' said Anthony, draining his whisky. 'Shall we say ten o' clock at the War Office, Captain?'

Knowle swallowed hard and glanced at Blatchford. 'That'll be fine.'

The valet cleared his throat. 'I don't think that's going to be possible,' adding, as a seeming afterthought, 'sir. You're going to the country tomorrow. You're going to be away for some time.'

Maurice Knowle looked like a hunted animal. 'I . . . I can go to the country after I've been to the War Office.'

'That would be best,' agreed Anthony smoothly.

The valet hunched his shoulders. 'That will be very inconvenient.'

Anthony put down his glass with a click. 'Nevertheless, I expect to see you there. That's an order, Captain.' He stood up. 'Until tomorrow, then.' He strolled over to the sideboard, picked up the visiting card that Knowle had written on and pocketed it.

Blatchford escorted him into the hall and helped him on with his coat. Opening the door, he watched Anthony walk along the hallway to the stairs.

Short of attacking the valet, there was nothing for it but to leave, but Anthony hated going. Should he take action? Violent action?

On the street outside he hesitated. Blatchford might be armed. That was one consideration but another, far greater, worry was that by attacking the valet he would send an unmistakable warning to the gang that they had been discovered.

If only he had more to go on! At the moment he and Talbot knew nothing apart from the stark fact that Milly, far away in an orphanage under enemy control, was threatened by a gang who had already murdered the Jowetts and an innocent old man. Who the gang were and what they intended was still a complete mystery.

And yet . . . The sight of Maurice Knowle's pale, anxious face worried him. The poor devil, with his shattered arm and lame leg, was clearly on the edge of a nervous breakdown. What were the chances of him being allowed to come to the War Office tomorrow? Slight.

Anthony grimaced. Blatchford had, in effect, not only forbidden the meeting but made a point of saying that Maurice would be away for the foreseeable future. Maurice Knowle needed rescuing, rescuing in a way that wouldn't alarm the gang.

If they only had time, they could ensure Knowle's fiancée, Edith Wilson, was safe, but they didn't have time. Come tomorrow, Maurice Knowle would be gone.

NINE

A t twenty minutes to midnight, Anthony swung himself over the wall at the back of Torpoint Mansions in Pipewell Lane, and dropped into the deep shadow of the yard. Above him loomed the bulk of the building, a few dim lights picking out the occasional window. As his eyes got used to the darkness, he could see the outline of the metal fire escape, zigzagging upwards, between the lights. As usual, the last flight of steps was raised up and chained underneath the platform of the first floor. He picked out the unlit rectangle of glass that was the kitchen window of number sixteen. Deep silence reigned. He just hoped they weren't too late.

In the shadows of the yard, Anthony raised his head and called softly, 'Travis! All clear.'

Lieutenant Travis of the Intelligence Corps quietly climbed the wall and dropped down beside Anthony. 'Any signs of life?' he whispered.

'Not yet,' Anthony breathed back. He indicated a darkened window. 'We're looking at the third floor, second window from the right.'

Anthony's first idea had been to arrest Blatchford, but that simply wasn't practical. For one thing, however dubious Blatchford's behaviour might be, he wasn't known to have committed any offence. There was nothing to charge him with. Even if he could've persuaded the police to arrest Blatchford, he would be freed virtually as soon as he'd been taken into custody. They might, in Blatchford's absence, be able to liberate Maurice Knowle, but in doing so they'd send a clear warning to the gang they were being watched.

Arresting Knowle, however, was a very different proposition. The Jowetts had died in suspicious circumstances and Maurice Knowle benefitted from their deaths. It was a pretty desperate solution but it was hard to think of a better plan.

If all went well, neither he nor Lieutenant Travis would be

called into action but Anthony wasn't taking chances. He glanced at his watch, seeing the luminous hands tick away the seconds, and settled down to wait.

The distant chimes of St Matthew's clock sounded midnight. Despite being in the heart of London, the night was quiet. Apart from the unmarked police wagon drawn up to the kerb, Gower Street was deserted, and the traffic on the Tottenham Court Road had slowed to a distant murmur.

Stifling a yawn, Sergeant McFadden climbed down from the wagon, glanced at Inspector Tanner and decided to risk a question.

The inspector had been in a foul mood ever since they'd left the station and all McFadden really knew was that they were going to arrest a geezer called Knowle in connection with the deaths of the Jowetts.

'So who is this bloke, Knowle, sir?'

'He's Jowett's stepson,' replied the inspector tightly. 'I had that case sown up. Jowett was guilty. I *proved* he was guilty, but apparently that's not good enough for our lords and masters, oh no.' He made a dismissive noise in his throat. 'I don't know what extra evidence Sir Douglas ruddy Lynton thinks he's come up with, but he hasn't seen fit to share it with me. No. I've got my orders, same as you, and that's all I know.'

'Will Knowle make a fight of it, d'you think?' asked McFadden, wisely not commenting on the ways of the upper echelons of the force.

Inspector Tanner shook his head. 'Him? No. He's a cripple. That's why he couldn't have done it.' He sighed deeply. 'Ours not to reason why, as they say. Our job's to pick him up and deliver him nice and snug to the station. And then, maybe, considering it was my case, someone will see fit to tell me what the blazes is going on.'

Anthony jerked forward as a roar of anger ripped through the night. Lights blazed from the kitchen window, followed by furious shouts.

In the dark yard, Anthony and Travis tensed for action. That was Blatchford's voice. More shouts, then another voice yelled, 'Drop it, man! Drop it!'

Three shots rang out, followed by a scream and more shouts, then with a splintering crash, the kitchen window shattered, sending a shower of glass into the yard. A bulky figure, black against the light, smashed through the window and onto the fire escape.

Travis started forward but Anthony pulled him back. 'Let him go!' he hissed.

Travis looked at him, startled, as feet pounded on the metal above their heads, but Anthony wrenched Travis back into the shadows. If they cornered Blatchford, the gang would be certain this was a set-up job. They had to let him go.

Blatchford swung himself off the bottom stairs and dropped to the ground with a grunt. Another figure looked out of the window. It must, Anthony knew, be one of the police officers.

'Stop!' the policeman yelled, clambering out of the window after Blatchford.

Blatchford raised his gun and fired. The policeman yelped, flattening himself against the wall. The shot missed, gouging into the wall, sending chips of brick zinging into the night.

Blatchford fired once more, the shot going wild, then he hurtled towards the gate, pulled back the bolts, and thudded out into the alley.

The policeman, oblivious of Anthony and Travis in the shadows, clattered down the fire escape, dropped to the ground and thudded after Blatchford through the open gate.

Torpoint Mansions came to life in a blaze of light. Windows creaked open, heads appeared and, from all over the building, sleepy voices demanded to know what was going on.

In the distance, a police whistle sounded, answered by more whistles from the surrounding streets and the window above.

'Come on!' yelled Anthony and, with Travis at his heels, jumped, caught hold of the platform of the fire escape, pulled himself upwards and raced up the stairs.

He shouldered his way in through the broken glass of the kitchen window, past the bewildered Inspector Tanner.

It was the scream that was driving him on, the scream that had come after the gunshots. Both Tanner and McFadden were obviously all right, therefore it had to be Maurice Knowle who had cried out.

Dread of what he would find filling him with sick fear, he raced out of the kitchen, leaving Lieutenant Travis to cope with Inspector Tanner's stream of questions.

Maurice Knowle was lying in the sitting room, sprawled out on the rug. He was fully dressed in a dark suit and white shirt. There was an ugly brown stain across the white.

His eyes flicked open as Anthony dropped to his knees beside him. 'He was taking me away,' whispered Maurice. *He* could only mean Blatchford. 'I had to do what he said.' His hand trembled and he grasped Anthony in a convulsive grip. 'You came just in time.'

'Quiet now,' Anthony said, his voice professionally calm. He tore open the shirt where the bullet had ripped it, wincing at the sight of the wound. Crunching his handkerchief into a ball, he pressed it firmly against Maurice's chest, trying to stem the flow of blood. Maurice whimpered with pain.

'Easy does it,' said Anthony softly. He could hear the calmness in his voice and a tiny distant part of his mind wondered how he could sound like that when he felt choked with black despair. He wanted to save Knowle, not have him murdered.

He could hear Travis and Inspector Tanner arguing in the kitchen. He raised his head. 'Travis!'

The argument stopped abruptly and Travis appeared in the doorway. His eyes widened as he saw Maurice Knowle. 'Sir?'

'We need a doctor with wound dressings and an ambulance as quickly as possible. University College Hospital is nearest. Hurry!'

Travis nodded and sped off.

Knowle's eyes flickered open again. 'Colonel?' His voice was painfully weak. Anthony had to strain to hear him. His fingers twitched in Anthony's hand. 'They threatened Edith.' His voice trailed off. 'Chocolate . . .'

'Chocolate?'

'They sent her chocolates. They were put on her bed.' Maurice's eyes opened wide and his grip tightened. 'They knew where she was. They knew how to get to her. They said they would kill her if we didn't co-operate.'

'We? You and your mother, you mean?'

Maurice gave the slightest of nods in agreement.

'What did they want?' Anthony's voice was gentle but he had to know.

'Diefenbach.' Maurice's face contorted. 'Diefenbach's a good man. Liked him a lot but Edith . . . They thought he'd write to me,' said Maurice, his voice thin. 'Contact me. I had to do what they said. Then you came. Blatchford suspected. Edith . . . Had to save Edith.'

He gave a convulsive shudder. His hand, which had gripped Anthony's, slackened and his eyes flickered shut.

Maurice Knowle didn't speak again. It seemed a long time before Anthony heard the ring of the ambulance bell in the street below.

'How's Maurice Knowle?' asked Sir Charles.

Anthony buried an enormous yawn and shook himself fully awake. It was three o'clock in the morning and the gurgling copper pipes that ran along the wall made the room soporifically warm. He had been offered the use of the consultant's office, where he had waited to see Talbot. Talbot, he knew, had been at Scotland Yard.

'Knowle will live, thank God,' said Anthony, rubbing his face with his hands and stifling another yawn. 'It was touch and go at one point, but he'll live. However,' he added, reaching for the cigarette box, 'I think it'd be as well if, as far as the public are concerned, he stayed dead for a while.'

Charles Talbot pulled up a chair. 'That's quite a big thing you're asking, Brooke. Why's it necessary?'

Anthony lit his cigarette and brought Sir Charles up to date. 'You see, Talbot, if Maurice Knowle lives, the gang will presume he's told us everything.'

'Miss Wharton, Knowle's fiancée, will be safe enough, though. They can't use her to threaten him any longer. There'd be no point.'

'Yes, but it puts us at a real disadvantage. The whole point of arresting Knowle was to rescue him without telling the crooks we knew he was in danger. If Maurice Knowle is known to be alive, we've failed. The gang will know that we know we're onto them, and we've lost the only advantage we have. Besides that,' he added, 'the poor beggar could do with some peace and quiet to recuperate. He's really been through it.'

Sir Charles nodded slowly. 'You're quite right. I'll have a word with the hospital and see there's a suitable announcement in the press.'

'Good. What about the valet? Did the police catch Blatchford?'

'No, more's the pity.'

'What the devil happened?' asked Anthony curiously. 'It all kicked off very quickly. Presumably Blatchford answered the door to Inspector Tanner and Sergeant McFadden.'

'That's where it went wrong. As soon as Tanner clapped eyes on Blatchford, he recognized him as one of their regular customers, so to speak. The recognition, I may say, was mutual. His real name isn't Blatchford, it's Stevenson, Johnny Stevenson. He's a nasty piece of work, who's been in and out of jail, with convictions for assault and robbery with violence. As soon as he saw Tanner and McFadden, he tried to slam the door on them – McFadden got his foot in the way – raced back into the flat, grabbed a revolver, shot Knowle, and made a break out of the kitchen window.'

'I wish I'd known he had a criminal record,' said Anthony ruefully. 'I could've nabbed him last night without anyone being any the wiser.'

'Never mind,' said Sir Charles. 'If we were all gifted with hindsight our job would be a lot easier.'

'Did he shoot Knowle because the poor beggar was in the way, or did he shoot him deliberately, as it were?'

'It's hard to tell,' said Sir Charles, his brow crinkling. 'To be honest, it more or less has to be the latter, doesn't it? It'd be easy enough for a tough like Stevenson to push Knowle out of his way.'

'In that case, I bet he was acting on orders,' said Anthony. 'Knowle told us that he'd always been friendly with Diefenbach. Knowle was forced to sack his previous valet and take on Blatchford after his mother and stepfather were killed. The gang hoped Paul Diefenbach would get in touch with him. They must be very keen nobody guesses that. I hope our friends buy the idea that the police were after Stevenson last night.'

Sir Charles rubbed his hands through his hair. 'I'll see there's a statement in the press to that effect. Why shouldn't they believe it? They don't know Father Quinet overheard them. Stevenson's a known criminal and a wanted man. I'd like to have a word with our Mr Stevenson.'

'I'd be surprised if he could tell us much. I think his role was that of a guard dog, pure and simple.' Anthony smacked his fist into his palm in frustration. 'Damnit, Talbot, I want to know what any of this has got to do with Milly. She's in danger but I don't know what the danger is or where she is. And what the devil has Paul Diefenbach got to do with it?'

'We'll find out,' said Sir Charles, with confidence.

Anthony gave a cynical laugh. 'You'll a good liar, Talbot, but I don't believe you're as certain as you sound.'

'Don't forget we know the identity of one of the gang,' said Sir Charles earnestly.

'Annie Colbeck,' said Anthony thoughtfully.

Sir Charles nodded. 'With any luck, we should know rather more about her soon. Stephen Mayer, of Mayer and Galbraith, has agreed to act as our cover and my advertisement for Annie Colbeck's fellow servants will be in the papers tomorrow.'

He rubbed his hands together. 'That should bring results and with the entire police force on his heels, we should nab Stevenson very shortly.'

Sir Charles' hopes that they would have news of Johnny Stevenson soon proved justified. It didn't, however, do them much good.

Johnny Stevenson was pulled out of the river near Blackfriars Bridge at eight o'clock that morning with a bullet through his head. It could, in the police surgeon's opinion, later echoed by the coroner, have been suicide.

For the time being, Sir Charles was content to let that opinion rest. There would be time enough later to set the matter straight.

After some debate, Anthony and Sir Charles decided against asking the bank for help. After all, argued Anthony, the bank had already been approached by Inspector Tanner in connection with the murder enquiry, and they had told him all they knew, which amounted to the fact that Diefenbach was headed for the jungles of South America.

Another possibility also proved a blank. Paul Diefenbach's rooms at his club, Addison's, had been searched and proved devoid of interest.

Apart from his clothes and a few books, mainly of travel, there was nothing of any personal interest, apart from his address book. Most of the entries were strictly business – the dentist, the doctor and work colleagues – but at the front of the book was the single name Yvonne and the address, 73, Elgin Road.

Yvonne, Sir Charles knew, was Yvonne Broussard, Paul Diefenbach's wife. As the couple were separated, she probably couldn't tell them anything, but it was worth trying anyway.

TEN

Anthony rang the bell of 73, Elgin Road, a small but elegant town house.

The visiting card he gave the neatly-dressed maid read *Andrew Atkinson. Private Detective.*

Yvonne Broussard came into the drawing room, holding his card in her hand. 'Monsieur Atkinson? You are a private detective?'

Anthony gave a mental and, thankfully, soundless, whistle of appreciation. Yvonne Broussard was absolutely lovely and her voice . . . Wow!

Dark, slim and attractive, she had a voice that could make even a plain woman beautiful and she didn't need any help. What was her accent? He'd assumed she was French but that wasn't quite right. It was an accent he knew quite well, though. Belgian? Yes, of course, that was it. That accent had become very familiar in London since the outbreak of war.

So this was Paul Diefenbach's wife, thought Anthony. Mind you, if a rich, young and handsome American – Anthony had seen his photograph – was going to get married, the chances are he wouldn't pick a frump.

He recalled his temporarily diverted wits and smiled. 'Madame Broussard? Thank you for seeing me.' He glanced at the open door. 'Excuse me, Madame, but could we speak in confidence please?'

Her eyes narrowed but she closed the door with a reassuring click. 'Now, Monsieur, what is this about?'

Anthony coughed. This could be delicate. 'Pardon me for asking, Madame Broussard, but are you acquainted with a Mr Paul Diefenbach?'

Her eyes rounded in surprise. 'But yes, yes of course. Paul is my husband. Is he safe? There has been a problem, an accident, yes?'

She looked at him anxiously. Despite the fact they were separated and she had resumed her maiden name, she still obviously cared for him. Lucky beggar, he thought wryly.

He met her anxious eyes. 'I'm afraid I haven't got any news, Madame Broussard. As far as I know, he is perfectly all right.'

She relaxed visibly, then shrugged impatiently. 'Why are you here? How did you find me? I no longer bear Paul's name.'

Granted her anxiety, it didn't seem very tactful to state there was a bunch of murderous crooks after her husband, or that the Intelligence Service had searched Paul Diefenbach's rooms.

'I have been retained by relatives of the Jowett family to investigate the recent tragic events.' This had seemed the best reason for asking a lot of questions. 'There was a note of your address in Mr Jowett's papers.'

She nodded, her expression grave. 'That news, it was *horrifié*. Paul will be very sad when he hears. He is very fond of Mr Jowett, yes?'

'So I understand. Apparently your husband dined with Mr Jowett before the tragedy. I was hoping Mr Diefenbach could cast some light on the sad affair. Perhaps Mr Jowett mentioned he was worried, or had an enemy, perhaps?'

She shrugged and put her hands out, palms upward, in a very Gallic gesture. 'Monsieur, I do not know. Who could have wanted to harm Monsieur or Madame Jowett? They were good people, you understand, kindly people.'

She obviously, thought Anthony, hadn't read the news about Maurice Knowle or, if she had, hadn't made the connection with the Jowetts.

'Doubtless, you will find it is a robber, a robber who was disturbed, yes?'

'Maybe,' said Anthony, as if considering the idea for the first time. As a matter of fact, she wasn't so far short of the mark. 'Would it be possible for me to speak to Mr Diefenbach?'

She shook her head. 'But no, Monsieur. Have they not told you at the bank? Ah, they are too secretive, they like to make the mystery where there is none. Paul, he is not here. He has gone to America, to South America, to explore a jungle.'

Anthony looked at her sharply. There was an edge of contempt in her voice that he couldn't explain.

She saw the question in his eyes. 'Before the war, then yes, if Paul desires adventure, to voyage himself to far-off places, to live in danger, then why not? He is a rich man, and brave, too. Although now he is married, he should become *établi*, he still desires adventure. But now?' She laughed cynically. 'No, Monsieur. He should fight.' She allowed her eyes to assess him. 'As should you?'

Anthony was prepared for this one. 'I'm afraid I was turned down for service. My heart is not strong.'

She flashed him a quick smile. 'But in the right place, as you English say, yes?' She grew serious again. 'Paul will not fight.'

'He is American,' said Anthony. 'He's a neutral, after all.'

She dismissed neutrality with a wave of her hand. 'Many Americans fight.' Her eyes grew fierce. 'I am Belgian, Monsieur, Belgian, I tell you. My country has been taken by brutes. Paul is American, yes, but his father is German and Paul supported Germany.'

'Did he?' asked Anthony, genuinely startled.

Many Americans of German descent did support Germany, he knew. That was understandable, but to find an American in London who supported Germany was virtually unthinkable. Anti-German feeling was so ugly, it wasn't, perhaps, so surprising that Diefenbach had left the country. There had been anti-German riots and some deaths in the East End of innocent shopkeepers who had a German name above their shop doorways. Even, revolting as it was, little Dachshund dogs had been stoned for the crime of being a German breed. 'That must have made life interesting,' he said cautiously.

She gave a very Gallic shrug. 'Mr Jowett, he tried to persuade Paul otherwise. As did I,' she added grimly. Her mouth set in a straight line. 'You English do not like the Boche. I hate them. I am a Broussard, a Belgian, once more. I do not care to be associated with the Diefenbachs. Perhaps it is better that he is far away.'

Anthony nodded. 'Perhaps.' There must be some reason why a bunch of crooks are so anxious to find him though, he thought. They aren't motivated by extreme patriotism. 'Excuse me, Madame

Broussard, but is there any reason you can think of why anyone should want to contact your husband? Urgently, that is?'

She seemed surprised. 'No. His affairs, they will be in order. He always saw to that. He is methodical, yes? Perhaps the bank? But no. Paul will have set affairs in order there, too. If there is anything urgent at the bank, they can always cable his papa.' She shook her head. 'I cannot help you.'

And really, there didn't seem anything more to add. Apart from hearing of Paul Diefenbach's pro-German sympathies, they didn't seem to be any further forward.

Another blind alley.

Anthony was much happier to receive a note that afternoon from Stephen Mayer, Sir Charles' tame solicitor. Both Eileen Chadderton and Winnie Bruce, previously employed as servants in the Jowett household, had seen the advertisement in the newspapers and would call at the solicitor's office at three o'clock the following day.

With any luck they would be able to show a way forward.

'Pro-German sympathies, eh?' said Sir Charles thoughtfully.

They were in Stephen Mayer's office, awaiting the arrival of Eileen Chadderton and Winnie Bruce. Anthony intended to slip out when the ex-servants arrived. He wasn't needed and the fewer people who could associate him with this business the better.

Sir Charles, on the other hand, with the agreement of Stephen Mayer, had arranged to act as clerk throughout the meeting, to get a first-hand account of what was said.

'Pro-German,' repeated Anthony. 'That's what his wife said. And obviously, I wondered if that was significant. After all, we know there's some sort of plot that involves the occupied territories.'

'You think the Germans are at the back of this?' asked Sir Charles.

Mr Mayer cleared his throat. 'If you'll excuse me for commenting, gentlemen, that doesn't make sense. You say that Paul Diefenbach has pro-German sympathies. If the plot, whatever it is, had been orchestrated by the enemy, they would hardly employ crooks of the like of Stevenson and the rest to lay hands on him.' He gave a thin smile. 'If the Germans are involved, surely Diefenbach would do the orchestrating, so to speak.'

'That's true,' agreed Anthony. 'I was toying with the idea that Diefenbach had somehow got himself over to Germany or the occupied territories, but the Germans wouldn't chase one of their own. They wouldn't need to.'

Sir Charles shook his head. 'He was on the passenger list for the *Union Castle,* sailing to New York. We checked. It's a puzzle, though,' he added in frustration.

Mr Mayer was about to answer, when a bell on the desk rang. 'That'll be Miss Chadderton and Miss Bruce,' he said. 'Perhaps this interview will provide some answers.'

Mr Mayer stood up as Eileen Chadderton and Winnie Bruce were announced.

'Ladies,' he murmured, taking their hands in turn and bowing over them with old-fashioned courtesy. 'Thank you for coming.' He turned to his clerk. 'Kelly, a chair for Miss Bruce and Miss Chadderton please.'

The two women swapped startled glances with each other, more alarmed than reassured by the solicitor's stately manners, but they allowed themselves to be escorted to chairs pulled out for them by Mr Kelly, a stout man dressed in sober black but with very twinkling eyes.

The temporary Mr Kelly summed up the two women. They were nervous, but that wasn't to be wondered at. Although both were well-dressed, in what were obviously new clothes, they looked tired. Edith Chadderton, at a guess, worked in munitions. Munitions workers were the highest paid of all factory girls, but their appearance suffered. Eileen Chadderton's complexion already showed that yellow tinge which had earned munitions workers the nickname of canaries.

'Make yourself comfortable, ladies,' he said reassuringly. 'There's some good news on the way. It's a matter of a legacy.'

They looked at him with a mixture of gratitude and apprehension.

'I told you,' said Eileen Chadderton triumphantly to Winnie Bruce. 'I told you it was something like that. It couldn't be nothing else.'

Mayer cleared his throat. 'Now, ladies,' he said, steepling his fingers together, 'I understand you were both lately in the employ

of Mr and Mrs Jowett of 4, Pettifer's Court, Northumberland
Avenue. Is that correct?'

Once again the two women swapped glances. It was Eileen
Chadderton who answered. 'Indeed it is, sir,' she said, leaning
forward earnestly. 'Me and Winnie, we kept in touch afterwards.
We always got on, didn't we, Winnie?'

Winnie Bruce nodded in agreement, obviously still feeling too
abashed to speak.

'Well, last night, Winnie came round and said had I seen the
advert in the paper? We were surprised, because we hadn't worked
for the Jowetts above a six month and we hadn't looked for
anything, but I said, well, you never know, they were a generous
couple, and here's hoping.'

'I liked it there,' said Winnie Bruce, speaking for the first time.
'They were nice.'

Eileen Chadderton took up the conversational baton. 'We both
liked it, didn't we, Winnie? Yes, we had some good times.' Her
face fell. 'You know about the tragedy?'

Mr Mayer nodded.

'I was shocked,' said Eileen.

'Awful, it was,' intoned Winnie.

'Awful,' repeated Eileen. 'Never in a million years would I have
believed that Mr Jowett – and him such a nice, well-spoken man
too – would ever do such a thing. I'd have sworn he thought the
world of the mistress, I would, honestly. It's my belief there's
more to that than meets the eye, and I'll go to my grave thinking
so. And now poor Captain Knowle, slain in his own house by his
own servant, and him a war hero and all.'

Tears came into her eyes and she sniffed as she dabbed them
away with her handkerchief.

Those were real tears, Talbot noted.

'Awful,' whispered Winnie Bruce in a croak.

'Did you know Captain Knowle?' asked Mayer.

Eileen nodded. 'We did, didn't we, Winnie?'

Winnie Bruce's expression changed from solemnity to distress.
'Yes, we did. He called regular and was always polite, you know?
He was very fond of his mother and the master, which is as it
should be.' She sighed deeply and repeated what seemed to be her
favourite word. 'Awful.'

'I'll say,' declared Eileen with feeling. 'When I saw the photograph in the paper of that hideous man who slaughtered the poor captain, I nearly screamed, and poor Winnie, you took on ever so, didn't you?'

Winnie couldn't speak but nodded earnestly.

Talbot cleared his throat. 'I saw the photograph in the newspaper too, miss. He was a rough-looking customer.'

'Yes, but we've *seen* him,' said Eileen Chadderton.

'You've seen him?' repeated Sir Charles. His pulse quickened. This was an unexpected lead. 'Was he with Captain Knowle?' He had intended, at the start of the interview, to leave all the talking to Mayer, but this was too good a chance to miss. He gauged that neither Eileen Chadderton nor Winnie Bruce knew enough of legal practice to be surprised at being questioned by a solicitor's clerk. His confidence was justified.

'No, he wasn't with the captain,' said Eileen, turning to him. 'I was surprised when I saw in the paper that he was the captain's valet because I knew the captain had a valet who acted as a nurse-attendant. I said to you, didn't I, Winnie, why ever has the captain changed his valet? It was worse for him, poor man, that he ever did such a thing.'

'Indeed it was,' agreed Talbot. 'But you say you saw his valet, this man, Stevenson?'

The two women nodded in agreement.

'Oh, yes, we've seen him,' said Eileen darkly. 'And what's more, if you could get hold of Annie Colbeck, her that we used to work with, she'd tell you more.'

Talbot silently cheered. To have the topic of Annie Colbeck introduce itself so naturally was more than he could've hoped for.

'I don't want to sound as if I'm speaking out of turn,' continued Eileen, 'and I don't wish to sound unkind, I'm sure, but I hope as how she hasn't been remembered in no will. Apart from not deserving it – I'm sure you won't mind me speaking plain – she wasn't there above six weeks and it wouldn't seem right.'

Talbot mentally congratulated himself on his restraint on not advertising for Annie Colbeck. Although it seemed the most straightforward way of enticing her in, it would definitely have aroused suspicion.

'Not right at all,' echoed Winnie Bruce.

'Did you not get on?' asked Talbot, more as a conversational gambit rather than seeking the answer to an obvious question.

Eileen Chadderton sniffed censoriously. 'Get on? Not half we didn't, not with her.'

'She gave herself awful airs,' opined Winnie Bruce.

'And graces,' completed Eileen Chadderton. 'Although what she had to be so pleased about, I do not know. I mean, we didn't know then what we know now, but to be courting that man, that horrible, rough man, who ended up a *murderer.* Well, I can hardly bear to think of it and why the poor captain had such a man in the house I can't think.'

Stephen Mayer raised an eyebrow. 'Courting?'

'Yes, courting,' affirmed Eileen vigorously. 'Courting, they were, although she denied it. I seen them together, more than once, walking out together, and thought then, you don't know what you're taking on, as he looked the sort who wouldn't think twice about raising his hand to a girl, no matter how sweet on him she was. But she said they weren't walking out and couldn't a girl have friends without a load of nosy parkers asking questions about it.'

'That's Annie,' agreed Winnie Bruce. 'Sharp, she was.'

'You could never have a proper chat to her like you could with Winnie, here, say,' continued Eileen. 'She never said nothing about where she came from or who her family were, nothing at all.'

'She spoke French,' offered Winnie Bruce unexpectedly. 'She said she'd lived in France and didn't half think herself posh on the strength of it. She thought it was a proper comedown, being a housemaid, with her able to speak French and all. She said she ought to be a lady's maid, as she could speak French, so I thought, well, go and be a lady's maid then, and leave us all in peace.'

Winnie Bruce glanced round, obviously startled she'd been surprised into saying so much, then subsided into silence again.

Sir Charles nodded. Here was the proof, not that he thought proof was needed, that Anthony Brooke had been correct in his deductions about the woman in the church.

What's more, she'd been seen with Johnny Stevenson. She could've been courting, to use Eileen Chadderton's expression, but Talbot thought it was unlikely to be romance that drew them together. Both Stevenson and Annie Colbeck were part of the gang.

Was Annie reporting to Stevenson? Or was it, perhaps, the other way round?

He dragged his attention back to the conversation.

Eileen Chadderton snorted in disagreement at the idea of Annie Colbeck being a lady's maid. 'You need training, proper training, for that. I can't speak any foreign lingo, but I wouldn't be seen dead with a type like Stevenson.'

'Was she a good worker?' asked Sir Charles. It was a bit of a blow to find that Annie Colbeck had been so tight-lipped about her origins, but he wanted to keep the conversation going.

Eileen Chadderton wrinkled her nose. 'She'd get away with what she could. She never put her heart and soul into her work. Mrs Harrop – she was the housekeeper – thought she was bold. Mrs Harrop didn't like her attitude at all. It was chippy, you know? Mind you, Mrs Harrop was in charge and didn't like us to forget it.'

'So how did she get the job? If Mrs Harrop didn't care for her, I mean?'

Eileen Chadderton laughed. 'It's easy enough to see you haven't got to staff a house, and no mistake. I stuck being in service because I liked Mr and Mrs Jowett, who always treated us fair and square, but what with the war and the factories wanting girls, there's not many now who choose service.'

She shook her head dismissively. 'It's the servants who choose the house and the mistress nowadays, not the other way round, and so it should be, I say. I can't deny I miss having a room and meals all found, as you might say, but the wages don't match up and I've got my freedom, such as you never have in service. I wouldn't go back.' She laughed once more. 'Catch me, I *don't* think, and Winnie thinks the same.'

'Was she recommended for the job?' persisted Sir Charles.

'Not that I know of.' She eyed him warily. 'Are you interested in Annie Colbeck? Special, I mean?'

Sir Charles thought quickly. Eileen Chadderton was bright enough to need a reason for his interest. 'If she knew Stevenson, the police might want to talk to her.'

Eileen put her head on one side, considering. 'Yes, I suppose they might, although what they hope to find out, I don't know. No, I don't know as how she was recommended.'

'She came from an agency,' said Winnie Bruce. 'I'd told the mistress as how the work was too much for me, in that big house and she said that a new girl was coming from an agency.'

'Which agency was that?' asked Sir Charles with a smile.

Eileen Chadderton and Winnie Bruce looked at each other. 'Which one?' repeated Eileen, puzzled. 'How should I know?' Sir Charles heard the unspoken question: why are you asking?

'I thought you might have heard the name,' he said easily.

Inwardly, he was alive with excitement. Here, at last, was the chance to get hold of some genuine information about the shadowy Annie Colbeck. Even if she'd left the agency – which, in view of the conversation Father Quinet had overheard, seemed likely – they were bound to have some information about her. They might even have her address and they'd certainly be able to give a description. He put these thoughts to one side. He had to give Eileen Chadderton a reason for his question.

'If she was walking out with Captain Knowles's valet, Stevenson might very well have used the same agency himself.'

Both Eileen Chadderton and Winnie Bruce accepted this fairly specious argument at face value, but to his disappointment, Eileen shook her head. 'I can't bring it to mind. Funnily enough, it was the master who suggested the agency, I do remember that, but I can't tell you the name.'

'You did know it,' said Winnie Bruce, speaking to Eileen. 'Which agency it was, I mean. Mrs Harrop mentioned it. You said she'd said something funny about it, but I can't remember rightly what it was.'

'Did I?' asked Eileen, frowning. 'D'you know, you're right, Winnie. Whatever was it? It wasn't the name of a person, such as Clarkson, who I used to be with, or Booth.'

'I was with Miss Booth's,' put in Winnie. 'That's not it.'

'No. Was it the Reliant? It was something like that.' She snapped her fingers. 'The Diligent, that's it!'

'That's right,' agreed Winnie. 'Diligent. That means working hard, doesn't it? You said so. You said that Mrs Harrop said if Annie Colbeck was their idea of diligence, they should buck their ideas up. It made me laugh, that did.'

'It tickled you, I remember,' said Eileen. 'Yes, Mrs Harrop said Annie Colbeck wasn't much of an advert for them, as far as diligence went. Very cutting, she was.'

The Diligent. Sir Charles concealed his satisfaction with difficulty. With both women agreeing on the name, it sounded as if he had a real, hard fact at last.

Eileen sighed and shook her head with a smile. 'It's done us good to talk about the old days, hasn't it, Winnie? It's a pity it all ended as it did, but we had some good times.' She sighed once more, as if drawing a line under the past and looked at Mr Mayer. 'I don't want to appear forward, but I think you said there was some good news for us?'

Mr Mayer cleared his throat. 'As executor of the late Mr and Mrs Jowett's estate, I am instructed to tell you that you have each been left a legacy of fifty pounds.'

Both Eileen and Winnie gasped. Fifty pounds amounted to nearly a year's wages for a servant. Eileen's eyes rounded. 'That's very generous. I wasn't expecting nothing. Winnie, yes, that's only as it should be, but I'd only been there a few months. That's very generous indeed.'

It would, in fact, have been very generous but was actually (with Sir Charles' sanction) a present from the Government. And, he thought with satisfaction, as he sat back and listened to Eileen and Winnie's exclamations of delight, to get the name of Annie Colbeck's agency was worth a hundred pounds of government money and no mistake.

ELEVEN

'So what are you going to do now?' asked Tara that evening as she poured out the coffee.

Dinner had finished and they were in the blue-and-white sitting room, looking out into the garden, rich with autumn colours. Anthony, who had put in an afternoon at University College Hospital after leaving the solicitors before the servants arrived, had called in at Angel Alley on the way home to get the latest news which he had faithfully recounted to a fascinated Tara.

Tara wanted to discuss the news, but he was feeling well fed, sleepy and content, and not at all in the mood to talk about house-maids, however murderous they were.

'What am I going to do?' He took the cup of coffee from Tara, put it on the table and drew her down on the sofa beside him. 'I'm going to sit on my own sofa in my own home with my own wife, while she tells me how wonderful I am and what she's done today, and forget about the whole wretched business.'

'No, you're not,' said Tara, laughing as she snuggled down beside him. 'Forget about it, I mean.' She kissed him lightly. 'I'll tell you you're wonderful, if I must, but I want to know what you're going to do now. Is Charles Talbot going to make enquiries at this agency, the Diligent?'

'I suppose so,' said Anthony, reaching out for his coffee. 'Do we really have to talk about it?'

'I'd like to,' said Tara seriously, resting her chin on her hand. 'I don't think Sir Charles should enquire at the agency.'

'Why not?' asked Anthony in surprise. 'Until we manage to track down Paul Diefenbach, the agency is the best lead we've got.'

'Don't you see, Anthony? The housemaid, Eileen Whatshername, said it was Mr Jowett who suggested the Diligent.'

'What about it?'

'That means someone who knew Mr Jowett wanted the Jowetts to employ a servant from that agency. There must be a reason for that. I think the agency is crooked.'

Anthony laughed. 'You're joking.' He looked at her serious face and shook his head. 'Come on, Tara, don't you think that's a bit far-fetched?'

'Is it? What are these crooks after?'

'Well, as far as we can judge, they're desperate to find out where Paul Diefenbach is. That's why Maurice Knowle, poor beggar, was kept tabs on, in case Diefenbach contacted him. Goodness knows where Milly comes into it.'

'And who is Paul Diefenbach?'

Anthony shrugged. 'You know as much about him as I do. He's a rich American, head of the Capital and Counties bank, with pro-German sympathies and a taste for adventure.'

'Rich,' repeated Tara. 'With a lot of money at stake, who knows what anyone would do?'

'Money's a powerful motive, I agree, but to say the entire agency is crooked is crazy,' protested Anthony. 'Look, these crooks want to find out about Diefenbach. They know Edward Jowett is a trusted friend of his and, presumably, believe he's got information about him. So they bribe one of the servants and the rest we know. That's a fairly straightforward way of proceeding.'

'It is,' agreed Tara, '*if* you know that one of the servants is crooked. But just think about what Annie Colbeck did, Anthony. You think she was bribed to search Mr Jowett's study, but she did far more than that. Not only did she help the murderer to escape, you believe she deliberately poisoned the butler with his own heart medicine.'

'She more or less had to, didn't she?'

Tara shook her head. 'Charles Talbot thinks it's inevitable, because he knows that's what actually happened. I don't think it's inevitable at all. It wouldn't seem like that at the time. I think a petty crook, the sort who'd take a bribe or a nice present, as she'd probably say, wouldn't think of murder. Remember, no one knew she was involved. You were the first to work that out. To turn to murder so quickly, to silence the old man, is something that would surely only occur to a hardened criminal. After all, no one knew she was anything but an innocent housemaid. I think that's a huge jump forward.'

Anthony drank his coffee thoughtfully. 'You might be right. It's a very big jump forward.'

Encouraged, Tara carried on. 'Add to that what the priest, Father Quinet, overheard her say in church. She didn't shy away from the idea of committing a crime, only the idea of being caught.'

'So she's a crook,' said Anthony. 'I don't disagree.'

'Don't you think the gang were lucky to find such a woman in the house? I think she was placed there.'

'But . . .' Anthony sat for a moment in silence. 'Even if the agency is dodgy, how could they be sure they'd get a servant into the house? For a start, whoever's setting this scheme up would have to know that the Jowetts needed a housemaid.'

His wife gave him a withering look. 'Anthony, of *course* the Jowetts needed a housemaid. Everyone with a house of any size is desperate for servants. It was easy enough before the war, but things are different now.'

'All right, I'll grant you that, but it's one thing to recommend a particular agency, it's quite another to know the advice is going to be followed. What if the Jowetts hadn't taken the advice?'

'What if they hadn't? As far as we know, all Annie Colbeck was asked to do in the first instance was to search Mr Jowett's study. The easiest way to do that is to have her employed in the house, but if that hadn't come off, they'd have found another way. They could've sent someone to inspect the gas pipes or see to the plumbing or even just broken in.'

Anthony laughed once more. 'It's a rum thing, Tara, but when you first suggested the idea, I thought it was barmy, but the more you've said, the more I agree. It's one thing to bribe a servant, it's quite another to have them turn to murder.' He frowned. 'I'll have to have a word with Talbot sooner rather than later.'

'Telephone him,' suggested Tara. She glanced at the grandfather clock. 'He's probably at his club. It's only a ten-minute walk or so away.'

'I'll ask him to call,' said Anthony. 'It's your idea. It's only right you should put it to him.'

Sir Charles listened intently to Tara, then, finishing his brandy, sighed deeply. 'I hadn't taken on board just how remarkable it was to find the likes of Annie Colbeck in the house.' He looked ruefully at Tara. 'You're quite right. She acted very quickly – to say nothing of ruthlessly – to let her comrade escape and cover up the Jowetts' murder.'

'So you believe it, then?' asked Tara.

'I do,' said Sir Charles simply. Tara couldn't help but look pleased. 'You've saved us from making a very grave error. If I'd enquired at the Diligent for Annie Colbeck, I might as well have sent the gang a postcard explaining what we're up to.'

He drummed his fingers on the side of the chesterfield. 'Unfortunately, it does beg the question of exactly what can we do. After speaking to the two servants this afternoon, I found out what I could about the Diligent. It seems perfectly legitimate. It's listed in *Kelly's Street Directory* at 64, Sullivan Place, off Charing Cross Road.'

'That's near St Mark's,' said Anthony in satisfaction. 'I thought it might be.'

'And you were quite right, my dear fellow. There's nothing in police records about them. I sent a man round to have a look at the agency. It was closed, but according to what was written over the door, it was established two years ago by a Mr Joshua Harper. In view of what you've worked out, Mrs Brooke, I'm guessing the name is false but the date, at least, seems to be genuine enough.'

'So it's a real agency,' said Tara slowly. 'I did wonder if the Diligent was set up with the sole purpose of getting Annie Colbeck into the Jowetts, but that can't be so, not if they've been going for the last couple of years.'

'They have,' said Sir Charles. 'The police officer on the beat confirmed it to my man. He knows Mr Harper by sight well enough and was able to give a description.'

'Which is?' asked Anthony.

'He's middle aged, about five foot seven inches tall, grey haired, wears spectacles, well-dressed with an affable manner with, as they say, no distinguishing characteristics. The only odd thing about him is his accent, which the police constable couldn't place.'

'The accent is probably American,' said Anthony. 'After all, Father Quinet thought the first man in the church was an American. What's the chances of that man being Joshua Harper?'

'He could be,' agreed Sir Charles. 'Granted that the agency is crooked, it seems likely that the boss himself would be the man to recommend Annie Colbeck to their client.'

Tara nodded. 'I did think of getting Father Quinet into the agency somehow, to see if he could hear Joshua Harper speak. He'd probably recognize the voice, but that would be very dangerous for him.'

'Very dangerous,' said Sir Charles quickly. 'We couldn't ask him to do that.'

'Besides that, there wouldn't be any reason for Father Quinet to go into the agency,' said Tara in an abstracted way. 'The priest's housekeepers are always women from the parish.'

'And more Catholic than the Pope,' agreed Sir Charles. 'You'd never get a Catholic priest using a domestic employment agency. But what's your point, Mrs Brooke?'

'It's this,' said Tara, hesitating. 'If the agency has been running for two years, with a crook at the helm and the likes of Annie Colbeck on the books, what have they been running?'

Sir Charles looked puzzled. 'I don't understand.'

'Are they running a legitimate enterprise?' asked Tara. 'It doesn't seem likely, does it? I know you said there was nothing on record about them, but why would there be? As soon as they come to police attention, they've failed. We've said they're crooks. What sort of crooks?'

'Murderous crooks,' muttered Anthony.

She turned to him. 'You can't make money out of murder, Anthony.' She looked at Sir Charles once more. 'We've assumed the agency is crooked. So what sort of crooks are they? What do they want?'

'Money, at a guess,' said Sir Charles. He grinned. 'That's the traditional root of all evil. A crooked servant is the ideal person to organize a robbery, as, indeed, has occurred to more than a few servants before now.'

Anthony ran his hand round his chin. 'They could be thieves, I suppose, but my guess is that they're blackmailers.'

Sir Charles pursed his lips in a whistle. 'That fits! After all, they blackmailed Mrs Jowett and Maurice Knowle.'

'Exactly,' said Tara in satisfaction. 'That's what I thought. You said a crooked servant is the ideal person to organize a robbery, but they're also the ideal person to gather the material for blackmail.'

Sir Charles reached for a cigarette from the box on the table. 'Blackmail,' he repeated slowly. 'The victim wouldn't contact the police. The chances are they'd keep quiet and pay up. So Annie Colbeck collects information . . .'

'And once she's got the information, the blackmailer calls,' said Anthony. 'That's what happened at the Jowetts. Presumably the blackmailer is our affable Mr Harper. He's the boss, after all. Annie Colbeck is in the clear. The first the victim knows about it is a visit from an unknown man who has some very damaging information.'

He looked at Tara enquiringly. 'I presume Annie Colbeck isn't the only servant employed by the Diligent. If the Diligent really is running blackmail as a business, what would happen if one of the Diligent people take a post at a house where everyone is completely above board? I know it's often said that everyone's got secrets, but I don't believe everyone is a candidate for blackmail.'

'They'd leave, I suppose,' said Tara with a shrug. 'And I imagine they'd only take a position at a likely house, where the employer is a businessman, say, not some little old lady scraping to make ends meet.'

'Fair enough.' Anthony glanced at Sir Charles. 'Can you find any proof of this, d'you think? Because it fits in with what we know happened at the Jowetts, I'm fairly sure it's the truth of the matter, but it'd be good to actually *know*.'

Sir Charles clicked his tongue. 'The trouble is, Brooke, is that blackmail victims, almost by definition, keep quiet. If this is organized blackmail, our blackmailers probably have the sense not to push their victims too far. It's like the protection rackets the New York gangs operate. Regular payments of what the victim can afford are the order of the day.'

Anthony snapped his fingers. 'We're back to America! Could that be a way of nailing him? If he's an American crook the Americans might have something on him.' He frowned. 'The trouble is, that'll take time.'

'Too much time,' agreed Tara. 'Besides that, he's bound to have changed his name. In any case, what if he does have a record in the States? That's not going to tell us what he's up to now.' She glanced at Anthony. 'We need to do something quickly.'

'Yes, but what?'

'We need to get them to show their hand,' said Tara, then added, in a distant voice, 'I'm Irish.'

Anthony blinked at her. 'I had noticed.'

'Lots of servants are Irish. I know how a household operates. I'd be a good servant.'

'What?' Anthony was horrified. 'Tara, if you've got any idea of getting these vicious crooks to take you on as a servant, then forget it.'

'It really isn't a good idea, Mrs Brooke,' put in Sir Charles.

Tara bit her lip. 'No, it probably isn't. By the time they trusted me to do a job, we'll have run out of time. It's a pity, but there it is.'

'Absolutely there it is,' agreed Anthony fervently. 'For pity's sake, Tara, these people are *dangerous*.'

'I know,' she said absently. 'We'll have to approach them another way.'

Anthony looked at her warily. 'Which way?'

Tara took a deep breath. 'It's obvious, isn't it? We'll have to employ the agency.'

There was a dead silence.

'What exactly are you suggesting?' asked Anthony at length. 'Because I can tell you now that inviting a servant who we firmly believe is a blackmailer into our house is not something that fills me with enthusiasm. I might not have a shady past but I've certainly got plenty of secrets.'

'I wouldn't invite them here,' said Tara. 'No, that's not my idea at all. You know Grace Russell?'

Sir Charles looked blank but Anthony nodded. 'Mrs Russell is a friend of Tara's,' he explained to Sir Charles.

'She's Irish, too,' said Tara. 'Her husband, Major Michael Russell, is serving in France, and I know her mother has asked her to come home to Waterford while he's away.' Sir Charles still looked blank. 'The thing is,' she continued, 'is that she's got a very nice flat in Chelsea. Now what I had in mind is this . . .'

TWELVE

The following afternoon, Tara turned off the Charing Cross Road into Sullivan Place. Sullivan Place was a quiet cobbled backwater, shaded by two plane trees, their leaves turning golden orange in the sun. The two facing rows of neat terraced houses were interspersed with small shops, a doctor's surgery and the occasional office. Tara took note of the shops as she walked past; there was a coal merchant, a greengrocers, a firm of glaziers, an ironmongers and a haberdashers before she came to number 64.

On the window facing onto the street was written, in ornate gilt lettering, *The Diligent Domestic Employment Agency*. Over the smartly painted maroon front door was the same legend, with the addition of *Established 1913. Proprietor Joshua Harper, Esq.*

The door stood open. Tara took a deep breath, put her shoulders back, and walked in. The tiled hallway was dark, tall and narrow and smelt of disinfectant and soap. As an underworld lair for murderous criminals – Tara had used the word *lair* unconsciously to herself – it was disappointingly mundane.

Halfway down the hall, opposite the flight of stairs, was another door. On the frosted glass of the upper half was written, again in ornate gilt script, *Inquiries. Please enter.*

As she pushed open the door, a bell tinkled above her head. A severely-dressed woman, her hair scraped back into an unflattering bun and wearing wire-rimmed spectacles, looked up from where she was seated at a typewriter.

She had a small port-wine birthmark on her left cheek, which she'd attempted to conceal with make-up. Apart from that, she would, thought Tara, be quite attractive if she allowed herself to be. It's a disguise, she thought, with quick insight. She's disguised as a lady clerk. She's playing a part. She's not *real*. Tara was suddenly aware of how unnerving that knowledge was.

The woman stood up and came from behind the desk. 'Good morning. I am Miss Anston, Mr Harper's confidential clerk. Can I help you?'

Tara swallowed, trying to get a grip on herself. She had to play a part too, the part of a woman in search of a domestic servant. I can do this, she told herself. I have done this. I've been to domestic agencies before. The memory of setting up house with Anthony came to her aid. She'd visited four agencies then and they all looked much the same as this one.

At the rear of the room was a door, slightly ajar, bearing the word *Manager* on a wooden plaque screwed to the door three-quarters of the way up. The room was furnished with three filing cabinets, a desk with a typewriter and a table with four hard wooden chairs. Even the individual notes in the room – the dark green Lincrusta wallpaper, the vase of flowers, and the fire burning cheerfully in the black-leaded grate seemed, in their essence of respectability, to be playing a part. It was a part she knew, though, and that helped to steady her nerves.

'Can I see Mr Harper?' she asked.

'I'm afraid Mr Harper is unavailable,' said Miss Anston. She flashed out an unconvincing smile. She pulled out one of the hard wooden chairs and motioned Tara towards it. 'However, I am authorized to deal with all enquiries in his absence, Mrs . . .?'

Tara gathered her skirts around her and sat down. 'I'm Mrs Russell,' she said. 'Mrs Grace Russell.' She opened her fussy little reticule, so different from the sort of bag she usually carried and, opening her card case, placed a visiting card upon the desk.

As Miss Anston picked up the card and bent to look at it, Tara felt a prickling sensation in the back of her neck. Tara trusted her feelings. She was being watched.

Nerves tingling, she allowed her gaze to wander round the room, hoping to convey an impression of bored upper-class haughtiness in the presence of underlings. She was in danger. All her senses seemed heightened. Very faintly she heard an almost inaudible rustle. It was the door. She was sure there was a watcher behind the door. She wouldn't usually have noticed such a tiny detail, but she saw, quite clearly, that one of the screw-holes in the *Manager* sign reflected the light. It was a glass spy hole.

Tara's fingers unconsciously wound themselves round the strap of her reticule. She had to play the part to perfection.

'Oakley Gardens,' murmured Miss Anston. 'Yes, I know the area. It's not far from Cheyne Walk, overlooking the Embankment.' She glanced up with an expression of unmistakable greed.

You enjoy this, thought Tara. You're jealous of anyone with more money than you. You'd really enjoy seeing me squirm. Behind those wire-rimmed spectacles, Miss Anston's eyes were very cold.

'How can we help you?' asked Miss Anston.

'I need a maid.' Tara leaned forward. 'A competent house parlourmaid who will also prepare simple meals.'

She didn't want to make her requirements too simple. If she was willing to accept anyone, that might seem suspicious.

'You require the girl to cook in addition to her other duties?' asked Miss Anston with a frown.

'I don't want anything elaborate. I usually dine out. I only want the one servant and I want someone who can do everything. I pay well, mind. Fifty or sixty pounds a year. Perhaps a little more for the right woman. My current maid does very well but she's leaving domestic service.'

She made a fluttering gesture with her hand and laughed dismissively. 'I don't want any young girl who has to be shown the ropes. I haven't time to be bothered with some country bumpkin who's never seen a gas light before and is frightened of electricity.'

Miss Anston permitted herself a wintery smile. 'All our staff are totally competent.'

'Are they?' said Tara, suddenly growing very Irish. 'Then you must be the most remarkable agency in London. Nobody I've tried yet seems to have exactly the sort of maid I'm looking for.'

'We endeavour to give satisfaction, Madam. Incidentally, what led you to us? I'm happy to say we have many satisfied clients. Was it a personal recommendation?'

This was a dangerous question. Tara had discussed it with Anthony and Sir Charles last night. If the Diligent really was a front for blackmailers, it was highly unlikely that their clients would recommend them. That was why she had noted the shops on Sullivan Place.

'I had business with Hardcastles', the glaziers, down the street, and I saw your office. I thought I may as well see if you had anyone suitable.'

Miss Anston's shoulders relaxed. Danger past.

Tara breathed deeply and looked around her, as if to ensure they were alone, then leaned forward confidentially. 'The thing is,' she said, her voice dropping, 'I'm not looking for a girl. What I'm really after is a mature woman who knows the ways of the world. Someone who can be trusted not to gossip, you understand?'

Miss Anston drew back. There was an unmistakable predatory gleam of satisfaction in her eyes. 'A good servant knows the virtues of discretion,' she said sanctimoniously.

'Yes, but . . .' Tara stopped, as if trying to find the right words. 'I'm not quite sure how to put this, but my husband's in France.' She dropped her gaze. 'Life can be very hard for a woman left alone.'

Miss Anston gave an unconvincing sigh. 'You're right. Naturally, one thinks first of the brave men at the front, but I often feel that the women left behind have made the greater sacrifice.' She gazed at Tara with intense and, Tara was sure, entirely false, sympathy. 'Women,' she added, 'suffer greatly from loneliness.'

Tara clasped her hands in apparent relief. 'That's exactly it! Loneliness is the greatest burden a real woman can endure. I have a sensitive nature. Without companionship, without kind friends, I shrivel.'

'But you have friends, surely?' asked Miss Anston with cooing sympathy.

'I do,' said Tara simply. 'And that's the difficulty, you see. I entertain the occasional visitor. Male visitors. Nothing untoward, you understand—' Miss Anston nodded – 'but my husband has a jealous nature. It'd be easy for him to jump to the wrong conclusions if any gossip came to his ears.' Tara looked down, twisting the ribbons of her reticule anxiously. 'It would injure his feelings, which I don't want to do, and yet I feel I have the perfect right to entertain guests in his absence.'

'Of course,' said Miss Anston, with a smile that, for the first time, showed genuine warmth. 'I'm perfectly certain we'll be able to find the exact person who'll fulfil your requirements very well, Mrs Russell.'

She opened the desk drawer, looked inside, then tutted in annoyance. 'I thought our ledger of available staff was here.' She drew her chair back. 'Excuse me. I must've left it in Mr Harper's office.'

Miss Anston stood up and went into the manager's office, shutting it with a click behind her. Tara strained her ears but could hear nothing. Nevertheless, she was convinced that Miss Anston had gone to get official sanction before she dispatched a maid to Oakley Gardens.

Miss Anston returned a few minutes later with the ledger. Resuming her seat, she opened the book. 'Here we are,' she said after a brief pause. 'Mrs Russell, you're in luck. It so happens that our Miss Bertha Maybrick is available. She's twenty-seven, a very experienced house-parlourmaid, and is skilled in preparing simple meals. She has excellent references.'

'And discretion?' asked Tara anxiously. 'She knows how to be discreet?'

Miss Anston smiled. It was exactly the sort of smile, thought Tara, that a cat would give on hearing a mouse enquire if it was quite convenient to pop out across the kitchen floor for a moment. It was funny, thought of like that, but the reality was chilling. How many others had walked blindly into the trap?

'Discretion,' said Miss Anston, 'is guaranteed. I may tell you that until the start of the week, Miss Maybrick was employed by Gloria Wilde, the actress. Miss Wilde has sailed for Hollywood.

She was, of course, anxious that Miss Maybrick accompany her, but Miss Maybrick preferred to stay in London.'

Miss Anston looked over the top of her spectacles. 'Actresses require complete discretion. Professional jealousy, Mrs Russell, can be cruel. Make no mistake, our Miss Maybrick will always have your best interests at heart.'

Tara gave a not entirely simulated sigh of relief. 'She sounds as if she may suit me. How soon can she start?'

'At once, if you require.'

'I do. My current maid only stayed on to oblige. I am happy to give your Miss Maybrick a week's trial. Shall we say three o'clock this afternoon?'

'Excellent,' said Miss Anston, making a note in the ledger. 'Your maid will be there, I trust? It would be helpful for Miss Maybrick to have an account of her duties.'

'I'll make sure of it,' said Tara, standing up to leave.

It was with a real sense of relief that she escaped the Diligent and back into the crisp autumn sunshine of Sullivan Place. Miss Anston's eyes had been very cold indeed behind those spectacles. She wouldn't like to be in her power.

What would happen if Miss Anston found out she wasn't Grace Russell? She thought enviously of the real Grace, now on her way to Bristol, *en route* to Waterford. Grace was a genuinely good person, devoted to her husband, Michael.

Grace, who knew of the odd straits that Anthony's work sometimes led him to, was perfectly willing to help, and, what's more, keep absolutely quiet about it. All the same, thought Tara ruefully, she'd better never know that her name had become, in some circles at least, a byword for adultery. Grace wouldn't like that at all.

THIRTEEN

'So you're the new maid,' said Miss Flora Shaw to the newly arrived Bertha Maybrick. The two women sized each other up.

Bertha Maybrick was thin and efficient-looking, neatly dressed in black with a coil of dark brown hair, watchful hazel eyes, and a painfully straightened cockney accent.

Flora Shaw, who had done many an odd job for Sir Charles, was stout, smiling and apparently easy-going.

'It's not a bad place,' said Flora. 'In a way I'm sorry to leave, but my sister has a shop in Silvertown and wants me to help. Well, family's family, but I'll be sorry to go.'

'Mrs Russell's husband is serving in France, I understand,' said Bertha. She paused. 'She must get lonely.' There was a faint question in the words.

Flora Shaw laughed heartily, then closed the kitchen door. 'He's serving in France all right, but I don't know about lonely,' she said, with a significant wink. 'A lovely looking woman like that, it's not to be wondered at. It takes all sorts as I always say.' She gave Miss Maybrick a swift glance. 'You don't have *views* do you? Anyone with views wouldn't suit at all. After all, she's not teaching at a Sunday school.'

Bertha Maybrick pursed her lips. 'I wouldn't like anything rowdy.'

'There's nothing like that,' Flora reassured her. 'Just visitors, you know? Polite enough, but you might have to cook breakfast for two.'

Bertha's lips compressed into a thin line. 'I see.'

'Just do your job and don't gossip,' said Flora. 'It can cause a lot of trouble, gossip can, and we don't want that.'

She didn't miss the avaricious gleam in Bertha Maybrick's eyes. 'No, of course not,' she murmured. 'Gossip is a dreadful thing.'

In that, at least, she was sincere. Bertha Maybrick had no intention whatsoever of gossiping about what she saw.

On the third morning of her new employment, Bertha was informed by Mrs Russell that she would be out to lunch. This didn't come as a surprise to Bertha. Hearing the faint ting of the telephone bell in the hall the previous evening, she carefully picked up the receiver in her mistress's bedroom and listened to a breathless conversation between Mrs Russell and a man she called Tony.

Tony, she knew, was the tall, grey-eyed, soldierly-looking man who had visited – and stayed – the first evening. Bertha had received a ten-shilling note the next morning, 'for the extra trouble'. Correctly identifying the wages of sin, Bertha pocketed it without comment.

Mrs Russell, as she had said on the telephone, was very anxious that Tony shouldn't be seen in Oakley Gardens. Tony's wife was very suspicious. She was sure Tony's wife was having the flat watched. They had to be very careful but she couldn't live without seeing Tony. There followed a declaration of undying love which Bertha Maybrick listened to with grim amusement.

Mrs Russell had had another visitor, an older man, an Irishman called Charlie, who had called Mrs Russell *mavourneen* and other terms of endearment when he thought the door was closed. Charlie hadn't stayed but, with her knowledge of the world, Bertha had no doubt that the old fool was paying the bills.

And she wouldn't like Charlie to meet Tony, thought Bertha, gently replacing the receiver after the call was ended. It'd serve her right, she thought with a self-satisfied twist of her lips. It's a disgrace, what's she doing. I don't hold with being immoral.

Oddly enough, Bertha really didn't hold with immorality. She had a fastidious distaste that amounted to aversion for all the frailties of the flesh. I'd like to see, she thought, her mouth tightening, any man trying it on with me! This had actually happened once. Ever since then Bertha had carried a small, sharp, kitchen knife in her handbag. That would show them, she thought with grim satisfaction.

No, she didn't hold with immorality. What she didn't object to was profiting from it.

'Surely I've given that awful woman enough ammunition to strike now,' said Tara over her chicken and bacon pie. They were lunching in the Trocadero on Shaftsbury Avenue.

She grinned ruefully at her husband. 'She's actually very good at her job. If I didn't know what she was up to, I don't think I'd realize she was listening in on the telephone. I'm sure she's picked up all the information we've fed her.' She giggled. 'Charles Talbot is such a good actor, you know. He acted the besotted boyfriend to the hilt.'

'Good for him,' said Anthony, who couldn't quite keep the reproof out of his voice.

Tara giggled once more. 'Are you jealous? You shouldn't be, after all I said to you on the telephone last night.'

'Wasn't that all persiflage?' asked Anthony, grinning.

'Not all of it.' Anthony looked understandably smug. 'I hope she does strike soon,' continued Tara. 'We can't keep it up for much longer. She's bound to twig I'm not the real Grace Russell sooner or later.'

'If you think there's the slightest danger, get out,' said Anthony alarmed.

'I've got your men outside,' said Tara. 'It's reassuring to know they're there. It was a very bright idea to say your wife had detectives watching the flat.'

'These people are professionals,' he said. 'If they do spot Talbot's men, I want them to have a convincing explanation of why they're watching the flat. Did you leave the letter, by the way?'

'I did. Four pages of highly actionable prose, addressed to you, my darling. I put it away hurriedly when she came into the room. It's hidden, of course, but she knows it's there. That should stir something up.'

'I hope so,' said Anthony. 'The sooner you're out of that flat, the better.'

Bertha Maybrick gave a little grunt of satisfaction as she looked at the desk. There was a studio portrait of Major Michael Russell on the desk, but it didn't interest Bertha. If anything, the portrait, and the crucifix that hung on the wall above the desk, increased her loathing of That Woman. She was nothing but a filthy hypocrite.

She knew That Woman had been writing a letter and, what's more, it was a letter she evidently didn't want Bertha to see. She'd thrust it away beneath the blotter when Bertha had come into the room. She thought she hadn't been seen, but Bertha had been too quick for her.

The letter wasn't under the blotter now, so where was it? A book, a cheap turgid romance, was lying on the desk. It was exactly the sort of book That Woman would read.

With a grim smile of satisfaction, Bertha opened the book. There was the unfinished letter, folded in two.

Bertha opened the letter and read it through with a growing

sense of moral indignation. It was disgusting what That Woman was doing, absolutely disgusting. She looked at the portrait of Major Russell with an indignant sniff. Fool of a man! He deserved everything he got, marrying a woman like *her*. And as for *her* . . . Well, she richly deserved everything that was coming to her. Picking up a pen, she set to work copying out the flowery phrases. She put the copy in the pocket of her apron and carefully replaced the original in the book.

Then, feeling as if she had done a really good hour's work, she went into the hall and picked up the telephone.

In Sullivan Place, Miss Anston hung up the receiver with a grim smile of satisfaction. Names, dates *and* a letter. All they needed was one more piece of information and Joshua would be very pleased indeed.

With Bertha Maybrick safely in the kitchen, Tara looked at the book lying on the desk. The single hair that had lain inside the cover was gone. Bait taken.

She finished the letter (the romance novel was a helpful inspiration), addressed it to a Mr A. Hamilton and stamped it. If the letter was ever delivered, it would find its way, via Mr Andrew Hamilton, to Charles Talbot. Sir Charles had far too much respect for his enemy to give them a fake address.

'There's a letter for the post on the hall table, Bertha,' she said, when the maid came in with afternoon tea. She didn't miss the gleam in Bertha's eyes. 'Could you post it at once, please?'

'Very good, Madam,' said Bertha, putting the tea tray on the table. 'I'll do so directly.'

Once Bertha had left the room, Tara slipped out into the hall and was rewarded by the faint ting of the telephone bell. That, she thought with satisfaction, was Bertha, envelope in hand, informing her boss of 'Tony's' name and address. Now all she had to do was wait.

FOURTEEN

Tara had never been blackmailed before. As she told Anthony in the restaurant that evening, what she was chiefly worried about was her ability to act as if she was really scared when the time came.

That wasn't a problem. Eleven o'clock the next morning Bertha informed her there was a Mr Smith to see her. Bertha couldn't quite hide her smirk as she showed him in. Despite herself, Tara's heart was racing as she stood up to greet the visitor.

'Mr Smith' was a man in his fifties or thereabouts, grey-haired with sharp blue eyes behind gold-rimmed spectacles. He smiled genially as he came into the room. Tara remembered the description Sir Charles had given of Harper from the local policeman. An affable manner? That smile – that snake's smile – was it. Her stomach turned over and her mouth was dry.

'Mr Smith?' she began. 'I don't think we've met?'

'And yet, Mrs Russell, I would like you to consider me as your friend.' His accent, the accent the policeman couldn't place, was American.

Without asking for permission, he sat down and regarded her gravely.

Tara remembered to act. She was surprised how nervous she was. I don't know what he wants, she told herself. I would be horrified if a complete stranger walked into my house and made himself at home. Her voice, when she spoke, cracked. That wasn't acting, but it fitted the part.

'How dare you, sir! I don't know who you are but I must ask you to leave at once!' Her hand stretched out to the bell, as if to ring for the maid.

'Don't!' said Mr Smith. His voice was commanding.

Tara paused, waiting.

Mr Smith put his head on one side. 'My dear Mrs Russell, you really do not want anyone else to hear what I'm about to say.' Again, the snake's smile flashed out. 'It's for your own good, my dear lady.'

Tara's hand dropped. 'What d'you mean? Who are you?' She knew her voice was trembling.

He rested his chin on his hand. 'Shall we say I'm here on behalf of Mrs Hamilton?' he said softly.

For a moment Tara was thrown. Who on earth was Mrs Hamilton? Panic must have shown in her face, because the snake's smile widened. Then she remembered the envelope Bertha had supposedly posted. 'Mrs Hamilton?' she wavered. 'Tony's wife?'

Mr Smith's smile widened. 'Precisely, dear lady.'

Tara stared at him.

'Mrs Hamilton has, I'm sorry to say, become increasingly suspicious of her husband's frequent absences,' said Mr Smith, examining his manicured fingernails. 'Hell hath no fury like a woman scorned, Mrs Russell, as one of the poets so wisely said.'

Tara sank into an armchair and nodded dumbly. Privately she was congratulating Mr Smith on his cleverness. By bringing the wronged Mrs Hamilton into the picture, he had neatly distracted suspicion from Bertha. The fact that Mrs Hamilton was a total figment of the imagination didn't detract from the cleverness of the scheme.

'I am a kindly man, Mrs Russell,' said Mr Smith, looking up from his fingernails. 'Mrs Hamilton would have undoubtedly been upset if she had seen the letters you have written to her husband.'

'Letters?' There was, of course, only one, but Smith didn't know that.

'Letters,' he repeated softly. He drew an envelope from his breast pocket and, opening it, unfolded a piece of paper. 'This is a copy,' he said. 'The original is, you will be glad to know, in safe keeping.' He cleared his throat. '"My darling Tony",' he began. '"How long do I have to wait before I feel the touch of your caress—"'

Tara threw up her hands as if to shield herself. 'No!'

'"Madness . . . Tender yearnings . . . Overwhelming desire".' He lowered the paper and looked at her over the top of his spectacles. The very purple prose of the letter owed almost everything to *Three Weeks* by Elinor Glyn, but fortunately Mr Smith did not appear to be versed in popular fiction. 'Shall I read more?'

'No,' she whispered.

'Now, to save Mrs Hamilton distress – which I am sure you are anxious to do – I could be persuaded not to contact Mrs Hamilton in return for a small sum. Shall we say a hundred pounds? I will, of course, keep the original letter. You need not worry it will fall into the wrong hands.'

'What about the other letters?' she managed to say. She wanted to keep the pretence there were other letters very much alive.

'We will deal with those in due course. A hundred pounds?'

She shook her head. 'I haven't got the money. I can't possibly raise that amount.'

'Maybe your friends could help?' he suggested softly. 'Charlie, perhaps?'

She gave a little yelp. That was partly acting and partly genuine. For a few moments she'd forgotten all about Charles Talbot. She was pleased, for once, to see his snake smile increase. 'You know about Charlie?'

'I know a great deal, Mrs Russell. You really had better co-operate, otherwise Mrs Hamilton will be so upset. To say nothing of Major Michael Russell or, indeed, Charlie himself.'

'I'll need some time to get the money.'

'You have until five o'clock this evening,' said Mr Smith. He replaced the letter in his pocket and stood up. 'I require one hundred pounds in five-pound notes in a plain brown envelope.' He glanced at the crucifix on the wall and grinned. 'I see you are a Catholic.' He seemed to be privately amused. 'That's very fitting. You know the church of St Mark the Evangelist? It's on Hob Lane, Soho.'

Tara's eyes widened. She couldn't help it. That was Father Quinet's church, the church where, as far as Anthony and she were concerned, this had all began. She had enough composure to shake her head.

'Find it. Inside the church, on the left-hand side, there is a statue of St Mark on a marble plinth. You will leave the envelope with the money behind the statue at five o'clock.'

It wasn't in the script, but Tara's temper suddenly flared. 'And what if I don't?' she snarled, her green eyes narrowed.

Mr Smith wasn't rattled. 'You will be an example to the others I . . . er . . . help. Every so often a lesson doesn't go amiss. Do you remember Lady Sylvia Newham? Or Mrs Isa Whitehope? Mrs Whitehope, I regret to say, chose to end it all when we were forced to inform her husband of her frailties. Lady Sylvia now lives permanently abroad. She was last heard of in a very insalubrious establishment in Naples, a place where no lady should ever go.' He smiled once more. 'So you see, Mrs Russell, I really do have your best interests at heart.'

Tara bit down her temper. 'All right. Five o'clock.'

Tara took a deep breath as she entered the church. She had never been in St Mark's before, but a lifetime of Catholicism made her surroundings comfortably familiar. At the front of the church, above the altar, dim in the slanting evening light, was a gilded scene of the Crucifixion, with the tabernacle beneath, the sanctuary lamp flickering in its red glass stand. The empty pews stretched out between the side altars, the occasional candle burning as a token of silent prayer. The evening sun, slanting through the windows, cast isolated pools of light on the glowing oak of the altar rails.

It was all very quiet, but she wasn't alone. She hadn't seen him at first, but at the front of the church knelt a man, his head bowed. Was it Harper? No. She let her breath out in relief as the man, an elderly priest dressed in a cassock, got up, genuflected stiffly and, biretta in hand, slowly walked down the aisle and through the open door. He idly glanced at her in passing. Tara knelt quickly and assumed an attitude of prayer.

Was that Father Quinet? Whoever he was, he had gone. Tara wanted to be alone before looking for the statue of St Mark. Not only didn't she want any curious eyes to see what she was doing, she felt oddly guilty about using a church for what could only be described as a plot.

St Mark had his own side altar. Book in hand with a lion at his feet, peering from behind his robes – a lion was the traditional symbol of St Mark, she reminded herself – St Mark stood on the other side of the altar rails. She was really glad the priest had gone. Slipping inside the altar, she groped around the base of the statue. She knew it was just her imagination, but she couldn't help feeling reproved by the stern, bearded, stone face above her.

There was a gap between the hem of the stone robes and the marble plinth. With another quick look round to see she really

was alone, Tara took the brown envelope containing twenty crisp
five-pound notes from her bag and slid it into the gap.

Now what she should have done next was leave the church and
go back to the flat in Oakley Gardens. Tara left the church, custom
prompting her to kneel and cross herself before she went out, but
she hesitated at the door.

Nothing would happen in church, she was sure. Anthony and
Sir Charles had dismissed the idea of telling Father Quinet or his
superior, Father Croft, that the church was being used for illicit
purposes. The time was short and there was every chance that
Father Croft would refuse Tara permission to leave the money
under the statue. Even if he did agree, Anthony had a shrewd
suspicion that Father Croft would insist on being present.

No; the church was merely the letter box. The action would
happen outside and Tara wanted to see it. Walking slowly down
the steps, she looked round for inspiration. A workmen's tent, with
a brazier full of hot coals on which a kettle was gently steaming,
was a short distance away. She could hide behind that, she
supposed, but what if the workmen asked her why she was lurking
behind their tent?

A few doors down and across the road, a tea shop called, accu-
rately but unoriginally, Church View, seemed a better prospect. Its
chief attraction, from Tara's point of view, was that it did indeed
command a view of the church.

Settling herself at a gingham-covered table in a window seat,
Tara ordered a roll and butter and a pot of tea. The waitress, who
was inclined to be chatty, retired, obviously slightly hurt by Tara's
abstraction.

There were very few passers-by on the street. Tara had time to
look at them all but there was no Joshua Harper. She glanced at
the clock. Quarter past five. He must be here soon. The base of
St Mark's statue was a good hiding place but he surely didn't want
to leave a hundred pounds lying around. Twenty minutes past five.
The tea arrived and Tara, hardly noticing what she did, poured
herself a cup and bit absently into her bread roll.

The minutes ticked on, then Tara cut short an exclamation. A
thin woman, dressed in black with a black cloche hat with a veil
that effectively hid her face, crossed the road towards the church.
Looking round, she mounted the steps. Bertha Maybrick!

Although Tara couldn't see her face, she was sure it was Bertha. Anthony and Sir Charles thought Harper would come. They weren't expecting Bertha. What if they missed her?

Tara pulled out her purse, put a ten-shilling note on the table, called, 'Keep the change!' to the startled waitress, raced out of the shop and across the road.

Gaining the shelter of the pillars at the side of the church door, Tara waited for her breath to steady.

Here she was! Bertha walked down the short flight of steps, her chin held high. The sheer smugness of her attitude infuriated Tara. She was a hair's breadth away from stepping out and accosting her, when a man in a trench coat briefly appeared at the top of the steps. He gave a thumbs-up to no one she could see, then everything seemed to happen very quickly.

Three men in khaki overalls and donkey jackets stepped out from the workmen's tent and the man in the trench coat came down the steps, blocking Bertha's escape.

They closed in, forming a loose ring around her. 'Excuse me, Madam,' said one of the workmen, 'we have reason to believe you are an accessory to blackmail and—'

He didn't get any further. Bertha screamed at the top of her voice, the sound utterly shocking in that quiet street. Plunging her hand into her bag, she drew out a wicked-looking knife. Screaming, she leapt at the nearest man, slashing out with the knife.

'Bloody *hell*!' He lurched back, narrowly missing the glittering blade.

Bertha whirled as one of the other men came from behind, catching him across the face. Swearing, he staggered back, a hand to his cheek, blood oozing between his fingers.

Still screaming, Bertha held the knife momentarily above her head, then turned and made a run for it.

Tara, who had stepped out, horror-struck from behind the pillar, made a wild grab for her as she ran past. She caught Bertha's veil, her hand twisting in the material. The veil tore but the hat, firmly pinned to Bertha's hair, didn't come off. Bertha gave a shriek of pain, stumbled and swung round, eyes wild.

'You!' she screamed and raised the knife to strike.

Tara hit out, then another man was there, a big man, the elderly

priest, Father Quinet. '*Arrête!*' he shouted, catching hold of
Bertha's arm. 'Madam! *Arrête!* Stop!'

'Men!' yelled Bertha. She wrested her arm free and struck out.
'*I hate men!*' The knife sank into Father Quinet's shoulder.
Groaning, he doubled over.

Freeing the knife, Bertha raised it to strike at his exposed neck,
but Tara chopped at her hand, catching Bertha on the wrist. The
knife flew out of her hand and skittered away across the cobbles.

Bertha made a dive for the knife, picked it up, then, seeing the
men coming towards her, ran.

Tara, with the wounded Father Quinet leaning on her, had to
let her go. Two of the workmen pounded after Bertha.

The third workman, the one who had been slashed across the
face, and the man in the trench coat came to Tara's aid, supporting
the elderly priest.

'You need help,' said Tara anxiously, looking at the blood still
trickling down the workman's face.

'I just hope they catch her,' the workman replied. He grinned
ruefully, then winced, holding a hand to his cheek. His voice, as
Tara had expected, was educated, at odds with his clothes. 'Good
God, what a wild cat! My name's Hoyland, by the way, Captain
Hoyland, and this is Lieutenant Staples.'

Lieutenant Staples gently undid Father Quinet's coat buttons,
examining the wound.

'It's just as well you were there, miss,' Staples said to Tara.
'She'd have murdered the priest if you hadn't got the knife off
her.'

'I shouldn't have been here at all,' said Tara guiltily. 'If I hadn't
tried to stop her . . .'

Staples shook his head. 'She'd have gone for the first person
to get in her way,' he said firmly.

Father Quinet's eyelids flickered. He muttered something in
French they couldn't catch.

'Come on, let's get him inside,' said Staples. 'We can telephone
for a doctor from the church. You too, Hoyland,' he added to his
companion. 'You'll need stitches in that wound.'

FIFTEEN

Bertha Maybrick ran the length of Hob Lane. She could hear the thud of feet behind her, but she didn't look back. She was heading for the safety of Charing Cross Road, for the anonymity of the crowd.

There were very few people on Hob Lane but there, coming towards her, was a policeman, burly in his official cape. He stopped and stared as she ran down the street towards him.

'What's . . .?' he began, when Bertha caught at his arm.

'Help! There's two men chasing me! Make them stop!'

The policeman blinked, looking down at her terrified face, then stepped out into the road. 'Leave this to me, Madam.'

The policeman blocked the way. Bertha slipped down a side alley, hearing furious voices behind her. She had seconds, nothing more. The back gate of the yard into a pub stood ajar. She could hear the men in the alley, but, straightening her clothing, adjusting her hat and steadying her breathing, she stepped into the pub confidentially and out of the front door. It led, as she hoped, onto Charing Cross Road.

A bus, caught in the traffic, was moving very slowly along the road. Catching hold of the brass pole, she swung herself on board.

'Here!' objected the conductor. 'This ain't an official stop.'

'Leave it out,' said Bertha, sitting down. 'I've just finished eight hours cleaning and I wants to get home.' Grumbling, the conductor took her tuppence for the fare.

With her hand shielding her face, Bertha was delighted to see two workmen, a policeman in tow, hunting the pavement outside the pub. She'd shown them. Men!

Where should she go? As the bus growled along Charing Cross Road towards St Giles and Tottenham Court Road, she reviewed her options. That cow, Mrs Russell, was obviously in on it.

Harper, who thought himself so clever, had obviously been stung. That Mrs Russell might seem like a pushover, but she clearly had hired some toughs to do her dirty work. What had the plan been? To give Harper a going-over and warn him to leave Mrs Russell alone? It was just her luck that she'd been collared while Harper got away with it.

What next? She couldn't go back to Oakley Gardens, that was for sure, not now Mrs Russell had seen her.

That wasn't a problem. Her box, her servant's box, which was at Mrs Russell's, contained a few clothes, that was all. All her things, the things she really valued, were safe and sound in her own house. She smiled grimly as she thought of her own house.

A nice little place, it was, paid for by her own hard work. Being in service was a lousy job, being treated like dirt, but being in service with blackmail – well, that was different. Secrets came expensive and had paid for her house. Besides that, she *enjoyed* it. She enjoyed getting her own back, seeing those posh buggers, who thought she was there just to run round after them, squirm and whine.

She'd better tell Harper that his precious Mrs Russell was finished. She fingered the envelope containing the five-pound notes in her handbag. Harper needn't know she'd collected them. She hoped this wouldn't put Harper off the blackmail lark. The blackmail scheme had worked well. Money for old rope, it was, but he'd had some big ideas lately. It was all secret, of course, but she knew what was going on.

She still wanted paying, though. She'd done her bit and no mistake.

Well, if Harper tried to get away without paying her, she'd have her revenge. That was a nice little scheme he was cooking up with Annie Colbeck *and* they didn't know she knew. Annie always got the plum jobs, the easy pickings.

'Bedford Avenue!' called the conductor.

Bedford Avenue? It wasn't far to Sullivan Place. Yes, first things first and tell Harper.

Bertha got off the bus.

It was only when she had turned into Sullivan Place that she realized there might be more to the Mrs Russell affair than she thought. Her stomach turned over as she saw the police wagon outside number 64. Policemen in uniform and men who she recognized as plain-clothes cops, were standing around.

Bertha Maybrick took a sudden interest in the newsagent's window, then, turning around, quickly walked away.

*   *   *

'Nothing,' said Anthony in disgust. 'We've got nothing.'

He had good reason to feel frustrated. True, the Diligent Agency had been raided and the files seized, but neither Harper nor Miss Anston had been on the premises. Added to that, although the files contained names and addresses and a note of the amounts paid, all the paperwork obviously referred to blackmail victims. There was no mention of France, Paul Diefenbach or – Anthony hadn't realized just how much he had been hoping for this – Sister Marie-Eugénie or Milly.

Sir Douglas Lynton looked pained. 'I wouldn't say we had nothing, Brooke.' It was seven o'clock in the evening. Anthony, together with Tara and Charles Talbot, were in Sir Douglas's office in Scotland Yard. 'After all,' said Sir Douglas, tamping the tobacco down in his pipe, 'we've flushed out as vicious a nest of blackmailers I've ever come across. I know the idea was to catch Harper and Miss Anston red-handed, but once the balloon went up at St Mark's, we had no choice but to act.'

'Yes, but we haven't caught them or Bertha Maybrick,' growled Anthony. 'They can always start again. They're dangerous.'

Tara shuddered. 'They are. I could hardly believe I'd slept in the same house as that woman. It was horrible when she stabbed Father Quinet.' She glanced at her husband. 'You're quite sure he'll be all right?'

Anthony nodded. He had visited the old priest in Charing Cross Hospital before coming to Scotland Yard. 'It was a nasty blow, but he's a tough old bird. Fortunately, he had a thick coat which took most of the blow and you stopped that lunatic woman killing him. That poor beggar Hoyland will probably have a scar for the rest of his natural though.'

'We'll pick Bertha Maybrick up soon enough,' asserted Sir Douglas confidently. 'We've got a first-rate description and the entire force is looking for her.'

'I wish we had some idea where to look,' said Tara fretfully. 'The first thing Anthony did after she'd arrived was go through her box and things, but there wasn't anything personal, was there? No photographs or books or anything to show us where she'd come from or where she might hide.'

'No,' began Anthony, then stopped. 'There were receipts in her purse,' he said slowly. 'All for purchases the week before. One for a coat, another for a pair of shoes but there was one for a pork chop, half a pound of sausages and so on. *Meat.*'

Tara, Sir Douglas and Charles Talbot stared at him. 'So we know she's not a vegetarian?' prompted Sir Charles.

Anthony waved him silent. 'No, it's not that. Damn!' He turned to Tara. 'I know Bertha Maybrick's box will still be in the flat, but I suppose she had her purse with her.'

'I imagine so,' said Tara. 'She certainly had her handbag. She was carrying the knife in it. Is it important, Anthony?'

He nodded. 'It could be. I'd like to see those receipts again. After all, why would she buy meat?'

Tara looked at him blankly. 'Why not? I know she's next door to a lunatic, but she's got to eat.'

'But where?' demanded Anthony. 'Where does she eat? When she was in Grace Russell's flat, you paid for all the food, didn't you? She didn't.' He jerked his thumb at the box of files taken from the Diligent. 'We know that story about her being employed by Gloria Wilde, the actress, is nonsense. She hadn't had a job for a couple of weeks. Where was she cooking her meals?'

Charles Talbot looked up, enlightenment dawning. 'In a boarding house?' he suggested. 'Residents usually buy their own food.'

Anthony shook his head. 'No, it can't be a boarding house. This was the bill for a week's worth of meat. If she lived in a boarding house, she'd buy each meal separately.'

Tara sat up, her eyes gleaming. 'Butchers don't give receipts for individual purchases. The butcher's boy comes every day with the delivery and the butcher sends a bill at the end of the week. She must've had it delivered!'

Sir Charles smacked his fist into the palm of his hand. 'That means she's got her own flat or house! It has to mean that! She must've made a deal of money from blackmail. Can you remember where these receipts were from, Brooke?'

Anthony sunk his chin into his hands, trying to visualize the thin pieces of paper. 'Fletcher's Drapers. High-quality Ladies' wear,' he said eventually. 'That was the coat. The shoes were from Mercers.'

'Mercers are on Oxford Street,' said Tara.

Sir Douglas picked up *Kelly's Street Directory* and turned to the trades section. 'And so are Fletcher's Drapers.' He looked hopefully at Anthony. 'The butchers?'

Anthony frowned, concentrating hard. 'Wilkinson! That's it! Ebenezer Wilkinson and Son, family butchers.'

Sir Douglas flipped through the book to the list of butchers. 'Walker, Widdecombe, Wilfred, Wilkinson – quite a lot of Wilkinsons – Ebenezer Wilkinson and Son!' he exclaimed triumphantly. '43, Melbourne Street, Paddington.' He put the book down and beamed at Anthony. 'Well done.'

Anthony stood up. 'I think I'd better pay a visit to Paddington.'

SIXTEEN

Mr Ebenezer Wilkinson lived over his shop and was none too pleased to be disturbed over his evening pipe and newspaper by a Dr Brooke in company with Constable Bryce and Sergeant Atkinson from Scotland Yard. How should he know, he complained, reasonably enough, the name and address of everyone he'd ever sold a pork chop to? A delivery? Well, that was different.

He supposed, he said, rising stiffly from his armchair, that they'd better come downstairs and look at the ledger in the shop, but he couldn't recall any Maybrick on the books.

Together the four men went downstairs to the darkened shop. As an afterthought, Mr Wilkinson called up the stairs for his son, Alan, a sharp-looking boy of fifteen. Alan, explained Mr Wilkinson, as he clattered down the stairs after them, was the delivery boy.

Mr Wilkinson lit the gas and opened the delivery book on the scrubbed beech butcher's block. 'Maybrick, you say?' he asked, wetting his forefinger and laboriously turning to the M's.

'We don't have any Maybricks, Dad,' put in Alan, disappointedly. He was obviously enthralled by the presence of Scotland Yard. 'I'd know if we did.'

Mr Wilkinson looked down the list of names. 'No more we do,' he agreed. 'I'm sorry, gents, but I can't help you. You must have the wrong shop.'

There was a printed block of blank receipts on the counter beside the till. Anthony picked it up. He recognized the receipt. 'This is the right place,' he said. 'The receipt I saw was from here. She's one of your customers, right enough. She's probably using another name.'

Alan's eyes rounded in awe. 'Is she a crook? Or a spy? A German spy?'

'She might be,' agreed Anthony quickly, ignoring Mr Wilkinson's snort of disbelief. To help track down a German spy was clearly the way to win Alan's co-operation.

'Cor!' Alan wriggled with barely suppressed delight. 'What did she order?' he demanded. 'I bet I can remember.'

Anthony stared at the blank receipt. The dimly lit shop with its row of gleaming knives on the wall, the carcasses on their metal hooks and the smell of fresh sawdust faded as he concentrated hard on the butcher's receipt in his hand. Scribbled pencilled words seemed to form on the paper. 'Pork chop,' he said slowly, 'half pound beef sausage, quarter pound pig's liver, half pound streaky bacon, two faggots. Three shillings and eightpence.'

Alan repeated the words with a frown, then looked up, his face alight. 'I knows it! I delivered that bill a fortnight come Friday. She's not called Maybrick, she's called Kylow!' He turned to his father. 'You know Miss Kylow, Dad. She lives on Draycott Road. Number 7.'

'Draycott Road?' said Constable Bryce. 'I know it.'

'Miss Kylow?' repeated Mr Wilkinson. 'Sour as vinegar, she is and argues about her bill. She's not here half the time. She says she's got a sick aunt who needs looking after.' He smiled slowly. 'I wouldn't want her looking after me.'

'I've seen her!' said Alan, nearly jumping with excitement. 'I seen her not half an hour ago! She was outside the shop, walking towards Draycott Road. She was with a man.'

Sergeant Atkinson looked at Anthony. 'A man?' he said quickly. 'I wonder if that's Harper?'

'Is he a spy too?' asked Alan.

Although anxious to be off, Anthony didn't want to disappoint him. After all, if the boy was right, he'd led them to Bertha Maybrick and, with any luck, Joshua Harper as well. He tapped the side of his nose with his finger and winked conspiratorially at the boy. 'Not a word.'

'Cor!' exclaimed Alan in absolute rapture. 'German spies!' He hugged himself in unadulterated joy. 'I've been delivering sausages to a *spy*.'

Number 7, Draycott Road was a small terraced house, fronted by a scrubby privet-hedged tiny rectangle of garden. Anthony sent Constable Bryce to the back of the house and, leaving Sergeant Atkinson on the street, carefully opened the iron gate and crouched down beside the front window.

Reinforcements were on their way. Sergeant Atkinson had telephoned Scotland Yard from the police box on the corner. Their orders were to make sure Bertha Maybrick and anyone else in the house stayed put until the police cars arrived, but Anthony wanted to make sure their quarry hadn't slipped away.

There wasn't anyone in the front of the house. He could hear the rise and fall of voices, but he couldn't distinguish the words.

The curtains were drawn back and he risked a quick glimpse into the darkened room. There was a strip of light from the open door into the hall.

The window catch was the old latch type. Anthony took out his penknife and quietly inserted the blade under the lock. He held onto the frame as the window swung open and listened.

A woman's voice, high and complaining, came from the room beyond the hall. '. . . Over? What d'you mean, over?' It was Bertha Maybrick.

'You knifed a vicar, you dumb hag!' Was that Harper? It seemed likely. 'If he dies, you'll swing.'

'Oh yeah? They've got to catch me first.'

The man laughed derisively. 'How long will that take? You're *known*, Bertha! That Russell woman could pick you out in a flash. You can't work for me now.'

'That's no great loss. The Diligent is bust. I seen the cops at the Diligent. You can't go back there.'

'So what? The Diligent's just a name. I can start again any time I like. You're finished. I might split on you myself.'

'Split?' Bertha Maybrick's voice was thick with scorn. 'You

want to shop me? For being a murderer? That's a laugh! What about you then?'

There was a sudden silence.

'What d'you mean?' Harper's voice was quiet and wary.

'Jowett, that's what I mean. I know a lot about you, Harper. Think you're so clever, don't you? Well, you're not. I ain't going quiet. You ain't getting rid of me.'

Again, there was silence. When Harper spoke again, his voice was too low to catch.

Anthony hesitated, then gripping the window frame, swung his foot over the sill and dropped silently into the room. Creeping to where the door stood ajar, he paused. The hall beyond was unlit, the light coming from a room he guessed was the kitchen.

Bertha Maybrick's voice was high and cracked. 'Don't say that! I *know,* you understand? Of course I know. I'd be stupid not to know.'

'What do you know?' Harper's voice was deadly.

'About Annie.' Bertha's voice dripped with disgust. 'Think I don't know why she always gets the plum jobs, the easy pickings? Well, let me tell you, if you have any thoughts of shopping me, I've got quite a lot to tell the cops about you and your precious Annie.' There was a pause. 'See this?' she cried triumphantly. 'If I were you, I'd think again.'

She was obviously showing Harper something.

There was complete, frozen silence.

When Harper spoke again, his voice was quiet, even gentle. 'Come on, Bertha. We've always been pals. Now you just give me that, like a good girl, and we'll say no more about it.'

Anthony couldn't see danger but he could sense it. Standing behind the door into the hall in the darkened room, the air seemed suddenly deadly cold.

There was a sudden, tremendous crash, as if something had been overturned.

'Keep off!' screamed Bertha. 'I'll use this knife, I means it! I've knifed one man today and I'll—'

There was a series of thumps, muffled grunts, a yelp of pain and then a horrible, drawn-out, choking gurgle.

It was enough.

Anthony was through the door and into the hall at a run. Flinging back the door at the end of the hall, he burst into the kitchen.

It was a small, cramped room with an empty black kitchen range and a table covered with a red check patterned oilcloth. The kitchen drawer was upended on the floor, forks, spoons and knives scattered across the linoleum. Even at that moment, Anthony knew that had been the crash he'd heard.

Bertha Maybrick, a hand to her throat, was slumped against the kitchen range, the other hand clawing uselessly at a black something on her dress.

Someone – Harper – shouted in terror as Anthony cannoned through the door. He had one glimpse of a white, startled face, then Harper wrenched open the back door and leapt down the steps, missing Anthony's grasping hand by inches.

'Stop him!' Anthony roared to the policeman outside.

He made to race after him, but Bertha Maybrick, in two staggering steps, lurched across the kitchen and fell, clutching his coat.

Blood pumping and desperate for the chase, Anthony went to knock her hand away, then she whimpered.

The sound brought him up sharp. He simply couldn't leave her. Catching hold of her, he laid her gently on the floor. The something on her dress was the hilt of a knife. He could see it move up and down as she frantically fought for breath. Her eyes were wide and unfocused and there was a darker stain on the front of her dark dress.

She gave a rasping croak – a hideous sound – then the hilt of the knife stopped moving.

Anthony sat back on his heels. He felt sick. Bertha Maybrick had blackmailed Tara, callously spied on those who trusted her, connived at the murder of Edward and Mrs Jowett and attempted to murder Father Quinet, but at that moment Anthony could've strangled her killer with his bare hands.

The shouting from outside seemed very remote. Wearily he stood up and shook himself back to the here and now.

He leaned against the open kitchen door, breathing deeply, and lit a cigarette.

As if the volume on a gramophone had been turned up, the sounds from the road outside increased as the drumming of the blood in his head diminished. He heard the creak of windows being thrown open as police whistles shrilled. Voices; lots of voices, neighbours shocked by the sudden eruption of violence on their

quiet street. More shouts, deep men's voices; he recognized
Sergeant Atkinson yelling orders. Pounding feet, dogs barking,
more whistles and then, against a hubbub of inquisitive, muttering
sounds from the street, the sound of the front door opening.

Constable Bryce stepped into the light from the kitchen door.

'We lost him, sir, . . .' he began, then took in the scene in the
kitchen. 'Good God,' he said softly. He gulped as he saw the life-
less, bloodstained body of Bertha Maybrick. With obscure decency,
he took off his cap and stood silently for a moment. 'So Harper's
wanted for murder, now,' he said.

Of course, Anthony reminded himself, Constable Bryce knew
nothing about the Jowett murders.

'I'll be back in a minute, sir.' Constable Bryce turned and,
retreating down the path, called for Sergeant Atkinson, leaving
Anthony alone with his thoughts.

He looked at the dead woman on the floor. *She'd known.* Harper
had killed her because she'd known.

What had she known? At first, it sounded as if she knew the
true story of the Jowetts' murders but was that all?

Anthony cast his mind back. *I've got quite a lot to tell the cops
about you and your precious Annie.* That had brought Harper up
short. Then Bertha had shown Harper something. What?

It could have been a knife, he supposed. Then, threatened with
a knife, Harper tried persuasion before wrenching open the cutlery
drawer and grabbing a knife himself. Was that it?

Maybe. Bertha Maybrick's handbag, a substantial brown leather
bag with a clasp, lay open on the floor by the kitchen range. He
looked inside. There, wrapped in a handkerchief, blotched with
the rusty colour of blood, was a bone-handled kitchen knife. So
it wasn't a knife she had shown him. No, it was something else.

See this? There had been a crow of triumph in her voice. What
had she shown him? Whatever it was, the sight of it had changed
Harper's tune. From being angry and dismissive, he had suddenly
become gentle and persuasive. *Now you just give me that, like a
good girl . . .*

Anthony lit another cigarette. He remembered the acute chill
of danger that had suddenly assaulted him. What was Harper
doing? He drew on his cigarette, seeing how it trembled in his
fingers.

His fingers. His hands! That was it! Harper, with that gentle voice, had advanced on Bertha Maybrick, hands twitching for the kill.

He knelt down beside the body and pulled away the collar of her dress. Finger marks and scratches. He was on the right lines.

That was when Bertha, mad with fright, had struggled free and wrenched open the cutlery drawer. Yes, that made sense. After all, it was her kitchen. She knew where the knives were. She'd grabbed a knife and threatened him with it. The knife she'd threatened him with had been turned against her and now she was dead.

That all added up, but it still left the question unanswered. What had she shown him?

She'd obviously had it in her hand. *See this?* Some significant object. Perhaps a ring or a key or a letter? There was the sound of footsteps on the path and he swore inwardly. He wanted to be alone, to have time to think this out.

Time. If he had time, Harper would have taken whatever it was with him, but Anthony's eruption into the kitchen hadn't left him time. So was it, whatever it was, still here?

Anthony glanced quickly round the kitchen. Bertha Maybrick had been a tidy woman. Apart from the spilled knives and forks, nothing was out of place. Knives and forks and a murdered woman.

He knelt down beside her and reached out.

'You shouldn't disturb the body, sir.' Sergeant Atkinson stood in the doorway. His voice was awkwardly respectful. 'We should wait until the doctor arrives.'

Anthony looked up. 'I am a doctor.' He rolled the body over. He felt a stab of disappointment. The linoleum where Bertha had lain was patterned in dark red and white flecks and stained with blood. Then he saw it.

It was a torn scrap of paper, sticky with blood and almost invisible against the lino. Anthony reached for a knife amongst the jumble of cutlery on the floor and, sliding the blade underneath, picked up the scrap and laid it on his palm.

The scrap had obviously come from a sheet of letter paper, torn down the side. Torn, Anthony thought, from Bertha Maybrick's hand by Harper before he made his dash for freedom.

Anthony stared at the jagged piece of paper thoughtfully. Written on it was what was obviously the end of five lines.

> *are of:*
> *nie,*
> *teu* [or was that *ieu*?]
> *nes,*
> *ain.*

'What's that, sir?' asked Atkinson, peering at the scrap in Anthony's hand.

'I'm not sure,' said Anthony thoughtfully. He took out his handkerchief and, laying the paper on the linen, looked round for something to protect it.

A few cookery books were on a shelf near the range. Standing up, he put the handkerchief between the pages of *The Bakewell Book of Practical Household Management* and slipped it into his jacket pocket.

Sergeant Atkinson shifted uncomfortably. 'I don't think you should do that, sir. Remove evidence from the scene of the crime, I mean.'

'Don't worry,' said Anthony, patting his pocket. 'This is going straight to the Assistant Commissioner.'

SEVENTEEN

Sir Douglas Lynton watched with keen interest as Anthony took his handkerchief from between the pages of *The Bakewell Book of Practical Household Management* and unfolded it on his desk.

His face fell as he saw the small scrap of paper. 'Is that it, Dr Brooke?' He prodded the handkerchief with distaste. 'It's very stained.'

'That's blood, I'm afraid, sir,' said Anthony quietly.

Tara gave a little cry. She and Sir Charles had stayed at Scotland Yard, waiting for Anthony to return from Paddington. Although it was only quarter to nine in the evening, she was desperately weary after the events of the afternoon. The sight of Bertha Maybrick coming at her with a knife and Father Quinet falling to the ground was one she would take a long time to forget. Yes, she was tired, but she knew that she wouldn't be able to rest until Anthony returned.

She'd hoped he'd return with answers. Ideally Bertha would have been arrested and even now be telling them what they so desperately wanted to know. Where was Milly? What was the plan? How could it be stopped? And now there was nothing. Nothing but another murder and this bloodstained scrap of paper.

Anthony turned to her and squeezed her hand. 'Don't worry,' he said softly. 'We know who we're looking for. Harper's a hunted man and I'm certain this paper can tell us something.'

'I admire your optimism, Brooke,' said Charles Talbot dryly. He adjusted the desk lamp so the light fell squarely on the paper. '"Are of"?' he said, reading the first line. 'Well, it's in English, at any rate. The rest looks French.' He clicked his tongue. 'It's not much, Brooke, you have to admit.'

It was the sense of unfairness that made Tara sit up. After what Anthony had done, it seemed wrong that all his efforts should have been for nothing and doubly unfair that Sir Douglas Lynton and Charles Talbot should dismiss the piece of paper as worthless.

Leaning forward, she glared at the scrap. She felt a mulish determination to make it mean something. 'It has to be important. When Harper saw it he stopped arguing and . . .' She broke off with a shudder.

'*I know*,' said Anthony softly. 'That's what she said to him. *I know.*'

'The question is, what did she know?' asked Sir Charles practically. 'Are you sure she didn't give any hint?'

'Did she know about the Jowett murders, for instance?' asked Sir Douglas.

Anthony nodded. 'Yes, she did.' Sir Douglas looked up alertly. 'She accused him of murdering the Jowetts. I couldn't hear what he said, but he certainly didn't deny it.'

Talbot cocked an eyebrow at Anthony. 'D'you think that's it? That she had proof Harper murdered the Jowetts?'

Anthony shook his head impatiently. 'I'm sure there's more to it. Harper asked, "What do you know?" and she replied with a tirade against Annie.'

'Annie Colbeck, I presume,' murmured Talbot.

'That's right. She was horribly jealous of her. She threatened to show the police the letter, or whatever it was, which would incriminate both him and Annie.'

'It's the Jowett murders,' said Sir Douglas confidently. 'I'm blest if I know why it's written in French, but that's my opinion. She'd got hold of some written proof of their complicity.'

Talbot looked at Anthony once more. 'Well, Brooke? Is that it?'

Tara stared at the paper. The second word leapt out at her: *nie*. 'It's nothing to do with the Jowetts,' she broke in. She was absolutely certain. 'Anthony, remember how this started. Annie Colbeck and Joshua Harper were plotting to kidnap Milly.'

Sir Douglas sighed disbelievingly but both Tara and Anthony ignored him.

'It has to be Milly they're after,' Anthony agreed. 'There can't be two children in the occupied territories looked after by a Sister Marie-Eugénie.'

'Exactly!' said Tara triumphantly. She tapped her finger on the desk next to the scrap of paper. '*Nie*! That's what the second word is. It has to be *Eugénie*.' She glanced at her husband and saw his faint smile. 'You thought so too, didn't you?'

'It occurred to me,' agreed Anthony. 'Of course it did, Tara, but how on earth can we prove it?'

'We can't,' she said simply. 'Not unless the police catch Harper, but we can guess. Eugénie,' she repeated fretfully and then, her finger beside the torn scrap, read the first words. '"Are of . . ."'

She shook herself in irritation. 'It doesn't make sense. "Are of", with a colon, something, something, *Sister Marie-Eugénie*.'

Maybe it was because she was so tired, but the words seem to blaze in her mind. *Are of. Are of . . .* She gave a little gasp. It all made sense! 'Anthony! It's not *are of*. It's *care of*!'

Anthony looked up sharply. 'Tara! You're a genius! *Care of.* Of course. And look! There's a colon after the *of*.'

Charles Talbot cleared his throat. 'Can you tell me why you're so excited about the punctuation?'

'Because a colon comes before a list. Tara, you're wonderful!'

Again, understanding seemed to blaze. 'The list,' said Tara, wriggling with excitement, 'it's an address! It has to be an address.'

'Has to be?' queried Sir Douglas doubtfully.

'Of course it's an address. Don't you see?' She fought to put her thoughts in order. 'The sentence probably said something along the lines of, "The child is in the care of" and then it gives Sister Whatsit's name and where to find her.'

'That's brilliant, Tara,' said Anthony enthusiastically. 'Talbot? Do you agree?'

Talbot cupped his chin in his hand. 'I think it's a reasonable supposition,' he said eventually. 'We know Harper and Annie Colbeck's scheme involves Sister Marie-Eugénie. It's very reasonable indeed they'd have a note of her name and address.'

'That's why the rest of the missing words are French,' said Tara. 'It's a French address, of course.'

Sir Douglas frowned at the paper. 'I'll grant you it's French, Mrs Brooke. I'll agree, too, that it might be part of an address, but what good is it? If it is an address, we need rather more of it.'

Charles Talbot lit a cigarette and leaned back in his chair. 'Let me get this straight. Harper and Colbeck plotted to kidnap a child, a plot that involves murder. Now, according to Mrs Brooke, Bertha Maybrick obtained written proof of the plot.'

'She'd have copied it out,' said Tara.

Anthony tapped the scrap of paper. 'She obviously treated it with care. She didn't have it in her handbag, or I'd have seen it when I searched her bag in Grace Russell's flat. She kept it at home.'

Sir Charles nodded once more. 'Agreed. The sight of that letter drove Harper to murder. He couldn't allow Bertha Maybrick to live in possession of that knowledge.'

He blew out a long mouthful of smoke. 'If we can work out the rest of this address, then we can find both Sister Marie-Eugénie and Milly and get to the bottom of this damned plot.'

Sir Douglas looked sceptical. 'That's a dickens of a lot of assumptions you're making, Talbot.'

Sir Charles shrugged. 'It's as Mrs Brooke said. All we can do is guess.' He pulled the scrap of paper towards him. 'We've got the first and second words, I believe. *Care of* and *Sister Marie-Eugénie*. How about the third? *Teu* or *ieu*. It must be the name of a place or town.'

Douglas Lynton puffed his cheeks out in dismissal. 'We've

fallen at the first fence. How many towns and villages in France are there that end in *teu* or *ieu*? Such as . . .'

He stopped as his knowledge of French place names came to an abrupt halt. 'Dash it, I don't know, but there must be dozens of places. Hundreds, even, if you include all the villages and hamlets. It doesn't even have to be in France! It could easily be in Belgium or anywhere else they speak French. The job's impossible.'

'Not in the occupied territories,' said Anthony. 'We know it's in the occupied territories. This is so important, surely it's worth setting a few clerks to work with a decent atlas.'

'I don't think it's a place name,' said Tara quietly.

The three men looked at her quizzically.

'I'm Irish and Catholic,' she said. 'I know about nuns. The name comes first and then the order they're in, such as the Little Sisters of the Poor or the Sisters of Notre Dame.'

'So what we're looking for,' said Anthony slowly, 'is an order of nuns that ends in *teu* or *ieu*.' He looked at Sir Douglas with a smile. 'I don't suppose Scotland Yard has a list of orders of nuns?'

Sir Douglas shook his head. 'No, we don't. I can't ever recall needing such a thing.'

'I wouldn't look to Scotland Yard to track down nuns,' said Talbot with a grin. 'After all, the good and holy nuns, as we used to refer to them in Ireland, are not the first group you'd look to for members of the criminal classes. No,' he added reflectively, 'I think you're right, Mrs Brooke.' He glanced at the clock on the wall. 'It's just coming up to nine o'clock. Let's pay a visit to Westminster Cathedral.'

Douglas Lynton stayed at Scotland Yard, hoping for news of Harper, leaving Talbot and Anthony to take Tara home – she was desperately tired – and go onto the cathedral. Sir Douglas didn't, Anthony could tell, believe their search would uncover anything useful.

Like most Londoners, Anthony had never been inside Westminster Cathedral. As a matter of fact, he thought, he couldn't remember even seeing the building. That was odd.

The oddity was explained as the cab left the bustle of Victoria Street and plunged into a maze of small streets and huddled houses to emerge a minute or so later, in front of a shallow flight of steps leading up to the arched doorway of a building that could only be described as huge. The cathedral might be huge, but it was completely hidden amongst the surrounding buildings.

Dismissing the taxi, they entered by the side door. Inside, the cathedral seemed, if anything, bigger. The interior, of undecorated brick and grey slabs, illuminated by small pools of candlelight, seemed to stretch into the far distance. Anthony changed his mental description from huge to vast.

As his eyes became accustomed to the gloom, Anthony saw there were people in the church, kneeling or sitting in silent prayer.

'We need a priest,' muttered Sir Charles. He brightened as he saw an elderly, aesthetic looking man in a dark suit with a clerical collar, book in hand, kneeling in a pew. He approached and stood politely by as the priest finished his prayers.

'Can we have a word, Father?' asked Sir Charles quietly. 'I need some assistance with an enquiry. I'm working with Scotland Yard.'

The priest's eyebrows shot up in alarm at the mention of Scotland Yard. 'We're bound by the secrecy of the confessional, you understand. If it's a criminal matter—' he began.

'We need to find a nun,' chipped in Anthony. 'It's urgent.'

The priest gazed at them, obviously wondering if he was dealing with the merely eccentric or outright lunatics. 'Scotland Yard is after a *nun*?'

Sir Charles smiled reassuringly. 'We're not accusing a nun of anything criminal, you understand, but she has some information that could be vital to Scotland Yard.'

The elderly priest eyed them cautiously, then stood up. 'You'd better come through to the house.'

The priest whose name, he told them, was Barrett, led them through a narrow doorway into a covered walk which joined the cathedral to the archbishop's house.

He opened a door and, going into the room, lit the gas. As the light flared, Anthony could see it was part office, part sitting room, with well-worn leather chairs and the familiar odour of pipe smoke.

'Now then,' said Father Barrett, ushering them in. 'What on earth is this all about?'

They started to explain. Anthony said nothing about Milly. It was far easier, as Sir Charles had said, to represent their quest purely as a desire for information appertaining to a murder enquiry. That made sense as the scrap of paper had been found in the dead woman's hand.

Father Barrett listened intently. When he heard that Bertha Maybrick was the woman who had knifed Father Quinet, he sat up alertly. 'I saw the assault reported in the stop press of the newspaper. To attack a priest on the steps of his own church is truly shocking. It's as bad as any story of the outrages in Belgium. And this woman, this Bertha Maybrick, has been murdered, you say?'

'By the leader of her gang,' said Anthony.

'A gang?' exclaimed Father Barrett in horror. He stared at them. 'You'll excuse me, gentlemen, but I fail to see how this Sister Marie-Eugénie or, indeed, any nun, will be of use in tracking down a gang of murderous criminals.'

Put like that, it did seem unlikely. 'I employed Bertha Maybrick,' said Anthony, editing the facts smoothly. 'That's how I know about Sister Marie-Eugénie.'

'Nevertheless, I cannot comprehend what connection Sister Marie-Eugénie can possibly have with this matter.' He ran his hand round his chin. 'Naturally I want to do everything in my power to assist Scotland Yard, but, on the other hand, I am loath to subject any lady, and especially a nun, to police questioning. In fact, I fear I must, with the greatest regret, decline to assist you.'

His thin face set in a worried frown. Anthony sighed inwardly. He felt he knew Father Barrett's type: principled, cranky, devoid of imagination and completely obstinate once his mind had been made up. The trouble was that even if they told him the whole truth he would never believe it. So . . .

'I'd be obliged if you would keep this to yourself, Father,' said Anthony, lowering his voice conspiratorially, 'as we don't want to cause alarm, but what we're really worried about is that this gang are maniacs – rabidly anti-religious French maniacs – who have a passionate hatred of the clergy. Roman Catholic clergy.' It was easier, he thought, to believe in a group of foreign rather than British lunatics. 'We have reason to believe Sister Marie-Eugénie could be their next victim.'

'God bless my soul!' exclaimed the priest. 'That seems utterly incredible.'

It was, of course, but they didn't correct his view.

'So if we could trouble you for a list of orders of nuns?' prompted Sir Charles gently. 'Sister Marie-Eugénie could be in grave danger.'

'Eh? What?' He wavered. 'In the circumstances, I suppose it would be permissible. French maniacs, you say? Incredible.'

Still muttering, he got up and walked to the bookcase and, after some deliberation, pulled down a directory. 'This will only list the religious orders, you understand,' he said. 'Records of individual nuns will be held by their mother house.'

'This will do fine,' said Sir Charles, taking the book. 'It is a complete list, isn't it, Father?'

'As far as I know.'

Sir Charles took the heavy book and laid it open so the gaslight shone on it. Anthony groaned inwardly as he saw the closely printed pages. He doggedly started to run his finger down the list of names.

'Which order are you looking for?' asked Father Barrett.

'We don't know,' said Anthony. With a glance at Sir Charles, he took the copied list of partial words from his pocket and laid it on the desk. 'We know this refers to Sister Marie-Eugénie,' he explained, pointing to the *nie,* 'but the other words, which we're assuming to be her address, are a puzzle. As I explained earlier, all we do know is that Sister Marie-Eugénie's order ends in the *teu* or *ieu.*'

'*Ieu,*' repeated Father Barrett, pulled, despite himself, into the search. 'The first French word that occurs to me which ends in *ieu* is *Dieu.*'

'God!'

'Exactly,' agreed Father Barrett.

Anthony sighed. 'There must be dozens of orders called the something or other of God.'

Father Barrett shook his head. 'No. Funnily enough, there aren't. Indeed, I can't think of any at all.'

'We need to find God,' said Anthony, bending over the list.

'So do we all,' said Father Barrett, with an unexpected flash of humour.

Anthony grinned and returned to the list. It seemed endless but, just as Father Barrett had said, there seemed to be no orders ending in the word *Dieu.*

'You're quite right, Father,' he said. 'These orders have names like the Sisters of Mount Carmel or the Society of the Divine Saviour.'

'The Carmelites and Salvatorians,' muttered Sir Charles, much to Father Barrett's surprise. Then both he and Anthony saw the name at the same time.

'*Sœurs de la Miséricorde Bénie de Dieu,*' exclaimed Sir Charles.

'Sisters of the Blessed Mercy of God,' translated Anthony slowly. 'Tara was right. The *ieu* is an order of nuns. Are there any other orders that end in *Dieu,* Talbot?'

They quickly ran through the rest of the directory. To Anthony's surprise but gratification, the Sisters of the Blessed Mercy of God were the sole order whose name ended in *Dieu.*

'Where's the Mother House?' asked Father Barrett.

'It's in St Maur,' said Anthony. 'It was established in 1803 by Eugénie Varennes,' he said, reading the entry, 'for the care and education of orphans. Orphans,' he repeated, looking at Sir Charles. 'That fits.'

'St Maur doesn't though. It's just outside Paris. We're looking for somewhere inside the occupied territories. What other words have we got?'

He pulled the list of words copied from the scrap towards him; '*nes* and *ain*'. He referred back to the directory. Anthony could see him tense with excitement. 'Look at this, Brooke! I don't know where *nes* fits in – maybe it's a street name – but there's three daughter houses. One in Limoges, and two in Belgium. Mechelen and Louvain.' He tapped the list of words. '*Ain!* Louvain!'

'Louvain!' exclaimed Father Barrett, shocked. 'Your Sister Marie-Eugénie lives in Louvain? The poor soul!'

Anthony swallowed hard. Before the war, Louvain had been a sleepy town, reminiscent of Salisbury or Canterbury, famous for its gothic architecture and university library, with a priceless collection of early books and medieval manuscripts.

Then, on the 19th August, 1914, the German army had invaded. The Belgian army had retreated to Antwerp, but the Germans were on edge. Hostages were taken, a curfew imposed, and the German

First Army established its headquarters in the town, swelling the numbers of troops to around fifteen thousand. For six days an uneasy calm prevailed, then came a single shot, a spark that caused an inferno.

Who pulled the trigger was never established, but it seemed probable that the culprit was a nervy German soldier, terrified of a lone gunman. Panicked by the thought of the hundred-thousand-strong Belgian army ready to mount a counter attack, the Germans went on the rampage.

Men were dragged from their houses in front of their terrified families, beaten and killed. An eighty-three-year-old was tied up, forced to watch his house burn, was bayoneted, then shot. In an orgy of arson, houses, shops and the medieval town centre were destroyed. At half past eleven that night, the university library was set ablaze with petrol. Anyone trying to save the books or douse the flames was shot. In the morning all that was left were four walls and a heap of ashes, just one building amongst the two thousand others in the fires that raged for the next three days.

Hundreds were shot as they tried to escape the flames. Ten thousand Belgians were expelled, some to be shot, and well over a thousand deported to Germany. The police force was rounded up and killed. The Catholic clergy and the university professors, who the Germans believed to be ringleaders in the opposition, were singled out for violence and, in many cases, execution.

It was no wonder, thought Anthony, as he looked at Father Barrett's appalled face, that the idea of a nun living in Louvain was a shocking thought.

'Are you sure the poor woman is still alive?' asked Father Barrett.

Sir Charles nodded. 'Fairly sure, Father.' He, too, looked shocked.

The first month of the war had left a swathe of desolation from the river Meuse over the border into France – the destruction of Leffe, Dinant, Reims and a raft of villages with their torched houses and heaps of corpses were vivid in everyone's mind – but the savagery inflicted on Louvain was absolute.

Farther Barrett gave a deep sigh, his lips moving in a silent prayer, then he shook himself. His eyes focused on the list of words on the desk. 'If Sister Marie-Eugénie really is in the Louvain house, then I worry for her safety. The Germans seem to have a hatred of our clergy. I once visited the cathedral of St Pierre in Louvain. The destruction of the cathedral was an act of absolute barbarism.'

Yes, the cathedral was no more, but, thought Anthony with a jolt of hope, surely the orphanage must still survive. No one would conspire to leave a child in a building that didn't exist. Milly was alive, Sister Marie-Eugénie was alive, and the building must still stand. The alternative was something Anthony could not bear thinking of.

Father Barrett pulled the list towards him and read it over the top of his spectacles. 'So what have we got?' He rested his chin on his hand, frowning. 'I believe,' he said after a few seconds thought, 'that I have a map of Louvain, a souvenir of my visit. Give me a few moments, gentlemen, and I should be able to lay my hands on it.'

He went to the bookshelf and, after a few minutes' search, pulled out a squat red volume. 'Here we are. *Baedeker's Belgique et Hollande.*' He rifled through the pages, then unfolded a map.

Anthony and Sir Charles bent over it. 'We're looking for a street name that ends in *nes*,' muttered Sir Charles. 'The trouble is that this map only gives the principal streets.'

'What about this?' said Anthony, pointing to a road on the outskirts of the town. 'The Rempart de Malines. That'd fit the bill.'

'So it would,' exclaimed Father Barrett, whose enthusiasm for the search had clearly grown. 'Let me write this down.'

He picked up a pencil and filled in the words in a neat, spiky, hand. 'Sister Marie-Eugénie, *Sœurs de la Miséricorde Bénie de Dieu,* Rempart de Malines, Louvain.'

Anthony took a deep breath and squared his shoulders. Looking up, he caught Sir Charles' expression and asked a question with his eyes.

Sir Charles caught his meaning and froze, working out the implications of what they had discovered. Then, with some reluctance, he slowly nodded.

Anthony understood. He had just been given permission to go to Louvain.

EIGHTEEN

A s they came out of the shadow of the surrounding trees, Anthony felt the warning pressure of a hand on his shoulder.

'Get down.' The words were a whisper.

Obediently Anthony sank to his knees, flattening himself into the boggy bare earth between the tall clumps of stiff marsh grass.

Beside him, the smuggler, Lucien Voltèche, dropped to the ground, remaining completely still as a searchlight picked out the uneven ground in blinding whiteness with sharp-edged black shadows. The searchlight moved on. Anthony, who'd been unconsciously holding his breath, breathed once more.

The series of events that had brought him to crouch in a muddy field on the border between Holland and Belgium had started three days ago.

The afternoon following their discoveries in Westminster Cathedral, Anthony received a note asking him to meet Talbot in the smoking-room of his club at half past six.

Anthony wasn't surprised by the choice of venue. Sir Charles had a theory that the more secrecy surrounding a meeting, the greater was the chance of being discovered.

The smoking-room, as Sir Charles predicted, was deserted. He had a guest with him, who he introduced as Peter Jager.

'It's not the name I was born with,' said Jager, settling into his green leather armchair. 'But these, as the Chinese apparently say, are interesting times, Dr Brooke.'

Anthony liked the look of Peter Jager, whatever his real name might be. He was a stocky, capable looking man, a South African Boer, one of the many who'd followed General Jan Smuts to fight with the allies against the Central Powers.

Jager lit the cigar Sir Charles had offered him and sipped his whisky and soda. 'I gather you speak perfect German, Dr Brooke.'

This wasn't time for false modesty. 'Yes, I do.'

'That's good,' said Jager in approval. 'Do you speak Dutch?'

Anthony hesitated. 'I've picked up some. Dutch has a lot in common with German and English. I can usually understand Dutch but I couldn't pass as a Dutchman.'

'That's a pity. You see, the place where you're going—' Jager carefully avoided the mention of Louvain – 'is a Flemish speaking area and anyone with good Dutch can pass for a native. How's your French?'

Anthony frowned. 'Not bad, but I doubt if I'd be able to fool another Frenchman into believing I was French.'

'That's a pity. My first idea was to send you in as a Belgian, but that's probably too risky.' Jager put his head on one side, sizing him up. 'I think you'd better be a doctor. A German doctor.'

Anthony turned to Sir Charles. 'Is that possible? Can you get hold of the correct uniform and papers and so on?'

'Leave it with me, Brooke.'

'That's a good plan,' said Jager. 'Your destination is out of the fighting line but there's at least one hospital there that's used for treating infectious cases.'

'A *Seuchenlazarette*,' said Anthony. He smiled at Sir Charles' expression. 'All the name means is disease hospital, but the Germans separate the classes of patients depending on their condition and allocate them to hospitals accordingly.' He stopped. 'Religious sisters – nuns – are often drafted in as nursing staff,' he added slowly. '*Seuchenlazarettes* are usually set up in suitable buildings, such as schools and convents.'

Jager looked at Anthony with respect. 'You know quite a lot about it, Dr Brooke.'

Anthony knocked the ash off his cigar. 'I worked in the university hospital in Berlin for the first months of the war.'

Jager nodded approvingly. He pulled on his cigar for a few moments, then sat forward. 'There's two ways of getting into Belgium. Flying and walking. Mr Monks has guaranteed the co-operation of the Flying Corps.'

'Isn't that risky?' asked Anthony.

'It can be,' conceded Jager. 'Aircraft are noisy machines and the distances involved make it tricky as regards fuel. For a short hop over the lines, that's the way I'd recommend, but we want more than that. How do you feel about a parachute jump?'

Anthony winced. He had never liked heights. 'Not great. Parachutes can fail to open.'

'We could have you in Belgium by tomorrow night,' prompted Sir Charles temptingly. 'You'd have to go at night, obviously.'

'Yes . . .' Anthony appreciated Talbot's desire to help, but he certainly wasn't leaping into the dark, parachute or not. If he had to fly he would, but he'd never been in an aeroplane and the idea that his first flight would be in the dark, over enemy country, with the petrol running low, didn't fill him with enthusiasm.

Jager looked at him appraisingly. 'It's obviously not your first choice, Dr Brooke,' he said, stroking his stubby beard. 'If you'll be guided by me, though, I'd recommend getting into Belgium on foot but using an aeroplane for your return. Even if the Germans realize one of our aircraft have landed, you can be miles away before they work out where it touched down.'

'All right,' agreed Anthony cautiously. 'That's a possibility. How about getting into Belgium? I thought I might go in under the cover of one of the American Belgian Relief convoys.'

Sir Charles gave a sharp intake of breath. 'We can't do that.'

'No, we can't.' Jager was definite. 'For one thing, the Americans wouldn't agree. The volunteers are all Americans and are kept under strict German observation. In addition, the Germans only allow the relief to enter the country because of America's absolute assurance that the sole purpose of the convoy is relief. If you're caught, you'd cause an almighty row between Britain and America, you and everyone with you would be shot, and the programme will be cancelled. Belgium would starve.'

Anthony raised his eyebrows. To be the man who starved Belgium, was responsible for a mass execution – himself included amongst the dead – and the cause of a major diplomatic row wasn't something he wanted to be remembered for.

'OK, so that's out.' He drew on his cigar. 'So how do I get into Belgium then?'

Jager glanced round the room, then hunched forward in his chair, lowering his voice. 'If you don't want to fly, the most practical way is to get you over to Rotterdam and introduce you to the White Lady.'

Anthony glanced at Talbot. He obviously knew who the White

Lady was, but Anthony had never heard of the woman. 'Who is she?'

Jager gave a short laugh. 'The Germans would love to know. They're frightened of her. The Hohenzollerns – the Kaiser and all his many relations – have a family legend, a myth, of the curse of the White Lady. They don't know if the White Lady is a real woman or a ghost, but her appearance is supposed to signal the downfall of their house. And I can only hope that's one myth that proves to have a foundation in fact.'

Anthony was impressed. 'So who is she?'

Jager's grin broadened. 'The White Lady isn't a woman but the Germans think she is. She scares them. The White Lady is actually an organization set up by my chief.' He nodded at Sir Charles. 'Mr Monks knows who my chief is and what the White Lady does.'

'The information the White Lady provides is priceless,' agreed Sir Charles. 'It's run under the auspices of British Intelligence and paid for by London, but it's an independent service.'

'We can be more flexible that way,' said Jager. 'We don't have to ask permission before we can take action. We have over a thousand Belgian and French men and women who monitor troop movements in the occupied territories.'

'That's right,' put in Sir Charles. 'Documents can be forged and agents can be fed lies, but you can't mistake the presence of divisions massing for an attack. That information is priceless.'

'Thanks,' said Jager softly. 'Naturally,' he continued, 'any information, no matter how pressing, is only of any use if we can get it into the hands of British Intelligence. That's where our couriers come into play.' He looked sharply at Anthony. 'You know about the border fence?'

'I've heard of it, certainly,' said Anthony.

In the first year of the war, the small Belgian army had been swelled by thousands of young Belgians who had braved the frontier and crossed into Holland. The German border guards, the *Landsturmers*, were drawn from the ranks of the recovering wounded. A return to full health meant a return to the misery of the front. Weary and disaffected, a generous bribe and an easy desertion into Holland was an attractive option for many *Landsturmers*. The Imperial Army, alarmed by the escape of so many Belgians and the constant loss of troops, took action.

The sentries were replaced by fully fit men, handpicked from those who had influential relations and large estates in Germany. They had far too much to lose by desertion. In addition, an eight-foot-high fence, running the entire length of the hundred and eighty-mile border between Belgium and Holland, was constructed.

'I know a good few men have been killed trying to get across the border,' said Anthony. 'The fence is electrified, isn't it?'

Jager nodded. 'The fence carries a charge of two thousand volts. The Dutch call it the *Dodendraad*.'

'Wire of the dead,' said Anthony.

'Exactly, Dr Brooke,' said Jager. 'The Dead Wire. It's a killer. In addition, there's sentries every hundred yards, searchlights, dogs, Secret Service Police and mounted patrols. Belgium is a prison and the *Dodendraad* is the prison wall.'

Anthony winced. 'So how do your couriers get across? If it comes to that, how do I get across?'

Jager smiled. 'We'll get you through, Dr Brooke, don't worry.' He swirled his whisky round his glass. 'The Germans rely on the lethal power of their fence. They've invested thousands of marks to make it impregnable. I'm glad to say that not a week goes by without us proving they're wrong.'

As the searchlight moved on, Anthony heard the crunch of booted feet. A dog barked from somewhere close at hand. Lucien Voltèche put his hand between Anthony's shoulder blades, pressing him down. The two men lay rigidly still. 'Patrols,' he murmured, his mouth close to Anthony's ear.

Even though they were still on the Dutch side of the border, they were in acute danger. The guards would shoot anyone within five hundred yards of the fence, no matter what side of the border they were on.

From his constricted viewpoint between the clumps of marsh grass, Anthony saw the dark outlines of two guards with a German Shepherd dog pause directly across from them, on the other side of the fence. The dog whined and pulled at the leash. Anthony hardly dared breathe.

The guards were about thirty yards away, but their voices carried on the still night air.

'The dog's restless,' said one. He clicked on his flashlight and swept it in a circle over the ground. The dog pounced forward, pulling the guard with him, as a hare, startled by the light, shot from behind the two guards and, terrified by the dog, leapt into the fence. There was an electric blue flash, a sizzle and a thump as the body of the hare was flung away from the fence.

The smell of burnt flesh and fire drifted towards them. That meant, thought Anthony with a stab of gratitude, that they were downwind of the dog.

The guard swore and pulled back the excited animal. 'Down, Berg!' he snarled. 'Leave the hare,' he said to his companion. 'They're never worth eating once they've been fried.' He flashed the light over the ground once more. 'Come on. No one's attempting the crossing tonight. No one's ever escaped through my sector.'

Beside him, Anthony heard Lucien Voltèche grunt quietly but dismissively. 'That's all he knows,' he whispered in Flemish as the two guards walked on down the line of the fence. Anthony knew enough Dutch to make sense of the words.

Voltèche waited for the searchlight to sweep past them once more, then pulled his knapsack off his shoulders and reached inside. He took out two pairs of rubber gloves and what looked like big rubber socks, gesturing for Anthony to put them on. Once more they waited for the searchlight to pass, then, re-shouldering the knapsack, Voltèche led the way, creeping towards the fence.

Even with the rubber gloves and socks, it was a nervy business getting through the fence. The strands of wire were about a foot apart. Voltèche held up the bottom strand and motioned to Anthony to wriggle under the wire.

Flattening himself as close to the ground as he could, Anthony went under. He tried not to think of the hare, of that blue flash and the hideous sizzle that the slightest brush against the wire would bring. Breathing deeply, he got to his knees on the other side.

Voltèche grunted in approval. Anthony lifted the wire and Voltèche first passed his knapsack through then, with seeming nonchalance, wriggled underneath. Taking off his rubber socks, he thrust them, together with Anthony's, into his bag.

'Step where I step,' he whispered. 'There are mines.'

Then, with a swift glance round and keeping hunched over, he ran for the trees about twenty yards away, Anthony at his heels.

Once in the shelter of the copse, Anthony sat with his back against a tree and breathed properly for what seemed to be the first time in hours. Voltèche looked up, grinned, then walked a few yards into the woods and hid the bag in the stump of a hollow tree, covering it with leaves.

Anthony understood. This was obviously something Voltèche had done many times before. If he'd been caught with those gloves and socks in his pack, a firing squad was the only outcome. He idly wondered how many caches of rubber gloves and socks Voltèche had hidden along the frontier. When he had first been introduced to Voltèche, he had been wary of an acknowledged smuggler who arranged a border crossing for the payment of a hundred francs. At the time, a hundred francs paid in advance seemed a lot of money. It wasn't.

Beckoning him to follow, Voltèche shouldered his knapsack and led the way forward. Although there was a crescent moon, it was dark under the trees and they had to pick their way over ground twisty with tree roots. Despite himself, Anthony felt ridiculously light-hearted. Even though the going was arduous, it felt safe under the rustling trees with the hideous obstacle of the Dead Wire behind them.

However, even with the wire behind him, he couldn't simply stroll across Belgium. Louvain was only a matter of thirty odd miles away but the river Muese lay across his path. The Muese was wide, its banks patrolled and its bridges heavily guarded, but the Muese was where they were headed.

It was nearly an hour later when Anthony saw the trees thinning in front of him. He'd felt the ground sloping down for some time. As the trees got more and more widely spaced, he saw the glint of the moon upon water in the distance and heard the faint sound of voices.

'Wait here,' Voltèche muttered quietly. 'If you hear an *uil* three times, come.' He spoke in Flemish. Anthony puzzled for a moment over the word *uil,* then it clicked.

'Terwitt-too-whoo?' he suggested with a smile.

Voltèche nodded. '*Uil,*' he agreed seriously. He cast a glance at Anthony's uniform. 'You look good, *Herr Doktor,*' he added. 'If you're spotted the Boche will think you're one of their own.'

He slid off into the darkness, leaving Anthony alone.

Anthony wasn't sorry of the rest. He itched to light his pipe, but that would be stupid. It had been hard going amongst the trees, although Voltèche always seemed to know exactly where he was. So the Boche would think he was one of their own, would they? What then? He'd probably get shot for desertion unless he could think of a good story. An owl hooted close by and he stiffened.

No, that was just one hoot. However, he could be a doctor with a passion for ornithology. That could be a convincing story, if he knew anything about birds. His identity disk gave his name as Erich Lieben and his identity papers confirmed him to be *Oberstabsarzt II Klasse* or Dr Lieutenant Colonel. On his shoulders were two golden stars in golden oak leaves and the familiar medical symbol of Asclepius' staff with a snake. Snakes could shed and regrow their skins. The ancient Greeks saw this as a sign of magical rebirth, of life renewed through healing.

Enough of snakes, he thought with mild irritation. Birds. *Oberstabsarzt* Lieben had a passion for birds, which was why he was wandering in the woods. Anthony fell to constructing the character of Dr Lieben in such detail that he nearly missed the hoot of an owl.

He stood up, poised and listening. No ornithologist could have paid keener attention. There it was again. And again.

Quietly Anthony made his way towards the gleam of water. There wasn't much high ground in this part of Belgium, but from a hummocky bit of ground he could see the Muese spread out before him. It was a big river, easily as wide as the Thames, he thought. The faint sound of voices grew more distinct.

Then the ground dipped again and he made his way cautiously forward, anxious not to slip and make a noise. He inched his way down, guided by the sound of lapping water.

He didn't see Voltèche at first. He was waiting for him, crouched in the shadow of a stone wall that banked up the earth and separated the trees from the river.

The voices were louder now. Anthony could pick out the occasional word and clink of crockery.

Voltèche put a finger to his lips and motioned for Anthony to get down. 'You will pay a hundred marks to get to Louvain, yes?' he whispered.

Anthony nodded. That had been the arrangement. A hundred to get through the wire and another hundred to get to Louvain.

'There is a barge train, one of the many river barge trains on the Muese. The captain and crew of the tug boat are Boche, but the bargees are Belgian.'

He jerked his thumb to indicate the other side of the wall. 'We have to watch for patrols. The barge trains don't travel at night but they are guarded. The barges are moored on the other side of the wall. There is a woman, *Mevrouw* Halleux, who will take you to Louvain. She is my mother's sister. She has taken my passengers before. You will go with her?'

'Yes,' Anthony agreed. He could hear footsteps on the other side of the wall and kept his voice very low. It wasn't just people on the other side of the wall. A dog whined and he froze. He knew the river bank was patrolled. If the sentries had dogs, that spelled trouble. He couldn't rely on a frightened hare a second time.

'It's all right,' whispered Voltèche, sensing, rather than seeing, his anxiety. 'The dog belongs on the barge. When you're over the wall, keep to the shadows.'

'How will I know which is the right barge?'

'*Mevrouw* Halleux will be on the towpath outside her barge with her dog. When the time seems right, get on board as fast as you can and hide straight away.'

He dropped his hand onto Anthony's shoulder to indicate he should stay put, then cautiously climbed up the rough stones of the wall and peered over the top. The footsteps – it sounded like two men – stopped a little distance away on the other side of the wall.

Voltèche dropped back down again. 'Get ready. You can go in a moment.'

'Wait.' Anthony took out fifty marks and pressed into Voltèche's hand. 'For you.'

Voltèche looked at the money for a moment, hesitated, then gave it back. 'No, *Mijnheer.*' There was a catch in his voice. 'I do this for Belgium.' There was fierce pride in the smuggler's voice.

Oddly moved, Anthony took back the money. You couldn't buy patriotism. 'For Belgium,' he repeated.

Voltèche squeezed his shoulder once more, then climbed the wall, turned and beckoned Anthony to join him.

Keeping his cap pulled low so as to hide his face, Anthony took in the scene on the other side of the wall.

The Muese spread out before him, the dark water hemmed in, on this side at least, by a broad canal bank with a towpath. A long line of barges lay moored alongside the bank, the water slapping against their hulls as they pulled against the mooring ropes attaching them to bollards fore and aft. They looked for all the world like overgrown versions of Noah's ark, with the hatches of the hold forming a triangular sloping roof.

At the front of the line of barges was a river steamer, the tug boat. It was a substantial craft, at least five or six hundred tons. That was where the sound of voices came from but his immediate concern was the two sentries.

They were about twenty yards away, looking out at the river. In their field grey uniforms, they might have been difficult to spot in the shadows of the trees in the fleeting moonlight of the river bank. However, both men had taken the advantage of not being under the eye of a superior officer and, lounging against the wall, were passing a cigarette between them. Its glowing orange tip shone bright in the darkness.

Anthony grimaced. Even though the two sentries were obviously not battle-hardened front-line troops, they'd certainly see him if he tried to cross the towpath. And where was *Mevrouw* Halleux?

Then came his chance. A dog, a little terrier, jumped over the side of a barge and, yapping ferociously, ran at the two guards.

'Now!' hissed Voltèche behind him.

Anthony swung himself over the wall, dropped to the ground and flattened himself into the shadows by the wall as the two sentries kicked out in alarm, swearing at the barking terrier.

Mevrouw Halleux, a stately presence, rose up from the deck of the barge. 'Leave that dog alone!' she called in furious and barely understandable Flemish.

'Call it off,' shouted a sentry, taking a swing at the dog with the butt of his rifle. The little dog missed the blow and, jumping up, managed a nip on the man's leg.

Amid the shouts from the guards, the frantic yipping of the terrier, and the shrill protests of *Mevrouw* Halleux, a platoon of men could have crossed the towpath undetected.

Anthony shot across the path, jumped down into the barge and crouched low on the deck. The door into the cabin stood open in front of him.

Down the steps into the cabin, he could see a boy, about eleven years old, sitting at the table. The cabin was illuminated by a single dim oil lamp above the table.

The boy stood up, looked at him with round eyes, and put a finger to his lips. Beckoning, he indicated Anthony should follow him to the back of the cabin to where two narrow wooden beds stood in opposite alcoves, shielded by curtains. The boy quickly drew back the curtains and lifted up one of the beds. The floor beneath it was hinged and the bed and floor swung up, leaving a narrow gap.

The boy pointed and Anthony scrambled into the hole. The boy closed the bed down and Anthony, lying on the unexpectedly soft floor, heard him walk away.

Although the space was cramped, he wasn't in total darkness. There were gaps in the floorboards above him which let in chinks of light. The softness of the floor was explained by a straw mattress, which covered most of the space and, Anthony was pleased to find, a couple of blankets.

Obviously *Mevrouw* Halleux had used this method before for transporting guests. That was a very well-trained dog she had. There was nothing quite like being attacked by a small, determined terrier to take a man's full attention. As a way of distracting the sentries, it was hard to beat.

It must have been half an hour or so later when he heard a creak above him and the bed was lifted up.

Mevrouw Halleux, oil lamp in hand, looked down approvingly at him. 'All is quiet,' she said softly. Her accent was so thick it was difficult to understand. 'You eat? Yes?' She passed him a sizable hunk of bread and, much to Anthony's delight, a bottle of beer. 'Stay there, *Mijnheer*. Till tomorrow.'

Anthony understood. Once they were underway, he could come out, as there was no danger of anyone coming on board. If they were moored up, he had to stay undercover. 'All right.'

She lowered the bed again and Anthony sat back with his bread and beer. The bread was tough and, although he couldn't see the colour, he was willing to bet it was grey. The bread, war bread, a mixture eked out with straw, took some chewing. If he hadn't been so hungry the coarse stuff would have revolted him, but the beer was good. Hunger abated, he drew the rough blankets round him. He spared a thought for Lucien Voltèche, alone in the woods, then, lulled by the lapping of the water on the hull, drifted into sleep.

His last conscious thought was that there were worse ways to travel to Louvain.

NINETEEN

Anthony had a cramped but enlightening few days on the barge.

When *Mevrouw* Halleux had lifted the hatch to his hiding place on the first morning, she had been so shocked by her first look in daylight at his uniform, she had promptly slammed the hatch down.

Anthony raised his hands above his head and heaved, emerging to the sight of *Mevrouw* Halleux, her son hiding nervously behind her and the dog prepared to spring. She, hefty spanner in hand, was quite clearly prepared to brain this wandering Hun.

It took all of Anthony's powers of persuasion to convince her that he wasn't German but, once convinced, she told him quite a lot about life in Belgium.

Her husband had been taken to Germany, one of the many deportees. She had no idea if he was alive or dead. He had been foraging in the fields for food and caught without his identity card. That was enough.

Every Belgian had to carry an identity card and if a man was of military age, between seventeen and fifty-five, he had to carry a military pass to show he'd been present at the weekly muster conducted by the German authorities. Internal passports were required to travel within Belgium and were very rarely granted.

Food was desperately scarce as the Germans took virtually everything. Potatoes, for instance, were three shillings a pound and who could afford such sums? The Germans took not only food, but coal, wood, oil, wool and all the necessities of life. Many hundreds – perhaps more – had either starved or literally frozen to death last winter. Machinery had been broken up and taken wholesale to Germany, forests had been levelled – the barges were carrying a load of pine from the Campine – and everything of any value, be it cotton, metal or leather, was impounded. Without the Americans and their food relief, many more thousands would be dead.

As Anthony listened to the catalogue of thefts and deprivations, he began to see why the sight of his uniform had such an effect on his hostess.

He had lived in Germany and, despite his experiences on the Western Front, liked and respected the country and its people. After all, war was war and brutality occurred on both sides. Along with the rest of the Allied world, he'd read reports of the savagery meted out to the occupied countries, but he'd assumed that the reports were hugely exaggerated. Maybe they were exaggerated, but the truth was very close to the reality.

Mevrouw Halleux considered herself fortunate. By helping her nephew, Lucien, she was able to make enough money to feed herself and Henk, her son.

It was the evening of the third day that the barge train arrived in Louvain. Anthony stayed that night on the barge, slipping away in the grey dawn of early morning.

The canal docks were at the edge of Louvain. Anthony, as neat and as shaved as he could contrive in the cramped conditions of the barge, walked along the towpath, out onto the Boulevard de Diest, and into the town.

The Boulevard de Diest ran as part of a rough circle round the town. Or what had been the town. It was now a man-made desert of desolation.

He had seen villages that had suffered from shelling, with one rickety wall still upright amongst a rubble of brick, timber and stone, but he had never seen anything on this scale.

The smell, the smell of stale, damp, burned things, was one he recognized immediately. It was one of the smells of the Front, and it was incredible that only a few short months ago, Louvain had been a place of elegant, ancient architecture, little shops, neat houses and grassy lawns. It was almost unbelievable to think that this devastation had been caused not by artillery shells, but by arson.

The streets had been only sketchily cleared of fallen masonry and debris. The wind had got up and every step filled his eyes with the dust from the heaps of dirt and ashes. He was heading for the train station, but the map, which he had brought from London and memorized on board the barge, seemed like a cartographer's fantasy in this desolation. The map was now in *Mevrouw* Halleux's stove. The fact it had been reduced to ashes seemed oddly fitting.

He briefly toyed with the idea of asking directions, but the very few Belgians he saw scurried away at the sight of him and he didn't relish the thought of asking the occasional groups of soldiers for directions. After all, the soldiers' natural assumption would be that he, like them, had arrived by train and it might arouse suspicion if he didn't know where the station was.

Guided by his pocket compass, he emerged from the ruins onto the Boulevard Tirlemont across from the railway station with real relief. The flames hadn't reached this far. The Germans needed the train station and had taken care to contain the fires.

Here, in front of the station, was an ordinary street with entire buildings, with enough people to be described as a crowd. He had seen very few people in what had been the town. Anthony felt so grimy after his voyage through the blasted rubble, that he felt as if all eyes must be on him, but very few passers-by, soldiers or civilians, glanced twice at the tall doctor in his army greatcoat.

His destination was a cafe on the platform, reserved for Germans. He pushed open the door marked *Officers Only* and for a moment felt completely disconcerted.

The bar, which ran the length of the room, was of dark wood with polished brass-ringed beer taps. A muted hum of conversation rose from the fifteen or so men sitting at the tables, drinking beer, coffee and small glasses of spirits. Some were reading newspapers and a couple were playing cards.

Anthony had lived in Germany. Before the war he had studied in Berlin and had, along with his German friends, visited many a German *bierkeller*. In the first few nervy months of the war, living in Germany, no longer as a friend but a spy, *bierkellers* had been prime sources of information. A *bierkeller* was a familiar place.

That was the trouble. He'd been subconsciously expecting a

bierkeller but this was a Belgian cafe, first cousin to an English pub.

For a couple of seconds, so recognizable was the atmosphere, so homely the scene, that Anthony felt a sudden, blistering, fury. This could be England. An England that had been invaded, where the conversation was in German and the conquerors wore field grey.

What's more, that ravaged wilderness outside could be the remains of an English town. He had a ridiculous urge to slam his fist into the face of the fat German *Hauptmann* swilling beer and, single-handed, fight everyone in the bar.

He hung up his cap and greatcoat on the hat-stand, forcing himself to pick out the details of the bar to prove to himself that this was Belgium, not Britain. For a start, a good few of his fellow officers – Anthony made himself use the term *fellow* – were drinking coffee. That wouldn't happen in Britain. Nor would the barman have such an elaborate moustache or be wearing a white apron.

He was in Belgium and he was Erich Lieben, Oberstabsarzt II Klasse, a doctor, a lieutenant colonel and a loyal German. When he turned round, he saw the German captain as not fat, but a solid, well-built fellow, doubtless a good officer, who thoroughly deserved his well-earned beer.

He pulled out a chair at a table and sat down. Glancing up at the bar, he rapped imperiously on the dark oak.

The barman hurried over, then stopped, taking in his uniform, his glance lingering for a moment on the medical staff with its snake. 'Monsieur?' he enquired.

It was the first time Anthony had heard French spoken since leaving England. He gave an almost imperceptible nod to the man and replied in French. 'Coffee and jenever.'

Jenever was a variant of gin and the national spirit of Belgium. It wasn't an impossible request but an unusual one. A German would tend to drink schnapps.

This time it was the barman's turn to give an almost imperceptible nod. 'A good choice, Monsieur. Does Monsieur require any cigarettes?' he enquired.

'Do you have Athikas?'

The barman was apologetic. 'I'm sorry, Monsieur, no. We have Eckstein.'

'I'll have two packets.'

'Certainly, Monsieur.'

Recognition, sign and counter sign complete.

With a glint in his eye, the barman gave a small bow, crossed to the bar and returned minutes later with a tray containing coffee, jenever and two green packets of Eckstein cigarettes. As usual, the barman had slit open the paper top of one of the packets of cigarettes.

Anthony drained the jenever at a gulp, wincing at the taste of the raw spirit, sipped his coffee, took out a cigarette and lit it, looking idly round the cafe. No one was paying him the slightest attention. He looked down at the note that had been put in the packet of cigarettes. It was written in French.

Ten o'clock. Becker. St Pierre side door. Go inside and wait.
The destruction is great. But not complete.

Technically speaking, the cathedral of St Pierre was still a building, if having the remains of walls and part of a roof constituted a building. The broken roof timbers drooped forlornly into the grey sky above him. What had been the steeple was an empty shell. The floor was a heap of rubble, with timbers and stone from the fallen vault. Mixed in with the rubble were pools of melted metal slag. Anthony crouched down and picked up a piece, weighing it in his hand. Where on earth had it come from?

Part of the metal had a familiar curve. Anthony ran his hand over the curve, searching for the memory. Bells! These had been the bells. Anthony dropped the piece of slag and stood up with a shudder. How fierce had been the fire to have melted bronze?

There was nothing accidental about the destruction. In what had been the side chapels off the nave, bonfires had been made by piling up altars, furniture and pews. Some of the bonfires had been infernos, others still clearly showed the charred remains of the wood tossed on them.

If anyone was interested, they could work out easily enough which direction the wind had blown that night, but Anthony suddenly wasn't interested but, for the second time that morning, furious.

A memory of Westminster Cathedral came to him and with it that choking anger that had possessed him in the cafe. This could be Westminster. He wanted to leave this smoke-blackened ruin with its bullet-pocked walls and hunt down every man responsible.

'*La destruction est grande.*'

He turned sharply as the voice spoke out of the shadows.

The destruction is great. He couldn't see anyone but remembered the countersign. '*Mais pas terminé.*' And the destruction wouldn't be complete, not if he could do anything to stop it.

A man emerged from the shadows beside the wall. 'Who are you, Monsieur?' he asked quietly.

'For the moment, I am Dr Erich Lieben,' Anthony replied. He spoke in French and kept his voice low. 'You are Monsieur Becker?'

'That's right.' Becker was dressed like a workman, in thick boots and a heavy jacket with a scarf instead of a collar, but his accent wasn't that of a labourer. The mere fact he spoke French singled him out in this Flemish town. 'What do you want, Dr Lieben?'

'I want to know where I can find a Sister Marie-Eugénie. I believe her to be in the convent of the Sisters of the Blessed Mercy of God.'

Becker raised his eyebrows. 'The orphanage?'

'That's right,' agreed Anthony, his spirits lifting. Although he was sure he was on the track of Milly and Sister Marie-Eugénie, he'd had plenty of time on the barge to worry that their reasoning was tenuous and his quest futile. To know there really was an orphanage was very reassuring.

'I don't know the nuns by name, but I know the convent.' Becker looked him up and down and nodded slowly. 'You'll fit in.'

Anthony was puzzled. 'Why? Why should I fit in, I mean?'

'Because you are a doctor,' said Becker. 'You are a doctor? In truth, I mean?'

'Yes, I am.'

Becker's face cleared. 'Good. The convent of the Sisters of the Blessed Mercy of God is now a hospital for infectious diseases. A *Seuchenlazarette,*' he added, using the German word.

Although this was a possibility that had been mentioned in London, it seemed extraordinary to have it confirmed in this burntout shell of a cathedral in Louvain.

'That's good. If it's a hospital, that could be a way in. What illnesses do they treat?'

Becker shrugged. 'Typhoid?'

'Do they, by George?' said Anthony in satisfaction. It wasn't surprising. Typhoid, highly contagious and almost inevitable in cramped, dirty, living conditions, was common in the trenches. It was a condition Anthony had become very familiar with over the last few months.

Becker's mouth twisted in an ironic smile. 'The hospital is supposed to be excellent. The Boche take good care of their own.'

That chimed in with what Anthony knew. Medical research had been highly advanced in Germany before the war. It was for that very reason that he had chosen to spend his meagre funds studying in Berlin.

Doctors were honoured in Germany, both in and out of the army. Unlike Britain, where, before the war, army doctors were viewed as the scrapings of a fairly unsavoury barrel by their professional colleagues and military superiors, German army doctors commanded respect. The Germans did, indeed, look after their own.

'When the Boche burnt Louvain, they killed many religious,' continued Becker, 'but the Sisters of the Blessed Mercy of God they spared. The convent is a large building and the Boche took up residence there. When the fighting moved on, it became a *Seuchenlazarette,* and the sisters became their nurses, working for the Boche. The sisters said they had no choice.' His mouth twisted. 'They said they had to protect the children in their care.'

From Becker's expression, it was evident he thought this was a pretty lame excuse. Anthony had a lot of sympathy for the nuns. Mind you, he reminded himself, he hadn't lived through the burning of Louvain.

Becker looked at Anthony appraisingly. 'You're dressed as a colonel. Why is that?'

'I've lived in Germany. Germans respect authority,' said Anthony.

'They do,' agreed Becker. 'So it wasn't part of a plan to get into the hospital?'

Anthony shook his head. 'I've only just confirmed that this convent is a hospital too. No, I haven't a plan yet. I was going to take a look around, see how the land lies and perhaps try and get in tonight, under cover of darkness.'

'It's possible,' agreed Becker. 'I wondered if it was part of your plan because Colonel Anschütz, who was in charge, died last month.'

'That's worth knowing,' said Anthony. 'If I'm spotted, I could say I'm on an informal tour of inspection, although I couldn't get away with that story for long. All in all, I think a better idea is to persuade one of the guards to swap clothes with me, if you see what I mean.'

Becker nodded. 'I think you're right.'

'Either that or dress up as an orderly or a male nurse.'

'Not a nurse,' said Becker. 'All the nursing is done by the nuns. You're too tall and broad to be a nun.'

Anthony grinned. 'I can't see myself taking the veil, that's for sure. Where's the convent? The *Seuchenlazarette*?' he asked.

'It's a large red-brick building set back from the road in its own grounds on the Rempart de Malines.'

Anthony recalled the map he had studied on the barge. The Rempart de Malines was on the western outskirts of the town, about half a mile or so away. If the town still resembled the map, he could probably find his own way. The trouble was that the Rempart de Malines was a long road which had boasted some of the finest and largest houses in the town. To pick out the hospital could be difficult.

'I can show you the way,' said Becker, much to Anthony's relief. 'I'll go in front and you can follow. We cannot walk together, as that would cause suspicion.' He smiled thinly. 'Belgians and Germans are not friends.'

TWENTY

B ecker left the cathedral first. Anthony gave him a couple of minutes, then slipped cautiously out of the side door after him. A quick look around showed him they were unobserved. Becker was waiting by a broken wall on the corner. Without exchanging glances, Becker set off, Anthony following some distance behind, picking his way through the blasted rubble of what had been the street.

Everything was broken, grey and dirty. The dust that the wind blew in clouds from the hollowed-out skeletons of the houses, choked him. The only new things were the posters that were fastened to every post demanding the requisition of virtually every good, from cotton and rubber to timber and tin. The penalty for hoarding, for withholding any demanded material, was death.

When he had lived in Kiel for those first few nerve-wracking months of the war, things had been tough for the Germans, suffering under the British blockade, but Germany was like paradise compared to this apocalypse.

They had been walking for about twenty minutes when a squad of Germans, herding a group of weary-looking civilians, swung round the corner. The captain, in charge of the squad, saw Becker.

'*Halt!*'

Anthony slid into the shadows, watching the soldiers surround his guide.

'Your papers!' demanded the captain.

Becker handed over his identity card. The captain gave it a cursory glance. 'You are under arrest. Do not resist.'

This wasn't in the plan. Anthony straightened his shoulders and marched towards the men. 'What is happening here?'

The captain took in Anthony's uniform and saluted. 'We have orders to round up able-bodied men, sir.'

Anthony nodded. 'Very good, Captain. However, I have need of such a man as this at the hospital.' He snapped his fingers at Becker. 'You! Come with me.'

Becker looked at him sullenly, playing his part. 'What about my work?' he mumbled.

'That is not important,' said Anthony icily.

The captain didn't look any too pleased either. 'I have orders to bring in twenty men, sir.'

'And I am sure you will fulfil those orders admirably, Captain.' Anthony inclined his head. 'Dismissed!'

The captain swallowed, turned, barked out an order at his men, and the squad marched off.

'Does that happen often?' asked Anthony, once they were safely out of earshot.

'All the time. They have deported thousands of us as slave labourers to Germany.' He shrugged. 'It happens.'

He could be mentioning that it might rain, thought Anthony, his admiration for Becker growing. 'Can't you escape to Holland?'

'I have work to do. The White Lady needs me. I'm a useful man. I speak German and it's remarkable what can be picked up by a good listener.' He grinned savagely. 'I can fight back.' Becker glanced at Anthony. 'I did wonder, when we spoke before, how you could be a German officer. Your uniform is excellent and your German is good, but you lacked arrogance. Arrogance is the mark of an officer.' He nodded slowly. 'You were arrogant then. Remember, my friend, be arrogant. I want you to succeed.'

The ground started to rise gently upwards and, quite suddenly, as if someone had drawn a line across the landscape, the blasted remains of the town were behind and they were amongst trees climbing up a gently sloping grassy verge.

Cresting the slope, Anthony could see a broad, unpaved road. The road was peppered with ruts and potholes but it was flanked with gracious houses that could've surrounded Oxford or Cheltenham. The contrast with the destruction behind them was astonishing.

A low thrum and a billowing cloud of dust in the distance made him step back into the trees. A car was approaching and that, of course, meant the enemy.

Becker had already taken cover behind a bush and together they watched as an open grey-painted Opel, cases strapped to the back, drove slowly past. Both the driver and the officer in the back were well wrapped up, scarves round their faces, against the choking dust.

A few yards up the road the Opel hit a pothole, gave a terrific jerk, bouncing both driver and passage high in their seats. Anthony winced as he heard the bang of a ruptured tyre.

The car ground to a halt. In the bush beside him, Becker gave a hiss of annoyance. They could hardly cross the road with the car there.

Up ahead, the driver got out of the car, ruefully inspected the wheel, then went to report to the officer in the back.

'I'm afraid I'll have to change the tyre, sir,' he said, saluting.

Anthony heard the passenger sigh. 'Oh, very well. I suppose there's nothing to be done about it. These roads are an absolute menace.'

Anthony frowned. That voice, with its slightly fussy, old-maidish quality, was oddly familiar. Who the devil was it?

'I'm very sorry, but you'll have to get out of the car, sir,' said the driver apologetically. 'I'll have to jack the car up to change the wheel, you see. I only hope the suspension isn't damaged.'

'I hope so, too,' said the officer. The driver opened the door and the officer got out, brushing the dust from his uniform. He pulled down the scarf from his face, coughing. 'Will you be long?'

'I'll be as quick as I can, sir, but it's going to take at least ten minutes, maybe longer.'

'Oh dear,' said the officer unhappily. He shifted on the spot, obviously uncomfortable. 'I think I'd better have a little walk.'

Baumann! It was Baumann! Talk about a small world. Anthony had known Baumann in Kiel, when, during the first few months of the war, he had worked at the university hospital as Dr Conrad Etriech. That period of Anthony's life had come to a sudden halt when, with his cover blown and the German army on his tail, he had escaped from Kiel.

Anthony couldn't help grinning. Baumann had a passion for coffee – even the ghastly ground acorn liquid that passed for wartime coffee – and many a conversation had been abruptly terminated because of Baumann's urgent desire to use the facilities.

His grin faded. Things must be getting pretty desperate if they'd rounded up the likes of poor old Baumann. Not that he was so very old, of course, and, like all Germans, he had served in the army and was in the reserve. It was only natural Baumann should be called upon, he supposed. But Baumann! He was a kindly, pernickety soul, generous and sentimental, devoted to his wife and five children. Anyone less like the stereotypical swaggeringly brutal Prussian officer it was hard to imagine.

What on earth was he doing in Belgium? As a matter of fact, thought Anthony, Louvain was probably the perfect posting. It was well out of the front line and Baumann was not a martial type.

A movement beside him made him look round. Becker had opened a large clasp knife and was feeling the blade with his thumb.

'No!' Anthony's whisper was urgent. 'We can't kill him.'

He really couldn't kill him. Yes, they were at war and Baumann was the enemy, but to kill the poor beggar was far too close to murder for Anthony's liking. He might be a spy in enemy country but before anything else, he was a human being and a doctor. *First do no harm . . .* To the best of his knowledge, he had always lived by the medical oath. Besides that, it was Baumann for heaven's sake.

He saw the disdainful look in Becker's eyes and tried for a reason the Belgian would understand. 'If he dies, we'll be hunted down. There'll be reprisals.'

And there would be. One dead German officer would mean quite a few dead Belgians, shot in revenge.

Becker sighed and lowered the clasp knife.

Up ahead, Baumann was inspecting the trees. There was very little undergrowth and Baumann obviously wanted some privacy. He always had been rather prim.

Anthony shrank down behind the bush. All he wanted was for that damn driver to change the wheel and summon Baumann back to the car.

Instead, to his dismay, he heard footsteps swishing through the grass. Baumann was getting closer. Not here, he thought urgently. Anywhere but here . . .

Baumann came round the bush. For a moment he didn't see them, then, his eyes widening in incredulous horror, he opened his mouth to call out.

Anthony sprang.

There was nothing else for it. He simply couldn't allow Baumann to call for help.

Taken completely by surprise, Baumann went down, flattened by Anthony's leap. Anthony sat astride him and clamped a hand over his mouth.

'Baumann? You recognize me?'

With bulging eyes, Baumann nodded. He looked terrified. Anthony knew what he was thinking. To Baumann he was Conrad Etriech, the spy. He'd never thought how his untimely departure from Kiel had affected anyone who'd known him there but, in the university at least, the truth about their erstwhile colleague must've been endlessly discussed.

'We are English spies,' Anthony continued.

Becker, kneeling beside Baumann, knife at the ready,

looked startled at his change of nationality but, thankfully, said nothing.

'If you do what I say, you will not be harmed.'

Baumann grunted in disapproval. He was a stubborn devil, remembered Anthony.

'Becker,' said Anthony, continuing to speak in German. 'Unwrap his scarf and gag him with it.'

Becker reluctantly put down the knife and, taking Baumann's scarf, quickly wrapped it round his face, knotting it tightly.

'Stand up,' said Anthony. He'd have to tie Baumann to a tree. There was nothing else for it.

He felt inside his tunic and produced a small automatic. Doctors didn't carry guns but Anthony had felt the need to be armed. He had no intention of using it, but Baumann couldn't guess that.

With one eye on the gun, Baumann allowed himself to be tied to a tree with his own belt.

'What now?' asked Becker quietly. A little way up the road, they could hear the driver whistling accompanied by the occasional clunk as he changed the wheel. 'And why did you say I was an English spy?'

'If it's known you're Belgian, think of the consequences. You'd be a hunted man and innocent people will be killed.'

'True,' acknowledged Becker. 'But will he believe it?'

Anthony jerked his thumb at Baumann. 'I knew him in Germany. He knows I'm English and it's a natural assumption that you are, too.'

Becker digested this in silence. 'So what now? I'd say you've got a problem on your hands.'

'Can you drive?' asked Anthony.

Becker looked at him quizzically then suddenly grinned. 'Yes.'

'In that case,' said Anthony, 'let's get you a car.'

He went forward through the trees and risked a glance up the road. The driver, his tools around him, was giving the wheel an experimental turn. Anthony waited until the driver, obviously satisfied, lowered the jack and tidied away his tools back in the car.

Anthony cleared his throat. 'Driver!' he called, in as good an imitation of Baumann's fussily precise voice as he could manage. 'Driver, come here! Come along!'

The driver rubbed his hands on an oily cloth, tossed it into the passenger seat, and came down the road. 'Where are you, sir?'

'Over here.' Anthony stepped behind a tree as the driver came into the thicket.

The man looked round, then plunged further into the woods. 'Sir?'

'Over here!' called Becker in German.

The driver went further into the wood. Anthony slipped out behind him.

The driver stopped and gasped in astonishment as he saw Baumann strapped to a tree.

At the same moment, Anthony, scarf in hand, gagged him from behind as Becker stepped from behind the tree and put the knife to his throat.

'Don't make a move,' growled Anthony.

The driver, his eyes fixed on the knife in terror, stood rigidly still as Anthony drew his gun. 'We need your clothes,' said Anthony. 'Take them off.'

The driver, his eyes bulging in fright, quickly stripped off his tunic, trousers and boots.

Anthony picked up the driver's belt and, gun in hand, waved him towards a tree. 'I'm afraid you're going to have to stay here for a while,' he said, tying the man up.

In addition to the driver's uniform, Anthony took both Baumann's and the driver's identity papers. The driver's name was Karl Hillgruber, he noted. You never knew when genuine identity papers might come in useful.

Becker, impatient at the delay, tapped him on the shoulder and motioned him to hurry up. 'I didn't want to say too much in front of those two,' he said as they walked away towards the car, 'but I don't think we have long. This is a very well-used road. Even tied up and gagged, they can probably make enough noise to be found. Have you thought of a plan yet, Dr Lieben?'

'I've got a couple of ideas,' said Anthony. 'What you need to do, though, is get me into the hospital, then make yourself scarce. The rest I'll leave to chance.'

TWENTY-ONE

With Becker at the wheel, the car turned into the gate of the hospital, swept up the drive, and came to a halt in front of the open main doors. The hospital was a long, narrow, red-brick building with steep Flemish roofs, probably built, thought Anthony, in the 1870s or thereabouts.

Two soldiers came out of the door as the car came to a halt. One stood smartly to attention while the other opened the door of the car for Anthony.

'I am Dr Lieutenant Colonel Lieben,' said Anthony, stepping down from the car.

He had wondered if he should use Baumann's name – he had Baumann's papers, after all – but a cursory glance at Baumann's identity documents had convinced him otherwise. Only a complete optimist could believe that the description of Baumann could possibly be taken for a description of himself. Besides that, what if someone in the hospital knew Baumann? That was always the risk in taking on the identity of a real person. On the short drive to the hospital he had compared his false papers with Baumann's genuine ones and had to hand it to the unknown forger. They really were very good indeed. No, on balance he'd better stick to being Erich Lieben.

The guard looked puzzled. 'Colonel Lieben? That was not the name . . .?'

Anthony sighed impatiently. 'You were expecting me, I take it?'

'Yes, sir, but . . .?'

The guard trailed off in the face of Anthony's stare. The way that the Germans respected a uniform really was extraordinary. That little piece of psychology had come to his aid before now. All he had to do was look the part and act the part. He needed to be absolutely self-assured. Or arrogant, to use Becker's word.

'I am expected? Then escort me in, man!'

The guard gave an almost imperceptible shrug and saluted smartly. 'Sir!'

Anthony waved a hand at the car. 'See that my cases are taken to my quarters.'

'Very good, sir.'

Anthony followed the soldier through the main doors. Behind him, he could hear the car being driven away. Becker had gone. He was on his own.

The soldier led him through the corridors of the house towards the gardens. Various crucifixes and religious paintings hung on the walls, testament to the hospital's previous existence as a convent. Pictures of the Holy Family, the Infant Jesus, and Jesus surrounded by children predominated. This had been an orphanage, after all. Anthony could only hope that Milly was still here. Through the various open doors they passed, Anthony could see rows of empty beds with the occasional black-clad nun busy at work with a mop and bucket.

'The patients are all outside at this time of day?' Anthony asked the soldier. Fresh air was important in typhoid cases.

'Yes, sir. All the patients who are fit to be moved are outside, together with most of the staff. Major Schuhbeck insists on open-air treatment whenever possible.'

'Very wise.' Major Schuhbeck was evidently in charge, pending the arrival of Colonel Baumann.

Anthony emerged from the house into a sunlit terraced garden. A statue of the Virgin Mary singled out the garden as a religious house. There must've been about eighty or so patients, either lying on camp beds or walking slowly round the garden.

The belt of trees that surrounded the garden acted as a windbreak and the air was pleasantly warm. The thing that made it different to Anthony's eyes from any other hospital was the fact that the nurses were nuns in long black habits, white aprons and long black veils with a starched white coif underneath. Nuns whose calling was nursing the sick were part of a long tradition, he knew – that's why nurses were called 'sisters' after all – but he had never worked with them.

A senior officer, a *Stabsartz* or major, a man who looked to be in his fifties, saw Anthony, and hurried over. He was a solidly built, red-faced man, running to fat, with a ferocious moustache and an expression to match.

He came to a halt and, clicking his heels, snapped out a parade ground salute. 'Colonel Baumann? We've been expecting you, sir. I am Major Schuhbeck.'

Anthony returned the salute. Better get it over with. 'Colonel Baumann?' he repeated enquiringly. 'There must be some mistake. I am Dr Lieutenant Colonel Erich Lieben.'

'Colonel Lieben?' Major Schuhbeck frowned. 'I apologize, sir. We were told to expect a Colonel Baumann.'

'Evidently you were given the wrong information, Major,' said Anthony dryly. 'I have known mistakes in movement orders before now.'

Schuhbeck nodded. 'So have I, sir.' He rubbed his hands together and smiled ingratiatingly. Obviously he was afraid of having made a bad impression first crack out of the barrel. 'No matter. We are very pleased to have you take up your post, Colonel.'

Anthony breathed an inward sigh of relief. So far so good. It could be called good luck to arrive to find a metaphorical welcome mat laid out for him. But that was a piece of good luck that would abruptly change if Baumann and Hillgruber were found. That would make life very interesting indeed.

He peeled off his gloves and slapped them thoughtfully across his hand. All he was really doing was playing for some time to think, but from the Major's expression, it was obvious he saw the gesture as a threat.

'Sir?' asked Schuhbeck nervously. He swallowed. 'Do you wish to be shown to your quarters or will you conduct an inspection first?'

Better go for the inspection, thought Anthony. Having breezed in on a fake name, it would be as well to lull any doubts Schuhbeck might harbour by establishing his credentials as a doctor. Add to that, the fact that he really needed to find Sister Marie-Eugénie and he couldn't do that stuck in his room. 'I'll conduct a brief inspection first, Major,' said Anthony.

He strolled across the courtyard, Schuhbeck at his heels. 'I am pleased to see that you have allowed the patients to enjoy the fresh air.'

'That is of first importance in typhoid cases, sir.'

'Indeed it is. As is the quality of nursing.' Anthony indicated the black-clad nuns. 'These nuns – they are Belgian women?'

Schuhbeck swallowed. 'It is necessary, sir,' he said apologetically.

'They are trained nurses?'

Schuhbeck swallowed once more. 'Colonel Anschütz instituted a rigorous training programme for all the nurses, Herr Commandant.'

'I see.' Anthony picked out an obvious flaw. 'Why are the nurses not wearing rubber gloves? Gloves are essential to prevent the spread of the disease.'

'Rubber gloves?' Schuhbeck looked startled. 'We cannot obtain them, sir.'

I should have known that, thought Anthony. 'Things are different in Germany,' he commented. 'You do insist that the nurses wash thoroughly with bichloride solution?'

From Schuhbeck's expression, it was obvious that the answer was no.

'See to it from now on,' said Anthony sternly. 'Hygiene is of the first importance.'

He stopped by a bed. The patient, a fair-haired boy in his early twenties, looked at him blankly from the pillows. The nurse stood by the bed, her eyes lowered.

Anthony looked carefully at the patient's skin. 'I can see no sign of the customary rash.' He turned to Schuhbeck. 'Have you considered this man may be suffering from pyaemia? Miliary tuberculosis is also a possibility.'

'It's possible, sir,' faltered Schuhbeck.

Anthony frowned at him. 'Do you not administer blood tests as a matter of course?'

'Not hitherto, sir,' said Schuhbeck.

Anthony sighed, a great deal more testily than he felt. 'You do have the facilities for blood tests?'

Schuhbeck nodded.

'Arrange for a test as soon as possible. If there is an absence of leukocytosis, then we can assume that the correct diagnosis has been made.'

'Very good, sir. I may say that I have always advocated performing blood tests on all our patients upon admission.'

A likely tale, thought Anthony. However, he nodded in stern approval. 'Excellent, Major. I can see you have the patients' interests at heart in accordance with the best traditions of our noble profession. It is that sort of attitude which wins both approbation and advancement.'

And that sentence, thought Anthony, as he watched Schuhbeck swell with conceit, could've won prizes for arrogance. Never mind. It was all to the good. First unsettle the Major, then dangle the carrot of promotion.

'What about diet?' demanded Anthony. 'Nurse! What has this patient had to eat?'

The nurse shook her head, not understanding the German.

'These women mainly speak either French or Flemish,' said Schuhbeck.

Anthony repeated the question in French, watching Schuhbeck's reaction out of the corner of his eye.

The nurse launched into a description of the patient's diet. Schuhbeck listened uncomprehendingly.

Anthony had an idea. It was evident that Schuhbeck couldn't speak French and Baumann could turn up at any moment. He didn't have much time. It was risky but it was worth trying.

Keeping a wary eye on Schuhbeck, he asked the nun a couple more questions in French, then added, in the same tone of voice, 'Is this building still an orphanage?'

The nun faltered in her account. Schuhbeck glanced up, alerted by the nun's change of tone, then resumed his blank stare of incomprehension as Anthony continued his questions in French.

Anthony, still with a watchful eye on Schuhbeck, talked about milk, bread and mashed potatoes then said, 'Please keep on talking. We cannot be understood. I cannot explain but I am a friend of Belgium and not what I seem. Please trust me. I have a reason for my questions. Is this building still an orphanage, Sister?'

The nun played along magnificently. Without pausing she answered. 'But yes, sir, it is. We were allowed to take care of the little ones in return for agreeing to work as nurses. The care of the sick is a Christian duty but the work is hard. Who are you?'

Anthony noticed that, despite being a young woman, how thin and tired her face was under the projecting white coif which framed her face. The word *English* was too risky. 'I come from over the water. You look after the children?'

'Yes. You ask about diet. Our poor children live because of the

Americans. They give us food.' Her face brightened. 'You are American? America must be a land of saints.'

Anthony toyed momentarily with the idea of being a saintly American then regretfully dismissed it. 'I am a friend of the Americans.' He hoped that would do. Never mind Americans, saints or otherwise, he needed to get in touch with Sister Marie-Eugénie and he needed to do it pretty sharpish. 'Please do not show any surprise at this question. Do you know a Sister Marie-Eugénie?'

Despite the warning, the young nun's eyebrows shot up. 'But yes, sir.' She moved as if to point her out. 'She's there.'

Anthony intervened hastily. 'Don't move. Just tell me where she is.'

'She is standing by the fourth bed along.'

'I see.' Anthony thought he was safe enough, but he didn't want the mention of Americans or Sister Marie-Eugénie to raise any suspicions in Schuhbeck's mind, so he threw in a few more comments about diet before moving on.

Sister Marie-Eugénie was a stout, middle-aged woman, who had evidently, judging by her loose clothes, once been stouter. She was bent over a patient, thermometer in hand.

Anthony looked at her hungrily. This was the woman he had come so far to see, the woman who could surely explain at least some of the mystery, the woman who – his stomach tightened – had care of Milly.

'What is the patient's temperature, nurse?' asked Schuhbeck, with a look at Anthony. He was obviously anxious to be seen to be doing something.

'High but steady, Herr Doktor,' replied Sister Marie-Eugénie. 'I think he will recover.'

So she spoke German, did she? That meant there was no chance of a secret conversation under Schuhbeck's nose, but he had to say something.

Anthony picked up the patient's wrist and felt for the pulse. 'I see dicrotism is well marked,' he said, feeling the irregular beats. 'Its presence is always suggestive in typhoid cases. See that this man receives a tepid bed-bath and ensure that he has nothing but a milk diet for at least the next three days.'

He dropped the man's wrist, smothered a yawn, and turned to

the Major. 'Everything seems to be running smoothly, Major. I congratulate you.' The Major, evidently very pleased, clicked his heels together and nodded. 'However,' continued Anthony, 'I am tired after the journey. Have a man escort me to my quarters.'

'Certainly, sir.' Schuhbeck turned his head and beckoned to an orderly who hurried over. 'Show the Colonel to his rooms.'

Anthony made as if to go, then stopped and clicked his fingers at Sister Marie-Eugénie in his best arrogant manner. 'And you, nurse, come to my office immediately.'

Both she and Major Schuhbeck looked surprised.

'I wish to question this woman about the nursing care and practices used.' The real colonel probably wouldn't have explained, but it was better than having Schuhbeck wonder what was going on. 'This woman evidently speaks German. I would prefer my questions to be answered in our own language.'

'I can send the Matron to you—' began Schuhbeck, but Anthony interrupted him.

'No doubt I will see her in due course, but for the time being, I will speak to this woman.' He smiled thinly. 'My office, Sister. Immediately.'

She looked put out, and no wonder, thought Anthony, as the major summoned an orderly to show him the way to his rooms. Anyone would be at being told to jump to it with a click of the fingers, to say nothing of being referred to as 'this woman' . Still, it was nice to know she still had that much spirit left.

Following the orderly, Anthony went back into the house. He was shown along the corridor and up two flights of stairs. Sister Marie-Eugénie followed on slowly behind.

To Anthony's annoyance, the orderly, an elderly private, and, Anthony realized, a real old potterer, followed him round, pointing out the various virtues of the various rooms, expressing the repeated hope that it was all to the Colonel's satisfaction.

The rooms consisted of an office, with the usual desk, filing cabinets and telephone. Leading on from the office, there was a sitting room, with a settee, two chairs and a dining table, should the Colonel wish to take his meals alone, a bathroom with a bath and sink panelled in gloomy mahogany and a high-cisterned lavatory that flushed. The lavatory, raised on its own mahogany step, was a genuine Victorian throne made, ironically enough, in London. The orderly seemed unduly proud of the lavatory.

The bedroom furniture consisted of a bed, a bedside table, a chest of drawers and a monumental wardrobe. Anthony could see it all for himself, but that didn't deter the orderly from expatiating on its virtues.

His cases – or, rather, Baumann's cases – were stacked neatly beside the bed. Was Baumann still securely out of action? Anthony thought. And where could he find Milly?

From the open bedroom window came the sound of children's voices. Anthony looked out. The window overlooked a private garden, evidentially the Colonel's own, separated by a hedge from a grassy space where children were playing.

The orderly saw where Anthony was looking. 'I apologize if the noise disturbs you, sir. Shall I instruct the children to be quiet?'

'No matter,' said Anthony, waving him away. A new colonel would surely comment on the presence of a load of kids. 'I know this building used to be an orphanage. I am surprised it still functions as such.'

'The children are kept entirely separate from the hospital, Colonel,' chipped in Sister Marie-Eugénie. Her mouth tightened. 'Their care is entirely in the hands of the order.'

'Good.' Anthony turned away from the window and nodded at the private. 'That will be all.'

The man saluted. 'Very good, sir.'

A thought occurred to Anthony. News would have travelled fast that the new colonel had arrived and, if he knew anything about military life, that would mean his adjutant would soon be knocking at the door, keen to run through the paperwork and impress the new boss with his efficiency. 'Who is my adjutant?'

'Sergeant Breynck, sir. Shall I send him to you?'

'Later,' said Anthony, pointedly smothering another yawn. Would the ruddy man never leave? 'I will send for him in due course. Dismissed,' he added firmly.

The orderly pottered out. Walking swiftly to the door, Anthony made sure it was firmly shut behind him.

'Now, Sister,' he began, when the telephone on the desk rang. Sighing impatiently, Anthony picked up the receiver. 'Yes?'

'This is Captain Malik speaking. Who is this?'

Anthony thought swiftly. If the call came from within the hospital, surely the caller would know that the new colonel had gone to his rooms. He wouldn't need to ask who had answered the phone. The phone call might concern an entirely routine matter about supplies and so on or . . .

Anthony blessed the instinct that had made him find out his adjutant's name. 'This is Sergeant Breynck, the colonel's adjutant.'

There was a startled gasp from Sister Marie-Eugénie. Anthony ignored her.

'His adjutant?' asked Captain Malik sharply. 'Has the colonel arrived?'

'Not as far as I know, sir.'

'Hmm. We have a report that Colonel Baumann and his driver have been found tied up on the Rempart de Malines road. They were attacked by two English spies. One of the spies was masquerading as a colonel.'

Some incredulity seemed called for. 'A colonel?'

'Exactly. Colonel Baumann believes that the spy may come to the hospital.' Anthony picked up the note of disbelief in Captain Malik's voice. 'Apparently he is a doctor.'

Although Baumann was, in fact, absolutely correct, Anthony could well understand why Captain Malik was sceptical. After all, just because an English spy in occupied Belgium happened to be a doctor, there didn't seem any very obvious reason why he should immediately gravitate to the nearest hospital.

'You think the spy will come here, sir?'

'It's possible, I suppose. Colonel Baumann will be with you shortly. Pass the message on to your superior officer and warn everyone to be on their guard. You will be informed when the spies are apprehended.'

The phone went dead. Anthony replaced the receiver. Things, he thought, were hotting up.

Sister Marie-Eugénie, who had evidently heard the gist of the call, gazed at him, open-mouthed. 'You aren't Sergeant Breynck,' she stammered, lapsing into French. 'You're Colonel Baumann. What is going on?'

There wasn't any time for subtlety. Anthony leaned forward, his hands on the desk. 'Sister Marie-Eugénie—'

Her eyes widened. 'How do you know my name?' she demanded.

Not only was there no time for subtlety, there wasn't any time for long-winded explanations either. 'Suffice to say that I do. Sister, I am not German. I am an English doctor.'

She gazed at him open mouthed. 'You are the spy?'

'You can call me that, if you like, but I have come all the way from England to find you.'

'To find *me*?' she repeated, her voice rising.

'And to find a child you have in your care.' Anthony reached inside his pocket and pulled out a photograph, the photograph of Milly. He laid it on the desk. 'This child.'

Eyes fixed on him, she pulled the photograph across the desk towards her. Glancing down, she stiffened, put her hand to her mouth, then looked at him in bewilderment.

Anthony's heart sank. Surely he hadn't come all this way for nothing? Yes, it had been a slender clue to follow, but surely this was the right place and Sister Marie-Eugénie was the right woman?

'You do have the child?' he asked urgently.

She paused then nodded slowly. 'Yes,' she said distantly.

'You have?' Anthony breathed again.

'Yes, she was given into my care. Forgive me, Monsieur, but this photograph was taken some time ago. At first I was not sure but yes, I know the child.' She looked up, and both her expression and her voice was sharp. 'What do you want with her?' She paused, looking at him shrewdly. 'Excuse me, but are you a . . . a relative perhaps?'

Even though he was desperate for speed, Anthony couldn't help smiling. The question had been very delicately put. 'No, Sister, I am not her father or any other relative. All I really know about her is that her name is Milly or Millicent. However, I also know that some danger threatens this child. I want to protect her from harm.'

'Millicent,' repeated Sister Marie-Eugénie. She eyed him thoughtfully. 'Yes, she was called that, I believe. When a child comes to us, they have a new life with a new name. Her name is now Agathé, so she may have the blessed St Agathé to guide and protect her.'

'Will you take me to Milly? Or Agathé as you call her?'

'Take you into the orphanage?' Sister Marie-Eugénie was

flustered. 'No. It is part of the convent, you understand? No Germans ever come into the orphanage.'

'Will you bring her to me then?'

Sister Marie-Eugénie sat frozen, her hand resting on the picture. 'Yes, I can do that,' she said eventually. She glanced at the door. 'I am free to go?'

'Of course.' Anthony opened the door for her. 'And please, Sister, hurry.'

She looked at him intently, then, gathering her skirts, went out.

Alone in the room, Anthony crossed to the window once more, looking down at the children in the garden. He swore softly. If he could be sure of identifying Milly from her photograph, then he could get into the orphanage – the sounds of the children playing made that possibility tantalizingly close – snatch her up and get her away from here.

But he couldn't do that. For one thing, he couldn't be sure of recognizing her. Milly had grown since that photograph was taken and for another, the orphanage, as Sister Marie-Eugénie had said, was separate from the hospital. It didn't sound as if any of the medical staff ever went in that part of the building. A German doctor – and a man! – would cause consternation in an orphanage run by nuns.

But even if he could get into the orphanage, that wouldn't be enough. As well as finding Milly, he wanted to know why she was threatened. He could hardly interrogate a five- or six-year-old child as to the nature of the plot she was caught up in. He drummed his fingers on the windowsill.

The clock was ticking and it was only a matter of time before Baumann arrived. He needed a plan.

TWENTY-TWO

Major Schuhbeck was feeling very pleased with life. To greet a new commanding officer was always a nerve-wracking experience. He had no illusions about the calibre of officer who was likely to be posted to the command of a typhoid hospital in what was now a remote sector, far behind the front lines.

He had expected a civilian in uniform, a man culled from private practice, probably a second-rate doctor, who resented their posting. He had expected a man who was unused to military discipline and more than ready to find fault with the hospital, its practices and, more to the point, its staff.

Instead the new colonel seemed smart, efficient and medically competent. What's more, he was obviously satisfied with the standards he, Schuhbeck, had maintained. Yes, he thought, smoothing out his moustache, it had all gone very well indeed.

He glanced at his watch. Lunchtime. It would be soup, sausage, bread and potato, as always, but he was hungry and . . .

He stood and gaped in disbelief as the door from the house was flung open and a squad of four soldiers, a lieutenant at their head, marched into the courtyard, guns at the ready. Bobbing along in their wake was a short, dishevelled man in a colonel's uniform.

Major Schuhbeck drew himself up to his full height and marched across the courtyard. 'What is the meaning of this?' he demanded. He stopped short as the lieutenant's pistol was levelled at him menacingly. 'Who the devil are you?' Schuhbeck barked. 'And what the devil's going on? This is a hospital!'

The soldiers, who were obviously well aware it was not only a hospital but a typhoid hospital at that, huddled together, clutching firmly onto their rifles, as if prepared to shoot any germ that dared approach.

The lieutenant kept his pistol raised. 'I am Lieutenant Keller. You are?'

Schuhbeck bristled. 'Major Schuhbeck, Lieutenant,' bellowed Schuhbeck. '*Major!*'

Military discipline reasserted itself. Lieutenant Keller lowered his pistol and snapped to attention. 'Sir!'

The stout little man in the colonel's uniform wriggled his way through to the front. 'Ask him to prove it! For all we know, he's in league with the spy.'

'The spy?' repeated Schuhbeck incredulously. 'What spy?'

Baumann almost danced on the spot in agitation. 'The country is awash with spies. Show me your papers! Prove who you are!'

It never did to disobey a senior officer, even one as agitated as this one, but Schuhbeck was at a loss. 'My papers are in my office. I can fetch them if you like. Sir,' he added reluctantly.

'No! You'll warn the spy, I know you will.' Baumann turned to the lieutenant. 'Arrest this man!'

Major Schuhbeck's eyes bulged. 'Arrest *me*? Lieutenant, *halt!*' he added in a parade ground bellow as the lieutenant moved as if to come forward.

Lieutenant Keller shifted uncomfortably. 'I can't arrest the Major, sir,' he said to the Colonel. 'He's not the spy.'

'What the devil is all this about spies?' Schuhbeck demanded curtly.

Colonel Baumann waved his hands distractedly. 'Spies! Two English spies! And I know one of them. *Conrad Etriech.*' He spat the name out. 'Etriech's a crafty devil but I got the better of him.'

Schuhbeck could make nothing of this. This little man might be dressed as a colonel but he didn't act like a colonel. How dare he come bursting in to his hospital with a bunch of guttersnipe soldiers and a lieutenant who looked as if he should be still in kindergarten? And how dare he threaten to arrest him? The thing was outrageous. Spies? Why should any spy want to come here? And why the devil should an English spy have a German name? The whole thing was ridiculous.

He glared at the lieutenant. 'What's going on?'

'Let me explain, sir,' said Lieutenant Keller. 'We were on a routine patrol on the Rempart de Malines road, when we heard a muffled shouting amongst the trees. We went to investigate and found the Colonel and his driver tied up and gagged.'

'I was attacked! Ruthlessly attacked!' put in Baumann. 'Conrad Etriech attacked me!'

'The Colonel,' continued the Lieutenant, 'told us what had happened. The driver had no uniform. The spies had taken it. I dispatched a man to inform Captain Malik what had occurred and, following the Colonel's instructions, came here.'

'You were attacked?' repeated Schuhbeck in bewilderment, looking at the Colonel.

'Yes, yes, yes, yes, yes! Attacked! Are you deaf, man?'

'No, sir,' said Schuhbeck evenly, 'but it sounds an extraordinary story. Excuse me, sir, but who are you?'

'Me?' shrieked the little man. 'I am Colonel Baumann. I am your commanding officer!'

'Colonel Baumann?' Schuhbeck shook his head in disbelief. He looked at Lieutenant Keller. 'There must be some mistake. We were expecting a Colonel Baumann to arrive but there was a mistake in the movement orders. Colonel Lieben has been assigned to this hospital. He arrived the best part of an hour ago.'

'I knew it!' yelped Baumann. 'That impudent devil of a spy has strolled in to my hospital! Didn't you suspect *anything*?' he demanded of the luckless Schuhbeck.

'No, sir, I—'

'Didn't you ask to see his papers?'

'No, sir. There didn't seem any necessity to examine the Colonel's papers.'

'He wasn't the Colonel! I'm the Colonel! You saw the spy, you fool!'

Schuhbeck had been engrained in the traditions of the Imperial Army and to question a superior was almost beyond imagination. However, the word 'fool' stung.

'You're quite right, sir. I should have asked to see his papers. Can I see yours?'

Baumann stared at him. 'I beg your pardon?'

'Your papers, sir. After all, I only have your word for it that you are Colonel Baumann.'

'I cannot show you my papers because they were stolen by the spy,' said Baumann in a voice that was chipped out of icicles.

'So we have no proof that you are Colonel Baumann.'

'I was attacked and *tied up*!'

'As you say, sir, but it could be a plan to gain entry to the hospital.'

'I don't need a plan to gain entry to the hospital,' Baumann snapped. 'I'm in charge!' He stopped and wearily wiped his forehead with a handkerchief. 'What did the spy do when he arrived?'

'He carried out a brief inspection and then asked to be shown to his rooms.'

Baumann whirled on the lieutenant triumphantly. 'After him, man! We can still catch him.'

Lieutenant Keller looked at Major Schuhbeck. 'Can you show us the way, sir?'

'Very well, Lieutenant.'

In his heart of hearts, Schuhbeck knew there must be some mistake. True, this little irate man was the sort of person he had expected, but the other colonel – the real colonel, he thought wistfully – was so very much more the sort of man he had hoped for. 'But why should any spy come here?'

'Who knows why a man like that does anything?' demanded Baumann. 'Come on!'

Schuhbeck was far too well disciplined to let his feelings show. He couldn't understand what had actually happened, but he hoped that they would find the colonel – the *real* colonel – in his rooms.

Then it would all be explained; this ridiculous talk of spies would be quashed, and, with any luck, this irritating jumped-up civilian would discover which hospital he'd actually been posted to and leave them alone. They could keep the real colonel and, at the very least, he could have his lunch. 'Very well, Colonel,' he said, with the merest suspicion of a shrug. 'Follow me.'

Schuhbeck strode along the corridor to the Colonel's rooms, Lieutenant Keller and his men behind, with Colonel Baumann bringing up the rear.

He was just about to knock when the Lieutenant intervened. 'Allow me, sir,' he said, drawing his pistol.

With a nod to his men, he opened the door and swung it back on its hinges. An empty desk and chair greeted his eyes. Relaxing slightly, Lieutenant Keller made way for Major Schuhbeck, who was radiating annoyance.

'He's somewhere in here!' asserted Baumann, pushing his way through to the front. 'Search the rooms and make sure you do it thoroughly.'

Under Baumann's increasingly febrile instructions, Keller's men searched the office, the bathroom, the sitting room and the bedroom. They paid particular attention to the monumental wardrobe, and looked both in and under the bed.

Schuhbeck stepped back as the men prodded the bolster with their bayonets. He took a malicious pleasure in the fact that the bed was not only empty but had been rendered completely useless for anyone wishing to sleep in it. Feathers filled the air from the ripped bolster.

'He's not here,' he said grimly. That was a shame. He really hoped the colonel would appear and put this ridiculous little man in his place.

Lieutenant Keller crossed to the open window. 'He must've escaped this way,' he said, looking down to the garden.

'That's it!' agreed Baumann excitedly. 'After him, Lieutenant!' He bustled back into the office. 'Quickly!'

The lieutenant saluted and, followed by his men, left the room.

'Not you, Major,' added Baumann, as Schuhbeck went to follow them. He drew out a chair from the desk and sank into it. 'Please ensure that I am informed immediately the spies are apprehended. I won't have a minute's rest until I know they are safely under lock and key.'

'As you say, sir,' said Schuhbeck.

Spies, he thought rebelliously. He didn't know what had really happened but the thought of English spies walking into his hospital was absolute nonsense. However, if this wretched little man said he was the Colonel, then perhaps he'd like to act as if he was the Colonel.

'Excuse me, Colonel, but will you inspect the hospital now or later?' From his tone, no one could have suspected Schuhbeck of anything other than an earnest desire to follow the correct procedure. He took an unholy delight in Baumann's reaction.

'Inspect the hospital?' Baumann's voice was a disbelieving squeak. 'Have you taken leave of your senses, Major? The spies are still at large and may appear at any moment. My life has been threatened. Threatened, I say! I will inspect the hospital when the spies are captured and I have sufficiently recovered and not before.' He lit a cigarette and pulled at it nervously. 'Send an orderly to me with a pot of coffee – good coffee, mind – and let me have some peace.'

Schuhbeck saluted. 'Very good, sir.' Spies! It was all such rubbish. But at least he could now have his lunch.

TWENTY-THREE

A nthony gingerly pushed back the panel of the bath and wriggled out.

He had heard the tramping of feet and the occasional snatch of voices, but his hiding place had worked. The men had hardly looked in the bathroom, as there was so obviously nowhere to hide.

He stole to the bathroom door and risked a glance through the hinge side of the door. Damn! Baumann was sitting at his desk, his head buried in his hands. 'Inspect the hospital,' Anthony heard him mutter with a groan. 'The idea!'

A respectful knock sounded at the door. 'What is it?' barked Baumann testily.

Anthony readied himself. If this was Sister Marie-Eugénie he'd have to take a hand, but it wasn't.

It was the elderly orderly, who didn't seem to be remotely curious about the change of superior officers. 'Your coffee, sir,' said the orderly.

'About time, too. Leave the pot, man!'

The orderly departed and various noises of clinking china followed. Anthony risked another glance. Baumann was steadily working his way through the pot of coffee and looked settled for the afternoon.

Anthony's heart sank. Ideally, he should regain his hiding place and stay until it was safe to leave. The disadvantage of hiding behind the bath panel, though, was that he couldn't see what was going on and he couldn't escape quickly.

At any moment, Sister Marie-Eugénie could arrive with little Agathé, as she called her. Baumann would naturally ask who on earth she was and what she wanted. Unless she was a very quick thinker, her part in affairs would be discovered and his chances of escaping with Milly were reduced from slim to zero. Unless, that was, he was on hand to take a part in affairs before Baumann gave the alarm.

What he needed was for Baumann to leave his desk, to go

downstairs or even into his sitting room or bedroom. Then he could escape from this ruddy bathroom, into the corridor, and find somewhere to wait to intercept Sister Marie-Eugénie on her way to the office.

There was a wooden-cased clock on the wall of the office. Anthony could hear the ponderous seconds tick by as the pendulum swung. He glanced at his watch. It was nearly quarter to twelve. It had been a very long morning, but it had started very early. And where the dickens was Sister Marie-Eugénie? He'd been stuck in the bathroom for nearly twenty minutes. She was certainly taking her time.

Then Baumann moved. With a jolt of hope, Anthony saw him push his chair back and stand up.

He walked towards the sitting room, then he stopped, turned and headed straight for the bathroom. The coffee had done its work.

There was nothing for it. Anthony only had fractions of a second. The bath panel was out of the question, so he did the only thing possible. He flattened himself against the wall where the door would shield him once opened.

Maybe Baumann, like most men, wouldn't bother to shut the door if he thought he was alone. Maybe . . .

The door swung back against his face. Anthony suppressed a grunt as the door hit his nose and, his vision occupied exclusively by the wood grain of the door panel, listened to the unmistakable sounds of Baumann using the facilities.

With the handle of the door in one hand and his automatic in the other, he heard a loud flushing noise as Baumann pulled the chain. He felt the oddest little stab of patriotic pride at the noise. That London lavatory really delivered.

There was the splash of water in the sink, a pause while Baumann presumably dried his hands, followed by a footstep.

A crash like a crack of thunder blasted the silence. At the same time, Baumann yelped and something hit the bathroom door hard.

Anthony made a desperate grab for the handle as it jerked out of his hand. The door swung slowly back.

Beside the bath, Baumann was bent double, nursing his foot. On the floor next to him was the fallen bath panel which he'd evidently caught with his boot. The panel had shot forward and crashed against the door, slewing off to one side.

Anthony waited for the inevitable. It seemed to happen in slow motion.

Baumann glanced up, gave a sort of gurgling gasp and started back, his eyes circled in terror.

'Hello,' said Anthony pleasantly, pointing the automatic. 'Don't shout.'

Baumann gurgled once more, then collapsed back on the lavatory seat.

'I'll have to leave you in here,' said Anthony. He opened the door with his left hand and backed towards it. 'I'm sorry to have to threaten you, Baumann, old man, but if you shout or try and escape, I will shoot. I intend to remain on the other side of the door. Do you understand?'

Baumann, frozen to the spot, nodded.

'Good. Then we have an arrangement. I'm going to lock you in. You don't move and I won't kill you.'

Baumann found his voice. 'Etriech,' he said in a hoarse whisper, 'why are you here?'

'Spying, old friend. I'll tell you all about it after the war. If,' he added, with a significant gesture of the automatic, 'you live that long.'

Baumann's gaze slid to the gun. He gulped and nodded.

Anthony walked backwards out of the bathroom, shutting the door behind him.

What the devil could he do now? Despite what he had told Baumann, he couldn't actually lock him in. There was a bolt on the inside of the bathroom door but, naturally enough, there was no lock or bolt on the outside. Fear would keep Baumann in the bathroom for a while but not forever. And where the hell was Sister Marie-Eugénie?

The best he could do was wedge a chair under the handle of the bathroom door. That would keep the wretched man safely out of the way for a while, at least.

Anthony had his hand on the back of the wooden desk chair to drag it across the room, when he heard footsteps in the corridor. Sister Marie-Eugénie? No. The footsteps sounded heavy and there was definitely more than one person coming.

Once more he had to hide and quickly.

* * *

When, Major Schuhbeck had, over what he thought of as his richly deserved sausage and potato, been nervously informed by Corporal Weber that a Hauptmann von Casberg and an Oberleutnant Krause wished to see him, his first response was to tell Weber that they could damn well wait. After all, why should he jump to it because two junior officers wanted to see him, even if one could call himself *von* anything? He was eating his lunch and wasn't going to be interrupted for a mere captain and a lieutenant. After all, who was the major here?

Corporal Weber squirmed on the spot. Daringly, he gave his opinion that it really would be a good idea to see Captain von Casberg and Lieutenant Krause now. At once. Quickly. Without delay.

Schuhbeck might have a just sense of his own importance, but he could read a situation as well as the next man. There must be something up to reduce Weber to such a quivering state of nerves. Grumbling, he threw down his napkin and strode outside.

And gulped.

Captain von Casberg and Lieutenant Krause may be junior officers, but they were junior *staff* officers.

Oh, my God.

It would take a far slower man than Schuhbeck not to realize that Captain von Casberg was someone he really shouldn't cross.

Every inch of Captain von Casberg, from his perfectly fitting flat cap with its dark crimson band, perfectly polished high boots and, in between, his perfectly-cut uniform with the distinctive double width dark crimson stripes, radiated steely authority.

His monocle, his duelling-scar, the way he flicked his gloves impatiently over his wrist, all told Schuhbeck that here was a man who was only a captain in passing. This was a man with influence and *relations* for heaven's sake and at that moment Schuhbeck could well believe that those relations included the Kaiser himself.

Lieutenant Krause, standing languidly a few feet away from his captain, was out of the same mould. He seemed to be a different order of being from Lieutenant Keller and his men, standing stiffly to attention a few yards away.

Lieutenant Keller and his squad looked completely wooden, which was, perhaps, the best response to Acts of God like von Casberg and Krause.

'Captain?' Schuhbeck said, and very nearly added, *sir*.

'Major Schuhbeck?' snapped the captain. 'You are harbouring spies.'

Schuhbeck swallowed hard. He hadn't believed in the spies but if Captain von Casberg said he was harbouring a spy, then he would harbour as many spies as the man wanted.

'Spies?' he wavered.

Captain von Casberg clicked his tongue impatiently. 'Yes, man, spies! The man purporting to be the Colonel is an English spy.'

The *Colonel?* Schuhbeck stared at him wordlessly.

The Captain seemed to swell with rage. 'Major Schuhbeck,' he ground out, 'I am a busy man. I have had very little sleep in the past few days. My time is precious and my temper is short. Take me to the spy. At once.'

'Of course,' said Schuhbeck, once more biting the *sir* off at the end of the sentence. 'Er . . . Follow me.'

Captain von Casberg nodded to Krause who beckoned to Keller and his men. They marched into the house, Schuhbeck leading the way.

Outside the office door they paused. Von Casberg came to the front, unholstered his pistol, then, tensing himself, slammed the office door back on its hinges.

The office was empty.

Von Casberg turned to Schuhbeck. 'I hope, for your sake, Major,' he said silkily, 'you have not allowed an English spy to escape.'

Schuhbeck hoped so too. 'Colonel Baumann?' he called, more from a desire to be seen to be doing something, rather than from any expectation his call would be answered. 'Colonel Baumann, are you here, sir?'

To his absolute astonishment, a voice called back from the bathroom. 'Of course I'm here! I'm locked in!'

Schuhbeck blinked. There was no lock on the outside of the door. Did the Colonel – the spy? – mean he had locked himself in?

Von Casberg strode to the door. With Krause beside him, he rattled the handle. 'Come out,' he said abruptly.

The door opened a crack. Von Casberg reached inside and, with one hand on his pistol and the other hand on Baumann's collar, hauled him out of the room.

'What is the meaning of this?' began Baumann furiously, then took in the full majesty of Captain von Casberg. 'Bless my soul,' he muttered weakly. 'Oh dear, oh Lord, oh bless my soul! Who are you?'

Von Casberg shook him like a terrier with a rat. 'I am Captain von Casberg. You would do well to remember that. I know exactly what you're up too, my English friend.'

'English!' yelped Baumann in indignation. 'What d'you mean, English? I'm German! It's the spy who's English! He's Conrad Etriech, and a dangerous man.'

Lieutenant Krause stirred. 'Conrad Etriech? Conrad Etriech of Kiel?' He turned to von Casberg. 'You remember hearing about him, sir? Last April he kidnapped an officer, stole his uniform and escaped under the very noses of the squad sent out to capture him.'

Von Casberg's eyes widened. 'So that's the man, is it? Conrad Etriech.' He repeated the name, rolling out the syllables. 'There was a generous reward for his capture. He's a clever man. Very clever indeed.'

Lying on the bed in the next room, hidden beneath the unholy mess Lieutenant Keller and his men had made of the bedclothes, Anthony listened to these biographical details with fascination. He had chosen to hide in the bed, not only because it was the nearest place available in the seconds he had, but also, because it had been so obviously searched, that he guessed it wouldn't be searched again.

'He is clever,' squeaked Baumann, who was probably grateful to find something that he and this living nightmare of a captain could agree on. 'He fooled everyone. He speaks perfect German. You'd swear he was German.'

'Would I, indeed?' drawled von Casberg. He released Baumann abruptly, who collapsed on the floor.

Von Casberg turned to Krause. 'I remember the Etriech affair. As you say, he stole a uniform and told a very convincing story to escape. We seem to have a pattern that's repeated itself.' He prodded Baumann with his foot. 'Get up, Etriech or whatever your name is! Your luck's run out.'

'I'm not Etriech!' Baumann scrambled to his feet, stuttering with indignation.

'Really?' Von Casberg curled his lip. 'You are an insignificant little man, not at all the sort of man anyone would notice. Exactly the sort of vermin who makes a good spy.'

'You've got this all wrong,' whimpered Baumann. He gesticulated wildly in the direction of Lieutenant Keller. 'He knows! He found me tied up. Etriech attacked me!'

'That means nothing,' sneered von Casberg. 'How easy would it be for you to be tied up by a comrade? Then you can arrange to be found in such a way that no one questions who you really are.' He glanced dismissively at Lieutenant Keller. 'Of course, this fool was taken in, but you can't fool me. That's exactly the sort of cunning trick I'd expect a man such as Etriech to try.'

Not bad, thought Anthony, from under the bedclothes. That idea hadn't actually occurred to him, but it wasn't at all bad.

'I'm not Etriech!' bellowed Baumann. He turned wildly to Schuhbeck. 'You know who I am. Tell him. There was another man, yes? Another man who said he was the colonel.'

Everyone looked at Schuhbeck.

'Well?' drawled von Casberg.

Schuhbeck cleared his throat. 'Dr Lieutenant Colonel Lieben arrived about an hour before Colonel Baumann.'

'You see?' said Baumann eagerly. 'He's the spy.'

Von Casberg laughed dismissively. 'I don't think so. I have no doubt that Colonel Lieben arrived, but he was not the spy.'

'I didn't think he was,' said Schuhbeck in some relief. 'When Colonel Baumann arrived, I asked to see his papers in accordance with proper procedures, but he refused to show them to me,'

'Etriech stole them!' yelped Baumann.

'How very convenient,' said von Casberg smoothly. 'Of course he did. I will interview Colonel Lieben in due course, but as for you, Etriech, we have proof positive that you are a fraud, a cheat and a spy.'

Anthony twitched aside a bit of ripped blanket, listening intently. What proof could von Casberg have?

'You made a grievous error in confiding in that woman. I have no truck with popish superstitions, but she acted wisely. What was her name again, Krause?'

'Marie-Eugénie, sir.'

'Exactly,' agreed von Casberg. 'She, I am glad to say, realizes who are the masters in Belgium now.'

Beneath the blankets, Anthony felt as if a cold hand had gripped his heart.

Sister Marie-Eugénie had betrayed him.

Yes, he had to work fast and yes, the situation had been desperate, but he would have sworn he could've trusted her. She was Belgian, for God's sake. More than that, she was a nun, a nun who must know how the occupying army had treated the priests and nuns of Louvain. Only hours ago he had stood in the ruined cathedral of St Pierre and seen the destruction of Catholic Belgium. How could he have been betrayed by her, of all people?

'She told us all about you, Etriech,' continued von Casberg. 'She told us that the man calling himself Colonel Baumann was really an English spy. You said as much to her, didn't you? For all your cleverness, that was remarkably stupid. You will come with us now, identify your companion, the second spy, if he is still to be found, and face the full consequences of your actions.'

Even though he felt sick with shock, Anthony numbly realized what must have happened.

A Colonel Baumann had been expected that morning. It was only the guards at the door and Major Schuhbeck who knew that the colonel who had turned up wasn't called Baumann but Lieben. While he was carrying out his brief inspection, Schuhbeck, if he had called him anything, had called him 'Colonel' or 'sir'.

Sister Marie-Eugénie knew him as the Colonel. Naturally enough, she believed he was the Colonel Baumann they had been waiting for.

If he had been capable of feeling anything at that moment apart from blank despair, Anthony could have felt sorry for Baumann. Without putting a foot wrong, he had landed himself in a mad tangle of misunderstanding. For Sister Marie-Eugénie he felt a cold knot of loathing twist his stomach.

'Take him away,' said von Casberg and Anthony heard the stamp of feet as the soldiers came to attention. A despairing wail from Baumann was the last he heard as the men marched out of the room and the door slammed behind them.

Anthony waited a few moments before throwing off the bedclothes. Practically speaking, it was to make sure that no one was in the office but, as much as anything, he wanted a couple of moments to gather his thoughts.

Sister Marie-Eugénie was an enemy. That was the stark, unpalatable truth. The only thing he could do was try and somehow find Milly and get out of here. He realized how much he had depended on trusting the nuns to help him. Dammit, he *needed* the nuns to help him. Milly had grown and changed since her photograph had been taken, that was obvious. How on earth could he find her?

The sound of the children in the garden below was maddening. One of them might be Milly. He could lean out of the window, call her name, see if one of the children looked up . . . No. That idea was appealingly simple but far too risky.

He had to get into the orphanage. Even if Sister Marie-Eugénie had inexplicably decided to side with the Germans, surely all the nuns couldn't be traitors? That young nun he had talked to in the hospital, for instance, could easily have given him away to Schuhbeck but hadn't.

Opening the office door a crack, he listened intently, but all was quiet. The whole top floor of the building seemed deserted. Von Casberg said he wanted Baumann to identify his companion. That meant, surely, that a parade of all staff would be called and Baumann would be forced to confront them.

Unless, that is, Baumann had managed to convince that swaggering bully of an officer he was who he said he was, but somehow Anthony didn't think Captain von Casberg was a man open to persuasion.

No. He could assume that, with any luck, the entire staff would be on parade in the hospital courtyard. Which meant, of course, that the hospital should be deserted. As long as he could keep out of sight, he was safe.

He slipped out into the sun-lit corridor and, walking as quietly as he could, reached the head of the stairs. From the open window at the top of the staircase he could hear the shout of orders. He had been right about the identity parade.

There wasn't a soul about as he went down the stairs to the ground floor. From what he had seen from the bedroom window, the orphanage garden was on the left-hand side. Turning left, he walked past deserted rooms along the arched hallway, until he came to a door.

It was a very solid door and it was locked. Anthony briefly

toyed with the idea of trying to shoulder-charge it open, but all he'd probably achieve was a broken shoulder. No, that wouldn't do. What else could he try? He looked around.

A few paces back was another door. Anthony opened it and saw it wasn't so much a room as a long, narrow store cupboard for mops and buckets. With a grin he saw the window, high up in the end wall. Reaching up, Anthony undid the latch and opened the window a crack, listening intently once more.

The parade ground noises seemed distant here. He should be round the corner from the courtyard. Standing on an upturned bucket, he grasped the stone sill of the window, pulled himself up and, with a terrific heave, got onto the sill.

TWENTY-FOUR

The wall separating the convent proper from the hospital was feet away. Anthony had been right about that solid door. It had led into the convent and orphanage.

The wall, the mortar between the bricks loosened with rain and sun, was an easy climb. Without much trouble, he swarmed up it, quickly checked the coast was clear, and dropped down on the other side.

On his left loomed the bulk of the orphanage. Anthony quickly ran through what he knew of the geography of the place. The orphanage garden, which he had looked down onto from his bedroom, must lie round the other side of the building.

Anthony came to the corner and risked a glance round. At a guess he was in the convent grounds. The sloping lawn was bounded by trees and shrubs. Halfway along the building was an elaborate portico across from which stood the almost inevitable statue of the Virgin Mary.

Outside all was still but, from within the building, he could hear an organ playing and voices singing what sounded like a hymn. The lancet windows fronting onto the lawn were of stained glass. This must be the chapel.

He had been married to Tara long enough to know about the

Catholic practice of saying the Angelus at midday. No wonder no one was about. All the nuns who weren't on nursing duty must be inside the chapel. Good.

What he needed to do was run the length of the chapel to get round to the other side. He was just about to set off when the hymn swelled in volume. He took another glance round the corner. The chapel doors were open and two nuns were standing outside.

He swore under his breath. The hymn finished and the garden, which had been so temptingly deserted, was suddenly full of black-clad nuns and chattering children as they came out of the chapel. If they came round the corner he'd just have to hope Sister Marie-Eugénie wasn't amongst them.

His luck held. From what he could hear, it sounded as if the nuns were taking the children off to lunch. After a few minutes, all was quiet once more.

Once more he glanced round the corner. The garden was deserted. Now for it!

He set off at a run. He had nearly reached the portico when the person he least wanted to see in the whole world came out of the chapel.

Sister Marie-Eugénie.

She started back as she saw him, her eyes wide with shock. Anthony knew she was going to scream.

He had to stop her. He had never laid rough hands on a woman in his life, but with one bound he had an arm securely round her shoulders and his hand clamped over her mouth.

Sister Marie-Eugénie was outraged. She wasn't strong but she was determined and very nearly struggled free.

'Quiet, Sister!' he hissed. 'If I take my hand away, will you be quiet?'

She glared at him ferociously but nodded. Anthony dropped his hand, ready to grab her again.

'Why did you do it?' he demanded, before she could say anything. 'Why did you betray me?'

She stared at him. 'What are you talking about?'

Anthony sighed impatiently. 'You promised to bring Milly – Agathé – to my office, yes? Instead you telephoned Captain von Casberg of the Staff. You told him I was an English spy.'

She continued to stare. 'But that's what I was told to say,' she broke out. 'Your people told me to say it.'

'People? What people? What on earth do you mean?'

She glared at him. 'Your people. You know who I mean.' Anthony shook his head, puzzled. 'The staff officers,' she insisted angrily. 'When the staff officers came a few weeks ago I was told I would be tested and what would happen to us – the sisters and the children – if I failed the test.'

'What would happen?'

'How can you ask?' Her scorn was withering. 'Louvain has burned. The house of God and the servants of God mean nothing to you and your kind. You destroyed the cathedral, murdered the clergy and killed anyone who begged for mercy. What could I do? You are in control.'

'I'm not in control,' said Anthony. 'I didn't burn Louvain. I'm not the enemy. Don't you understand? I'm English. Everything I told you in the office is absolutely true.'

She blinked. 'I don't believe you . . .' she began but, for the first time, her face and her voice were doubtful.

Anthony pressed home his advantage. 'Look, Sister, I'm not a Catholic, but my wife is. A few days ago I stood in Westminster Cathedral. This morning I stood in the cathedral of St Pierre. St Pierre could be Westminster. I was sickened by its destruction. I'm on your side.'

She put her hands to her mouth, staring at him. 'Can it be true?' she muttered, when they were interrupted by a nun hurrying round the corner.

'Sister!' she called. 'Sister Marie-Eugénie!' She stopped short as she saw Anthony.

'It's all right,' said Sister Marie-Eugénie quickly. 'What is it?'

The nun, a young woman, approached cautiously and, looking warily at Anthony, dropped him a curtsey before speaking. 'It's the German officer, Sister,' she said breathlessly. 'The Captain. He's arrested the Colonel, but the Colonel says he's never met you. The officer's coming to take you to him to confront him. I wanted to warn you.' She looked nervously over her shoulder. 'I ran to get here. He's right behind me.'

'Thank you, Sister Thérèsa,' said Sister Marie-Eugénie. 'You'd better get back quickly.'

As the young nun hurried away, Anthony leapt up the steps, into the portico, and hid behind the pillar at the entrance. If von Casberg caught sight of him, the fat would really be in the fire. 'Why do the Germans want Agathé?' he asked softly from behind the pillar.

'The child is . . .' she began, then stopped. Anthony heard the crunch of footsteps on the gravel. Von Casberg was here.

In a carrying voice she called, 'Yes?'

'Marie-Eugénie?' There was no mistaking von Casberg's voice.

'I am Sister Marie-Eugénie,' replied the nun coldly.

'Come with me.'

'Must I?' Her voice rose slightly. 'The child is safe. She is with Sister Angelica. Sister Angelica will give the child to you.'

Thanks, Sister, thought Anthony, hiding in the shadows. That was as helpful as she could possibly be in the circumstances.

'For the moment, the child is not my concern,' said von Casberg. 'My concern is the spy. He insists he has never met you. You must confront him.'

'Confront the spy?' Sister Marie-Eugénie sighed theatrically.

Don't overdo it, begged Anthony silently from the shadows.

'What spy?' she asked. 'I don't understand,' she added, sounding genuinely puzzled.

And, of course, she would be. The Germans had warned her that she would be tested. That was clever. It meant that should anyone turn up – as, indeed, he had done – she would immediately assume they were part of the enemy's plan. It was a practically foolproof way of ensuring her loyalty.

However, she didn't know anything about Baumann. She must wonder who on earth was this spy who von Casberg wanted her to confront.

'I don't understand,' she repeated. 'It was a test.'

'There was no test,' said Captain von Casberg grimly. 'The man you met is a spy.'

She gave a little cry. 'No!' then added anxiously, 'what if the spy escapes? Am I safe? Are we safe? You know I have done everything you asked.'

'He will not escape,' said von Casberg. 'Come with me.'

'Tell me I am safe,' she insisted. 'Upon your word of honour as an officer, promise me I am safe. I have been a loyal servant to Germany. Tell me you know this.'

Again, it was all a bit theatrical, thought Anthony, but he could understand why she was worried. If he did, by some miracle, manage to get out of here with Milly, she'd want as much assurance as she could get that there would be no repercussions.

'You have my word,' said von Casberg impatiently. 'You have proved you are loyal. That is just as well. Come along. Now, woman!' Anthony could hear his quick, impatient sigh. 'Far too much time has been wasted already. I am tired. Do you want me to lose my temper?'

'Very well,' agreed Sister Marie-Eugénie, her anxiety clear in her voice.

Anthony breathed a sigh of relief as their footsteps crunched away along the gravel. Now to find this Sister Angelica and, fingers crossed, find Milly too.

Outside was evidently hopping with Germans, so staying inside seemed like an attractive idea. The chapel was small and quiet, with the hushed silence of a sacred space. He quickly walked up the nave to the altar rails. He spared a glance at the painted crucifixion scene at the back of the altar and said a rare, quick, but fervent prayer. He needed all the help he could get, both material and spiritual.

With a slight feeling of sacrilege, he unlatched the little gate on the altar rails and stepped onto the altar. There didn't seem to be any doors leading out of the chapel apart from the main entrance, but he had hopes.

What he was looking for was the sacristy where the priest and the altar servers put on their vestments. The door was set in the wall behind the pillars that framed the altar. It opened onto a small functional room, containing a wardrobe, a sink with vases stacked on the drainer, a cupboard and – thank God! – another door. By the door was something that made him pause.

It was a coat-rack with a couple of raincoats, presumably for the benefit of visiting clergy. Anthony took down a coat. It was old and shabby but it covered his uniform.

The fact there were coats here told him something else, too. He must be near an outside entrance.

Buttoning up the coat, he opened the door. It led out onto a tiled hallway, which, by its size and grandeur, looked like the front entrance to the convent. A short distance away, he could see sunlight through the glass panels set into the oak door of the porch. Presumably that led to the garden.

An impressive oak staircase led up from the hall, but Anthony didn't think he'd find Sister Angelica upstairs. Besides that, if any nun found a German officer wandering round what presumably were the bedrooms, she really would have a fit of the jim-jams.

He was desperate to get on, but in the silence of the hallway he consciously forced himself to be still.

From along the hallway, away from the front door, he could hear the faint chinking of crockery. It sounded as if a meal was in progress but he couldn't hear any voices. Hold on. This was a convent. They probably ate their meals in silence.

He walked along the hallway in the direction of the sounds of crockery and came to a large double door. That must be the dining room.

Across the hallway from the dining room was another, much more modest door. That opened onto a tiled kitchen.

The kitchen, bright with copper pipes, had a cavernous black oven, a stove, cupboards and a scrubbed table but what it chiefly contained were two nuns washing up.

They stared at him in amazement.

'Good afternoon,' said Anthony, with as much suavity as he could muster.

'Monsieur,' said one. 'This is the convent. You should not be here.'

Anthony couldn't agree more. At least with his uniform covered up by the raincoat, the women weren't reacting with stark terror, which was something.

'I know, Sister,' he agreed. 'But the matter is urgent. I have just spoken to Sister Marie-Eugénie. She knows I am here. I need to speak to Sister Angelica. Would you bring her to me?' He tried a winning smile. 'Please? At once?'

'Sister Marie-Eugénie sent you?' said the nun doubtfully. The women looked at each other and shrugged.

'If Sister Marie-Eugénie says it's all right, I suppose it is,' said one, wiping her hands on a towel. 'I'll ask Sister Angelica to come and see you.'

She hung the towel up and left the room. The other nun regarded him doubtfully for a few moments, then resumed the washing up.

A few minutes later, the nun came back into the room, followed by another nun, leading a little girl by the hand.

Anthony stood up. 'Milly?'

He scarcely believed his luck, but . . . Although he had longed to see her, he'd never have recognized her from her photograph. With an odd tinge of disappointment, he repeated her name. 'Milly?'

The little girl looked at him blankly, then hid behind the nun's skirts.

'Her name is Agathé,' said the nun.

Of course it was. Anthony had concentrated so much on Milly that he hadn't really looked at Sister Angelica but, at the sound of her voice, he snapped his head up.

Sister Angelica was the nun he had spoken to in the courtyard.

'Colonel?' she asked, her eyes wide. 'What are you doing here?'

At the mention of his title, the two other women hissed in alarm.

Anthony smiled reassuringly. 'Sister Angelica, the less you know, the safer it is.' He turned to the two nuns by the sink. 'I am working for Belgium. For Belgium's sake and for yours, please forget you have ever seen me. If I am caught, I will be executed.'

At this fairly stark sentence, both women crossed themselves.

'It's hard to explain,' said Anthony. Time was passing. Captain von Casberg could only spend so long on his identity parade. Once Sister Marie-Eugénie had spoken up for poor old Baumann – as she was bound, in all conscience to do – the hunt would be on for the elusive Colonel Lieben. 'Sister Marie-Eugénie will tell you everything after I am gone.'

Sister Angelica studied his face for a few moments. 'You are the English spy,' she said quietly.

Anthony nodded.

'Sister Marie-Eugénie told me the new colonel had put her to the test, that he had pretended to be a spy.'

'There was no test,' said Anthony. 'I am the spy. I am English. I have come for Agathé.'

The nun looked alarmed. 'Sister Marie-Eugénie asked me to take care of Agathé.'

'Sister Marie-Eugénie told me to come to you,' said Anthony. 'I want to take Agathé back to England. Will you let me?'

Sister Angelica put her hand to her mouth. 'I can't,' she whispered. 'The Germans told us to keep the child safe. If anything happens to her, we will all suffer. I cannot let you take her.'

This was awkward. Anthony thought for a few moments. 'Have the Germans taken a keen interest in Agathé?'

She shook her head blankly. 'No, Monsieur.'

'Do the Germans know how many little girls of Agathé's age you have here?'

Again, the nun shook her head.

'Could you pretend another child is Agathé?' he asked. 'It's a deception, yes, but an innocent one.'

She frowned at him. 'It's possible,' she said slowly.

'The cause is good,' urged Anthony. 'Please let me take her.'

The nun studied his face once more and, to his relief, nodded slowly. 'How will you get away?' she asked simply.

'If you can take me to where the cars are parked, I can escape. But, Sister, we need to hurry. I haven't got much time.'

She took a deep breath. 'Come with me,' she said and, still holding the little girl by the hand, looked out of the kitchen door, turned and beckoned to him to follow.

'Do you know why the Germans are so interested in Agathé?' he asked as they walked along the hallway.

'No, Monsieur. I only know there is a mystery about the child. Sister Marie-Eugénie kept her very close.'

'She's nice,' piped up Milly. 'Sister Marie-Eugénie is nice.' Those were the first words she'd said.

Although anxious to get on, Anthony stopped and went down on one knee, so he was at eye-level with Milly. 'Sister Marie-Eugénie wants me to look after you,' he said. 'Will you be a good girl? Will you come with me and do what I ask?'

She regarded him solemnly, then nodded. 'All right. You're nice, too.'

'And what name do you like best?' He really did want to know what he should call her. 'Milly or Agathé?'

She put her head on one side. 'Agathé, of course. Agathé's a saint. She's important.'

'You're quite right,' said Anthony, giving her hand a gentle squeeze. 'Agathé it is.'

After the events of the past couple of hours, Anthony expected to be challenged on the way to the cars, but they reached the back of the house without seeing anyone.

Almost as equally incredible, the old stable yard, where two cars were parked, was deserted.

Leaving Agathé with Sister Angelica standing in the doorway of the house, he walked towards the two cars parked in the cobbled yard. One, a black Mercedes, had a Staff flag on the bonnet. The other was the Opel Becker had driven.

Anthony lifted the boot of the Opel and took out the jacket and cap of the driver's uniform Becker had left there.

'It was part of the plan,' he said in answer to Sister Angelica's enquiring look as he quickly stripped off his colonel's jacket and replaced it with the driver's tunic. And the astonishing thing is, he commented to himself, that this part of the plan, at least, came off.

Which car should he take? The Opel had obviously seen better days. The Mercedes, a sleek black machine, looked easily the better of the two. If he was going to continue his career as a car thief, he might as well pinch the better car.

He picked up Agathé and, with Sister Angelica's help, draped the coat over his shoulders to hide her.

'I want you to sit in the front of the car, but on the floor. I don't want you to be seen,' he explained.

'Is it a game?' asked Agathé.

'Yes, it's a game. But a serious game. Don't say a word.'

Holding the little girl close, he sat her down in the front footwell of the Mercedes. He draped his colonel's jacket and the coat round her. She'd be warm at least, if not very comfortable.

Scarcely believing his luck, Anthony walked round to the driver's side, when there came an interruption.

'Get out of my way, woman!' snapped a voice from inside the house and Captain von Casberg strode into the yard.

Behind him, Sister Angelica shrugged her shoulders with a 'what can I do' gesture.

Anthony stood by the car with as wooden an expression as he could muster.

'Here! You!' barked von Casberg, snapping his fingers at Anthony. 'Take me to headquarters.'

'Yes, sir!' said Anthony, saluting. There really wasn't anything else for it. He opened the back door. Von Casberg got in the car with very bad grace. Things, Anthony thought as he went to swing the starting handle, had obviously not gone well with the identity parade.

He had absolutely no choice but to drive von Casberg to headquarters. Fortunately the Captain wasn't a man to register unimportant details such as a driver's face. That was a plus. The minus was that he had absolutely no idea where headquarters were.

At the gate of the convent, he had a straightforward choice of left or right. A wayward memory of a song came to him. *Keep right on to the end of the road . . .*

He turned right.

The situation, to put it mildly, was interesting. He was trying to make as quick a getaway as he could and it was difficult to see how he could, granted there was a staff officer with a rocky temper in the back of the car.

He reached out, adjusted the driving mirror at the side of the windscreen and looked into the back of the car. Von Casberg had leaned back on the seat, his eyes closed. He said he was tired, thought Anthony.

A vague plan of parking the car and slipping away came briefly to mind and was immediately dismissed. The Captain was bound to notice the car stopping. No. He had to lose von Casberg and the quicker the better.

TWENTY-FIVE

The Rempart de Malines described a big circle around Louvain. It was flanked by large houses and was far too populated for Anthony's liking.

A turning about a mile along the Rempart de Malines looked as if it headed into the country. It was deserted. Anthony turned as smoothly as he could and drove along it.

He had got no more than half a mile or so when the road gave up being anything that could be described as a road – this was the country, after all – and deteriorated into a track.

The suspension of the Mercedes was excellent, but Anthony had only driven a few hundred yards before the gaping holes and unmissable ruts in the road tested the car's ability to the fullest.

It certainly got a response from von Casberg. He woke up with a start and looked around him. 'Driver! Where are you taking me, you fool!' he yelled. 'This isn't—'

He broke off as Agathé, who must have been nearly shaken to bits, climbed out of the footwell and on to the front seat.

'It's very bumpy,' she said plaintively.

Anthony reached out, pushed her back into the footwell, turned the steering wheel hard, slammed down on the clutch and pulled up the handbrake. The engine screamed a protest as the car skidded round in a tyre-shredding turn and came to a shuddering halt.

Anthony hurled himself out of the car and, pistol in hand, wrenched open the back door. Von Casberg was flung across the back seat.

'Get out,' he said curtly.

Utterly bewildered, von Casberg stared up at him.

Agathé crept onto the front passenger seat and, kneeling on it, looked at the two men with large, frightened, eyes.

Anthony reached for von Casberg's holster, unclipped it, took out the gun and threw it into the front of the car. 'Don't touch it, Agathé,' he warned, not taking his eyes off von Casberg.

Von Casberg's eyes narrowed to gimlet points. 'You are the spy,' he said softly.

Anthony shrugged. 'If you say so. Get out. And keep your hands up.'

He stepped back as von Casberg scrambled awkwardly out of the car.

One thing Anthony was sure of, and that was although the man may be a posturing, arrogant bully, he wasn't a coward. A coward would have whimpered, blustered and then crumpled. Von Casberg stood by the car, muscles tensed, his eyes never leaving the barrel of the automatic. He was a dangerous man.

'You have come for the child?'

'Obviously,' replied Anthony levelly. 'Tell me, von Casberg, exactly why is she so important?'

Von Casberg stared at him, then started to laugh. He seemed genuinely amused, which was quite a feat in the circumstances.

'You don't know? I'd ask your bosses, errand boy, to explain things to you.'

Anthony knew 'errand boy' shouldn't have stung but it did. 'Perhaps you don't know either.'

'Perhaps not,' agreed von Casberg. 'Or perhaps I do. I might even tell you, if we could come to an agreement.'

'Not a chance.' Von Casberg couldn't be trusted an inch.

'I see. In that case, what are you going to do?'

That was the question, thought Anthony ruefully. The sensible thing to do would be to shoot the man, but he wasn't a killer. He could – he would – shoot if his life or other lives depended on it, but he simply couldn't shoot a man in cold blood.

The countryside around consisted of rolling fields and deep ditches, without any handy trees to tie the man to. In any case, that needed two hands and he'd have to put down the gun. Von Casberg would certainly fight back if his assailant was unarmed. If the Mercedes had any luggage space to speak of, he could've been stowed in the boot, but it didn't. However, if von Casberg was stripped of his clothes, he was, to a large extent, stripped of his authority.

A completely naked man, alone in the countryside, would have some explaining to do. Without his uniform or any identification, it would take some persuasion for von Casberg to be accepted for the sprig of nobility he undoubtedly was.

It would certainly take him time to get back to headquarters. Lots of time. Without boots it would be difficult for a man to pick his way over the stony ground.

Anthony might not be a killer but he had a good idea of who he was up against. If von Casberg wanted to try walking with a bullet in his foot, that depended entirely on how much resistance he put up.

'Where are headquarters?' demanded Anthony.

Von Casberg looked surprised. 'Why d'you want to know?'

'That's my business.'

Von Casberg shrugged. 'Headquarters are . . .' He looked round, as if to point out the direction, then hurled himself into the car, making a grab for Agathé.

As Agathé screamed, Anthony, with supreme self-control, stopped himself from firing. Agathé was in the way. He couldn't get a clear shot.

With a triumphant laugh, von Casberg held onto Agathé.

'Drop the gun or I strangle the brat,' he gasped, groping for his revolver that Anthony had tossed onto the front seat. His hand was round Agathé's neck. There was no doubt he meant it. Agathé struggled furiously as the grip tightened. 'Now!'

Agathé's mouth opened in a soundless cry as her struggles lessened.

'Drop the gun!' he snarled.

For Agathé's sake Anthony had no choice. Reluctantly he bent down and put his automatic on the ground. His fingers closed around a stone. It wasn't much but it was all he could think of.

Von Casberg flung the child away from him as he brought the gun up, pointing it at Anthony. His finger tightened on the trigger. 'Hands up! I want to have you interrogated, Mr Spy. I want to know who you are and where you come from, but try anything and I will kill you.'

Anthony's shoulders drooped. 'All right,' he said dejectedly. 'You win.'

He raised his hands then flung the stone as hard as he could into von Casberg's face. His aim was good. Von Casberg screamed as, his face covered in blood from his broken nose, he reeled back, stumbling into the car. The revolver exploded in his hand.

'Agathé! Out of the way!' yelled Anthony, lunging forward as the bullet whistled wildly over his head.

His leap took him over the side of the car. He thudded his fist into von Casberg, catching him on the chin. Von Casberg fell back but brought up the gun.

Anthony twisted von Casberg's wrist as the gun fired once more. This time the bullet found a home.

Von Casberg's eyes opened wide in disbelief. His fingers scrabbled vainly at his chest, then, with a choking grunt, he fell back.

Agathé burst into tears.

'It's all right,' said Anthony, catching her up in his arms. 'Agathé, it's all right.'

He held her tightly, waiting for her sobs to subside. They had to get out of here and fast. Even though the fields seemed deserted, he couldn't count on the shots not being heard.

And then there was the matter of von Casberg's body.

He forced any urgency out of his voice as he carried her across the road and to the grassy verge that ran along the side of the ditch. 'Agathé,' he said as gently as he could, 'I'm going to put you down. I want you to wait here, like a good girl, and then we'll go for a drive. Yes?'

'Is the nasty man dead?' asked Agathé unexpectedly.

'Er . . . Yes, he's dead,' said Anthony, taken aback.

'My kitten went to sleep and wouldn't wake up and Grandmamma said that was being dead and I could ask the Sacred Heart of Jesus to look after her because I was sad but Sister Marie-Eugénie said we mustn't pray for kittens, only for people. Do I have to say prayers for the nasty man?'

There are those who deserve our prayers and those who need them, thought Anthony wryly. Von Casberg was very much in the latter category. And who the dickens was Grandmamma? It struck him again how little he really knew of Milly.

'I don't *want* to say prayers for the nasty man,' said Agathé, determinedly.

Anthony put aside this theological conundrum. 'No, sweetheart, you don't have to say prayers for him. You could say some for us, though.'

And that would, hopefully, keep her occupied while he got rid of the body. He put her down at the side of the road where she clasped her hands together. 'I'm saying my prayers,' she announced.

'Good,' called Anthony as he walked back to the car.

Von Casberg's body, with its staring eyes, broken nose and bullet-torn chest didn't inspire any prayer in him, only a fervent desire to get rid of it as quickly as possible.

He hauled the body out of the car and stripped off the uniform, stuffing it in a bundle beside the back seat. He pocketed von Casberg's identity disk and identity papers, then paused. Von Casberg had a ring with a heraldic eagle emblazoned on it. That had to be important, surely.

Feeling like a grave robber, Anthony tugged the ring off the dead finger. Then, bracing himself, he heaved the body up the steep grass verge and rolled it into the ditch.

The ditch was deep, waterlogged, and thick with rushes. Bracing himself, Anthony trod the body down into the mud. If anyone knew it was there, they could find it, but it was concealed

by the reeds and, with any luck, it would be a long time before
it came to light.

He wiped his boots down with von Casberg's handkerchief,
tossing the dirty cloth down beside the uniform in the back of the
car. 'Agathé,' he called, 'we've got to go now.'

'Are we going back to Sister Marie-Eugénie?' she asked
hopefully.

'No, I'm afraid not.'

'To Grandmamma's?'

'No, we can't go there either. You've got to be a good girl and
sit in the car in secret again.'

The little girl climbed unenthusiastically back into the
footwell and Anthony set off, turning at random at the next
likely-looking crossroads. Rocky though the road was, it took
him away both from Louvain and the ditch where the Captain
lay concealed.

Quarter of an hour later they arrived on the outskirts of a tiny
hamlet. Anthony could see two German soldiers, lounging by a
brazier by a hut at the side of the road. There was a pot of coffee
warming on the brazier.

Warning Agathé to be quiet, he drew the car to a halt and got
out.

The two soldiers, who had snapped to attention at the sight
of the car, relaxed as they saw Anthony, apparently alone and in
his driver's uniform.

'Are you lost, mate?' called one of the soldiers, a burly, thickset
man.

'Too blinking right,' said Anthony morosely. 'Anyone'd get lost
in this bleeding country.'

The soldiers laughed. 'No one'd come here on purpose.'

Anthony shared the laugh and took out the packet of Ecksteins
he had bought in the station bar that morning – was it really only
that morning? – and breaking a cigarette in half, lit it. 'Want a
fag?' he asked, tossing them a cigarette.

'Cheers, pal,' said the burly soldier, breaking the cigarette in
half as Anthony had done and passing the other half to his
companion. 'Have a coffee,' he said pouring out some steaming
liquid into a battered tin mug. Anthony didn't want it, but he knew
better than to seem in a rush.

The cup was passed round between the three men. It wasn't exactly coffee but it was hot.

'So where are you trying to get to then?' asked the thin soldier.

'Anywhere with a wireless set will do. I've got to ask for orders, see?'

'Does it have to be Staff?' asked the burly man, looking at the car. 'Because the nearest Staff is over by Louvain.'

'No, just the nearest place with a wireless.'

The other soldier scratched his chin. 'I reckon that'd be Elewyt. Straight down this road and turn left at the crossroads. I hope you don't mind waiting though, pal. Major Kabel is a real swine. He won't go out of his way to help the likes of us, oh no.'

'Thanks for the warning,' said Anthony, throwing the miniscule stub of his cigarette into the brazier. 'I'd better be off. I'll catch it if I don't contact my unit soon.'

Elewyt, thought Anthony as he strolled back to the car. Elewyt and Major Kabel. He drove until he was out of sight, then pulled over.

Agathé scrambled out of the footwell. 'Please let me sit on the seat,' she begged. 'It smells all petrolly.'

He didn't want the poor kid passing out because of petrol fumes and it must be really uncomfortable down there. 'All right,' he agreed reluctantly. 'But if I say get down, you have to get down at once, yes?'

Anthony took a map from the map case beside the driver's door as Agathé settled herself on the seat beside him. He recalled the information Talbot had given him. With a grunt of satisfaction he pinpointed the spot on the map. Field number thirteen was about twenty miles beyond Elewyt. That would do very nicely.

At Elewyt, Anthony took the bull by the horns. Dressed in his colonel's uniform, he strode into the village hall that housed the army post.

Last August the Belgium Army had nearly reached the village but now the tide of war had moved on, leaving the little village in a sullen peace.

'Major Kabel?' he snapped at the corporal at the door. 'I wish to see Major Kabel at once.'

Swallowing, the corporal escorted him inside the hall, where, after a short interval, Major Kabel, a second-rate appointee if Anthony had ever seen one, hurried towards him.

'Colonel?' he began, then stopped, his eyes widening as he took in the medical insignia on Anthony's uniform.

Anthony smiled thinly. 'Do not be deceived, Major. As I am sure you are aware, things are not always what they seem.'

The Mercedes, with its Staff flag, was parked outside the door. Anthony could only hope that Agathé wouldn't choose this moment to poke her head out of the car.

'Take a glance outside.'

The Major did and gulped. 'Sir?'

'I wish to send a wireless message. The wording must be precise, you understand? I will supervise the transmission myself. It is to our Embassy in New York.'

'Yes, sir . . .' The Major seemed in an agony of indecision.

'Is there a problem, Major?'

Major Kabel writhed. 'I'm very sorry, sir, but we have received a report of an English spy masquerading in the uniform of a Dr Lieutenant Colonel. Can I see your papers, sir?' His voice trailed off as he met Anthony's icy stare.

Von Casberg would never show his papers to a mere major. Anthony glared at him then, peeled off his gloves, revealing von Casberg's ring. 'Is this good enough for you, Major, or do you need further reassurance?'

At the sight of the ring, Major Kabel paled. Von Casberg must've had people react like this all the time. Anthony was careful not to show any emotion except impatience as the Major virtually grovelled.

'Very good, sir. Let me take you to the wireless transmitter. I do apologize, sir.'

Minutes later, Anthony had the satisfaction of seeing his message encrypted and on its way to New York. What the German Embassy in New York would make of it, he could only guess, but Room 40, the Admiralty code breakers in Whitehall, would certainly intercept and read the German code.

Hansel and Gretel number thirteen.

'Well done, Agathé,' he said quietly as he got back into the Mercedes. 'We're going to take another drive and then we're going to wait for an aeroplane.'

There was a very satisfying completeness, thought Anthony, as he nosed the Mercedes out onto the open road once more, about using the German wireless system to summon an aeroplane to escape from German occupied territory.

Hansel and Gretel were on their way to field number thirteen and on their way home.

TWENTY-SIX

Tara tucked the eiderdown round the sleeping little girl. Stepping away from the bed she looked round what had been the spare room and was now an impromptu nursery. The fire in the grate, safely encased behind a fireguard, cast a flickering but reassuring light into the room, and the nightlight in its saucer of water was on the bookshelf, safely out of reach. Looking down at little Agathé, (Tara still thought of her as Milly) with her new fluffy toy lamb snuggled up in the bed beside her, she felt a lump in her throat.

She shook herself as the doorbell rang and hurried to the door, intercepting Ellen, the maid.

'I'll answer the door, Ellen. I know who it is. Can you keep an eye out for little Agathé? I don't think she'll wake up, but come and tell me if she does.'

'Very good, ma'am. I'll see to the little one.'

She opened the door to find, as expected, Sir Charles Talbot. Anthony had wanted to see him as soon as he had got off the boat train in London. In the hubbub of St Pancras Station, Tara had insisted that a couple of hours wouldn't make any difference. At the very least, he should come home and have a bath and dinner first. And, she added, picking up the little girl and giving her a hug, it would give Agathé the chance to get settled into her new home.

'It's good to see you again, Mrs Brooke,' said Sir Charles, coming into the hallway. He hung up his hat and coat on the stand and followed her into the sitting room, his face creasing in a smile as he saw Anthony. 'Brooke! I can't tell you how glad I am you got back safely.'

'The feeling's mutual,' said Anthony, walking to the sideboard. 'Whisky? And Madeira for you, Tara?'

'I knew it was dangerous,' said Tara accusingly, as she took her Madeira. She turned to Sir Charles. 'I can't get much out of him, apart from the fact the journey home was long-winded.'

'Well, so it was,' countered Anthony. 'Don't worry, Tara, you can have as many details as you like, but the main thing is, both little Agathé and I are here.'

'Agathé?' questioned Sir Charles.

'It's Milly's preferred name. That's what she was called by the nuns in the orphanage.' He stretched out his feet towards the fire and sipped his whisky contentedly. 'My word, Talbot, it was a relief when I heard that aeroplane come into land.'

'You knew you'd be able to get home, though, didn't you?' asked Tara, suddenly worried. 'There was no doubt about that?'

'Not really, Mrs Brooke,' Sir Charles reassured her. 'Any agent of the White Lady could carry a message back to us.'

'And I knew that Room 40 could read the German transmissions,' put in Anthony with a grin. 'Even so, it took some brass neck to stride into a German post and whistle up a British aeroplane. The rest of the journey really was just long-winded, with about fourteen different trains, a boat and another train. Poor little Agathé was horribly seasick.'

'Like Mrs Brooke, I'm anxious to hear the full story of your adventures,' said Sir Charles, 'but first of all, we need facts.' He cocked an enquiring eyebrow at Anthony. 'What's the plot? Do you know why the Jowetts were murdered? And why Harper and his crew wanted to kidnap Milly?'

Anthony shook his head. 'I'm afraid I don't know. On that score, I'm no wiser now than when I left England.'

Sir Charles groaned. 'Surely you must have found out something? Didn't you meet Sister Marie whatever her name was?' Anthony nodded. 'Couldn't she tell you what it was all about?'

'I'm sure she could, but I wasn't able to ask her,' said Anthony dryly. 'I'm sorry, Talbot. You'll understand, once I've explained.' He took a cigarette from the box on the table. 'Have you caught Harper? He'll be able to tell us what's going on.'

'I'm sure he could, *if* we could lay hands on him,' said Sir Charles glumly.

Anthony paused in the action of striking a match. 'You mean you don't know anything?'

'Not a thing.'

Anthony lit his cigarette and threw the match into the fire with a savage gesture. 'We're back where we started,' he said in disgust. 'The whole thing's ruddy well hopeless. We don't have a clue what it's all about. We haven't got any further forward. We've achieved precisely nothing.'

'That's not true, Anthony,' protested Tara. 'We've got Milly. She's safe. And so are you.'

Anthony looked at her and grinned reluctantly. 'There is that,' he conceded, 'but I really wish I knew what was going on.'

Sixty-four miles away, James Dunwoody, chauffeur in the employ of *Automobiles de Luxe Ltd* of Islington, was asking himself the same question.

Mr Dunwoody enjoyed his job. There was no questioning the deluxe nature of his car. It was a Rolls-Royce Silver Ghost, which, according to the adverts, was the best car in the world. Mr Dunwoody agreed. Mind you, the customers paid to enjoy it.

For the princely sum of six pounds, six shillings a day, of which Mr Dunwoody received eighteen shillings, Mr Dunwoody would drive the Silver Ghost at the customer's bidding. Usually that bidding involved waiting patiently outside hotels, restaurants and West End shops, but that was all part of the day's work.

A job such as this, a straightforward drive along the Great Dover Road to Canterbury, was unusual but that wasn't any of James Dunwoody's business. His client was unusual, too. His customers were usually actors, Americans or aristocrats, but this woman was a servant, a nursemaid, with a little girl in tow.

James Dunwoody was inclined to be friendly but the nursemaid, a stiffly correct, snooty sort of creature, obviously didn't want to chat. The little girl – James Dunwoody liked children – sat in crushed silence beside her nurse. Poor kid, he reflected. Her parents obviously had more money than Creosote, as he'd heard it expressed, if they could afford to waft their servants and offspring around in Rolls-Royces, but, if it was him, he'd want a kindlier nurse in charge. Rich people could be very rum.

It was when they were driving through the silent village of

Lower Harbledown that the nursemaid, Miss Springer, spoke for
the first time in miles.

'Driver! Where are we?'

'Lower Harbledown, Miss, in Kent,' replied James, who resented
being addressed as 'Driver' by a mere nursemaid. Who did she
think she was? A ruddy duchess or something? Still, it was conversation of a sort, he supposed. 'It's Upper Harbledown next.' He
recalled something that always went down well with his American
passengers. 'This is the old Watling Street what the Romans built.
We should reach Canterbury by—'

'Very good,' said Miss Springer repressively. 'Please stop after
Upper Harbledown.'

'Upper Harbledown?' repeated James in surprise. 'Do you want
to go to Upper Harbledown?'

He couldn't think why anyone would want to go to Upper
Harbledown. It was an unremarkable little hamlet without anything
to attract a visitor, especially on a cold night in autumn.

'I do not wish to go to Upper Harbledown,' said Miss Springer
icily. 'I require you to stop the car after we have passed Upper
Harbledown.'

Well, he was the driver and she was the customer, and it wasn't
his place to ask questions, he supposed, but what on earth was
going on?

The village came and went. James Dunwoody obediently
brought the car to a halt.

'Is this all right for you?' he asked, an edge of sarcasm in his voice.

'This will do nicely, thank you.'

After a couple of minutes listening to the wind in the trees and
watching the grass on the verge picked out by the headlights,
James tried again. 'Are we waiting for something, Miss?'

'Yes,' she replied tightly. 'Please be quiet.'

James swallowed a reply and sat in silence. Then he heard it.
It was a car engine, close at hand. He turned his head, looking
back along the road.

A big car, a Vauxhall at a guess, had come out of a side road
and was approaching slowly.

Miss Springer opened the back door and stepped down onto the
verge. Reaching back inside the car, she picked up the little girl
and waited on the roadside.

'What's going on?' asked James in bewilderment.

The Vauxhall drew to a halt.

Without a word, Miss Springer crossed to the waiting Vauxhall, opened the back door of the car and, putting the little girl on the seat, climbed in after her and closed the door.

James Dunwoody wasn't alarmed yet, but he was seriously puzzled. Miss Springer was an odd customer, but even the oddest of his customers had never calmly stopped the Rolls mid-journey, got out of his car and into another like this.

'Oy! What's going on?' he repeated and then stopped.

The driver of the Vauxhall got out of the car.

As he walked round the front of the Rolls-Royce, James could see his face was covered by a black scarf.

James knew real fear at that moment. 'What's . . .?' he said again and then gasped as he saw the gun in the driver's hand. 'Is . . . Is this a hold-up?' he gasped, raising his hands.

'No,' said the driver, raising the gun. 'This is murder.'

Anthony treated himself to a late breakfast that morning. As always, at breakfast, he had the *Telegraph* propped up on the coffee pot. He scanned the headlines quickly but the war had come to a standstill, politics were dull and the stop press announcement of 'Upper Harbledown, Kent. Chauffeur found shot in Rolls-Royce' carried no further details to awake anyone's curiosity.

He was far more interested in Tara's account of what Agathé had done and said that morning to both Tara and Ellen, the maid.

'. . . And, of course, although she speaks French, and poor Ellen hasn't a word of French, Ellen forgot she couldn't understand and told her to bring her lamb. Would you believe Agathé went and got it straight away and said "lamb" as clearly as anything! Ellen was tremendously impressed.'

'So it's going to be all right, d'you think?' asked Anthony. 'Ellen acting as nursemaid, I mean? I know she offered, but, after all, she's not trained.'

'She's the eldest of a family of eight, though, and she's very kind-hearted, if awfully sentimental. When she saw Agathé saying her prayers, even if they were in French, she nearly broke into tears.'

'Lots of prayers,' said Anthony with a grin. 'That's what growing up in a convent does for you. By the way, Tara, can she have a kitten? Apparently she had a kitten called Minou she was awfully fond of. She wants another Minou.'

'Minou?' repeated Tara. 'That's the French pet name for a kitten, isn't it? We'll have to explain the name to Ellen,' she added. 'Of course she can have a kitten. It might even grow up to be a decent mouser. We'll choose one from the pet shop this morning.' She broke off as the telephone rang. 'I'll answer it,' she said, pushing her chair back. 'Ellen's in the nursery.'

It was Sir Charles Talbot. 'Good morning, Mrs Brooke! I'm sorry to trouble you, but can Brooke come along to Scotland Yard? Right away, I mean? I'm with Douglas Lynton now.'

'I'll pass the message on, Sir Charles. What's it about, or shouldn't I ask?'

'It's about the chauffeur who was shot in Kent. It's in the papers.'

TWENTY-SEVEN

'What's all this about a chauffeur being shot?' asked Anthony, as he pulled out a chair and sat down. 'There was an item in the stop press, but that's all.'

'A fuller story is in the later editions,' said Sir Douglas Lynton. He glanced across the desk to Sir Charles Talbot. 'Talbot has got some ideas about it. Quite fanciful ideas, in my opinion.'

'I'll be surprised if Brooke doesn't agree with me,' said Sir Charles equably. 'Eh, Brooke?'

Anthony shrugged. 'If I had the slightest idea of what you're talking about, I very well might.'

Sir Douglas picked up a copy of the *Daily Mirror* and passed it across the desk. 'This account is as good as any of the others.'

Anthony picked up the paper.

> Murder in Rolls-Royce. Ploughman's Appalling Discovery.
> Further to our earlier report, we can now reveal that the police are treating the death of Mr James Dunwoody, 46, of Kenner Road, Islington, as murder.

Mr Dunwoody, a chauffeur for *Automobiles de Luxe Ltd* of
Islington, was found in the early hours of this morning, slumped
at the wheel of his car, a Rolls-Royce Silver Ghost, on the
Great Dover Road, near Upper Harbledown, Kent.

The gruesome discovery was made by Mr Clarence Wistow, 53,
ploughman at Abbot's Farm, Upper Harbledown. Mr Wistow,
who at first assumed that Mr Dunwoody had been taken ill,
went to his aid, and was appalled to discover the chauffeur was
dead, killed by a gunshot to the head.

The police, who were immediately summoned to the scene,
called in the local doctor, Dr W.R. Leighton, who pronounced
life was extinct and estimated that the death had occurred
around ten o'clock last night. Self-destruction was immediately ruled out as a cause of death, both because of the angle
of the shot and the absence of any weapon.

Mr Dunwoody, who was married with three children, has
been a servant of *Automobiles de Luxe Ltd* for four years and
has a spotless record of service.

A regular attender at Offord St Methodist Chapel, Islington,
Mr Dunwoody, a lifelong teetotaller, had no enemies and was
respected by all who knew him. No robbery was attempted
and no motive can currently be ascribed to this ghastly outrage.

Anthony looked up from the paper. 'Well, it's all very sad, no
doubt, if a trifle wordy. It's damned odd, as well. There doesn't
seem to have been any reason to have killed the poor chap.'

'Precisely,' said Sir Charles. 'As you know, I keep an eye out
for odd happenings and this seemed odd enough for me to want
to know more details.'

'So you came to me,' said Douglas Lynton with a sigh. 'Well,
you're perfectly right about one thing, at least. It's all very odd
indeed. There wasn't any sign of violence at the scene and whatever
the motive was, it wasn't robbery. All the *Automobiles de Luxe*
drivers carry five pounds in cash in the car, for petrol and other
expenses, in addition to which, Mr Dunwoody had nearly three
pounds in cash in his wallet. Add to that is the fact that a Rolls-
Royce is well worth stealing, but the car was untouched. For all
the world it looks as if Mr Dunwoody parked his car and placidly
waited to be shot.'

'Hold on,' said Anthony slowly. 'If he was a chauffeur, who was he chauffeuring? There must've been someone else in the car. Unless he'd dropped them off and was on his way home, I suppose, but either way, there must've been someone else in the car last night. There's no mention of them in the paper.'

'No, there isn't,' agreed Sir Douglas, 'but I thought exactly the same thing. Major Barnes, the Chief Constable of Kent, passed the case to us as James Dunwoody is a London man. Naturally enough, the first thing we did was to check with Dunwoody's firm, *Automobiles de Luxe Ltd.* Mr Dunwoody did have a client in the car, or should've done, at any rate. He called for her at The Rutland Hotel, Mayfair. Dunwoody picked her up at half past five. His instructions were to take her to The Lamb and Flag in Canterbury – it's an old coaching inn – where a room had been booked.'

Sir Charles wriggled impatiently. 'There were two clients,' he broke in. He paused significantly. 'A nursemaid and a little girl. The Rutland Hotel confirmed that.'

Anthony's head shot up. 'A nursemaid?' he repeated.

'Now you understand why I wanted you here, Brooke,' said Sir Charles.

Anthony swallowed. 'Was the nursemaid Annie Colbeck?'

'I think so,' agreed Sir Charles to a snort of disapproval from Douglas Lynton.

'The nursemaid gave her name as Springer,' he said.

Sir Charles shook his head. 'Anybody can call themselves anything, Lynton. You know that. The description, such as it is, from the Rutland Hotel fits that of Annie Colbeck well enough. Unfortunately, we don't know who the child is. The hotel registers, both for the Rutland and the Lamb and Flag, have them listed as Miss Springer and charge. We only know the child's a little girl because the Rutland Hotel people told us so.'

'Who booked the car?' asked Anthony.

Sir Charles shrugged. 'It could have been Annie Colbeck – all right, Lynton, Miss Springer – herself. The booking had been made that morning in person by a Mrs Marston. Again, the description, such as it is, could easily be that of the nursemaid. Her only really distinguishing feature was a small red mark on her left cheek. She covered it up with make-up but the lady clerk at *Automobiles de*

Luxe noticed it all the same. I don't know if Annie Colbeck had a birthmark, but that's something we could check with the Jowetts' housekeeper, I suppose. Mrs Marston, to call her that, paid the cost of the car in full, so *Automobiles De Luxe* didn't ask for her address.'

'Hold on,' said Anthony slowly. 'A birthmark, you say? That rings a bell.' He thought for a couple of moments, then looked up. 'Miss Anston had a birthmark! Miss Anston of the Diligent. Tara noticed it when she called into the agency.'

'Did she, by Jove?' said Sir Charles in satisfaction. 'What d'you think, Brooke? I think this is the plot, the plot that Father Quinet overheard.'

'But where does Milly come into it?' asked Anthony.

Sir Charles shrugged. 'I don't know, but we've got a murdered man and missing child.'

Sir Douglas snorted in disgust. 'Dammit, Talbot, if someone wanted to murder James Dunwoody, they could shoot him any time they fancied. They need hardly plot and plan weeks beforehand. Dash it, man, the idea's ridiculous!'

'Of course it is,' said Anthony quietly. 'I think poor Mr Dunwoody was incidental to the proceedings. What about the fact that this so-called Mrs Marston had a birthmark? Don't you find that significant?'

Sir Douglas sighed. 'I certainly don't find it as compelling as you seem to.' He turned to Sir Charles. 'Lots of women have birthmarks, so there's no need to be so excited about it. I don't know where the nursemaid's got too, but if there was a man waving a gun about, she very likely took fright and ran off.'

'So where is she now?' demanded Sir Charles. 'Why hasn't she come forward?'

'Damned if I know,' muttered Sir Douglas, 'but dash it, Talbot, this can't be your precious plot.'

'Why not? According to Father Quinet, the plot was to murder a man and endanger a little girl. I think she's been kidnapped.'

Once again Sir Douglas snorted in disbelief. 'Kidnapped? My dear sir, this is London, not New York. We don't *have* kidnappings here.'

'That's not a natural law,' said Anthony mildly. 'That's a case of custom and habit, surely.'

'Joshua Harper, who's in league with Annie Colbeck, is American,' said Sir Charles softly.

'But . . .' began Sir Douglas, when the telephone on his desk rang. With a brief excuse, he picked it up.

'Well,' said Sir Douglas, replacing the receiver after a short conversation. 'We've got your Mrs Harrop downstairs, Brooke.'

'My Mrs Harrop?' began Anthony blankly, then stopped. 'The Jowetts' housekeeper, you mean? What does she want?'

'We asked her to bring any post that arrived for the Jowetts to us,' said Sir Douglas. 'It is a murder enquiry, after all, for all you seem to have lost sight of it, what with plots and kidnaps and heaven knows what. She usually leaves any letters at the desk but she was insistent that this particular letter should go to someone in charge, as she put it. Apparently it's got a foreign stamp.' He grinned. 'That means it has to be important.'

'She might be right, at that,' said Anthony, standing up. 'I'll see her.'

Mrs Harrop was waiting in an anti-room. She looked up with surprised delight as Anthony and Sir Charles came in.

'Colonel Ralde? I never thought I'd be lucky enough to see you, sir. It's good to see you again, indeed it is.'

'And it's a pleasure to see you, Mrs Harrop,' said Anthony. 'I happened to be with the assistant commissioner when you called. I'd like to introduce you to a colleague of mine, Mr Monks.'

'How d'you do,' said Sir Charles. 'The Colonel has told me how helpful you were with the sad business at Pettifer's Court.'

'I'd do anything I can to help,' she said, clearly reassured by the warmth of his Irish brogue. She heaved a sigh. 'It makes me so sad to think of it, especially now poor Mr Maurice has been taken as well. I was in floods when I seen that in the paper.'

'It does credit to your feelings, Mrs Harrop,' said Anthony gently. He would've liked to have told her that Maurice Knowle was making a full recovery, but that would never do.

'Are you still at the Jowetts' house?' asked Sir Charles.

'Yes I am, sir. The solicitor, Mr Hawley, he told me to stay put and look after things until it could all be sorted out. Mind you,

it's a lot better since Colonel Ralde laid the ghost to rest. To think
I'd got myself so worked up about that room being haunted, and
all the time it was the old skylight off the latch!'

'It was a very natural thing to think under the circumstances,
Mrs Harrop,' said Anthony reassuringly.

'It's good of you to say so, sir. I was that relieved.' She sighed.
'But still, I mustn't take up your time like this.'

She reached into her capacious handbag. 'It's about this letter, sir.
It's addressed to Mr Jowett. I thought as how it had to be important,
coming as it does, from foreign parts. I'm not one to make a fuss,
but if it is important, I didn't want it to be overlooked.'

As she produced the envelope, Anthony could see the French
stamp. 'I think you've done exactly the right thing, Mrs Harrop.
Can I see the letter?'

She put it into his outstretched hand.

Anthony slit it open and took out the single sheet it contained.
The letter was written in English and the signature consisted of
two initials: P.D.

P.D.? Who was P.D.? Then he froze as the answer hit him.
Paul Diefenbach.

Anthony stared at the letter. The address – the only address – was
Brussels. Brussels for Pete's sake? Brussels, deep within occupied
Belgium. What the devil had Diefenbach been doing in Belgium?
He was supposed to be in South America, not across the channel
in Belgium.

He became aware of Mrs Harrop's puzzled frown.

'Is everything all right, sir?' she asked tentatively.

Anthony forced himself to smile. 'Perfectly all right, thank you,
Mrs Harrop.' He folded the letter up and put it back in its envelope.
Whatever Diefenbach had written, he wanted to read it without
the housekeeper's concerned gaze upon him.

Sir Charles came to his aid. 'You've done exactly the right thing
to bring it to us, Mrs Harrop. Can I show you out? It's easy to
get lost in these corridors.'

Taking her by the arm, he led her gently away, leaving Anthony
with the letter.

It was dated the 4th of September. That was eighteen days
ago.

Dear Ted,

I'm writing this in the hope it'll reach you before I get back.

I'm not sure what's happening, but the facts are these. I arrived at Mme. Legrand's to find Rosie has gone! It might be all right – Mme. Legrand showed me a letter Yvonne had written which the nursemaid had with her – but even so, I'm very uneasy.

Apparently, the nursemaid, a Miss Springer, spun Mme. Legrand a yarn about being granted free passage through the border, which sounds like nonsense to me.

Can you write to Yvonne or even, old friend, see her and get the truth of the matter? As always, don't say a word of this at the bank – as you know, I can't prove anything but I have my suspicions.

Regarding the official business, my mind has been made up. I know I argued the toss with you, but I was wrong. Germany has turned Belgium into a slave state. Conditions here are worse than anything we've read in the papers and I'm going to tell the old man as much. The people are literally starving and scraping by on American handouts. I might have to see him in person to get the message through but he can't go ahead.

P.D.

Anthony looked up as Sir Charles came back into the room. 'It seems as if our Mr Diefenbach has had a change of heart,' he said, handing him the letter.

'Diefenbach? Paul Diefenbach?' exclaimed Sir Charles, taking the letter. He read it through quickly. '" *Don't say a word of this at the bank*",' he quoted softly. 'What the hell's going on there?'

'Something both Diefenbach and Edward Jowett suspected but couldn't prove, by the sound of it,' said Anthony. 'It has to do with money, obviously. Have you approached them officially, Talbot?'

Sir Charles shook his head. 'No. The only official contact with the Capital and Counties was when Inspector Tanner interviewed the bank officials in connection with Jowett's death.'

Anthony breathed a sigh of relief. 'That's something.'

Sir Charles was still staring at the letter. 'I can't get over it,' he muttered. 'Damn it, Brooke, he had a passage booked on the *Union Castle* for New York! We've had the dust thrown in our eyes and no mistake. Who the devil is this Madame Legrand, I wonder?'

'I don't know,' said Anthony, 'but we know who Rosie is. She has to be the child who the nursemaid, Miss Springer, took from James Dunwoody's Rolls-Royce.'

Sir Charles nodded. 'I agree.' He read the letter through once more, then put it on the table. 'Well, there's one thing. At least we know what to do next, and that's to see Yvonne. Yvonne has to be Diefenbach's wife, of course.'

'Yes, she is,' said Anthony absently.

Sir Charles picked up his coat. 'Come on!'

Anthony held a hand up. 'Talbot, wait! We can't walk in on Yvonne Broussard.'

'Why the devil not?'

'Because she's Paul Diefenbach's wife and if we do, we'll give the whole game away.' Anthony clasped his hand to his chin, his mind racing. After a couple of moments he sighed and lit a cigarette.

'Look at the letter,' he said. 'It's dated 4th September. That's nearly three weeks ago. If this child, Rosie, was taken three weeks or so ago, how come she was only kidnapped last night?'

'Because . . .' Sir Charles stopped. 'Coincidence?' he suggested.

'Coincidence, my foot! Look how anxious the gang have been throughout to know where Diefenbach is. They planted that thug, Stevenson, on Maurice Knowle in case Diefenbach got in touch with him. I bet you anything you like they've got a spy planted on Yvonne Broussard, too. Read the letter again. What would be the first thing Paul Diefenbach would do after arriving back in this country?'

'See his wife, even if they are separated,' Sir Charles replied.

'Exactly. And once the gang know he's in the country, they can start the ball rolling by kidnapping the child. As much as anything else, this is a plot to get *him.*'

Sir Charles sat down. 'So what do we do?' he asked. 'If there is a spy at Yvonne Broussard's, we can't interview her at home. Can we ask her to come into Scotland Yard?'

Anthony shook his head. 'It's too risky. Only us and Harper

and his gang know there's a connection between this child's disap-
pearance, James Dunwoody's murder, Paul Diefenbach and Yvonne
Broussard. The fact that they don't know we know is about the
one advantage we have. If we ask her to come into the Yard, they
might not be able to overhear the conversation, but they'll sure as
hell know we've had it.'

'So what can we do?' demanded Sir Charles in frustration.

Anthony took a last pull at his cigarette, then ground it out in
the ashtray. 'Let's ask Tara,' he said.

TWENTY-EIGHT

The door of 73, Elgin Road opened.

'Well?' said the maid, looking at the representative of
the Women's Defence Relief Corps standing in front of
her. 'What do you want?'

Tara, secure in her severe grey uniform and official badge, drew
herself up to her full height, regarding the maid coldly.

She knew perfectly well that visitors from the WDRC were not
popular. Despite doing some sterling work, they could be, not to
put too fine a point on it, officially sponsored busybodies.

The WDRC kept a close watch on public houses, maintained
the morality of the nation by hunting down romantically inclined
couples in parks and any man out of uniform had learned to
dread the grey-uniformed women presenting them with a white
feather.

As far as most householders were concerned, the Women's
Defence Relief Corps spent their time checking that all the seem-
ingly countless regulations of the Defence of the Realm Acts were
being followed. That could mean anything from checking that
waste paper was properly collected to forcibly suggesting that too
many servants were kept who would be better off otherwise
employed.

'If you're here to check on our pig-swill, or to say that I should
be working in one of those nasty factories, you can clear off,' said
the maid truculently. 'This is a decent house with decent people,

for all that the mistress is foreign, and we do everything right, see?'

'I'll thank you to keep a civil tongue in your head, my girl,' said Tara, imperiously. 'Your mistress is foreign, you say?'

'Yes, but she's a Belgian. Thems who we're fighting for, ain't it?'

'I need to see her, all the same. Be so good as to tell her I'm here. And I am not accustomed to being kept waiting on the doorstep.'

The maid bridled, but the tone of voice, the uniform and the badge had its effect.

After a few moments Yvonne Broussard came into the hall. She looked, thought Tara, with a quick stab of sympathy, dreadful. She was pale with dark shadows under her eyes.

'What is it you want?' she began quickly. 'I am busy, you understand, busy. I can see no one.'

Tara glanced at the dining-room door and slipped her hand into the pocket of her coat. She sensed, rather than saw, the maid behind the partly open door. She was listening. 'Can we speak in private, Madame? It's a matter of regulations.'

'I can see no one, I tell you,' began Yvonne Broussard, then glanced at the paper Tara was holding out. There was one word written on it.

Rosie.

Yvonne gave a little cry. Tara put her finger to her lips, indicating the dining-room door.

Yvonne swayed on the spot. For a moment Tara thought she was going to faint, then, with a supreme effort, Yvonne collected herself.

'Regulations?' she repeated in a distant voice.

'Regulations,' repeated Tara for the benefit of the listening maid.

An hour later Tara, having shed her grey uniform, admitted Yvonne into the flat. Yvonne grasped her hands, staring pleadingly into her eyes. 'Please, tell me what you know! You said nothing – nothing!'

That was true. At 73, Elgin Road, Tara didn't know who was listening and couldn't trust Yvonne to keep quiet after she'd gone. Realizing she sounded exactly like a crook, a kidnapper or a blackmailer, she had told Yvonne Broussard to say nothing to anyone, but to come along to the flat in an hour's time.

'I'll tell you everything I know, and welcome,' said Tara, moved by the Belgian woman's evident anxiety, 'but we can't talk in the hall. Come into the sitting room.'

She led the way. As they came into the room, Anthony and Sir Charles stood up.

Yvonne gasped at the sight of them, then turned accusingly on Tara. 'I thought we would be alone.'

'It's all right,' said Tara reassuringly. 'We're all here to help you.' She indicated Anthony and Sir Charles. 'This is my husband, Dr Anthony Brooke, and Mr Monks, who is working with the police.'

Yvonne stared at Anthony. 'I know you! You're the private detective. You came to see me, to ask about the Jowetts.' She looked at him with frightened eyes. 'Your name, it was not Brooke!' She looked about her wildly. 'You mean to keep me here, to harm me?'

'Not in the least, Madame Broussard,' said Sir Charles soothingly. 'We have your best interests at heart. But please, can we all sit down? You're among friends.'

Yvonne sat down tentatively on the edge of a chair. She glanced to where the French windows opened onto the garden, obviously weighing up the chances of escape.

'Now, Madame Broussard,' said Sir Charles, 'perhaps you'd be so good as to tell us what your relationship with Rosie is?'

Yvonne didn't answer, but gazed at him.

'She's your daughter, isn't she?' said Tara.

Yvonne closed her eyes for a moment, then nodded slowly.

Anthony cleared his throat and spoke for the first time. 'We appreciate how worried you are. We are right, aren't we? It was Rosie, your daughter, who was kidnapped last night? She was with a nursemaid, a Miss Springer, in a Rolls-Royce. The chauffeur, James Dunwoody, was killed and your daughter has been taken.'

Yvonne's eyes widened in terror. Her lips moved silently, but she said nothing.

'The thing is,' continued Anthony, 'is that we believe that your husband, Paul Diefenbach, saw you recently. There is some sort of plot surrounding both your husband and your daughter and we want to prevent any harm coming to either of them.'

Again, Yvonne's lips moved silently, then she drew herself up and shook her head. 'I can tell you nothing, Monsieur,' she said, picking her words carefully. 'Nothing at all.'

'Please, Madame Broussard,' said Sir Charles earnestly. 'Your husband may be in very great danger.'

She bit her lip, then shook her head. More questions followed but she remained silent. Tara felt acutely sorry for her. Even though they were trying to help, it was horrible to try and drag information from a woman who was so clearly unwilling to give it.

'I can tell you nothing!' Yvonne Broussard said eventually. She picked up her bag. 'Please, I must go.'

Anthony sighed deeply. 'Madame Broussard, perhaps you will understand if I tell you the whole story.' It was, he thought, the only possible way to make her appreciate the issues at stake. 'This started with the deaths of Mr and Mrs Jowett and their butler, Hawthorne.'

He launched into the story of what happened that day. Yvonne Broussard gazed at him intently, then broke off.

'*Mon Dieu!* Who is that?' she asked breathlessly. 'Who is that?'

Through the open window came the voices of Ellen, the maid, and little Agathé from the garden.

A squeaky meep of a meow told them that Ellen and Agathé were playing with Minou, the new kitten.

'*Minou, Minou,*' they heard Agathé call happily. '*J'adore petit Minou.*'

Yvonne Broussard, her face frozen in apprehension, walked to the French windows, her steps jerky and uncoordinated. She stepped out into the garden, then gave a heart-rending wail.

'*Rosie!*'

Anthony and Tara swapped glances, then ran to the window, Sir Charles behind them.

Yvonne Broussard was on her knees, sobbing, with Agathé in her arms.

'*Maman,*' said Agathé, over and over again. '*Maman.*'

After what seemed like a long while, Yvonne scrambled to her feet. Picking up Agathé and holding her close, she turned to face them. Although glowing with happiness, her eyes were fierce as she glared at Anthony, Tara and Sir Charles.

'You had Rosie!' she said accusingly. 'Why did you keep her from me? And Paul? Where is Paul?'

'Come inside,' said Anthony. 'I think we all have some explaining to do.'

Reluctant as she was to let her child go, Yvonne Broussard consented to let the little girl sit on the hearthrug, rolling a paper ball for Minou to chase. 'How did you,' she demanded, 'come to have Rosie?'

Anthony lit a cigarette and told her.

'You went to *Belgium*?' she said incredulously. 'And rescued Rosie?'

'Yes, Madame. But you understand I didn't know she was Rosie. Her name in the convent was Agathé.'

Sir Charles nodded. 'You'll appreciate, Madame Broussard, that Dr Brooke faced considerable danger to rescue little Rosie.'

Even though, Anthony commented to himself, I thought I were rescuing an entirely different child. My God, what a mix-up!

'We've been very frank with you, Madame,' continued Sir Charles, looking concernedly at his friend. 'Will you tell us what you know?'

'But of course, Monsieur,' she said, beaming at him, Tara and Anthony. 'Dr Brooke, he has been so brave, I owe it to you to tell everything.' Her expression grew serious. 'This is what happened . . .'

Yvonne's story was easily told. She and Paul married seven years ago. Of course she knew that Paul's father had been born in Germany. What of it? There were many thousands of Germans in America. What she hadn't realized was how deep the old man's patriotism ran and how he had passed onto his son his pride in both his family and all things German.

Paul wanted a German name for their daughter, Yvonne a Belgian. They compromised by calling the baby Roswitha, after Paul's mother, and Agathé, after Yvonne's. For the first year after Rosie was born, they lived in America. Then Paul organized an expedition to Brazil. The expedition was cut short by the death of his good friend, Richard Cooper. Cooper's last request was that Paul should contact his only relative, Edward Jowett.

Paul Diefenbach might have a taste for adventure, but he had inherited his father's business instincts. The Capital and Counties bank was moribund and the Midwest Mutual and Savings wanted a London branch. The takeover was arranged to everyone's mutual satisfaction. Edward Jowett, who Paul came to regard virtually as an uncle, was retained as Chief Cashier, the bank prospered, and Paul and Yvonne made their home in London.

As tension in Europe grew, Paul took the German side. Yvonne disagreed. Matters had come to a head the previous summer.

Yvonne left Paul for an extended holiday and, taking Rosie Agathé with her, went to stay with her grandmother, Madame Legrand, at the family home in Brussels.

At first, the news that an Austrian Archduke had been murdered in Serbia seemed to make little difference. Yvonne paid no attention to the news; Rosie was ill, struck down by the much feared summer flu, or meningitis.

Then, on 4th August, as Rosie was, thank God, starting to get better, their peace was shattered by the appalling news that the German Imperial Army had invaded Belgium.

Yvonne, said Grandmamma, must return to London at once before the Boche arrived. Rosie wasn't fit to travel. She could stay with her until this stupidity of a war was over. It wouldn't last long and Rosie would be perfectly safe. An old woman and a little child posed no threat to anyone's army.

So Yvonne left. When, back in London, she found that Paul still supported the German invasion, in spite of the terrifying reports coming from Belgium, she took back her own name and left him. When he returned to his senses, she would return to him, but not before.

Then, a few weeks earlier, Edward Jowett had called to see her. He was desperately worried. Rupert Arno Diefenbach, Paul's father, had been approached by the German ambassador in New York. Germany needed money for the war; could he oblige with a loan?

Anthony, Tara and Sir Charles swapped startled glances. Money. This, felt Anthony, was getting to the heart of things.

'You'll excuse me for asking, Madame Broussard,' said Sir Charles, in his most persuasive voice, 'but what was your husband's reaction to this request? Did he agree with the idea of a loan?'

Yvonne nodded. 'Yes, he did. That is why Monsieur Jowett came to see me, so I could argue against the idea with Paul. There is, Monsieur, a considerable amount of gold in the vaults of the Capital and Counties. The bank, she has prospered, yes? Paul proposed to loan the German government twenty million dollars in gold.'

Charles Talbot stared at her blankly. *'Twenty million dollars?'* he repeated in a hushed whisper. 'Dear God. That's what? About four million pounds?'

Yvonne shrugged. 'If you say so. Mr Jowett, he was worried, you understand? Paul was stubborn, then something changed his mind.'

She leaned forward. 'Paul, he is a free spirit. He does not like to be spied upon, and the conviction grew on him that there were spies in the bank. There are Americans in the bank, you understand, Americans who worked for Paul's father. Paul became convinced that at least one of these men had been put there to spy upon him. So he consulted Mr Jowett, and they worked out a plan. Mr Jowett, he had always tried to persuade Paul that the Germans were not the innocent victims of lies and propaganda.'

She shrugged. 'Perhaps, I do not know, he had been swayed by Mr Jowett and by me. Paul always wanted to know the truth and we told him he was ignoring the truth about Belgium. So, he did what, knowing Paul, I should have expected him to do. He went to see for himself.'

'He went to Belgium?' asked Anthony.

'Yes,' she agreed. 'He told me – he told everyone except Mr Jowett – that he was off to South America, and I believed him.'

Sir Charles lit a cigarette. 'That answers a lot of questions, doesn't it, Brooke? Paul Diefenbach's whereabouts is the information Harper and his crew blackmailed out of poor Mrs Jowett. Once they knew he was actually in Belgium, he'd become a complete loose cannon. They needed to keep tabs on him and he'd disappeared.'

He raised an eyebrow in Yvonne's direction. 'We've seen a letter your husband wrote to Edward Jowett, Madame Broussard. We know that what he saw in Belgium made him change his mind.'

'That is so, Monsieur,' she agreed. 'But, in the meantime, I thought I had committed *une grosse erreur.'* She smiled happily at Rosie. 'Thanks to the brave Dr Brooke, all is well.'

That was stretching the facts more than a bit, thought Anthony, but he didn't contradict her. 'What do you mean, Madame?'

'A few weeks ago a man came to see me. He was very nice,

very respectful, and my heart, it was overwhelmed when he showed me photographs of Rosie with Grandmamma.'

'I can imagine you were overwhelmed,' said Tara.

Yvonne turned to her eagerly. 'But yes! Imagine! This man – his name was Smith – said he was part of the American Relief Fund and could travel in Belgium. He had talked with Grandmamma and Rosie. He said that for three hundred pounds, he could bring Rosie to me.'

The three hundred quid was a good touch, thought Anthony. If he'd offered to do it for free, even the most besotted mother would be suspicious.

'The money was needed, he said, to smooth the way, to pay bribes and so on, and also to pay for his trouble, but he could do it. All I had to do was write a letter to Grandmamma, explaining that she was to give Rosie in the charge of the nursemaid who would be sent to Belgium to collect her.'

'Didn't you suspect anything?' asked Tara.

Yvonne shrugged. 'I was uneasy, yes, but, Madame, I ask you, would you refuse? The photographs, they proved he had seen Grandmamma and Rosie, yes? If I knew Paul was in Belgium, I would have left it to Paul, for he loves Rosie very much, but I did not know. I paid Mr Smith the money and wrote the letter and then . . .'

She gulped. 'I waited. The night before last, Paul returned. He, like me, thought there was a chance that Rosie still could be safe. Then, this morning, he received this letter.'

She took a letter from her handbag and handed it to Sir Charles.

He unfolded the letter. It was typewritten on a single piece of plain paper. He read it out loud.

> This morning's newspaper contains a report of the murder of James Dunwoody, shot at the wheel of his Roll-Royce.
>
> His death was not an accident. We murdered him.
>
> James Dunwoody was chauffeuring your daughter, Rosie, and her nursemaid. We have taken your daughter and will hold her hostage until you have fulfilled your father's wishes.
>
> Be at the Grey Street entrance of the Capital and Counties bank at ten o'clock this morning.
>
> Tell no one. If you do, your daughter will die. We murdered

James Dunwoody and will murder your daughter without hesitation.

You have one chance to save her. Take it.

There was stunned silence. 'That,' said Sir Charles eventually, 'is the most evil letter I've ever read.'

'They wanted to be noticed,' said Anthony heavily. 'They hired a Rolls-Royce and murdered that poor beggar, James Dunwoody, to be noticed. They made sure that it'd be in the newspapers and you'd take their threat seriously.' He looked at Yvonne. 'I take it your husband obeyed the instructions, Madame?'

'Yes, of course,' she agreed. 'How could he do anything else?' She looked at Tara. 'When you came this morning, I thought you were one of them, these evil people, but now – now I know that you are good.'

She smiled happily at Rosie. 'Now Rosie is here, there is nothing to worry about, yes?'

'No,' said Anthony. Although Yvonne Broussard didn't seem to realize it, there was one certain way for a bunch of killers to ensure that Paul Diefenbach couldn't tell anyone what had happened. And, of course, there was another life at stake.

She frowned at him, puzzled. 'But what is wrong? Germany will get the money and that is bad, yes, bad, but they cannot harm Rosie.'

'There was a child in the car with the nursemaid,' said Anthony.

Tara's face was pale. 'It's Milly, isn't it, Anthony? They've got Milly.' She looked at him imploringly. 'Can we save her?'

Anthony got to his feet. 'I'm going to damn well try.'

TWENTY-NINE

A phone call to Scotland Yard brought the co-operation of the official force. Sir Douglas Lynton met them outside the Capital and Counties, on the junction of Chambers' Row and Grey Street.

Despite Sir Charles' reluctance to approach the bank, they didn't have any choice. As Anthony said, if Paul Diefenbach was ordered to be at the bank at ten o'clock this morning, the bank was the only place they had a hope of finding out what happened to him.

Sir Douglas's first idea had been to raid the bank with a show of force, but both Sir Charles and Anthony disagreed.

'I hope we're doing the right thing, Talbot,' said Sir Douglas unhappily as they walked towards the entrance. 'Say the word and I can have every man in the bank arrested and every piece of paper impounded. We can stop these people dead in their tracks.'

'It might come to that,' said Sir Charles, 'but this way, we've got a chance of working in secret. It's not just the gold that's at stake.'

'Exactly,' agreed Anthony. 'They murdered James Dunwoody. I just hope Milly's still alive.' He swallowed hard. 'There's no real reason why she should be.'

Sir Charles grasped his arm. 'Think what Father Quinet heard the woman say, Brooke. She didn't want to be party to killing a child.'

The clerk at the mahogany counter received their request to see the manager politely enough.

'You wish to see Mr Crichton, gentlemen? May I ask what it concerns?'

'Say it concerns a large account,' said Sir Charles with a smile. 'But we do have to see Mr Crichton himself, you understand.'

After a few minutes wait, they were shown into the green leather and oak-rich office of the manager.

Mr Crichton, a portly, balding man, looked worried to death. He knows something's going on, thought Anthony as he rose to greet them.

Sir Charles made sure the door was firmly closed before he sat down.

Mr Crichton blinked at him. 'How can I help you, gentlemen? I understand your business concerns a large account.'

'Very large,' said Sir Douglas, placing his official warrant card on the desk. 'A matter of twenty million dollars in gold.'

The manager gave a little cry and started back from the desk. Sagging in the chair, he clapped a hand to his mouth with a horrible retching noise.

Anthony thought Crichton might very well be sick or faint or both. He clapped a hand on his shoulder, undid his collar button and loosened his tie. 'Come on, man. Breathe deeply. I'm a doctor,' he said, authoritatively. 'Do what I say. Mr Monks, pour me a glass of water.'

Sir Charles poured a glass from the heavy glass water carafe on the desk, adding a generous measure of brandy from the decanter next to it.

The manager gulped down the brandy and water with shaking hands. After a few moments his breathing steadied. He tried to speak and eventually managed a hoarse whisper. 'Am I under arrest?'

'That depends,' said Sir Douglas. 'I need hardly ask if you know what happened this morning. Perhaps you would give us the details.'

Mr Crichton shut his eyes briefly. 'I knew something was wrong,' he said. 'Ever since Brown and Forester arrived, I knew something was wrong.'

'Brown and Forester are . . .?' prompted Sir Douglas.

'Americans,' answered Mr Crichton. 'German-Americans, from the Midwest Mutual.' He glanced at them. 'You know about the Midwest and Mutual?'

Sir Douglas nodded. 'Go on. We'll ask for any details we need.'

The manager nodded. 'I call them Americans, but they were German, sure enough. German-American perhaps, but German.'

Brown and Forester? Anthony thought. Make that Bruhn and Förstner, perhaps.

'They arrived about two months ago,' continued the manager, 'posted here by Mr Diefenbach – Mr Rupert Diefenbach – himself.' He gazed at them earnestly. 'Gentlemen, believe me when I say that I have not known an easy moment since. Poor Mr Jowett was unhappy about their presence and although I cannot prove it, I believe they know far more about his tragic demise than they should.'

'Where are they now?' asked Anthony quickly.

'Gone. They departed this morning with Mr Diefenbach. Had not Mr Diefenbach himself been present, I would have resisted their actions with all the authority at my disposal.' He raised his hand and let it drop. 'But as Mr Diefenbach was in charge, I had no choice but to comply with his orders.'

'Get to the point, man,' said Sir Douglas brusquely. 'What happened?'

Anthony frowned at Sir Douglas and dropped a reassuring hand on the manager's shoulder. 'Let Mr Crichton tell the story his own way,' he warned. He knew the man was on the verge of a breakdown. Any attempt to bully him could send him over the edge.

The manager looked at Anthony gratefully. 'As you will appreciate, I was surprised to see Mr Diefenbach, as we thought he was in South America. I was delighted to see him return, but, as a matter of fact, gentleman, he was very far from his usual self. He is usually a most affable man, but this morning he was unusually curt and off-hand.'

He lit a cigarette with trembling hands. 'As soon as I heard Mr Diefenbach had returned, I hastened into the lobby to greet him, but he hardly seemed to know I was there. Brown and Forester met him and I overheard him say, "I thought I was right. It's you, isn't it?" and they replied, "Yes. Remember these are your father's instructions." They had a brief conversation, which I couldn't catch, then Mr Diefenbach took them into his office.'

'Yes?' said Anthony after a pause. 'What happened then?'

The manager's lip trembled. 'They took the gold,' he said in a whisper. 'As you can imagine, I protested, but Mr Diefenbach reassured me everything was in order. He supervised the loading of the gold into a van.'

'It must have been a jolly large van,' commented Sir Douglas, but Mr Crichton shook his head vigorously.

'Oh no, sir.' His voice took on an oddly reverential tone. 'The gold is composed of eighteen bars weighing four hundred troy ounces apiece. Gold. Solid gold.'

'What size are the bars?'

'Approximately seven inches by four inches. They are small, but heavy, of course. As I said, each bar weighs four hundred troy ounces.'

'That's what?' asked Sir Douglas. 'In ordinary pounds and ounces, I mean.'

The manager shrugged. 'I imagine it would amount to thirty pounds or so.'

'Where did the van go?' asked Anthony.

Mr Crichton put his hands wide. 'I don't know,' he said

miserably. 'They refused to tell me. Despite Mr Diefenbach's reassurances, I knew something was amiss. Why, Brown and Forester wouldn't even have one of our drivers. Brown drove the van and Forester sat in the back with Mr Diefenbach, in place of our guards. The whole procedure was most irregular.'

His face was a picture of misery. 'If Mr Diefenbach had not been present, I would have certainly informed the police. Ever since the van drove away, I have tried to convince myself that all was well.'

He glanced at Sir Douglas's warrant card and shuddered. 'What could I do? I have always had the most profound respect for Mr Diefenbach. He is young, yes, and sometimes unorthodox in his views, but the bank has prospered under his guidance and I entertain the warmest feeling towards him.' He hesitated. 'Tell me, gentlemen. Has – this is so incredible I can hardly say it – has the Chairman, Mr Diefenbach himself – actually robbed the bank?'

Sir Douglas pursed his lips, unwilling to answer, but Sir Charles nodded. 'Unfortunately, that's what it amounts to.' Mr Crichton closed his eyes in horror. 'However,' he continued, 'Mr Diefenbach was acting under duress. No court of law would find him guilty.'

Sir Douglas raised his eyebrows in disagreement, but Mr Crichton seized on Sir Charles's words.

'The Chairman was forced to act, you say? He is an innocent man?'

Anthony could see hope dawning. Mr Crichton sat upright, braced himself, and, when he spoke, his voice was far stronger. 'Who forced him? Brown and Forester?' His face grew grim. 'By George, gentlemen, this needs to be stopped!' He glared at Sir Douglas. 'You, sir! You represent the police. You must do something!'

'That's exactly what I intend to do,' snapped Sir Douglas. 'However, in order to do so, we need information. Have you no idea where the van was headed?'

'Did you overhear anything?' put in Anthony. 'Any clue would be useful.'

Mr Crichton frowned. 'No . . . That is, I think a woman was involved. I heard them say a name. Jane Fleet.'

'Jane Fleet!' exclaimed Anthony. He and Sir Charles swapped

glances. 'That's the name Father Quinet overheard in St Mark's. Did they say anything about her?'

Mr Crichton shook his head. 'No, I just heard the name.'

'Did Brown and Forester have their own offices?' asked Anthony.

'Indeed they did,' said Mr Crichton, standing up. 'If you think it will help, I'll gladly show you to them.'

Both Brown and Forester's offices were of the same pattern. Virtually identical rooms, they were linked by a connecting door.

Mr Crichton looked on with fascinated interest as Anthony examined the rooms. A few minutes' search was enough to convince him that neither room concealed any hidden drawers, cupboards or safes. Such things, especially in a building such as this, always ran to a pattern and he knew exactly where to look.

That meant that if there was anything to be found, it must be in the paperwork on the desk. Fortunately, there were very few files to look at.

'What are you looking for?' asked Mr Crichton watching Anthony flick quickly but methodically through the papers. 'Incidentally, sir, you would have made a superb bank clerk.'

'Thanks,' said Anthony with a grin. 'That's never a career I considered. I'm looking for anything that will give us a clue as to where the gold has been taken.' He drummed his fingers on the desk. 'And unfortunately, the place is as clean as a whistle.'

An exclamation from the next room made him look up. Douglas Lynton put his head round the door. 'We've found a receipted bill from the Diligent Employment Agency. Apart from that, there's nothing.'

'The Diligent?' said Mr Crichton with interest. 'That rings a bell. Oh yes, I remember. Forester went to them when he first arrived in London. He recommended them highly.'

'Did he recommend them to Mr Jowett, perhaps?' asked Anthony.

'I believe he did, now you come to mention it,' said Mr Crichton after a few moments' thought.

'I thought as much,' said Anthony, lighting a cigarette. 'I'm afraid we're out of luck. The only other place to search is Mr Diefenbach's office.'

Mr Crichton drew back. 'The Chairman's office? Really, sir, I must protest. You assured me Mr Diefenbach was an innocent man.'

'And that's what I both hope and believe,' said Anthony smoothly. 'However, he might have left a message there.'

He didn't think any such thing, but at least it gave Mr Crichton the moral prod he needed to escort them to the Chairman's room.

The large oak desk didn't contain a message or note, of course. Mr Crichton looked on disconsolately as Anthony walked to the fireplace and started to run his hands round the heavily embossed hearth and mantle. 'What are you doing?' he asked.

'Looking for a secret cupboard. This fireplace looks very promising.'

Mr Crichton made an unhappy noise.

'There is a secret cupboard, isn't there?' said Sir Charles. 'Come on, man, out with it.'

Mr Crichton sighed impatiently. 'Oh, very well. It's part of the bookcase. I've seen it open, but I don't know how the mechanism works.'

Anthony's searching fingers paused, then pressed the top of a wooden pineapple. There was a click, and a door that formed part of the panels separating the heavy oak shelves of the bookcase swung open.

'Bingo,' he muttered.

Douglas Lynton and Sir Charles seized a file of papers. 'They're letters,' said Sir Charles, putting the file on the desk and opening it. 'They all seem to be written in German.'

Anthony read through the first letter and whistled. He quickly flicked through the other letters. There were seven in all. 'These prove,' he said softly, with a weather eye on Mr Crichton, 'that our Mr Diefenbach was hand in glove with the Germans.'

'So was Diefenbach acting under coercion or not?' demanded Sir Charles.

Anthony shrugged. 'Things might not be as they seem,' he said quietly. 'Hello! What's this?'

It was a letter from a lettings agent, Chaucer's of Sittingbourne, dated two months previously.

Anthony read it quickly. 'Well, I'll be damned. Jane Fleet isn't a woman. It's a place.'

'What?' roared Sir Douglas. 'A place?'

Anthony handed him the letter. It confirmed the letting of

Jainfleet House, Jainfleet, Kent, to Mr Paul Diefenbach. 'See for yourself.'

He picked up the next document in the pile, a large-scale ordinance survey map of Kent. 'And with any luck, this will tell us exactly where Jainfleet is.'

He unfolded the map and held it up to the light. There were pinpricks at each corner, where it had been pinned to a wall and, on the coast between Margate and Herne Bay, another pinprick on the tiny village of Jainfleet. Jainfleet House was a short way off, on a headland above the village, at the mouth of an inlet.

'Got it,' breathed Anthony. He looked to where Sir Charles was holding a small black notebook. 'Anything interesting?'

Sir Charles nodded. 'There's a series of numbers.' He tilted his head to look at the map. 'They look like – yes they are – a map reference for Jainfleet. Then there's a note. "Light above and below. Three hours before high tide at Margate" .' He put the notebook down. 'That'll be tonight, of course. They'll need the cover of darkness to bring a boat in.' He rubbed his hands together. 'So once we find the time of the high tide at Margate, we've got the where and we've also got the when.'

'The when of what?' asked Mr Crichton, bewildered.

'When the gold's going to be picked up, I imagine,' said Sir Charles. He turned to Mr Crichton. 'Now, sir, you'll understand that it's vital that you mention nothing of this to anyone. Anyone at all, you understand? Lives may hang on your silence.'

Mr Crichton looked thoroughly confused and depressed, but he nodded all the same.

'We're also,' said Sir Douglas, 'going to impound all these documents and lock the door to this room. No one must enter without my express authority. This is a police matter, Mr Crichton, and I'm sure I can rely on your complete co-operation.'

Once again, Mr Crichton nodded.

'And now,' said Anthony, 'let's get off to Jainfleet.'

THIRTY

They couldn't, of course, set off for Jainfleet right away. A trip to the Admiralty office, where Sir Charles spent some time with Admiral Cunningham, confirmed, amongst other things, that high tide at Margate was seventeen minutes past two that night.

Which meant, thought Anthony, looking at the looming bulk of Jainfleet House on the headland, black against the raggedy moonlight, everything kicked off at seventeen minutes past eleven. Lying on his stomach on the bleak, flat cliff, he glanced at his watch, shielding the luminous face with his hand. Ten past eleven. Seven minutes to go.

With him, silent and virtually invisible, was a hand-picked platoon of soldiers, fifteen strong. Their officer, Captain Calcutt, was under orders to co-operate with the civilian authorities, which meant, of course, Charles Talbot. For once, Anthony was glad of his colonel's uniform. It gave him some military clout.

He shivered. Margate and Herne Bay may be popular holiday resorts, but no one in their senses would holiday in Jainfleet. The scatter of fishermen's cottages which made up the village were half a mile along the coast. Jainfleet House stood bleakly alone, facing the sea.

Beneath him, at the foot of the cliffs, he could hear the black sea rise and retreat from the pebble beach in a giant's breath of sound. If he was cold, the men on the beach must be freezing. The wire-grass of the headland blew against his face as the minutes ticked on.

There was a grunt and a thud as a shape settled beside him. It was Captain Calcutt.

'I don't like this, sir,' he whispered. 'It's nearly seventeen minutes past eleven and there's no signal from the lads below. If the enemy were going to land a boat on the beach, they'd have done it by now, surely.'

Anthony bit his lip. Captain Calcutt's orders were to let the

boat land and wait until the crew had come up the cliff-path to
Jainfleet House. Then, once the crew were safely on the headland
and with their retreat barred by the men below, attack.

He glanced at Jainfleet House. It seemed deserted. Had the
papers in Diefenbach's secret cupboard been planted there to
mislead them? But why, for heaven's sake? We weren't meant
to find the papers, he thought.

He came to a decision. 'I'm going into the house,' he said softly.
'If this is a wash-out, we need to know.'

'Will you take Sergeant Granger, sir? He's a good man.'

Anthony hesitated. He trusted himself to be able to scout out
the house without being overheard but he couldn't answer for
anyone else. 'No, thanks, I'll go alone.'

From the grunt Captain Calcutt gave, he was obviously going
to argue the toss, so Anthony added, 'When the boat crew do land,
you'll need every man you've got.' That was true enough. 'Tell
Mr Monks what I'm doing.'

Captain Calcutt subsided. 'Very good, sir.'

Anthony crept up to the wall surrounding the house. The closer
he got to Jainfleet House, the more it looked not only deserted,
but ruined. The occasional gleams of moonlight from behind the
scudding clouds shone through the exposed rafters of the roof
where the slates had fallen. The broken-down wall enclosed a
cobbled yard and the remains of a scrubby kitchen garden that
obviously hadn't been tended in years.

Anthony slipped into the old yard and waited. Silence. He
breathed a sigh of relief. He had been dreading the bark of a dog,
but the only sounds were of the wind and the sea.

Across the yard was a door, presumably the old kitchen door.
The door had been repaired with new wood and had a very service-
able lock. The metal on the lock was untarnished. So the place
wasn't abandoned, after all. That did leave, however, the question
of how he was going to get in.

He could always break a window, of course, but the thought of
the noise put him off. Keeping in the shadows, he stole round the
side of the house, coming, after a couple of minutes, to the front
of the house.

Again, everything was in darkness. A low wall enclosed a square
of wind-blown shrubs and patchy grass that had once been a

garden. The front of the house, only fifty yards or so from the cliff edge, commanded what must be, in daylight, a magnificent view of the sea, stretching out to the horizon.

Anthony ignored the view. In the centre of the garden, a path led up to a grandiose front door. It stood at the top of a flight of steps between two pillars, but beside it, under one of the blank black windows, was what he had been looking for. It was a stone lintel, the lighter coloured stone standing out against the dark brickwork in the fleeting moonlight.

Anthony climbed over the wall and quietly approached the stone lintel. In a house this size, it was what he had hoped to find. Underneath the house were the cellars. The front cellar rooms were lit by windows that opened onto a small rectangular pit, dug out of the earth and covered above by thick glass, resting on two iron bars. Those windows, if he knew anything about it, were secured by simple catches that could easily be turned back with the blade of a penknife.

He knelt down and, putting his hands on the edge of the thick glass, heaved. The glass shifted, then, with another heave, came away all together.

Anthony looked down into darkness. It was a narrow gap between the iron bar and the wall, but he should be able to swing himself down to the window.

He braced his hands against the lintel, then took one last look round.

And froze.

There, close into the shore, was the unmistakable black bulk of a submarine. Any minute now, they'd launch a boat. Any minute . . . but nothing happened.

What should he do? Briefly, he thought of going back to the cliff top where Charles Talbot, Captain Calcutt and his men waited to ambush the boat crew, then, just as quickly, decided against it.

Something must be happening inside Jainfleet House and he wanted to know what. He swung himself into the hole and, risking a gleam from his electric torch, found the clasp of the window. Seconds later, he was standing in the cellar.

He risked the torch again. The cellar, a large, low, stone room, contained an ancient washing copper and nothing of interest, but the sounds he could hear, a distant swooshing and roaring, puzzled him. The sea? Yes, of course, but oddly enough, it sounded louder in the cellar than it had outside.

Across the cellar was a door, opening onto a square stone flag-stone, with a flight of stone steps leading upwards. There was a dim light at the top, as if the door was open.

Cautiously, he crept up the stairs. He'd been right. The open door at the top of the stairs led into a cavernous kitchen. It was deathly quiet. He snapped on his torch, illuminating a table and chairs and an ancient kitchen range, thick with dust. There were footprints on the dusty flagstones. He tried the kitchen door into the house but it was either locked or bolted from the other side.

Anthony bit his lip. So far, he had accomplished nothing and the sight of that damn submarine told him things were hotting up. He'd better retrace his steps and join the others on the cliff. That's where the action would be.

By the light of the torch, he made his way down the cellar steps, hearing once more the distant surge of the sea. He walked into the cellar and paused. The sound of the sea really was louder on the stairs. And why, in a house this size, was there only one cellar?

He turned back to the doorway, shining his torch at the floor. Footprints. Footprints in the dust, that apparently led right through the wall.

There was an empty stone shelf attached to the wall. Anthony grinned as he saw the handprints on the edge of the shelf. Wedging his torch under his chin, he grasped the shelf with both hands and tilted it.

The wall was a disguised door and swung back easily. Evidently the hinges had been recently oiled. Anthony examined the catch on the other side of the door. From this side it was obvious how it operated and was simple enough to open. Should he shut the door? Yes. If anyone came down the stairs from the kitchen, he didn't want to advertise his presence.

He quietly set off down the steps. In the middle of the stairs ran a flat ramp, perfect for rolling barrels up and down. This place must've been a smugglers' paradise. The sound of the sea filled his ears, but the stairs were deserted. Two flights down he came to a level passage. The walls were damp and the smell of salt filled the air.

Cautiously he crept to the end of the passage. The passage

ended in a door, beyond which the sea churned. He stiffened. He could hear voices, voices with a distant, open-air quality.

Turning off his torch, he opened the door a crack. He looked out into a small natural sea cave. A smugglers' paradise? Absolutely.

Beyond the rocks of the cave was a pebble beach with the sea lapping the shore. Four hurricane lamps, balanced on the rocks, provided enough light to show a rowing boat drawn up on the beach with three men round it, loading a box into the boat. Although small, it was evidently very heavy. The gold.

Realization hit him. The submarine wasn't launching a boat to the shore.

The boat was being launched from the shore to the submarine.

He swore under his breath. Charles Talbot, Captain Calcutt and all the men could wait for hours for the boat crew from the submarine, because there *was* no boat crew from the submarine. What's more, although he couldn't swear to it, he guessed that the rocks of the inlet would prevent the boat being seen until it was well away from the shore.

'What the hell's happening on board the U-boat?' he heard one of the men say. 'They're showing lights. That's not in the plan.'

'They want us to hurry up,' was the impatient reply. 'Come on, we're running late.'

'Blame Diefenbach,' was the answer. 'He very nearly got away.'

So Diefenbach was with them. As Anthony's eyes adjusted to the dim light, he took in other details. Two of the men by the boat were strangers to him. At a guess they were Brown and Forester, but the third man he had last seen in a kitchen in Paddington, where he had just murdered Bertha Maybrick. Joshua Harper.

Standing beside him was a woman. Who was she? She didn't look like the descriptions of Annie Colbeck. Was this Miss Anston from the Diligent? Maybe.

So if Brown, Forester, Harper and Miss Anston were accounted for, where was Paul Diefenbach?

Even as he asked himself the question, it was answered. Harper stepped away from the boat and picked up a hurricane lamp, holding it so the light fell on a fair-haired man slumped with his back to the rocks, hands behind him.

Anthony slipped out through the door and, keeping to the deep shadows at the back of the cave, wormed his way round the beach and through the rocks to Paul Diefenbach. Getting as close as he could, he risked a whisper.

'Don't say a thing.'

Undoing his penknife, Anthony cut through the rope that bound Diefenbach's wrists.

He heard Diefenbach's hiss of satisfaction as the ropes parted and could feel, rather than see, him massaging life back into his wrists.

The men by the boat stood up with grunts and sighs.

'That took longer than we expected,' said one of the men, wiping his forehead. He spoke with an American accent. 'Harper, give us a hand to push the boat out.'

'Wait a moment, Forester,' said Harper sharply. 'We've only got half the money we're owed.'

'You'll get the rest when sonny boy is truly no more – and when Daddy buys the story. Don't worry, Harper. You'll get what you're owed.'

'I'd better,' growled Harper. 'If you want to work for Rupert Diefenbach again, stick to your promise. Otherwise he'll be very interested to know exactly what happened to his blue-eyed boy.'

Forester's companion, Brown, shifted impatiently. 'Come on, guys. Enough of this. You'll get your money, Harper. Let's get this boat launched. We're running out of time.'

Forester didn't move. 'I don't like being threatened. Harper, do as you're told, otherwise it's worse for you. By tomorrow morning I want to hear that our Mr Paul Diefenbach has been found dead. Get me? That's all you've got to do. Kill him.'

'Like hell you will!' yelled Paul Diefenbach.

To Anthony's horror, Paul Diefenbach rolled away from the rock and, scrambling to his knees, launched himself at the men by the boat.

Taken utterly by surprise, Harper, Brown and Forester were hurled away from the boat. In the dim light it was impossible to see who was fighting who.

Then the deafening roar of a shot rang out, echoing round the cave. It was Miss Anston, automatic in hand.

All four men stopped fighting as she stepped forward. 'Diefenbach, stand up and step away, otherwise I'll shoot.'

Diefenbach raised his head from the pebbles but didn't move.

Miss Anston took aim and fired another deafening blast, sending the bullet close to his head in a spray of pebbles.

Harper kicked him in the ribs. 'Do it!'

With a yell of pain, Paul Diefenbach doubled up.

'Who the hell let him go?' demanded Forester, wiping blood from his mouth.

Anthony stepped out, gun in hand. 'I did. Miss Anston, drop the gun!'

Forester tried to back away. Anthony zinged a bullet past him. 'It's just as easy to hit you,' he said grimly. 'Miss Anston, I won't tell you twice. Drop the gun. Diefenbach, come here. You four, stay exactly where you are.'

'Do what he says,' said Harper, his voice breaking. 'He's army.'

Reluctantly, Miss Anston dropped the gun.

Harper swallowed hard. 'Look, friend, I'm American, okay? These guys might speak English, but they're German, sure enough. They made me go along with them. I'm a neutral, yes? But I'm on your side.'

'Don't give me that,' said Anthony curtly. 'I know exactly who you are.'

Brown and Forester looked uneasily at each other. 'What are you going to do?'

Inwardly, Anthony was asking himself the same question. All four captives were as dangerous as a black mamba. Despite the fact he was still spoiling for a fight, Paul Diefenbach had been beaten up and couldn't be much use.

Then, unexpectedly, Harper started to laugh. 'Do yourself a favour, pal, and look round.'

Anthony smiled grimly. He was too old to fall for that one – and then a shot blazed out from behind.

Spinning round, he dropped to the ground, flattening himself on the pebbles, the gun skittering away from him.

In the flickering light, he could see the figure of a woman framed in the doorway to the cave, a gun raised in her hand.

As she crunched across the beach towards him, he could see her other hand firmly gripping the arm of a little girl, who she dragged along behind her.

Milly.

Even in that moment, Anthony's heart leapt. Of course this was Milly! Yes, she'd grown – of course she'd grown – but she was unmistakably Milly.

Behind him, Harper and the others had dived from the gunshot. 'Careful, Annie,' said Harper, getting up cautiously. 'That was too close for comfort. And why,' he added, his voice rising, 'have you bought that kid along?'

'Because she keeps trying to escape, that's why,' said Annie, giving Milly an impatient shake. Gun in hand, she glared down at Anthony. 'Get up. Who the hell are you?'

'Never mind,' cut in Forester urgently. 'We have to launch the boat.'

For a fraction of a second, Annie Colbeck's attention was diverted as she looked at the boat. That's all it took. In a swift movement, Anthony kicked out, sending Annie Colbeck's gun into the air. He snatched the pistol as it fell and turned it on Annie.

'Join the others,' he said, indicating Harper, Forester and Brown with the barrel of the gun.

Annie Colbeck took two reluctant steps back away across the beach, still dragging Milly.

'Milly, come here,' said Anthony.

'Milly?' Paul uttered in confusion.

The little girl shook herself free and started towards Anthony, when she was grabbed by Annie. 'Not so fast!' With one hand on her arm, the woman's other hand closed round the child's throat.

Milly yelped in a strangled gasp of pain.

'I'll kill her. I've killed before *and* enjoyed it. I'll wring her neck.'

Annie Colbeck's voice was ice cold. Anthony remembered Hawthorne, the butler, an old man who'd just got in the way. Milly's eyes bulged.

'Give me the gun,' ground out Annie, lifting Milly off her feet.

Anthony couldn't stand it. Milly would be dead in seconds. 'All right!' he yelled, throwing the gun to her.

Annie laughed, dropped Milly, and bent to pick up the gun.

Milly sank her teeth into Annie's hand. Annie yelled and, shaking her hand free, drew her arm back for a stinging slap as Milly wriggled away.

'You little cow!' screamed Annie and, pointing the gun at Milly, fired. At the same moment, Paul Diefenbach caught hold of her arm, sending the bullet wild. Furiously, Annie whirled, bringing the weight of the gun across the side of his head.

He fell back, unconscious, as Milly ran down the beach, out of the cave, into the sea, scrambling away over the rocks.

'Let her go!' yelled Brown, as Harper started after her. 'She's just a kid. We're running out of time. We have to launch the boat!' He snapped his fingers at Harper. 'Take care of Diefenbach and his pal. If you don't, it'll be the worse for you.'

'Don't worry,' said Harper with relish. 'It'll be a real pleasure.'

Miss Anston stooped and picked up her automatic. 'You!' she said motioning to Anthony. 'Pick up Diefenbach and back against the rocks. Move!'

Anthony moved. With two guns pointed at him, he didn't have much choice.

Harper, Forester and Brown set their shoulders to the boat and, grunting, pushed it into the sea. The water had already risen appreciably round the prow. Taking two of the hurricane lamps, they climbed on board and started to row steadily out of the cave onto the open water. Two lamps. That was the signal to the submarine.

Harper smacked his hands together and smiled. It wasn't a nice smile. 'Now, to take care of you two. But first, army boy, where did you come from?'

Anthony had his answer ready. 'I live in Margate. I've known this house for years. I was walking along the cliffs when I saw the kitchen door wide open and thought I'd better take a look.'

'He's lying,' said Annie Colbeck furiously. 'I closed that door.'

'It's certainly closed now,' said Anthony. 'I closed it.'

Miss Anston shifted impatiently. 'Does it matter? Let's tie these jokers up and get out of here.'

Harper cracked his knuckles. 'Okay.' He picked up a coil of rope from the beach and motioned to where a ring, evidently for tying up a boat, was set in the rock. 'One wrong move and the girls will drill you,' he warned.

Harper lashed him and the unconscious Diefenbach to the ring. Anthony felt the bonds. They were very efficient.

The water was surging into the cave. In the short time it had taken to tie them up, their ankles were already covered.

Harper stood back and grinned. 'You're going to drown, pal. In about six hours' time, when the tide's gone out, we'll come and untie you. Not that you'll know anything about it, but I'll do it, all the same. You can be lost at sea, I think, but as for Mr Diefenbach here . . . Well, he'll have been killed by the British.'

'No one will believe that,' said Anthony.

'His daddy will,' said Harper with a grin. 'Nice knowing you. So long,' he added and, with Annie Colbeck and Miss Anston following, crunched up the beach.

A few minutes passed in silence, broken only by the onrush of the tide.

Once over the rocks shielding the inlet, the water was rising fast. Each black wave seemed to mount higher and higher. Anthony's thighs were covered, but Diefenbach, slumped unconscious against the rock, was nearly underwater. Anthony managed to get a knee under his body and lift. Diefenbach groaned.

'Come on,' Anthony urged. 'Stand up, man!'

Diefenbach blinked his eyes open. 'Sorry,' he muttered. 'Can't.'

Anthony fought against the water. The undertow of the tide was pulling at him, knocking him off balance.

'Come on!' yelled Anthony. Straining on the rope, he managed to wedge Diefenbach's body between himself and the rock, as the tide mounted another assault. 'Stay on your feet!'

The water was up to his chest. In desperation, he threw back his head and yelled. 'Help!'

'*Les voilà!*' said a small, shrill voice excitedly. '*Les voilà!*'

It was Milly. She scrambled onto a rock and sat out of the water at the mouth of the cave. Behind her were two soldiers.

The beach party. Thank God.

'We're tied up!' yelled Anthony.

'Hang on, sir, we'll soon have you out of there,' shouted one of the soldiers. Bayonet at the ready, he slid down the rock into the sea, his companion following.

'Did we get the submarine?' gasped Anthony, as the bayonet sawed through the rope.

'Yes, sir. All safe and sound in the hands of the Navy. We've had a signal.'

He jerked his thumb backwards at Milly. 'This little one turned up on the beach, scared to death, and insisted we came along. We didn't understand her lingo, but it was obvious what she wanted. I reckon you'd have been goners for sure without her. We'd heard gunshots but couldn't work out where they were coming from. It's just as well she showed us the way. To get here from the beach you have to squeeze through a gap in the rocks. We'd never have found it without her. She's a good kid.'

'She certainly is,' said Anthony, helping to heave Paul Diefenbach to safety on the rocks. He held out his arms to Milly. 'Come on, sweetheart, down you come.'

She looked at him shyly, then Anthony picked her up and lifted her onto his shoulders, out of the water.

With the two men helping Paul Diefenbach, Anthony sloshed his way up the beach to dry land.

'What now, sir?' asked one of the men, a corporal, looking back at the sea. 'I'm from Reculver, just down the coast. The currents are tricky round here on a rising tide. We can't risk going back until the sea's gone down but we've got a good few hours' wait.'

'We can do better than that,' said Anthony, gently lifting Milly off his shoulders. He smiled for what seemed the first time in an eternity. 'We can walk up through the house.'

To the soldiers' complete astonishment he led the way through the door, along the passage, and up into the kitchen.

It was a crowded room. Charles Talbot, Captain Calcutt and a party of soldiers were guarding three very sullen prisoners.

'Brooke!' yelled Sir Charles. He bounded across the kitchen and shook him vigorously by the hand. 'Glory be, man, where did you spring from?' He looked down at Milly. 'And the little girl, too. Is that Diefenbach?' he asked as the two soldiers, supporting Paul Diefenbach, came into the room. 'It's like a miracle.'

Milly took one look at Annie Colbeck and, with a little whimper, buried her face against Anthony's leg.

'Milly saved us,' said Anthony, putting a protective arm around her. 'She led the men straight to us. They'd left Diefenbach and myself tied up to drown.'

'Did they, by jingo?' said Captain Calcutt. 'That's something else to add to the charge sheet. I'm very glad to see you safe and sound, sir.'

'Thank you, Captain. Diefenbach's been treated pretty badly by our pals over there. Is there any brandy?'

Sir Charles had brandy in a hip flask. After a few minutes, Paul Diefenbach had some colour back in his face. Anthony took a long draught and, feeling new life course through him, brought Sir Charles up to date with what had happened in the cave.

'Will Diefenbach be all right, Brooke?' asked Sir Charles.

Paul answered for himself. 'I'll be fine,' he said. 'But, my God, I'd like to get my hands on Brown and Forester.'

'You'll get your chance very shortly,' said Sir Charles. 'The navy should be here any minute now with the prisoners from the submarine.' He cocked his head to one side as a challenge was shouted from outside, followed by the crunch of feet.

A party of sailors, led by a lieutenant, came into the kitchen, bringing with them the dejected Brown and Forester. Their dejection turned to utter dismay as they saw Paul Diefenbach.

Anthony caught Paul's arm as he got to his feet, fist clenched. 'You can't hit them,' he warned. 'They're prisoners.'

'It's just as well for you two you're under guard,' Paul snarled. 'I always knew you were spies.'

Forester wasn't cowed. 'Spies? Ask yourself why we were needed, Diefenbach. If your father could've trusted you, he wouldn't have needed us to see that you'd stick to the plan.'

'What was the plan?' asked Anthony, cutting off Paul Diefenbach's furious retort. 'There's a lot I don't understand.'

Paul slumped back into the chair. 'It was my father's idea,' he said wearily. 'I was brought up to believe that of all the nations on God's earth, the tops were America and, way ahead, Germany.'

He shrugged. 'I bought it. I never thought about politics, but I bought it. When the war started, everything got serious. Yvonne tried to talk sense but I wouldn't listen. Ted Jowett, a good man if there ever was one, tried too, and something of what they said got through. Then my father was approached by the German ambassador in New York, who requested a loan. As far as my father was concerned, it was simple. The money would come from the Capital and Counties. I was uneasy about the idea.' He jerked his thumb at Brown and Forester. 'That's when these two clowns arrived.'

'That's when Annie Colbeck went to spy on the Jowetts,' said Anthony slowly. He didn't miss the quick smirk that passed between Brown and Forester. 'No, wait.' He looked squarely at

Forester. 'Somehow you must've known about Harper and the Diligent. What happened? Did Harper try and blackmail you?'

He nodded with satisfaction as he saw the expression on Forester's face. 'I'm right, aren't I? Only Harper found he'd bitten off more than he could chew. You made him a deal. You used the Diligent to spy on the Jowetts and Yvonne Broussard.'

Diefenbach looked up sharply. 'There's a spy in Yvonne's house?'

'Not for long,' said Sir Charles.

'And these are the people my father trusted,' said Diefenbach bitterly. He took another swig of brandy. 'I thought there was only one way to find out what was really happening in Belgium, and that was to see for myself. Ted Jowett helped. We told everyone I was off to South America.' He glanced up at Brown and Forester. 'How did you know I wasn't?'

Forester sneered. 'Simple. Your father had the ship met and you weren't on it. We needed to find out where you were. We never intended Jowett to be killed. We only wanted information.' He pointed at Harper. 'That's your murderer.'

'Hey!' yelled Harper. 'Don't pin this on me!'

'It's true, Harper,' said Anthony. 'We know you murdered the Jowetts. I saw you murder Bertha Maybrick and I'm willing to bet you murdered James Dunwoody too. Annie Colbeck, whatever her real name is, murdered old Hawthorne, the butler.'

She looked at him in stunned silence. 'You can't prove that.'

'I can try. When it went wrong at the Jowetts, that's when you came up with the plan to kidnap Rosie from her great-grandmother's.'

Paul cut off Annie Colbeck's protests. 'I don't get it,' he said, turning back to Brown and Forester. 'My father might have backed the wrong side in the war, but he'd never agree to anything that could harm Rosie.'

Forester laughed. 'You think so?'

Paul flung his chair back and made a sudden grab for Forester. 'Where's my daughter? If she's harmed—'

Anthony pulled him away. 'She's safe!'

Forester laughed once more. 'Safe? Yes, safe where you'll never find her.' He looked at Sir Charles, hope dawning. 'You want to cut a deal? If you don't want to be responsible for what happens to that kid, let's talk.'

'You cynical bastard,' breathed Anthony. He tightened his hold on the struggling Paul. 'Diefenbach, stop it, man! These scum haven't got Rosie. I have.'

Paul froze. '*You* have?'

'Yes. She's with your wife, safe in my house in London.'

'Don't give me that,' said Forester. 'He's lying, Diefenbach.'

'She was,' said Anthony, still keeping a firm grip on the furious Paul, 'in a convent in Louvain.'

Paul stopped struggling. 'Where?'

Forester stared at him without speaking.

'It's true,' said Anthony. 'I understand it now. After the Jowett murders, our pals here knew you were in Belgium and thought you'd come back with a very different view of the war.'

'That's true,' Paul shuddered. 'Yes, I changed my mind, sure enough.'

'As they knew you would,' said Anthony. 'But you're quite right. Your father wouldn't endanger Rosie. He knew she was with your wife's grandmother in Brussels. Our friends needed a way to put pressure on you when you returned.' He pointed to Annie Colbeck. 'So they got this woman to take Rosie from Madame Legrand's and place her in the care of Sister Marie-Eugénie in Louvain.'

'Was she safe?' demanded Paul.

'Perfectly. Sister Marie-Eugénie is a good woman. But the gang needed a little girl to take her place, so you would believe that your daughter was threatened. Good, credible witnesses testified there was a little girl in the Rolls-Royce with a nursemaid. The kidnap wouldn't have been very convincing if there hadn't been a little girl in the car.'

He squeezed Milly's shoulders. 'So they substituted Milly for Rosie in the convent, brought her here from Belgium and kept her under wraps until they knew that you, Diefenbach, were back in England. That's the Prussian mind for you. They could've used any little girl from that orphanage, but because they'd used Milly once before, they used her again. Thinking what happened in the cave, it's just as well for us they did.'

Paul buried his head in his hands. 'Rosie's safe,' he repeated. 'Safe with Yvonne.' He looked up. 'You're right. If it wasn't for the threat to Rosie, I would never have gone along with their plan.

If I hadn't been there to authorize the shipment, Crichton at the bank wouldn't have agreed to let the gold go.'

'We saw him earlier today,' said Anthony. 'He was delighted when we told him you were acting under coercion.'

Out of the corner of his eye, he caught Forester's smug expression. 'Yes, he was delighted,' repeated Anthony, louder. 'Even when we found a stash of false papers in the secret safe in your office, he still believed in you.'

'What papers?' asked Paul, puzzled.

'The papers that seem to prove, beyond doubt, that you were working for the German government.'

'*What*?'

'That was, I might say, a bit of an own goal,' said Anthony, turning to Brown and Forester. 'Those papers were meant to be found after Diefenbach had been reported missing together with twenty million dollars in gold. However, for the plan to work, amongst the papers were accurate directions to where this place was.'

'I just don't understand,' said Paul.

'Don't you? These crooks wanted to get rid of you, Diefenbach. You'd changed your views. You were a dangerous man, with first-hand knowledge of Belgium and a great deal of influence in America. You might even change your father's views. He'd probably never support the Allies, but I bet you'd dissuade him from supporting Germany.'

'That's for sure,' agreed Paul.

'Now just think what should've happened. The gold had gone, supposedly taken by you, but where are you? Not in your office in the Capital and Counties, but drowned in a cave on the east coast.'

'I'm beginning to get it,' breathed Paul. 'Dad would never believe I'd been killed by his people.'

'Yes,' said Anthony. 'It's obvious, isn't it? By the time your body was found – and our two pals left us directions so your body was certain to be found – there wouldn't be any doubt in your father's mind that you'd been murdered by the British, especially after Brown and Forester had sworn they'd left you safe and well. That cellar door would've been left open, as an invitation to explore below, and there you would be. Drowned, of course, but you'd expect the British to make sure you'd died of natural causes.'

Paul nodded slowly. 'You're right. Dad would have gone to his grave believing I'd been murdered by the British.' His mouth set in a thin line. 'He's going to hear the truth and by the time I've finished, not one cent more will find its way to Germany.'

Anthony carefully wrapped a blanket round the sleeping Milly and settled her down in the car.

Sir Charles gave instructions to the driver and climbed into the back seat beside Anthony. The car bumped off down the cliff path, away from Jainfleet House.

'It's funny how things work out,' said Sir Charles, looking down at Milly. 'She's such a little scrap of a thing, no one would ever believe she could overthrow the plans of that cold-blooded bunch of crooks.' His voice was oddly soft. 'You went to Louvain to save her, and she ended up saving you. We must see she's looked after, Brooke. She's a great kid.'

'I hope so,' said Anthony, resting his hand on Milly's hair. 'She's going to be my daughter.'

AUTHOR'S NOTE

In their landmark book, *German Atrocities 1914: A History of Denial*, the Trinity College, Dublin, historians, Alan Kramer and John Horne discuss how retrospective disillusionment with the war (the depression of the 1930s fuelled the mood) and skepticism of wartime propaganda led to the belief that German atrocity stories were the invention of the wartime Allied governments. Although there were, of course, exaggerations, a few minutes' conversations on the subject with almost any Belgian will bring up stories of what their grandparents and great-grandparents endured.

It was the scale of the deprivation in Belgium that led to the founding by Herbert Hoover (the future USA president) of the extraordinary American Relief Administration for Belgium. He persuaded the German authorities to allow him to import food to Belgium and persuaded the British authorities to export it from British ports. At its peak, the organization was feeding ten and half million people daily. The references to 'saintly Americans' in the story are taken directly from contemporary accounts, as is the description of the destruction of St Pierre.

The White Lady was also a real organization, founded by Henry Landau, a South African. His book, *The Spy Net*, which he had to publish in America because of the British Official Secrets Act, gives some astonishing accounts of the bread-and-butter work done by his spies – some of whom were nuns! Lucien Voltèche, the people smuggler who got Anthony across the *Dodendraad,* was a real person whose exploits are recorded in *The Spy Net*. His escapade with Anthony and his aunty, the bargee, are, however, figments of my imagination.

In a historical mystery, it can be fun to draw from real life. *Automobiles de Luxe* was a genuine firm, hiring out Rolls-Royces at the stated price. I'm glad to say, though, that as far as I know, none of their employees were murdered at the wheel. That, too, was a figment of my imagination.

I hope you enjoyed the book. Thank you for reading!